For Stuart

For gold in physic is a cordial; Therefore he loved gold in special.

CANTERBURY TALES: PROLOGUE GEOFFREY CHAUCER

CONTENTS

IN WHICH DR ROBERT GUNN GOES ASHORE

Robert Gunn was a tall man, and when he came up on deck the mahogany treads of the companionway creaked beneath his weight. He had to bend to clear the archway that opened on to the sharp, bright sunlight.

He leaned on the ship's rail, feeling the wood's welcome warmth on his bare arms. It was his birthday; May the fourth, eighteen hundred and thirty-three, and he was twenty-five. The stinking, spiced air blowing from the Chinese mainland made him wrinkle his. face in distaste and spit. The Pearl River, yellow and oily, carried the spittle beneath the bows of the clipper *Trelawney,* and away to the South China Sea.

The ship lay off Whampoa Island, a few miles from Canton, the only port on the Chinese coast where Europeans and Americans were grudgingly allowed to land, however briefly, for trading purposes.

At Whampoa, cargoes had to be offloaded into junks and sampans and rowed or taken under their matted sails, like giant fans, up-river to Canton. The Barbarians, as the Chinese contemptuously called all Westerners, were allowed brief leave ashore, and then back on board again, lest they should corrupt any of the subjects of the Emperor, Tao Kuang, the Son of Heaven, who ruled his celestial empire from his remote palace in Peking, the forbidden city, nearly fifteen hundred miles away; on the northern extremity of his kingdom.

In Canton, a small group of waterfront buildings, known as factories, but in fact warehouses and agencies rather than places where goods were manufactured, were the only bridge-head of European and American traders to three hundred mil-lion potential Chinese customers. The possibilities of trade were indeed dazzling, but the reality was rather less impres-sive. China was a closed country, virtually sealed off from the rest of the world, and content to be so. What need had Tao Kuang's subjects with the cotton goods, furs and scrap iron which the sweating Western Barbarians so assiduously tried to sell them? Chinese merchants were willing to ex-port their surplus tea and silk and rhubarb; but even this was done through compassion, because they believed that with-out rhubarb the inhabitants of the Western world —shown on their maps as little more than a scattering of islands around a central China, the ruler of the universe — would die from constipation.

But Robert Gunn, lately graduated from St Andrews Univer-sity in Scotland, and on his first visit to the East as a ship's sur-geon, was not thinking about this unlikely medical problem. He was thinking about himself.

He saw, as though for the. first time, the yellow water gurg-ling and sucking greedily at the-slimy timbers of the ship, and he was back once more in the little fishing port of Herne Bay on the Kent coast, walking along the shingle. The wind from that green sea felt fresh on his face, not warm and scented as here.

Marion, the' girl he was going to marry, to whom he had just given an engagement ring bought with the few guineas he had earned helping the local general practitioner, was by his side.

'I'll be back within the year,' Gunn had assured her. 'Then we will marry. One trip east with the chances of preferment I may find in Bombay or Calcutta, or even in China, and I'll be able to buy a house and put up my plate.'

'How *wonderful,*' Marion had said, and he believed she meant it, for she rarely enthused about anything. She smiled and patted his arm, and he had looked down fondly at her from his greater height.

They had kissed then, or rather she had turned up her face to submit to his kiss, and he had felt the outline of her small breasts through her bodice. There was no fire in her response, and there never had been, he admitted now; he might have been manipulating the rubber likeness of a woman. But then ladies did not show their enjoyment of such things as a doxy might. They simply endured coarse male advances; and, if married, as their wifely duty. Yet Gunn had seen labourers and girls picking hops, and their eyes glowed at each other with animal longing. There had never been such feeling between Marion and him. He had told himself that no doubt it might grow, but now he knew it never would; he had been deluding himself.

Only hours before, the mail from England had been handed up into the ship. The letters had come by fast new steamship to Alexandria, and then overland by camel caravan to the other side of the Red Sea, where another of these vessels, just coming into service, had belched its smoky way to Bombay, then on to Calcutta and Singapore, and finally, here; the farthest East that any Westerner could travel. There seemed something symbolic in this fact. Gunn had reached the end of a journey; after this, wherever he sailed, he would be returning. Now, he felt no need to hurry back.

He put his hand in his pocket, took out the letter, screwing up his eyes against the glare of the sun reflected from the river flowing to the estuary known as the Bogue or the Bocca Tigris — the Tiger's Mouth — the name that early Portuguese voyagers had given to it three hundred years earlier.

His father's familiar handwriting made his throat tighten with a sudden wish to be home in the little house that overlooked that other gentler sea. Gunn's father was the local schoolmaster; his mother had shared his delight when Robert had won a place at a Scottish university, for she was Scottish. They would both have discussed this letter which already was months out of date. He spread the opening page on the warm, rounded rail and read it again.

'My dear son Robert,

'It is with a heavy heart and a most reluctant hand, that I write to give you news of Marion.

'As you know, it was our wish and yours that you would both be wedded on your return from the East, but something has happened which I must relate, although it grieves me to be the agent, however unwilling, of hurt and pain to you.

'In brief, Marion has run away with a married man. You will remember Joss Cartwright, who had the general store in our village, and a branch of the same in Whitstable? His wife being, brought to bed for the fourth time in as many years, he has suddenly renounced her, his family and his business, and has gone away with Marion, no-one knows where.

'Your mother and I heard this news from his brother, who is running the shops, pending whatever legal outcome there may be. We were both as astonished as he was. The man is nearly twice as old as Marion and of comfortable means, and a warden in our church.

'There is only one consolation. Both your dear mother and I feel you will draw what comfort you can from it. Better to know the apple is rotten before you bite it. Better that this should have happened, hurtful as it is, before you married Marion, than after. No-one here has any news of where she may be, or where they intend to settle. Should news come to hand, I will most urgently post it to you. In the meantime, be assured of a place in the hearts and prayers of your mother and me.'

Gunn could almost repeat the words off by heart; he had read them a dozen, two dozen times, since the letter had arrived. He remembered Cartwright's shop well. As a boy he had often bought a pennyworth of liquorice, or a ha'porth of bull's eyes, kept in a giant, huge-mouthed bottle. Cartwright he remembered as a small, round man, with a beard, always wearing a white, stiff collar, and a gold watch-chain; he was like a thousand other tradesmen in a middling way of business, unremarkable and unremarked on. Yet some spark had caught unlikely fire and blazed between Marion and him. The chemistry of attraction had reacted so fiercely that Cartwright had abandoned everyone and everything, and taken Marion out of Gunn's life for ever.

He straightened himself up and pushed the envelope into his pocket. He would go ashore tonight and drink; first, to remember Marion, not as she was, but as he imagined she had been, as he had told himself repeatedly she was. Then he would drink to forget; alcohol was a powerful passport to oblivion.

A sound of shouting scattered his thoughts like the seagulls swooping over floating offal in the river. Griggs, the first mate, came across the deck to him; a swarthy, stocky man with bushy eyebrows and tattoos on his arms. He had been a sailor since his teens, always on the China run.

'We've' just had permission to land at Canton,' he said. 'We're taking a longboat up now. Care to join us, doctor?'

'Certainly,' said Gunn; anything to be away from his thoughts. 'Who's given us this permission?' he asked.

'The Hoppo.'

'The *who?*'

'Oh, the Emperor's man in Canton. That's the nearest we get.to pronouncing his Chinese title. He has the job of controlling foreign trade in the city for-three years. In that time, he *has* to make a fortune — because it's cost him a fortune in bribes to get the post in the first place. So he squeezes every possible source of income. Mooring fees, permission to unload, harbour dues, duties on all sorts of things.

'He has to pass on a good whack of his takings to the mandarins and other officials, and no doubt a lot also towards the Son of Heaven's expenses up in Peking. This means there's always a lot of bargaining before we agree on a price for unloading. If he was in a bad mood, we could have been stuck here for weeks.'

'Why is the Hoppo so corrupt? If he's the Emperor's man, isn't he .paid a salary?'

'Shouldn't think so for a moment. The Emperor doesn't care to become personally involved in sordid considerations of trade. He's above all that. We're the *hung-mao-fan,* the Red-Bristled Ones to him, the foreign devils who've sailed from our tiny islands across the seas — *his* seas by the way — simply to pay tribute to him.

'The Hoppo is the man we must deal with. He controls a group of Chinese merchants who are the only ones allowed to trade with foreigners. They're called the Hong merchants. Rather like a music-hall turn, Hoppo and Hong, eh? The Emperor doesn't really want our money — or us. Especially us.'

'Then why do we trade here at all? It seems a long way to sail just to be fooled about with.'

'So it is. But one day this ridiculous business may end, and then the trade will go to the people .who have contacts here.

'We make a profit on the tea and silk. The rhubarb which we're forced to take, we're not so keen about. Often we dump the whole cargo out at sea. But we have to humour them, and they believe it's their mission in life to see our bowels run freely. At a price, of course. And *our* mission is to get as much trade as we can.

'Do you know that only a hundred and fifty years ago our total imports of China-tea were two pounds and two ounces weight exactly? And for the past ten years they have been worth nearly three and a half million pounds sterling every year? Why, the drink is so popular that the East India Company has to keep a year's supply always in stock in England by

Act of Parliament. That's an indication of how the China trade could grow—if the Chinese allowed it to.

'There are other reasons, too, of course. Mainly the Coast Trade.'

'What does that involve?'

'Mud. Foreign mud, which is what we call opium,' said Griggs. 'We don't usually shout much about this business, and no East India Company ship carries it, so the Company can deny all knowledge of the traffic. But it's the forbidden trade, and the richest in the world.

'The Company makes a million a year out of it—a sixth of all its profit from the East. They've sown hundreds of thousands of acres in Bengal and Patna with poppies to grow the stuff.

'But opium can have terrible effects on the poor devils who smoke too much, so the Chinese Emperor has forbidden all imports, which means there is a great risk in smuggling it. If you're caught selling or buying mud, you can face death by strangulation or decapitation.'

'Opium possesses considerable medicinal value,' Gunn pointed out. 'It isn't all bad.'

He had frequently prescribed it himself for a wide range of complaints: travel sickness, toothache, neuralgia, ulcers, insomnia; even for hysterics in women. Nearly all the patent medicines on which nannies relied so heavily in Britain — Mother Bailey's Quieting Syrup, Godfrey's Cordial, Galby's Carminative and McMunn's Elixir — contained opium; sometimes as much as half a grain to a fluid ounce. Poor mothers, distracted by crying children, also fed their infants these elixirs by the spoonful. It quietened the children immediately; sometimes for ever. But then one could say the same for almost any other medicine, which was harmless in the right quantities, yet lethal if you swallowed too much of it.

'I always thought opium came *from* China, not went to it. And I never imagined I'd ever be closely involved with it,' he went on.

'We're not—personally,' said Griggs. 'But a lot here are, and the old Hoppo knows which side his bread's buttered on. He'll make ten times as much dealing illicitly in opium as he gets from our legal trade. Anyhow, that's nothing to do with us. If the Chinese are going to kill themselves smoking mud, they might as well do so at a profit to our Company as anyone else's.

'Don't forget. Longboat's leaving in five minutes. It'll take us two hours to Canton if we catch the tide. If not, twice as long. Can you be ready?'

'Of course.'

Gunn went below decks to his cabin, a. small hutch, barely twelve foot square. A round porthole looked out over wash-boats with split bamboo roofs and curtained walls, each crewed by three or four girls, cheerfully calling out to the crew for any clothes that needed washing or mending. They were refreshingly honest. Sometimes, so Griggs had told him, when a ship sailed unexpectedly before all the crew's clothes had been laundered, the wash girls would keep them safely until the ship returned, twelve or eighteen months later. They were all shouting now.

'Ah, you missee chiefee mate, how do you dooa?... I missee you long time.... I makee mendee youah shirt, yes? . . .'

Gunn closed the porthole, and locked it, for his cabin was not only a sleeping place, but also the ship's surgery. Two rows of shelves had wide holes to accept his big round-stoppered bottles of tinctures and lotions. He also kept a stained wooden trunk, always locked, beneath his bunk, for his instruments and dangerous drugs,

He poured water from a ewer into the zinc basin, washed his hands quickly, dashed some over his face, combed his hair and was back on deck within minutes. Already, as he watched sailors ferrying food or unloading cargo, Marion's memory was fading, and the hurt diminished. In its place a new hardness was growing, like fresh skin over a wound.

He had never possessed much money, and this shopkeeper

fellow Cartwright was obviously richer than his family. However, Gunn had one important qualification; he was a doctor. This did not rank particularly high in the social strata, of course, but it gave him a possible edge on some rivals. He was paid nearly two hundred pounds a year and his keep as ship's surgeon, and he should also find opportunities of making money by trading ventures. Few men who sailed East did not return to England wealthier than they left.

I'll grow rich *somehow,* he thought. Really rich. Then women will be proud if I just look at them, let alone offer them my name in marriage. Money alone might not guarantee happiness, or even a place in society, but provided you had enough, gold was a card of entry that eventually everyone honoured. For then you could buy your estate .and become a country squire, arrange for a seat in Parliament, maybe even a title.

He would make Marion sorry she had ever spurned him for a shopkeeper who dealt in peppermint bull's-eyes and aniseed balls. He felt more cheerful now; maybe Marion, quite unintentionally, had done him a good turn.

The longboat drew alongside. Gunn climbed down the white ladder and the *Trelawney* soared above him like a sheer tarred wall from her gilded figurehead to ornamented stern, both freshly painted and shining with new varnish. The rigging, made a rope lattice against the blue sky, and the black and white chequers beneath the deck reflected the yellow water like a chess board. Well, if it *is* a chess board, Gunn told himself, then I will be king; never the pawn.

Griggs and he sat in the stern. Twenty oars dipped and raised as the tars bent broad backs to their task. As they rowed, girls sculling small sampans shot out from shore, their boats laden with oranges and bananas. They cried out:.'You wantee fluit? Olanges, yes?'

Some of the crew shouted back bawdily: 'You know what we want! We want fruit with hair on it!'

These girls, using a single scull at the stern, twisting it

with their wrists, could keep up for a hundred yards or more, until .finally they realized that the sailors were making fun of them, and fell back to await another boat, shouting: .'You all stinkee lying Englishmen!'

The sun was very bright. What had seemed a yellow river, oily and scummy, from the *Trelawney,* now glowed like liquid gold. On either side, rice fields grew greener than an English lawn; there were temples and pagodas, and in the distance, mist had painted the hills pale blue. They passed lacquered house-boats, passenger vessels. with streamers and - paper lanterns, and war junks with eyes lacquered on their bows to see an enemy, and red and blue demons on their sterns to frighten them away.

Canton was crowded with sampans; house-boats and junks were moored in mid-stream, packed with men and women and children. On one, half a dozen people in rags came out to watch them row by. Or»ᵉ threw a bucket of faeces and orange peel into the water after them. A naked child of five or six stood on a box and slowly raised her. right clenched fist, as though lifting a severed head by its hair. She drew her other hand beneath it in a horizontal cutting motion, as if slitting a throat, and then everyone shouted in English, in a chorus ob-viously learned by rote, 'Foreign devils! Demons! Red Bristled Barbarians!'

"They don't think much of us,' said Griggs. 'Never mind. They sell the strongest drink in the world in Canton. We'll be lucky if we get half our fellows back tonight to row us.'

'What happens to those left behind?'

'If they're on their own, they'll probably be robbed, and left in the gutter. If they're in a crowd and put up a fight, then they should escape. Either way, there will be some sore heads in the morning!'

Moored close to the shore, Gunn saw several long house-boats with gilded roofs and painted decks, their roofs heavy with flowers in terra cotta pots. On balconies reached by carved staircases and shielded by ornate bannisters, young women sat dressed in purple silk, strings of bright jewellery, round their necks. Some stood up and tip-toed to the edge of the craft to wave to the new arrivals.

Gunn saw with horror that their feet were bound so tightly, their toes curved beneath them like claws, so that they were barely the size of a child's clenched fist. The girls could only totter or toddle. It was quite impossible for them to run, and difficult enough to walk.

'They do that here, from birth,' explained Griggs. 'It's a mark .of class. Only peasants walk well.'

'It's a terrible custom.'

'No worse than stays and tight lacing.'

'.Who are these girls, anyway?'

'Whores. But don't pay 'em a visit. They all have ponces or protectors aboard and they will kill you for your wallet.'

They were running in now between sampans and barbers' boats, others selling toys and burning charcoal, towards wooden piers, bearded with seaweed. The crew shipped oars, and pulled their way along by boathooks on to other craft already moored.

On land, the noise after the gurgling of the river was suddenly intense. Gongs boomed; firecrackers whirled; men carrying trays of melons shouted their wares. Servants, pushing their employers in wheelbarrows, screamed hoarsely for others to make way, and a band marched along the quay, leading a funeral procession. Gunn knew that the noise was to drive off demons and devils; the louder the bangs, the more frightened such devils became.

The longboat bumped against the wooden piles, the sailors made her fast, and Gunn and Griggs climbed up an iron-runged ladder. After the slow rolling of the *Trelawney,* the earth seemed to heave beneath Gunn's feet: He stood still to steady himself, eyes narrowed against the burning brilliance of the day. Hundreds of people were milling about. At various points, raised high on lattice scaffolds of bamboo, stood little bamboo watchtowers. Each contained a policeman watching for fires or any other disturbances.

Canton was divided into areas separated after dark with locked gates guarded by watchmen who beat a tom-tom every hour to mark the passing of the night. By dividing the city in this way the authorities believed that robbery or insurrection could be localized.

Gunn had heard that each area held one citizen responsible for the good conduct of all the residents. This man subdivided his responsibility to other individuals in each street who became responsible for the good behaviour of their neighbours. Because they knew they would be punished if no other culprit were apprehended, these headmen invariably discovered the guilty men—and so saved the police (and themselves) a great deal of trouble.

At the far end of the quay, three-quarters of a mile away, he could see the Union Jack, then the Dutch and French flags, and the American Stars and Stripes.

'They're the factories,' Griggs explained. Their pillars and porticoes faced a garden known as the English Garden, which, in turn, ended in Jackass Point and the river. Between these factories ran three narrow alleys, Hog Lane, Old China Street and New China Street, all leading to a wider road behind them. This was called, from the number of foreign factories that had originally traded, Thirteen Factories Street.

In the past, Swedish, Spanish, Austrian, Danish and other companies had been represented in Canton, but they had gradually withdrawn, although the names of their companies were still engraved on the buildings. All had three stories; the ground floor given over to counting-rooms, vast store-rooms, and a treasury built of granite, with iron doors, for Canton possessed no banks that would do business with Barbarians.

The first floor contained sitting-rooms and dining-rooms; the bedrooms were on the third.

Opposite their landing place stood a factory narrower than the rest, on the edge of a scummy stagnant river, fouled with bloated bodies of dogs, pigs, and branches of dead trees. Children squatted in the yellow mud, defecating amid crowds of blue flies. Above the front door, in. black raised letters, were the words: Creek Factory.

'That's privately owned,' Griggs explained. 'By two of our countrymen. One, William Jardine, is a doctor, like you. Used to be a ship's surgeon, too. The other is James Matheson, the son of a Scots baronet. They're probably the richest European merchants out here. They trade as Jardine and Matheson.'

'What do they trade in? Tea?'

'Yes. And lots of other things. But they probably make more out of opium than all the rest put together.'

'A doctor,' said Gunn musingly. 'I must meet him.'

Maybe Jardine had also yearned for wealth, and had been goaded to prove himself in a way his fellow men would be forced to admit and admire?

'He doesn't practise now,' Griggs added. 'Doesn't need to, of course. You'd probably meet him if you were staying here.'

'Pity I'm not.'

'I don't think so. Couldn't stand this place myself. Give me the sea. Something clean about that. These factories are like monasteries. They've hardly any windows, and no women are allowed whatever. Then the Chinese have a guard-house on the corner of Old China Street, either to see we all behave ourselves, or to protect us from the locals who can't bear the sight of Foreign Devils. Or maybe for both reasons.

'Anyhow, each year, as soon as the trading season is over, they insist that all foreigners move to Macao—the island the Portuguese have owned for two hundred years in the mouth of the river.

'The Chinese Emperor fears that if we're allowed to stay here for twelve months in the year then we'll all gradually acquire more space, more land, and more concessions. Which he's no intention of giving in case we take over the whole country, as we've done in India and Burma. So he only allows foreigners about three hundred yards frontage for all their factories, and a depth of four hundred. And this in a country with more inhabitants than, any other in the .world, and a potential trade that is staggering!

'So far as the merchants are concerned, they feel like men dying of thirst on the edge of a locked reservoir. They are more concerned about the fortunes they're *not* making than the ones they are.'

'Then why don't they come to some better arrangement?'

'The mandarins are afraid to. They have a strictly ordered society here—-more so than with us. The mandarins treat, the peasants like dirt, and the peasants don't object, because they don't know anything else. Now if you allow all kinds of Europeans in, and the peasants hear how well labourers live in the West, then they'll demand more for themselves. And that would mean less for the mandarins and the Emperor.'

At the edge of the quay, half a dozen Chinese, naked except for blue drawers, had looped a rope around the bloated carcase of a pig floating in the river. Very carefully, for the rope was old, they began to haul it up, faces beaming.

'They'll have that for dinner tonight,' said Griggs, and spat into the sea. 'But don't let it put you off your food,'

'I won't. But I'll be damned careful what I eat.'

The smell of spice, overlaid with scents of tea and spices and the salty stench of the river, was suddenly overpoweringly strong. He turned away in case he was sick.

Griggs called to the men.

'Liberty boat will return to *Trelawney* at' nine .o'clock tonight. Anyone not here will be left behind. Any of you lot ever landed here before?'

'Yes, sir,' called a young man with a fresh country face.

'Well, you know the place, but to the others I'll give you this advice. Keep off those flower boats. You'll only catch the pox, and more than likely you'll also lose your wallets. With your money, you'll be worth a year's income to them.

'And if you must go in the grog shops, keep near the door. Otherwise, if there's a fight, you'll be dragged out the back way. Last voyage, we lost two men like that. Never saw 'em again. Any questions?'

'No, sir.'

'Well, see you at nine o'clock. Here.'

'Aye, aye, sir.'

They went off, followed by a crowd of children, hands out for coins, and old beggars with swollen legs and bloated trunks, propelling themselves along painfully on wooden trolleys.

A handful of Englishmen in light trousers, black jackets and black stove-pipe hats walked down from the factories along the quay. Behind came a retinue of servants; small tough men, heads entirely shaved except on the crowns from which sprouted strong thick black hair, fibrous as a horse's tail, and plaited in a pigtail to their waists. Some wore cone-shaped rattan hats against the heat, but most were bare-headed, wearing nothing but cotton drawers. Already, junks were unloading bales of cargo on the hard, trodden earth of the quay. Chinese supervisors marked off each item on scrolls of paper. Servants held umbrellas over them to shield them from the sun.

Gunn saw one supervisor beckon to a servant and incline his head briefly. The servant produced a small square of paper from a. pouch, and held it up to the supervisor's nose. He blew into it. The servant folded it up and threw it away. Then the servant began to feel in his master's clothes for nits and lice. He held up an insect triumphantly. The supervisor put it in his mouth, ground it between his teeth and swallowed it; the unloading continued.

On all sides, women and. children were scrambling about on hands and knees for scraps of grain that burst from a loose bag. Several boys dived into the filthy water to rescue crusts and apple peelings. Yet they all looked bland and cheerful. They might be poor beyond anything Gunn had ever imagined, but, incredibly, poverty did not mark their character. They laughed and joked and shouted at each other in high spirits.

'No point in hanging about here, with just these slit-eyed swine to look at,' said Griggs, wrinkling his nose. 'Let us have a drink. Pity it's not allowed to go into Canton.'

'Anyone ever tried it?'

'Lots. But they've always been brought back. So they concentrate on getting drunk here.'

'On what?'

'Mixtures. Served in the gin shops. Old Jemmy Apoo. Tom Bowline. Old Sam's Brother. Jolly Jack. You can see their signs written up in English, as well as Chinee characters. Each sells his own speciality. Some of their drinks are so strong we've had men go blind or mad, or just stay drunk for days—and no wonder.

'What they call their first chop rum number one curio is about a pint of neat rum, with aphrodisiacs, alcohol, tobacco juice, sugar and a touch of arsenic to give it colour and tang.'

'And you are suggesting we drink here?' asked Gunn with a grin.

'Look behind you,' Griggs said sharply, ignoring his question. 'There's a mandarin coming past. Get back to the side of the road. Quickly. He's the Hoppo.'

Gunn turned, surprised at the urgency of Grigg's voice, and shaded his eyes against the blazing sun. A dozen servants carried a palanquin on long gilded poles through the crowd. Their bodies were bent double by the weight, for the mandarin was not a slim man. Giant moths, flies and mosquitoes fluttered and buzzed about their sweating flesh as they trudged in step to the beating of a brass gong.

Ahead of them, on either side, walked lictors with long moustaches, wielding leather whips and staves at everyone in their path to force them down on their knees.'

The Hoppo was plump and squat, his face impassive as a bladder of lard; mouth small and pursed, eyes dark slits in shining skin. His hands were folded in front of his paunch, and his fingernails, an inch long, were especially sharpened to show that he never condescended to physical labour.

He wore a heavily embroidered gown of purple and gold with the design of a quail worked on its back and front. On his head he had a round hat, like an inverted plate, with a gold button on the top.

'That's one of the high ranks,' whispered Griggs. 'The only one better is a prince of the blood. The lowest mandarins wear a crane embroidered on their coat and a red button in their caps. This fellow has bought his way up, of course. Not born to it.'

Gunn was fascinated by the instant attitudes of respect that the Hoppo's approach had caused. Shopkeepers were flinging themselves down on the filthy road, faces pressed eagerly into the dirt. Others already on their knees turned away, as though the passage of such privilege was too much for their eyes to bear.

'How rich is he?' he asked.

'Impossible to say. But his predecessor amassed one of the largest commercial fortunes in the world. His gold was not just a button in his hat! He had the equivalent of *ten million pounds sterling*.'

'But how *could* he have done, out here?'

'By applying himself to all the opportunities of his post, that's how. Remember, doctor, he takes a cut on every item that comes ashore from the ships *and* every item that goes back on board. Even drinking water. Of, course, he makes most out of opium. Turning a Nelson eye to a trade he should be stamping out.'

'And he achieved this fortune in three years?'

'Yes. And this fellow will make more, for the opium trade's

increasing.'

'But I can't understand it. He's only a Chinese.'

'*Only* is hardly the word I would use, doctor, especially round here. Some, of these fellows know more English than they admit. The Hoppo is *the* most important man in the East. And everyone in these factories—the Americans, Parsees, Russians, Austrians and ourselves included—would do almost anything rather than offend him.

'You really have no conception how absolute this man's power is. Some years ago, a British ship, the *Lady Hughes,* fired a gun in salute on some Chinese holiday—and the shot accidentally, killed a Chinese boatman noone had seen.

'At once, the Hoppo threatened to stop all trade with *every* Western country unless the British sailor who had fired the shot was delivered over to them. So he was. The Chinese gave him a secret trial, and sentenced him. The poor devil was ceremoniously strangled by an iron chain—and all through an accident.

'Odd for an Empire as strong as ours to submit to that blackmail, eh? But so much money is involved— and the hope of millions, more if only we can extend trade throughout the country with an ambassador in Peking, and the use of other ports—that we tolerate all kinds of indignities rather than jeopardize our chances.'

'Maybe,' replied Gunn, grimly. 'But I'm still not going down on my knees for anyone, except to pray to God.'

'As you wish,' said Griggs, 'but at least, salute. It's a matter of courtesy, remember. You'd do the same for the Lord Mayor of London if he passed.'

Reluctantly, Gunn's right hand went up to his cap and down again. The Hoppo turned and looked at him. He gave no indication that he had seen the salute; his eyes did not widen and no shadow of feeling or interest crossed his face, which was impassive as a painted mask. All the same, Gunn felt a strange shiver in his spine, as though dead hands had touched him.

It seemed—quite absurdly, of course—that the mandarin had looked at him closely because he wished to recognize him again. But—why? Or was he imagining the incident?

The procession passed by, the shopkeepers stood up, and returned to their booths and stalls.

'What do we do now?' Gunn asked. To have set foot in the world's most remote and secret country, and then just to stand bowing—*kowtowing,* as the Chinese said—to some native merchant, seemed an absurd anti-climax. He yearned for excitement to purge from his mind the memory of Marion and his father's letter. He could imagine the shopkeeper's pale hands about her body, exploring secrets he had never known, for he was innocent of such things, imprisoned by his own strict upbringing. He shook his head sharply to rid himself of these torturing images.

'That drink,' said Griggs, watching hjm closely. 'First drink ashore is always the best. Like the first girl.'

'But you've just said they'd offer us arsenic'

'That's only for sailors. They'll drink anything. I'll take you where they serve Chinese wine and food you can trust—not old pig pulled out of the river!'

They walked up a narrow alley off Hog Lane, where singing birds jumped frantically in tiny bamboo cages, and into a wooden building. A gilded dragon breathed painted fire above the doorway. A screen hung in the opening, with space to pass on either side.

'That's to keep the demons out,' Griggs explained 'The Chinese believe demons can only go forward and back, like the shuttle on a loom. They can't slip round the side like the rest of us.'

Scrubbed wooden tables with benches were set out inside. In the far corner, Chinese women in shapeless black trousers and blouses sat smoking clay pipes and chattering together. They did not even turn to look at them. A roly-poly Chinese man, his huge paunch held in by a red sash with tassels, bowed to them. His feet flickered like mice under his robe, so that he appeared to glide rather than walk.

'Chop, chop. Fetchee good number one wine, all clean cup. Number one nice chow, heap big fellow - prawns. Quicklee running,' said Griggs, and then turning to Gunn he added proudly: 'It helps to speak their lingo.

'Of course,' he admitted, 'that's only pidgin. When we first started trading here, years ago, the Chinks couldn't pronounce the word "business." They called it "pidginess." So since then this cudd lingo we talk when we're discussing business with them has been called pidgin.'

'Do many of our countrymen speak the proper lingo - Cantonese?'

'No. It's death for any Chinese caught teaching a foreigner his language. But one or two of our crowd still pick it up somehow.'

'There's no cutlery,' said Gunn, sitting down on the nearest bench.

'They eat with chopsticks,' Griggs explained. 'Chop means food—or, any business of any description. And China is full of bamboo sticks, which are a lot cheaper than knives and forks.'

Beggars and touts for peep-shows, tailors, cobblers, and men carrying trays of nuts and beakers of hot tea pushed hopeful faces in at the door, eager for trade.

'Wantee talking bird?'

'All hot tea, mighty fine drinkee?'

'What you want, new number one suit made first-class cloth, two hours work time?'

Griggs waved at them irritably.

'Trouble here is that you buy something from one man, and you're immediately surrounded by dozens of others. And in the middle of all the crush, someone else lifts your wallet. They've got the world's lightest fingers in Canton.'

The chop-house man reappeared with a tray piled with bowls of grilled prawns, plovers' eggs and roasted snails and rice, and porcelain cups of pale wine made from green peas, with a china spoon for Gunn and chopsticks for Griggs. As he set this down, with special silver stands to hold the cups, a great beating of brass gongs boomed outside.

IN WHICH A PARSEE MAKES AN UNUSUAL PROPOSAL

Through the bamboo screen at the door, Gunn could see men on the quay lighting fireworks and strips of red paper, and throwing them up into the air like leaves. A ship was leaving harbour.

'They always do that,' Griggs explained condescendingly. 'It's to appease their heathen gods and give the _ ship safe passage. They call it chin-chinning joss. A bit of joss pidgin —which means God business. A kind of insurance, I suppose. They're great fellows for omens, here.'

The meal tasted surprisingly good, but as Gunn chewed the prawns, he suddenly remembered the coollies hauling up the bloated body of the pig; and thereafter none of the food held any further attraction for him.

He pushed away his bowl, and swallowed a cup of wine. It tasted sharp on his tongue. He had never drunk much wine; as a student, beer had been all he could afford. He decided he liked wine more, so poured himself a second cup; and then a third.

The room was filling up with Chinese coolies, bodies varnished with sweat, searching in folds of their clothes for clay pipes and pouches of tobacco.

Then some British sailors from another vessel came in, - and several better class Chinese, wearing wide, cone-shaped hats and robes, edged with gold thread. One glanced at Gunn, and instantly he had the same uneasy feeling as when the Hoppo had met his gaze; the man was watching him because he wished to recognize him again.

Gunn drank a fourth cup of wine. His nerves must have been affected by the news about Marion; he was imagining things. Maybe he should prescribe himself a dose of laudanum—or as they would call it here, opium, or mud. Jugs of Chinese wine and toddy were now appearing on other tables. Some of the sailors, who had already been drinking elsewhere, began to sing. Outside, the sun slid down the sky, and the brief Chinese dusk painted the quay with indigo. Within minutes, it would be dark.

Already, paper lanterns were glittering above shop fronts and over stalls; candle flames trembled in glass jars. It was suddenly and unexpectedly cool. The clatter and bustle had died with the heat of day; and with them, something else: the sense of adventure he had enjoyed on the quay.

Sitting in the tiny room, with sweating sailors shouting for more grog, and beating the table tops with their fists to accelerate the service; with Chinese carefully ignoring them and pecking away expertly with their ivory and bamboo chopsticks, Gunn felt alien and vulnerable. There was an immense distance, not measured in miles, between the safe homely atmosphere of England (the little house overlooking the sea at Herne Bay, the tweeny making tea, the familiar hiss of the soot-encrusted kettle on the kitchen stove) and this isolated civilization, which only tolerated his presence, and that but barely.

After all, for centuries, China had produced the world's best food, rice; tea, the universal beverage; and superb clothing of cotton, silk and fur. They had literally no need to bother with other goods they did not want, or the red-faced perspiring people who sought to force their wares upon them. Yet the East was the golden land. From the time of Marco Polo, it had been the magnet for those who sought wealth and what money could buy and bring. And Gunn knew that within hours of his arrival, it had laid bare this hitherto unknown power. He was already under its ageless spell; what secrets it held, he meant to uncover; what treasures it concealed, he determined to make his own.

'Didn't like to mention it before, but you were looking gloomy when I saw you on deck,' said Griggs, watching his set face and pouring out more wine. 'Saw you had a letter. Not bad news, I hope?'

'In a sense,' said Gunn shortly. The pain involving Marion was still too tender to be touched roughly or prodded by discussion.

'Well, what I say is, if it *has* happened then it won't happen again. Lightning never strikes the same place twice. Got to look on the bright side.'

'I am looking. After all, it's my birthday, too!'

At this, they emptied two more cups of wine. The drink seemed to be stronger than Gunn had imagined at first, but it was certainly welcome. His gloom gradually melted in its friendly strength. The proprietor cleared away their dishes, and brought bowls of warm water with linen napkins to wipe their hands and mouths. As he set them down, a great cry came from beyond the doorway.

A drunken British sailor staggered in, shouting at someone behind him in the street. His jacket was soaked with grog and fouled with yellow gobbets of vomit. He slipped and fell clumsily across a table where three .coolies were eating.

They leapt to their feet, screaming abuse at him. Rice spattered like hot confetti. One seized a steaming bowl of beanshoots and threw it into the man's face. Roaring from the unexpected pain, the sailor lurched to his feet, grabbed the dish and smashed it over the coolie's head. Instantly, the other two were at him, jumping up and down on their small feet, kicking him rhythmically and ferociously in the groin with their bare toes. The sailor groaned in an extremity of unendurable agony, and folded forwards over the table, scattering the remnants of their meal.

Three other British sailors, eating at another table, now jumped up angrily.

'That's Bert Martin!' one shouted. .'Give 'em what they gave'im!'

He picked up the bench and hurled it at the coolies.

'You slit-arsed bastards!' another sailor yelled furiously, and suddenly everyone was standing up, armed with bowls of rice, plates, jugs of wine and benches as weapons. One sailor, leaping to avoid a blow, slipped and grabbed the bead curtain that separated the kitchen from the dining-room. Thousands of tiny beads scattered like glass grain across the tiled floor under their feet.

The proprietor rushed out of the kitchen, waving a bamboo club, his previously impassive face contorted with rage at the disturbance.

The room, which only seconds earlier had been quiet and peaceful, now erupted in chaos and anger. Faces creased with hate and anger floated phantasmagorically in and out of Gunn's vision. He ducked down by the wall, Griggs by his side, shouting: 'Steady there, I say! Back to your seats!'

But no-one heeded him. The sailors were delighted at the prospect of a fight. Months of being cooped up in creaking, rolling ships, in cramped wooden quarters, exploded volcanically into a hatred of these yellow-faced Chinese, with their contemptible heathen customs, their ridiculous clothes and, worst of all, their ludicrous and totally unwarranted superiority.

Anger also poured its xenophobic message through the blood of the Chinese coolies. Here were the *fanquis,* the foreign devils, the red-bristled hogs from the west, drunkenly defiling them and their country—just as their rulers had warned them they would do. They fought back silently and ferociously.

Gunn watched, fascinated and astonished, yet feeling curiously uninvolved, as though this was happening somewhere else altogether; rather like watching play-actors on a stage. Soon it would all be over and he would go home. But where was his home now? In Herne Bay or aboard the *Trelawney*, off Whampoa Island? Or had he really no home? Was he already a wanderer, with his home wherever he might hang his hat?

Some instinct made Gunn turn. The Chinese man he had seen only minutes earlier was also uninvolved in the fight. He was standing with his back against the opposite wall, arms folded, while the figures fought furiously between them. And he was *still* watching him ... watching him ...

Gunn was lying somewhere, but he did- not know where, or why, nor did he greatly care. He felt cushioned by swansdown dreams; nothing seemed particularly important.

He moved his hands at his sides and felt the straight edges of cold tiles. He opened his eyes and looked up at a tessellated ceiling. Gold plaster dragons stared back at him with round red eyes the size of apples. On one wall, a picture in a cork frame showed a pale blue mountain above a deep blue sea, and a ship with a fan-shaped sail. The other walls were white and blank as empty pages. Oddly, the room had no windows. Above the door was a pagoda-shaped archway, all curves and gold paint, and more dragons with long tongues and fierce curving claws.

Gunn moved his head very slowly and carefully because suddenly it seemed to be beating with a heart and pulse of its own. He put up one hand to his chin and was surprised at the roughness of his beard. He had shaved as usual that morning, so what had happened to him? Had he been injured—and, if so, when and how long had he been here? And where the deuce was he?

He sat up. He had been lying on a rush mat. A pewter dish of water and a china cup engraved with blue flowers was by his right hand. He smelt the water suspiciously; a doctor could not be too careful. But it seemed fresh enough, and he drank greedily, and splashed another cupful over his face. Then he felt in his pockets in case he had been robbed. But his handkerchief was still in his right trouser pocket, the keys of his medicine chest in his left. The German silver watch his father had given him as a present when he qualified had stopped at half past three, but on which morning or afternoon?

He stood up and called out: 'Who's there? Where am I?'

There was no answer. He beat on the door with open palms. The wood was several inches thick, and only boomed with the effort of his futile blows. He stopped, wearied by the sudden effort, bile sour in his throat. Maybe he had drunk too much? That pale, green-pea wine ...

Something made him turn.

Another man was also in the room, standing behind him, watching him. He had entered from a door concealed so cunningly in the far wall that no edge was visible. This man was Chinese, of medium height, wearing a dark green robe. He kept his face down, hands folded across his body and concealed under wide sleeves. He had the familiar cone-shaped hat, the pigtail, the drooping oiled moustaches.

'Who are you?' asked Gunn suddenly uneasy. 'What's happened to me?'

The other man raised his head. Gunn recognized him; he was the man in the chop-house who had stared at him.

'You have been asleep,' he explained in English.

'But why am I sleeping *here*? What *is* this place? I am a ship's doctor. I should be on board *Trelawney*.'

The man bowed.

'We were both in a chop-house, off Hog Lane,' he explained. 'There was, regrettably, an unexpected uncouthness, and then fighting. You were injured. You were brought here.'

Little fragments of memory began to piece themselves together in Gunn's mind. Griggs pouring wine. A sailor falling drunkenly across a table. The sudden explosion of violence. And then this man watching him.

'Where is here?'

'You will be told in good time.'

'I want to be told *now,*' said Gunn firmly. 'I am a British subject, and if you rescued me, I thank you. But it seems to me I am being held as some kind of prisoner.'

'We are all prisoners of circumstance and experience. You have been here for one night and one day, doctor.'

'What time is it now?' asked Gunn.

'After the Hour of the Cock. Five o'clock in the afternoon.'

'I had better leave for my ship.'

'Later.'

Gunn walked over the tiles towards him. He-was about a foot taller. This fellow might keep a key to the door in a pocket, or maybe he could be persuaded to explain how the secret door opened; persuaded or forced.

'Do not be so foolish as to offer me violence,' the man said quietly. 'Or I will be compelled to defend myself by the ancient arts of China. Then you might be injured, and this I would lastingly regret.'

'One minute, you say you rescued me. Now you threaten me.'

As Gunn spoke, he jumped, meaning to tread hard on the other man's feet, then seize him by the throat and bring up his knee into his groin. But the man stepped to one side with a speed that astonished Gunn. He felt a sharp hard punch in his own stomach, and then he was somehow being propelled through the air, arms and legs flaying like the spokes of a wheel. He collapsed untidily on the hard floor, and lay breathless and bruised. Painfully, wearily, he pulled himself up.

'Please do not attempt any further foolishness,' warned the man. 'I am not wishful to harm you.'

Gunn bit back a retort; there was no point in antagonizing the fellow.

'I *must* know where I am.'

'You are in a house in Macao.'

'Macao!'

This was the island Griggs had mentioned. The Portuguese enclave across the Canton Bay. Was he being held to ransom?

'Do not ask any more questions, Englishman. I will arrange for you to have a bath and new clothes. Then you can speak to my master.'

He took a step backwards and slightly to one side. In so doing, he trod on some catch concealed beneath a tile; the hidden door opened in the wall.

Gunn followed him through, and along a corridor. A smell of curry hung faintly on the air. There must be Indians here; but the only Indians Gunn had seen on his voyage East were dockside coolies or low-caste shopkeepers, and this house bore the imprint of wealth.

The man opened another door and ushered Gunn inside. In a room lined with blue Portuguese tiles, stood a zinc bath full of warm water, with a white towel, sponge, a bar of English yellow soap. From a peg near the mirror hung a white towel bathrobe.

On a marble-topped table lay a razor, a metal comb, two brushes with tortoiseshell backs, a shaving brush with a bone handle, a jug of hot water, a stick of shaving soap. The water in the bath smelt of pine essence. Gunn breathed deeply. The steamy room felt infinitely relaxing.

'I will leave you, Englishman. When I return, you will be washed and shaved.'

'What if I'm not? I tell you, I'm not a slave. I'm a British subject. Do you realize what you are doing?'

'I am fully aware. And so is my master. The way of heaven is fairness to all. Let us leave all words to him.'

He bowed and backed out of the door, Gunn heard the lock shoot on the other side. He wound his watch, set it at five o'clock, and looked at himself in the mirror.

His eyes had sunk deeply in his head, his face was sallow, his hair matted. He pulled down the skin beneath his eyes. The pupils were dull, the whites putty-coloured. Maybe he was ill with a fever. Or he had been drugged?

This was the most reasonable explanation — but why should anybody drug him? Of course, a British subject could command, a considerable ransom. And yet surely the man who owned a house like this would not need a ransom, for he must be rich already?

Gunn took off his clothes, sour and damp with sweat, transferred his watch, a few coins, notes and his father's letter into the pocket of the robe, and climbed into the bath. By the time he had washed, shaved and brushed his hair, he felt relaxed, The warm scented bath soothed his spirit as well as his body.

The door opened.

'Are you ready?' the Chinaman asked him.

'What about my clothes?' said Gunn. 'That is my best uniforrn.'

'They will be, washed, and pressed and brought to you.'

'What is going to happen?'

'Nothing of violence. You, have no need to feel alarm!'

He walked ahead in the curiously silent, snake-like progression of the Chinese. Gunn followed him down the corridor into a flagged hall with black and white marble pillars supporting a gilded ceiling painted with huge pictures of stone temples and foaming rivers. They climbed a marble staircase with a golden balustrade, and his guide opened two double doors eight feet tall with crystal handles, and motioned Gunn to enter.

The room beyond was large and airy. High windows opened on to a verandah shielded by a white canopy from the glare of the late afternoon sun.

A man of indefinite age — he could be fifty or seventy — stood looking out through the windows at a bay alive with junks and small boats. Gunn could see two churches and a terrace of houses with baroque fronts; a carriage sped along a road by the edge of the sea. Then the doors closed behind him and they were alone.

The man turned to face him. .

'You are Surgeon Gunn?' he asked in English, in a powerful voice. Gunn saw that his face was neither yellow nor brown nor white, but rather a mixture of all three, the colour of creamy coffee.

'I am. And who are you, sir?'

Something about this man compelled reluctant respect. He wore a loose white jacket, white cotton trousers, gold rings on both hands, and gold sandals with thongs around the big toes. His flesh was soft and scented.

'My name is unimportant, doctor,' he replied. 'It would mean nothing to you. It is an Eastern name, a Parsee name, and as such very common. Your name, on the other hand, means a great deal to me, because I have consulted the various records which you English so assiduously cause to be printed.

'From them I learn that you are twenty-five years old and unmarried. That you were born in the county of Kent and have qualified as a doctor. You are also in first-class health, mentally and physically. These are things important for me to know.'

'But why? I seem to have been kidnapped and brought to your house — for what purpose?'

'Sit down, Dr Gunn,' the man said gently.

Gunn drew up a chair by the side of a marble-topped table. The Parsee sat opposite him, poured out two cups of black tea from a samovar, and added slices of lemon with silver tweezers.

'First of all, Dr Gunn, rest assured that we mean no malevolence or harm to you. I have a task for which I have selected you — out of many other possible candidates — because of your bearing and your education.

'When you have completed this task to my satisfaction —

and to the satisfaction of one other person involved — you will be rewarded with a present of gold coin equal to five hundred English sovereigns. You will also be taken back to Canton to join your ship.'

'My ship may have gone.'

The man inclined his head.

'That is true. She leaves tomorrow on the morning tide. But she will be back. She is only sailing to Lintin Island, across the bay.'

He nodded towards the window. On the far horizon, Gunn saw a dark smudge of land with a long thin spire of rock, looking from the distance like a giant factory chimney.

'Lintin,' the man continued. 'Or as the Chinese say, because of the strange rock formation, the Island of the Solitary Nail: And also as you may or may not be aware, the centre of the forbidden opium trade. Your ship, having discharged one cargo, now proceeds there to discharge another of much greater value, which you probably do not even know about. One grown with infinite care as a prime export in the best land in all India by your own Honourable East India Company.

'My information is that the vessel will return to Canton within two or three weeks. You should be back in time to join her. What account you give for your absence, I leave to your own imagination and ingenuity. But, as I say, you will have the equivalent of five hundred English pounds in your pocket. And I understand you had only six and a half sovereigns in your pocket when you arrived here. So you will not lose money, doctor.'

He smiled, and Gunn closed his eyes for a moment. The room seemed to be turning slowly like a top; the man's voice had an oddly soporific effect.

'What is it you wish me to do?' he asked, and added: 'Before you tell me, I must say I will do nothing that would dishonour my profession or the dignity of the King.'

'You speak like a man.'

'So what if I refuse to do whatever you may ask me?'

The other man smiled almost sadly, as though such a faint possibility had also briefly entered his mind, but very quickly removed itself.

'You will not refuse,' he replied.

'You seem very confident, sir. But what if I do refuse?'

The dark-skinned man glanced down at the tiles on the floor and pointed a ringed finger at one of them. Gunn followed his gaze. A black ant, hardly larger than a moving speck of dust, was diligently crossing the smooth, glazed surface. The man took off his left slipper and flung it down on the tile. When he picked it up, the ant was only a tiny stain on the blue porcelain.

'As that ant is in our eyes, so is a single human life against the background of eternity. It is as nothing, a voice spoken against the winds of evening, a lost echo .we shall never hear again. *If* you are foolish enough to refuse, doctor, you will disappear as that ant has disappeared.

'Look out at that bay. The sea seems smooth as glass, does it not? But under that blue surface it is alive with sharks and pirhanas, waiting to skin the flesh off bones before a body has sunk a foot beneath the waves.

'This is not your country, doctor, with laws and regulations in case anyone is hurt. Values here are not the same — and the first difference you will discover is in the importance we in the East place on human life. It is not high, doctor. Quite the reverse. Life here is very inexpensive. One might almost say, cheap. Everyone has to die one day - so why should it be a matter of importance if they are persuaded to leave, this world rather sooner than they intended?'

'But that's murder,' said Gunn, his voice suddenly hoarse at the thought.

'You can call it by any name you like. But such things frequently happen here, as you could prove very easily for yourself if you stayed long in this latitude. And that is what awaits you if you decline my assignment'

Gunn took another sip of tea. Either this Parsee was mad, or he was; or they both were. His heart was pounding with alarm. He had better humour the fellow.

'What is it you wish me to do?' he asked as quietly as he could.

'I wish you to make love to my daughter, doctor. To mount her, and mount her again, until she is with child by a white man.'

IN WHICH DR GUNN DISCOVERS HE HAS MUCH TO LEARN

Gunn stared at the Parsee in astonishment. Was this some quaint Oriental idea of a jest?

'But I don't even *know* your daughter,' he said in astonishment. He did not add that he had never known any woman in the sense the man suggested. And to do what he proposed would be unthinkable on moral and religious grounds. This damned heathen native *must* be mad. It was the only possible explanation.

'Your face reflects with credit the turmoil of your thoughts,' said the Parsee, with a slight smile. 'You have never been East before?'

'Never.'

'Well, I will explain to you something of this custom. I am a Parsee. I follow Zoroaster, the God of Fire, from whom all blessings flow. Originally, we came from Persia, from which country we take our title, Parsees. Like the Jews, we have ability in commerce and as merchants. We are also, like them, a proud, people. And we are especially proud of the colour of our skin.

'We are not white or red-bristled as the Chinese call you Europeans. Nor are we black as Ethiops, nor yet dark brown like Indians. Our blood is a mixture from many races. And this unique colour of our skin can only be maintained by judicious marriage, and sometimes by deliberate breeding in alternate generations.

'My daughter's husband is a man of honour and ability, a banker of great wealth. But his seed is barren. My daughter has been married to him for three years, and she is still without child.

'You will remedy this situation, doctor, and more than that. With your fair skin you will ensure that her child is fair. I pray to my god she will bear her husband a son.'

'Does she know about this proposition?'

'It was her suggestion. All I had to do was select the right partner — a man of physique and learning. I have chosen you.'

'What about her husband?'

'He knows nothing of this. He is, in fact, on business in Bombay, where a large community of us have houses. On his return he will be overjoyed when his wife tells him she is with child. However, we waste time with words when you have a decision to make.'

'I have made it. The answer is, no.'

'Then you have decided too soon and wrongly. You have not fully considered the alternative.'

'I know little of your customs, but is not adultery held to be a serious offence, in your religion as in mine?'

'You speak the truth, Englishman. It is a most serious offence, yet its evil can be mitigated. The man who commits adultery can atone for his sin by helping with gifts of money to bring about the lawful marriage of four poor couples, by paying for the proper education of poor children, who have none to care for them, by bringing others to a knowledge of God, and by performing certain specific religious rites.

'All these things I will do in your name.'

'But surely, if I refuse, as I do, you would not murder .me? What good could this do you, sir?'

'It is not a question, young man, of doing me either good or evil. It would simply be the only, satisfactory solution to a situation that could otherwise cause embarrassment. If you went back, you might foolishly tell the story to other people. My daughter's name, and that of her husband, might be discovered, and my family insulted on the lips of insignificant persons.

'I would not, of course, kill you myself. There are professionals who do that kind of work. As a matter of fact, I personally abhor all physical violence. Now, what is your answer?'

'No. I cannot do it.'

'Are you adamant that you wish to die?'

'Of course I am not. But this is a disgusting proposition.'

'There are men who would not view it in that light,' said the Parsee sharply. 'Is it more money you wish, but are too gentlemanly to suggest? We who are schooled in commerce have no such scruples. Would the equivalent of a thousand sovereigns change your mind about the value of my proposal?'

This was a fortune, more than Gunn could hope to earn in five years. And there was no middle course between this and the incredible and ludicrous alternative, of death. But his strict upbringing did not make acceptance easy, and to fornicate was a sin, although obviously these *might* be extenuating circumstances.

No doubt to fornicate would be considered a lesser evil than to acquiesce in his own destruction? And, for that matter, who would ever know about this sin, unless he told them? Of course, God would know. But then He knew all things, past and future; He had created him, and already knew what course Gunn would take.

A thousand pounds in gold. With such a sum Gunn could afford to treat poor people who would otherwise suffer and even die. Out of evil, might not some good grow — as the Parsee himself proposed — as flowers sprouted from a dunghill? He was wavering; he realised it. He poured himself another cup of tea. Obviously, this Parsee fellow would like him to agree. Otherwise, he would have to begin fresh negotiations and then arrange another abduction, and possibly a further journey from Macao for his unsuspecting son-in-law.

It might be possible to turn, these facts to his own advantage; at least, he could try. If he *had* to commit this sin, then he would do so on the best financial terms he could arrange. If this Parsee were as rich as he appeared, then he must pay dearly for an Englishman's seed.

'I am young and without wealth,' said Gunn, surprised at the strength of his own voice. 'You are rich, and I am in your power. But I have something that you wish for your daughter. And you have something I also need. Money. Since you tell me you have no scruples about bargaining, you teach me to abandon my own. I will do what you ask. But not for one thousand sovereigns. For *five* thousand.'

'What would you do with so much money, Englishman?'

'I would send one thousand sovereigns to my parents in England. It would buy them many things they have gone without all their days.'

'And how would you explain your sudden affluence?'

'I hadn't thought of that,' admitted Gunn. But he would; he was learning fast.

'You see, doctor,' the Parsee went on in his gentle voice, 'wealth has its own obligations. One should never be too greedy in acquiring it. You seek to acquire a fortune, and one day, too late, you will find that it has acquired you. But I admire your courage, and how you say, your cheek. *Three* thousand. That is my last price.'

Three thousand pounds. Fifteen years' pay. For doing something that most other men from *Trelawney* were spending a month's pay to do with some prostitute, heedless of pox or robbery.

'How do I know you will keep your word?' asked Gunn. 'If you hold life so cheaply, why will you not kill me when I have done my part of the bargain?'

'Because I am a man of my family's honour. I will give you

the coin, or a letter on any bank in India or your own country - for three thousand sovereigns, which would be more convenient for you. You can trust me, doctor. To a Parsee a promise is a debt. Broken promises mean broken faith and broken friendship.'

'How did you choose me?'

'I have told you. Because of your intellect, your physique and, I understand, your abstemious life.'

'But why me? You don't know me. You've never seen me before.'

'True. But we merchants have our contacts in all the great cities of trade — in London, in Bombay, in Calcutta and Singapore. I asked for a suitable person to be found. Several candidates were proposed, but they failed in some way. You did not.'

Gunn thought back to the *Trelawney's* short stay in ports on the outward voyage. An English family had asked him to dinner in Bombay. In Calcutta, while at a regimental dance (to which he had unaccountably been invited) someone had introduced him to one of the city's richest jute merchants, a Scotsman. Gunn had not been particularly interested or impressed; how, looking back, he was. He remembered the Hoppo looking at him in Canton. The links of trade and money were stronger than he had ever imagined. But how had their reports reached Macao?

'By letter. In your own ship,' the Parsee said, guessing his thoughts.

'How long will this take?' asked Gunn. He had already made up his mind. There was no going back now, no way of retreat; and, surprisingly, no wish to find one.'

'You as a medical man know the intricacies of the feminine rhythm better than me. I would say you would be here for at least a fortnight.'

'*Where*, exactly?'

'In another part of this palace. You will have a suite of

rooms with a bathroom and a courtyard, where you may walk or sit in the sun. But you will not be allowed out onto the Praya. You will also have your own personal servant, who will bring you your food and drink and wash your clothes.'

'It's like being at stud,' said Gunn musingly. But for three thousand pounds who wouldn't be a stallion? What would his parents think of him now, in some Eastern potentate's palace, about to sell his manhood for three thousand sovereigns? What would Griggs think? Gunn immediately knew the answer and smiled at it. Griggs would be in there before him!

'You find this situation amusing?' asked the Parsee coldly.

'Amusing, no. Unusual, yes. I have no alternative but to accept. And, as Iago said to Othello, "I'll do it, but it dislikes me".'

Now the Parsee smiled.

'I have never found the act of love to my disliking.'

'How do you know I will not speak of this?'

'You may. That is your decision. But in so doing, you would lay yourself open to calumny and contempt. And, in any case, what good would it do either of us? What English gentleman would accept money from a native to mount his daughter, and get her with child? And what would your medical colleagues think of such behaviour, should it ever reach their ears? In any case, you will never see me again.'

'But if I am still a ship's doctor, we might call here?'

Odd, how he had said 'still.' Was he already contemplating another career, not at sea and maybe not even in his profession?

'My daughter will leave when she bears the child. She and her husband will live in Bombay.'

Gunn stood up; there seemed nothing more to discuss. The door opened, and the man who had guided him here stood inside, hands folded, head down.

'Here is your servant. And while you are my guest, I would warn you against trying to overpower him to make an escape. In view of the importance of your task, Dr Gunn, and the high fee you are receiving, we would not wish to risk injury to you — or tire you unnecessarily.'

The Parsee crossed to a table, wrote out a cheque and handed it to Gunn. It was drawn on Grindlays Bank in Bombay for three thousand sovereigns. 'Your name is on the cheque,' Gunn pointed out. 'I .could easily trace you.'

'We have already discussed that eventuality. Now, I have other matters to attend to.'

The Parsee bowed. Gunn followed the servant out of the door, along a different corridor, up more stairs, until they reached a landing where small palm trees in flowered blue urns carved with dragons stood outside another set of double doors.

'Here are your quarters,' the servant told him. 'You will find a bell inside. Ring it, and I will bring whatever you need.'

Reaction had dried Gunn's mouth. His heart fluttered like a bird beneath his ribs. He felt suddenly nervous and shy. He was a virgin, and this_ woman, however unsatisfactorily married, would instantly know this. It was one thing to be acquainted with the written techniques of love, to know the names and intensities of the erotic zones, just as it was to be acquainted with books on medicine and surgery. It was altogether another to have to practise satisfactorily with a stranger what others had written about, and what you had only read.

Gunn walked slowly into the room. Another wide window overlooked the bay. He was about a hundred feet above the Praya, and he looked down on people foreshortened by the height. A horse whinnied, and half a dozen coolies jog-trotted past, huge bundles on their heads. There was no drainpipe, no convenient gutter to which he could cling, or climb down. But why try to escape - and where could he go if he did? Also, he had given his word; he had taken the Parsee's money. Now he had to do what had been agreed. The floor was white marble, covered with sheepskin rugs. Two wide divans were separated by a table, with bottles of whisky, crystal goblets, a glass bucket of ice. To one side were bowls of shelled prawns fried to an unusual crispness, and peeled lychees and small oranges.

He sat down, poured himself a Queen Anne, then examined the next room. This contained a wide double bed, and plain unpainted furniture. Beyond this was a bathroom. So here he was: Gunn at stud. And, incredibly, his fee could buy a grand house, a carriage and pair, a medical practice in Herne Bay, and still leave more to spend. It was a staggering amount of money. But, as he remembered Herne Bay, he realized that the prospect of being a country doctor there seemed suddenly much less attractive than it had appeared only days before, aboard *Trelawney.*

If he could make three thousand sovereigns in a fortnight in the East, what might he make in a year or in a lifetime, if he set his mind to trade and commerce, like the Parsee?

The prospect of wealth, of the power it could bring, its comforts and pleasures, had never greatly occupied him before. He had never been in a position to command it. But now, quite unexpectedly, he was. To the devil with going back to being a ship's doctor for a few pounds a month and his keep of hard-tack and rum and lime juice, examining sailors for pox and scurvy. *This* was where his fortune lay. Here, in the East, where for centuries wealth had been beyond accounting; where mandarins were millionaires and what was strange and fabled by any other standard, was accepted as commonplace. As he was about to prove conclusively.

Gunn heard a door click, and walked back into the main room. A girl was standing in the other room, her arms folded, head down modestly. She was of medium height, and wore a white sari with a gold edge, and gold chaplis. Her fingernails and toenails were painted. Long gold rings dangled from her ears.

As Gunn came to the door, she looked up at him; she was smiling slightly. She was younger than he was, possibly only twenty, but there was a fullness about her mouth and face that gave her a maturity beyond her years. Gunn held out his hand awkwardly. She curtsied, and taking it between both of hers, raised it to her lips. This must be the woman he was to seduce for three thousand sovereigns — or, rather, who was to seduce him.

'I don't know your name,' he said.

'I know yours,' she replied in English.

'So you have the advantage over me?'

'No doubt it is the only one. Please sit down.'

They sat at each end of one of the settees. She poured out two glasses of fruit juice and handed one to him.

'You must think the East has strange customs?' she said.

'Yes,' he agreed. 'Some are, shall we say, unusual?'

'But you *might* grow to like them?' she went on, smiling.

'That is possible,' he agreed again, still ill-at-ease, but much less so. She was easy to talk to, and gentle and warm in a way Marion had never been. His tension melted.

'When did you last have anything to eat?' she asked him. Gunn saw that her brown eyes were unusually large; the lashes were darkened with kohl.

'Days ago, I suppose. I was drugged in Canton, I think.'

'We must get you something.'

She leaned to one side and pulled a bell tassel and, as she leaned, Gunn could see the nipples like dark stains through the tightening silk across her breasts. The whisky and the sight and scent of her moved in his blood. He could feel warmth spread to his loins.

The servant appeared silently in the doorway. She spoke to him quickly. The man bowed and went away.

They had another drink, and then the servant was back with a companion wearing a white uniform with a red belt and gold buckles, carrying a tray. On this were dishes of rice and curried prawns, silver jars of chutney, and plates of chopped eggs and beetroot and carrot and coconut.

The servants bowed and withdrew. The plates were kept

warm over a spirit flame. They served themselves.

'You have everything?' she asked, smiling.

'Everything,' he said, suddenly conscious of the *double en-tendre.*

They ate, and as Gunn swallowed the food, rich and spiced and satisfying, a feeling of complete relaxation swept over him. With Adam and this girl as his guides, he would not disgrace himself.

The servants returned and wheeled away the trolley.

'Tell me about your home,' said the girl.

'There's not much to tell, really,' said Gunn. 'Except it's different from this.'

He suddenly recalled the semi-detached villa; cold mornings when bedroom windows were damp with condensation; summer days when the only sounds were the hum of bees and the distant cries of seagulls.

He glanced out of the window; the heat was draining from the day. Within minutes, it would be dusk.

'Have you ever done this sort of thing before?' he asked, suddenly nervous again.

'Never,' she said, still smiling. 'Have you?'

'Goodness, no.'

Gunn was shocked at the idea, and then faintly amused. He stood up and walked to the window. The Praya seemed full of people walking in the evening air. What would they say if they knew what he was about to do? He smiled at the idea, and then sat down, this time much closer to her.

He stretched out his left arm tentatively along the back of the sofa. She was really very beautiful. Although her skin was coffee-coloured, in the deepening darkness of the room, this did not matter at all. Indeed, it seemed to suit her better, to be a greater contrast to the whiteness of her sari.

She leaned slightly towards him.

'You're good-looking,' she said.

'Oh? Thank you. You're very good-looking yourself, if I may say so.'

'You may and you have. Are you married in England?'

'No. I was engaged. But not any more. She preferred some-one else.'

'Tell me about her.'

'There's nothing much to tell,' said Gunn, and of course there wasn't. Just a letter he had read, a feeling of emptiness inside that was fast fading.

His fingers had reached her hair, which was soft and dark and long, and quite different from Marion's brittle hair on the few occasions he had touched it. But then this girl was altogether different in every way. Or was she? Perhaps this was how Cartwright, the grocer, had started with Marion. Perhaps he should have been bolder with her? But what did any of these possibilities matter now? The present was what counted; the present and the future. Three thousand sover-eigns was a solid initial payment of a far greater fortune.

Gunn moved his hand, which rested on her far shoulder; his arm had gone to sleep. She slid slightly against him.

'What colour was *her* hair?' she asked, as though it mat-tered.

'Brownish,' he said, and as he tried to recall Marion's fea-tures, he found with surprise he could hardly remember any-thing about her. She had always been indeterminate; a charac-terless face in a crowd.

Now she was gone, lost in a crowd of more important sensa-tions.

He could feel the warmth of this girl's body through her thin sari. His grip tightened. He turned slightly, and her face came up against his, so that he could see it and nothing else: her enormous dark eyes, the glisten of white teeth through parted lips, her smile.

He kissed her then, and it was different from the short pas-sionless pecks he had exchanged with Marion in another coun-try, another life.

Her tongue moved gently against his mouth, soft as a night-moth's wings, and then probed between his lips in a fierce, electrifying way. His hands went round the bodice of her sari, and hers slipped under his robe against his bare body. The touch of flesh on flesh was burning, like fire.

She drew back briefly and he saw her face again, still smiling, enigmatic and her fingertips brushed magically and mesmerically down his spine. Her tongue was now a dark honeyrose that flitted in and out of his mouth at will.

His fingers found a dip at the back of her bodice, which was the easiest thing in the world to undo. She gave a sigh of relief and content, and wriggled free. Her breasts were firm in his hands, pointed, rounded, altogether wonderful. It was not nothing to hold these heavy globes, paradoxically soft yet firm, two round worlds with a life of their own. She moved against him and it was the most natural thing in the world to cover her with his body. His robe slid open, and her legs entwined about his, so that it seemed they were not two bodies but two parts of one. Then she was feeding him gently into her other soft, moist mouth, and suddenly he was rearing like a beast, thrusting as though he must die if he stopped; not heeding her first stifled cry, nor the soft moanings she uttered.

Her fingers gripped his shoulders, digging into the firm muscles like hard claws as he thrust like a god. The sweat from their flesh ran together and mingled in the anonymity of dusk. Then the long hot thread of his life poured into her, and they sank, sobbing for breath, side by side, in a welter of robe and sari, on the rough canvas of the settee.

They lay until the thunder of Gunn's heart receded. From far away, he heard sweetmeat sellers call their wares on the Praya. They had been calling before he started this apocalyptic journey he had begun as a youth and ended as a man. How elastic had time become! He dozed, half between sleep and dreams, content and relaxed.

The girl was the first to move.

'Come into the bedroom,' she said softly. Her eyes in the

dark room were luminous, like stars, and she was smiling. 'You have things to learn. And I want to be the one to teach you.'

IN WHICH THE SON OF HEAVEN UTTERS AN IMPORTANT PRAYER

The procession had set out some time before dawn, so that when the sun came burning up over the four cities that constituted Peking, the leading marchers were already near the Altar of Heaven — a huge open marble dais in a park near the main gates.

People had packed the narrow streets of the capital for hours, climbing up on the roofs of the gaily painted shops for a better view. Outside teahouses in side streets, so narrow that two wheelbarrows could barely pass, comedians went through their patter, and acrobats and jugglers flung themselves about furiously while colleagues touted busily for coins from the crowds.

The sun gilded the curved tiles on the towering gatehouses that guarded the city entrances, turning their red shutters, quaintly painted with pictures of cannon, to the colour of dried blood. Steam rose from the sluggish river and hung like fog in streets already heavy with the stench of sewage. In China, all household waste was collected in pails and then carried to the fields to fertilize the crops, along with hair gathered daily from the floors of barbers' shops. It slopped over and was trodden through the streets.

At the head of the procession marched the Emperor's imperial bodyguard, tall, broad-shouldered men, sweating in the suffocating, stinking air. They marched in leather skirts and black helmets, and carried quivers of sharpened arrows on their shoulders. They, held whips in their right hands, and to the rhythmic boom of a brass gong beat back people who had poured from their stews and alleys and hovels to see the passage of the Son of Heaven, the Emperor of the Celestial Kingdom.

Behind the bodyguard came standard bearers with flags and streamers on golden poles, and then a pig-tailed mandarin in blue robes, wearing the red cap of his rank, holding a gold umbrella, the symbol of royalty. Court eunuchs, each six feet tall, their faces plump as capons, and other lesser mandarins marched after him. All intoned the Emperor's praises in a strange high chant.

Tao Kuang, Glorious Rectitude in the Chinese translation, Emperor of China for the past ten years, sat on a golden throne, its legs carved in the likeness of talons. This throne was carefully shielded by glass and borne on gilded poles by sixteen men. The Emperor's hat was shaped like a scholastic mortarboard, and from it twenty-four pendentives swung with every step of his bearers. His yellow gown and purple coat were special garments worn by succeeding Sons of Heaven when acting as High Priests of the Children of Han, and about to address themselves to Heaven, as only they were privileged to do. For this procession had neither political nor military significance; it was a religious pilgrimage of national importance. Tao Kuang was on his way to the Altar of Heaven, near the Hall of the Blending of Heaven and Earth and the Palace of Heavenly Purity, to pray for rain.

China lay in the grip of a ferocious drought. Reservoirs were empty; cattle had died for lack of water; crops stood parched and stunted. Many rivers had dried up altogether; only a few contained enough water to keep fish alive.

This in itself was an omen of more terrible things to come, for fish were most important symbols of life, and how they fared was a sure indication of what awaited the whole Kingdom.

For weeks, priests had lamented and prayed for rain; but no rain had fallen. So now the Son of Heaven would speak to Heaven, his Father, and, begging forgiveness for his grievous sins, would ask that rain should fall, and quickly, and in abundance.

As befitted, the supreme dignity of such an occasion, the Emperor's coat was embroidered with the Twelve Ornaments, each symbolic and significant of some part of China or Chinese life. First, the sun; then the moon and the stars; fire; grass; a pheasant; a key-fret; the head of an axe; mountains; the dragon; cups of wine and milk; rice grains, that represented both food and drink.

The Emperor wore a leather girdle, studded, and glittering with sacred gems, each big as a man's eye, and hanging with clattering metal pendants. His black leather boots, soft as silk, had white leather soles three inches thick.

Behind him, through the tortuous streets of the city, followed thousands of his subjects. They felt supremely honoured that they had set eyes on the man whose power and word were infinite; who usually spoke to other men only through intermediaries; who alone could speak to the gods; whose wisdom was the wisdom of all the ages.

Tao sat with his hands loosely on the gold arms of the chair. He was in his fifties, a quiet man who, in another situation, might have been an academic or a teacher, for he lived a surprisingly austere life. At three o'clock each morning he was carried to his private pagoda to worship Buddha. Then he would walk in his palace garden, in the Purple Forbidden City, at the heart of Peking, before work with his Secretaries or Grand Counsellors. After a light meal of, rice and fruit, he would relax for an hour or two writing poetry with a brush dipped in Royal vermilion ink.

He would retire to bed at seven each evening, and outside his room eunuchs stood on perpetual guard, ready to summon to him any of a hundred concubines and eight queens whose lives were devoted to his whims and his pleasures. These women were all adept at different attitudes of sexual gratification. One, her front teeth removed, would take his penis in her mouth; another, with large, firm buttocks, would, delight on being penetrated from the rear; a third, hands kept perpetually moist in gloves of scented ointment, would massage his phallus to the muted music of harps.

But the Emperor was not thinking of such things now. He was pondering the speech he would have to make when the procession reached the Altar of Heaven. Sinister signs had been seen in the heavens —falling stars, strange glowing lights — which soothsayers could read as ordinary men read books, and all pointed relentlessly to a time of terrible change and war. The ancient rules of Confucius, by which all civilization must live or die, had been flouted and this drought was only one of the results.

There were also other signs of anarchy, equally serious and closer to his heart. Earlier that year, a rebel in Canton, who called himself The Golden Dragon King and claimed he possessed magical powers, had defeated a regiment of the Imperial troops that the Emperor had sent against him.

The Emperor knew from his own spies that this had happened because many Imperial soldiers were opium smokers, living in their private, flowery world of ease and dreams.

But the Governor of Canton, in reporting their humiliating defeat, had prudently not mentioned this addiction, lest his own vast income from trading in the forbidden drug should be questioned. Instead, he had declared that The Golden Dragon King had possessed demoniacal powers against which human troops had been powerless.

This was a falsehood, of course, and Tao had dismissed the Governor instantly and brought him in iron chains to his court in Peking. His possessions had been seized, and then he had been banished to the wild, cold, frontier country in the north, to ponder on his misdeeds. But his punishment did nothing to change the ignominy of Imperial defeat; another regiment had been required to subdue the insolent rebels. The Emperor's palanquin jogged on. The streets were hotter now, and he felt the vague unease he always felt on these occasions. What would happen if he prayed — and no rain fell? What would happen if, next time, not two hundred but *four* hundred of his troops were opium addicts?

Why, even in Peking, a manure gatherer who scratched up horse dung with a wooden shovel, had saved a little money, and gathered together some discontented old soldiers, whose pensions were in arrears, some professional beggars and paupers, and then had the effrontery to style himself the reincarnation of an Old King.

He claimed he had reigned before the Manchus took power, and now had returned to claim his throne.

Fortunately, the Emperor's spies had told him the date of the uprising, so the manure gatherer had been arrested on that same morning and strangled ceremoniously and in public with iron chains. There had been other attempts at rebellion, too, which had fortunately fizzled out like damp fireworks on an autumn evening. But they all were significant, for Tao knew that many still regarded him as a stranger, an interloper.

His family, the Manchus, had ruled China for barely two hundred years, and so were still not accepted in a land where time stretched measureless as the Outer Seas. And because of this feeling he believed that his officials did not fight corruption as fiercely as if he had been a native king.

If his prayers for rain failed, then all kinds of other revolutionaries would instantly rise, like frogs in a marsh, and croak their criticism. He dare not fail, because he could not afford failure — but how could he be certain of success?

How different life had been in the past, he mused, when

honest men held office, and corruption was virtually un-known! Once, in the golden days of long ago, a friend of a pro-vincial governor, Yang Chen, had remonstrated with him for not leaving a fortune to his sons, and Yang Chen had replied: 'If posterity speaks of me as an incorruptible official, will *that* be nothing?'

And again, when someone else had offered Yang a bribe, ex-plaining: 'It is dark, and no-one will know,' Yang had replied in surprise: 'No-one will know? Why, Heaven will know. Earth will know. You will know. I will know.'

In memory of this man's integrity, the Ancestral Hall of his family was still called the Hall of the Four Knows. Where in all his Kingdom now could Tao find a man like this?

I must have more spies, he thought, and I must pay larger rewards for information, so that I can discover which offi-cials are taking bribes from these Barbarians. Or what about getting rid of the Barbarians altogether? This was a most at-tractive idea. It was very possible that their presence in the Heavenly Kingdom was in large measure to blame for famines, for this present drought — and even for the serious floods of the Yellow River which earlier that year had drowned hun-dreds of people.

Truly, since the arrival of the earliest Barbarians, the Portuguese three hundred years before, China's troubles had multiplied and grown graver. Somehow the Portuguese had persuaded the Emperor of that time to allow them trading facilities. They had spoken with honeyed tongues and prom-ised him all kinds of benefits. Finally, he had allowed them the use of Macao, a barren, mosquito-ridden island in the Canton River.

But hardly had they set up their warehouses than the Span-ish had arrived to break their monopoly. First, the Spanish had seized the Philippine islands and subdued the savages there. Then, sailing from Mexico by way of Manila, the Spanish used Macao to turn round their ships, and re-load them with new cargoes.

Early in the seventeenth century, the Dutch had arrived in Java. They renamed the island Batavia, and almost immediately sent envoys to Peking, impudently asking for the use of a port in China, and permission to trade. But of course the Dutch were only pirates; they had nothing to offer, and they were given nothing in return. The Emperor had explained to them courteously that while it was right and proper for them to come to admire China and worship the Son of Heaven, he did not need their ambassador or their trade, and nothing would change this view.

After this discomfiture of the Dutch, the British had arrived, and the Americans. They were strange peoples, often swearing and shouting, and fighting among themselves, speaking the same language, yet absurdly claiming to be two separate nations. The British were the more politically dangerous, for although his cartographers assured him they came from a tiny island, yet from this faraway foggy place on the edge of a mainland, they had subdued countries a hundred times their size, and thousands of miles away.

Now they pressed impatiently against the shores of his Kingdom. So far, he and his predecessors had managed to confine them with the other foreign devils to a small area in Canton, but they were determined to advance these narrow frontiers, and would use any means to do so.

They had tried with gifts, sending noble lords as ambassadors to him bearing presents, astrolabes, telescopes with huge lenses, and brass howitzers. They had even presented his predecessors with two carriages on springs. These were unusual, for Chinese conveyances possessed no springs, but what strange values Europe must admire if the humble coachman took preference over the owner of the carriage, by sitting above him *and* in front of him!

Tao smiled again at the absurdity of this idea. But what else could one expect from sweating Barbarians, with bristled chins and red hair, who belched after drink and not after food? This was truly the ultimate mark of their crudity, for to belch after food was to acknowledge to your host how much pleasure it had given you. But to belch after drinking was to equate yourself with grunting hogs in a swamp.

These unlikely foreigners had subdued India and had swanned into Burma and Malaya, but their greatest prize would be China itself.

The Americans were even landing men and women with the declared intention of converting his subjects to their strange Christian religion. No wonder the gods were angry with him and withheld rain while he allowed them to prosper, and their strength and influence to increase!

Perhaps his officials also took bribes to allow this, as along the southern coast they took money from the suppliers of opium?

His Imperial Displeasure must flash against them like flame, and be as lightning and thunder over the Purple Mountains. He must show all corrupt administrators how long was his arm and how hard and crushing his fist. Clearly, he had failed to be ruthless enough.

'The quality of the rulers,' so Confucius had taught, 'permeates society to the dregs.' If their quality was good or bad, then the calibre of the entire country must be coloured accordingly. Did he not recall the example of Emperor Chang K'an, in the first century, who was so just a ruler that nature had responded and made every blade of corn grow two ears instead of one?

He became aware that the procession was about to stop. The rhapsodists and eunuchs had ceased their songs, and were now humming a hymn of praise to him. At the tap of a drum, his sixteen bearers, with one well-drilled movement, slid the poles from their shoulders, bowed, and prostrated themselves until his palanquin was resting on the ground.

Tao climbed out and, walking with the stiff ceremonial gait he had been taught as a child, as rigorously defined as the steps of a formal dance, every step made on the beat of a gong, he approached the altar to pray. All around him, people flung themselves, faces down, in the dust.

'Wu Hu, oh, alas, Imperial Heaven, were not the world afflicted by extraordinary ills, I should not dare to present extraordinary supplications,' he began, in a ritual sing-song voice. 'But this year the drought passes all precedent. Summer is past and still no rain has fallen. Mankind is bowed beneath calamity, and even the beasts and insects cease to live.'

Tao paused, hands outstretched, looking at the thousands of his subjects lying still as the dead. A few dogs and hogs grouted and grunted among them, but even those people they pressed against did not dare to move.

'I, the Son of Heaven, am Lord of this World,' he went on. 'Heaven looks to me that I preserve tranquillity. Yet, though I cannot sleep, though I cannot eat with appetite, though I shake with grief and anxiety, my grief, my fasts, my sleepless nights have obtained but a trifling shower.

'Have I wanted in respect for you? Has pride or prodigality too deep a place in my heart, springing like weeds by my neglect?

'Have I been negligent in public business, lacking in the diligence and effort that was due? Have unfit persons been appointed to official posts? Have magistrates declined their ear to petitioners?

'I implore Imperial Heaven to pardon my ignorance. Summer is past, autumn is close at hand, truly to wait is not possible. Hasten and confer clement deliverance. With speed send down the blessing of rain. Wu Hu, oh, alas, Imperial Heaven, give ear to my petition!'

Tao paused, head down now that his prayer was over, hands by his sides. Then he turned and walked back to his palanquin and climbed inside. The sixteen men took the strain on their shoulders again and raised him up. The procession began to march back to the palace, and the crowds stood up on their feet.

Above them all, the sun still burned like a flame in the sky; there seemed neither sign nor hope of rain. The Emperor sat, face composed and expressionless as a mask, but his mind in a ferment. If no rain fell, his power would be doubted, his whole authority questioned. For this reason, he had delayed making his prayer for weeks; for the longer he waited, the nearer rain must be. Yet he could do no more than pray in the ancient, stylized way, using phrases as old as his religion.

Perhaps he should have promised something specific in return for rain? Perhaps he should have made a private vow to Heaven that he would do some great and worthy act — like driving the Barbarians out of his kingdom?

But how could he force them to go? His Viceroy in Canton had repeatedly assured him that they were harmless; that foreign ships were leaky, and because European soldiers wore such heavy uniforms, they were unable to run without falling over on their backs like beetles, and so offered no challenge to Chinese troops.

Tao doubted this, for the Portuguese, the British and the Americans had sailed these same contemptible ships for thousands of miles; and some of their ships were now propelled by fire and steam, and not by wind or oars. Also, their soldiers had stayed upright in many hard campaigns elsewhere. So, lacking direct force, he would have to use guile. He thought about the problem during the long journey back to his palace, bowing mechanically from time to time, not seeing any of the people who flung themselves, heads down, in front of his procession.

He had passed the Palace of Heavenly Purity, the Hall of the Blending of Heaven and Earth, and was going through the Archway of the Purple Forbidden City, at the centre of which was his palace, when he realized what he must do.

He could not demean himself by attempting to deal with Barbarians and Foreign Devils direct. Instead, he would make all opium dealers liable to instant death if dealing was discovered. The trade was already illegal, and this Imperial Edict, if enforced rigorously and without exception, would soon stamp it out, as a man in heavy boots can beat down a fire before it spreads and sets a whole forest aflame.

He would also appoint a new Viceroy in Canton, a man who had reached high rank by his own endeavours, whose honesty was not suspect. He would give this man strict orders to deal harshly with the Foreign Devils. They would react in some violent and un-Confucian way, as they had so often reacted in the past, and he would strike and banish them all. And then China and all his empire could return to peaceful things, and life would be as it had been in the olden .times. He would promise Heaven he would do this great deed, worthy of all his ancestors; now Heaven would relent and allow rain to fall.

The procession stopped as it approached his palace. Gently, his palanquin was lowered, and the singing died to a whisper. A servant prostrated himself and then opened the door.

The Emperor stepped out. As he turned his face to look up at the sky, rain began to fall; thin scattered drops at first, like tiny fingers tapping on a drum, and then in a torrent of water as the skies opened.

Now the gongs and drums beat triumphantly and the singers took up their song. The crowds shouted with wild delight. Truly, the Son of Heaven's prayer had been answered with unusual and amazing swiftness.

But only the Son of Heaven knew why.

IN WHICH A REVEREND AMERICAN GENTLEMAN RECEIVES AN IMPORTANT VISITOR

At the same hour that rain fell in Peking, the Reverend Selmer Mackereth knelt piously at prayer in his room in Macao. It was not raining there, and the room was warm, and he was praying to another God.

Mackereth was a squat, broad-shouldered man, with hair turning grey and cropped short against the heat. In the half light of evening, his head looked as though it had been dusted with iron fillings.

Mackereth's hands were broad and the nails bitten down to the quick. His eyes, unusually, were open, for he had run out of anything further to say to the Almighty. As he knelt, elbows tucked into his round stomach, looking at the opposite wall of the room where Christ hung on an ivory crucifix, the thought struck him that he had been praying like this in Macao, morning and evening, for seven years, and he. was still as far from converting the Chinese heathen to the ways of the one true God' as when he had arrived from New York. Perhaps this was God's way of informing him that he was in the wrong place, and had answered the wrong call? Or perhaps he had only imagined he had ever heard a call?

He struggled to his feet, stiff in his joints, confused and disappointed, and sat back thankfully in a wicker chair. He poured himself a neat whisky. I have laboured in the vineyard, he thought to himself, but there are no grapes yet worth gathering, nor any foreseeable harvest worthy of the name.

His mind ran back for a moment over the chequer-board of his life. His family had sailed from Bohemia to the United States, where his parents had both died when he was in his teens, and on money he inherited from his father, who owned a market garden, he had qualified as a priest of a small and unfashionable order, the Sons of Zebedee.

Priesthood in this order was no bar to marriage, and he chose as his wife a dull, mousey woman who sang in the tabernacle choir. She was a widow, in poor health, as it turned out, and had died within months of their marriage. Mackereth then discovered with surprise, and some relief, that her first husband had left her thousands of acres of wheatland. Mackereth sold this, banked the money and lived comfortably off the interest.

He liked travel and had visited England, but the climate and the welcome were both too chill for him; also, England already had enough priests. He had moved on to France and Germany, then back to Bohemia; next, on to Egypt. His rank and his money assured him of respect, but friends he would have to make himself, and this he had always found difficult.

He rented a villa on the outskirts of Cairo near the Nile, but the weather was hot, and the rasping dust from the desert and those endless burning days, irritated his throat and made him cough. Also, it had been difficult to find companions among either the English or the French community. He had been disturbed by critical remarks from irreligious people who doubted that he was a priest, for the Sons of Zebedee were not widely known. So he had sailed even farther east to India; then on to Burma. A brief stay in Java followed, and finally, he had reached Macao, the farthest East that he could travel. If he left Macao, he could only go back, not forward, and there was nothing and no-one to return to in any of the countries he had visited.

Mackereth had established himself as a missionary in Macao, printing Bible tracts with his own money, and distributing them to the Chinese. They accepted them politely enough at street corners, but once out of his sight either threw the paper into the gutter, or else carried it home to patch up a hole in one of their ramshackle houses.

Mackereth had really achieved nothing, and now as he sat in the evening of middle age, dwelling on his past and contemplating the present, he knew the future would be similarly full of failures. How disappointed Our Lord must have felt, he thought, when He had walked round the shores of Lake Galilee and spoken to the multitudes in parables, and even performed miracles for them, and yet *still* they remained unbelievers, or even worse, disbelievers!

Mackereth sipped his drink again, and poured himself another. He was running away, of course. He could admit this to himself only after a few drinks; but never to anyone else. He was running away from that terrible vice which every nation gave to a neighbouring country. In England, it was the French complaint; in France, the English vice. In Germany it was said to belong to Italians; Italy blamed it on the Slavs. Only in the comfortable acceptability of Cairo and in some of the anonymous back streets of Bombay, had Mackereth been at ease, out of his dark suits and imprisoning white collar; for he was a homosexual. He had realized this as soon as he was married — before, if he was absolutely honest — but the Lord in His infinite mercy, in gathering his wife to the Eternal Blessed, had saved him the further degradation of connection with a woman.

He sat, legs apart, head flung back, remembering the Chinese and half-caste Portuguese boys he liked to think of as his friends, with their fresh clean complexions and firm young limbs, their flat bellies and rounded buttocks. At the thought, he squirmed in his seat, and the familiar arrows of desire dug well-sharpened barbs in his loins.

Of course, he was not alone in this private battle. Had not St Paul suffered from these same agonies of lust? Mackereth had adopted all kinds of allies in his war against these forbidden longings. He had endured cold baths, purges, sea-bathings. He had drunk foul-tasting elixirs and swallowed pills, but beneath these extremes of drugs and discomforts, his need burned oh like fire below a covering of burnt-out ash.

He told himself he was helping the boys, that he was teaching them Christianity. If, in return, they shared his bed or fingered him, or allowed him to finger them with his brown, nicotine-stained hands, while his breath throbbed and rattled in his throat, perhaps they would forget these physical indignities, and remember the spiritual introduction he had given them to the Kingdom of Heaven?

There had been complaints against him, but he had bought them off. In Macao, this was not difficult to do. Officials of every kind and every rank had their price, just as in Canton and Lintin the mandarins had theirs.

He was a labourer in the vineyard of the Lord, and of all the millions in China, surely a handful would eventually accept the message of the Gospels he had come so far to spread? Then everything would be worthwhile, but to achieve this, he needed money, more than his means would allow, and only that week he had heard the shattering news that the bank in which he had placed his money had found itself unable to meet its commitments.

He read the letter time and again, before the horrible, unspeakable message filtered through to his understanding. They had lent more money than they possessed; there had been a run on their funds, and they had closed their doors.

Mackereth was therefore not a rich man with private means, but a frightened, worried, middle-aged man with rent to pay, a housekeeper to pay, boys to pay, bribes to pay; and no money for any of his debts. So he had been praying for help to the God he had served in his own way. Had not Our Lord Himself advised: Take no thought for tomorrow, what ye shall eat or what ye shall put on, for the Lord shall provide? Now was His chance, thought Mackereth.

He poured a third whisky, and its rough fire began to burn in his veins. There were many rich families in Macao. Perhaps one would hire him as a tutor for children; perhaps they might even have young boys? Maybe he could be a confessor? The Catholics had done very well out of that for centuries. There was no reason, surely, why a Son of Zebedee could not follow where they had led. The Lord would provide for him somehow, he kept telling himself, assuring-himself, but how?

He poured himself a fourth whisky and sat, head sunk down now on his chest, as the shadows grew longer and darker. His Chinese servant appeared silently in the doorway; he often watched his master thus. How odd that these Barbarians found such comfort in this fiery, angry water! Of course, he had sampled it when Mackereth was away, but he had not found its heat at all to his liking. Now Mackereth owed him a month's salary. He would have to steal some whisky to sell or some food. He had never been owed a month's salary before.

He gave a gentle cough and Mackereth looked up, his hooded eyes trying to focus in the dimness of the room.

'What do you want?' he asked.

'Dr Jardine is here to see you,' he said.

Jardine. Mackereth tossed the name on the wheels of memory. Of course, Dr William Jardine, a ship's surgeon from England, who had left his ship some years previously., to go into trade along the Chinese-coast. And now, he and James Matheson controlled a most astonishingly successful firm, Jardine, Matheson & .Co. They traded in all kinds of things. They owned warehouses in Macao, a factory in Canton and their own clipper fleet. Of course, they traded most in the most profitable cargo of all, what the Chinese contemptuously called foreign mud. Opium.

'Show him in,' said Mackereth, 'and light the lamps.'

The servant lit two oil lamps, trimmed the wicks, bowed and went out. He returned with Jardine, a handsome man in a dark suit. He and Mackereth knew each other, of course; everyone knew everyone else worth knowing in Macao, and there were few secrets on the island. You paid your servants to pass on what they learned from the servants of your neighbours. Information was always worth money; news of cargoes, local shortages, the going rate for bribing officials, whose wife was being unfaithful It is odd, Mackereth thought, how the poor will spend time to save money, while the rich pour out money to save time, and as he rose to shake hands with Dr Jardine, he thought ironically, I'm running out of both time and money.

'What can I do for you, sir?' he asked in his ecclesiastical voice that boomed mellifluously like a rich brass gong in the small room. 'Will you take a whisky with me, or a little wine perhaps?'

He hoped he had some wine left, that the servant hadn't drunk it all. You couldn't trust these fellows; you couldn't trust anyone.

'No thank you,' replied Jar dine. 'This is not a social call, much as I appreciate your kindness. And in any case, I rarely drink intoxicants. I came to see you, sir; on a private matter.'

'You wish to consult me in. my religious capacity?' asked Mackereth, whisky slurring his vowels.

'Yes and no,' replied Jardine cautiously. 'Can we speak freely without being overheard?'

'Of course.'

Mackereth opened the door quickly, in case his servant was eavesdropping, but the corridor was empty. He shut it and nodded to Jardine to take a seat. Then he sat down himself.

'I am at your service, sir.'

'I wonder,' began Jardine, 'whether you know the Reverend Dr Gutzlaff?'

'Of course,' said Mackereth. Everyone knew Gutzlaff. He, like Mackereth, was one of the few men in Macao to speak Chinese well and to read the characters. Gutzlaff had come from Pomerania years ago, a burly man with a wide-brimmed straw hat and cold eyes. He had enjoyed more success as a missionary than Mackereth, for he was also a doctor, and so could help people with physical as well as spiritual problems.

Gutzlaff would go off for weeks on end, touring villages along the coast, distributing his own translations of Bible passages and religious tracts; 'The Word of Life' and 'Saints' Rest', along with bottles of Lee's Anti-Bilious Compound and Cockle's Pills, against all kinds of aches and infirmities. But then Gutzlaff had a source of income denied to Mackereth, which allowed him to spend heavily on his tracts and even, to order Bibles in bulk from England, Jardine's clippers employed him as an interpreter with the Chinese. Now a glimmer of hope gleamed like a welcome star in Mackereth's clouded brain. The Lord had worked in Jardine's mind; truly His ways were wonderful and marvellously worthy to be praised.

'Yes, I know the doctor well,' he said.

'We've had an unfortunate experience,' said Jardine. 'As you may know, we have given Dr Gutzlaff safe passage in one of our vessels from time to time on his missionary travels, and in return he has acted as our interpreter with the mandarins and others with whom the present situation in China insists we deal.

'We have paid him generously and so he has been able to buy medicines for the poor people among whom he moves, and also more Bibles to bring them into the way of eternal salvation.'

'I know that,' said Mackereth hastily. Why did the man not touch on the purpose of his visit?

'Dr Gutzlaff is unfortunately ill. He is therefore unable to sail with us on our next trip. I wonder, sir, whether we could prevail upon you to take passage with one of our clippers in his stead?'

'What would I have to do?' asked Mackereth.

'We would give you a cabin to yourself, and full board, of course. And we would also be pleased to pay you the sum of one thousand pounds for your services as interpreter during the length of the voyage.'

'How long will this take?'

'Possibly three weeks.'

'What is the cargo?'

'Opium.'

'Are there any bad effects of opium?' asked Mackereth pontifically. 'I am not a medical man like Dr Gutzlaff, you understand. I would like my conscience to be at ease before I agree.'

'Of course. I respect you for that, sir. As you may know, opium is used widely in medicinal drugs in England. In fact, as a doctor myself, I can say I have prescribed it in a very high proportion of the cases I have been called upon to visit — including children who cannot sleep, older people who sleep badly, and patients of a nervous disposition.

'It has soothing qualities, Mr Mackereth, but it is idle to pretend that, if taken to excess, it may not cause some mental trouble and even instability. But then, of course, that is the same with the whisky you are drinking now — which I know you-do not take to excess. But were you to drink a bottle a day, then naturally that would gradually have deleterious effects on your mind and body.

'Equally, if I were to eat sodium bicarbonate in large quantities, this could also have serious consequences. But in the proper quantities, it is ideal for relief in indigestion. It is precisely the same with opium. We sell it because, to be honest with you, this is an important part of our business. We make a profit that allows us to lower the prices of other commodities we carry. People who buy our opium also draw comfort from it. Many work in the rice-fields, up to their knees in water, and so suffer the most excruciating agonies in their joints. They smoke a pipe of opium and immediately they know peace and calm, and feel goodwill to their fellow men. Then they sleep, and rise refreshed to work for another day.'

'So, in fact, Dr Jardine,' said Mackereth, sipping his whisky, 'you would consider this drug to be of help to those who buy it?'

'Provided they do not take it to gross excess, yes. We fulfil a need. And if we did not do so, someone else would. I am sure that most of us would agree that in these circumstances it is right that our nation should benefit?'

'I am American,' said Mackereth coldly.

'Of course. Forgive me. You have so many qualities which I think of as English that, temporarily, I forgot you were not — ah — one of us. Do I take it then, Mr Mackereth, that you will be of our number when we sail?'

'When do you sail?'

'I personally will not be with you. The clipper *Hesperides* is owned by a company with which we have connections. She leaves on Tuesday on the evening tide. Eight o'clock precisely from the main quay.'

'I will be there.'

They both stood up at the same time and shook hands, and then Jardine went out into the warm Chinese evening. He was happy that Mackereth had agreed. Rumour said that Mackereth was a drunk and a perverter of boys. But Mackereth spoke Cantonese and Mandarin fluently and also the dialects which were most widely used. For while the Chinese language had one set of characters, it possessed so many dialects that someone from one province might not understand a man from a different district. Mackereth would tell, from the inflection in an official's voice, whether a bribe was too much or too little; or even whether it had been offered to the wrong man.

So, until Gutzlaff recovered, he, would use him. After all, Gutzlaff charged much more than a thousand pounds for his services on each voyage, because he thought he had the monopoly. But he had forgotten about Mackereth. Well, Jardine had remembered. And if Mackereth earned his money, he would play him against Gutzlaff.

Jardine had learned this essential lesson early on; you played one man against a second, both against a third. Then you set them all against each other — and picked up the profits yourself.

He had learned the hard way, from the old China traders; men like Daniel Beale, who nearly half a century earlier had been a purser in a Company ship, and then laid the foundations for all their fortunes. Beale had seen the possibilities for trade in the East, but of course, the East India Company held the monopoly in China as in India; no British outsiders could squeeze more than a bare living from what petty trade they were allowed to conduct.

But the Company could not prevent foreigners from trading, so Beale had somehow acquired Consular papers from a friend at the court of the King of Prussia, and then set up in Canton and Macao as an Agent of the Prussian Government. Although he was simply a merchant, the East India Company could neither expel him nor harass him, as they would have done had he not possessed this invaluable diplomatic protection.

A Scotsman, David Reid, next saw further possibilities for trade and, armed with a captain's commission in a Danish infantry regiment, which also gave him immunity from the Company's monopoly, he arrived in Canton and joined forces with Beale.

Jardine, as a ship's surgeon at the age of eighteen, first visited India aboard an East Indiaman. He decided he liked business better than medicine and, on his return to London, he became a trader and then returned to the East. In Canton, he met James Matheson, twelve years his junior, who had previously -worked for a Spanish firm, which enjoyed certain trading concessions at Amoy, farther up the coast, which they never used. Matheson turned these concessions to his own great advantage by selling the locals there a cargo of opium for thirty-three thousand pounds.

This transaction changed not only his career, but the whole course of Eastern history. Others speedily learned of the astonishing profit he had made, and began to peddle opium along the China coast. The Coast Trade had begun.

Matheson also recognized the value-of diplomatic status, and became Danish Consul. His diplomatic duties were limited to acting for any Danish ships in port, and the real value of the post was that he could run up the Danish flag if any East Indiaman or British Navy ship approached to inquire about the nature of his cargo.

At first, Jardine rented living quarters from Matheson; soon they were partners. Until they began operations together, the ships ferrying mud from Calcutta were old-fashioned, heavy vessels, called country wallahs. Built of teak and displacing between five and eight hundred tons, they were replicas of seventeenth-century caravels and galleons and carracks, built with a roundhouse over a cuddy, and a short waist for guns.

Jardine and Matheson scrapped these ancient vessels, some of which had been at sea for a century and a half, and. took three months for the trip from Calcutta to Lintin, and a month even with the monsoon wind behind them.

Both men realized that their success depended on moving as much mud as possible and as quickly as possible. They needed ships that could easily make three round voyages from Calcutta to Lintin every year, vessels capable of sailing against the wind, even in the monsoon. Jardine soon commissioned the first, *Red Rover,* a copy of an American privateer, displacing only two hundred and fifty-four tons, with three masts; she was so swift, she sailed from Calcutta to Lintin in eighteen days, against both tide and wind.

The Coast Trade was the most profitable side of their business, but it was only one side. They traded in virtually anything; snuff-boxes (called 'sing-songs' because they contained jewelled mechanical birds inside that sang when the lid was opened); furs from North America; camphor, tea and rattan and birds' nests from Malaya; elephants' teeth and raw cotton from India; cut price machinery from Britain. Nor were they simply content to trade; they took a genuine interest in what they sold, and when they found they could improve it, they did so.

Matheson, for example, discovered that the Chinese would buy more blue bandanas if they were woven with white lines in them, instead of being blue with white spots as the mills supplied them.

Jardine capitalized on the fact that East India Company's officers sailing east usually occupied cabins far larger than they needed. He sublet their unwanted space and stacked his goods around their bunks.

For years the East India Company had held the monopoly of shipping direct from Canton to London, but Jardine, Matheson & Company found a loophole in this arrangement. They sailed Chinese cargoes to Singapore, a free port, and unloaded them. Then they reloaded them in the same ship, and sailed on to London. Legally, no monopoly had been infringed, and several thousand pounds more profit had been paid into their bank account.

Not many could teach them much when it came to pruning expenses and increasing profits; and now, with more opium arriving from India aboard their clippers, they had to find new markets farther up the coast.

Mackereth knew this, too, but he also knew that without this unexpected money he would have faced ruin and disgrace, and for some time after Jardine had left, he sat in his chair, watching the moths blunder blindly against the dim globes of the oil lamps.

It was astonishing that literally only minutes before he had been wondering where he would find funds to continue with his work, and even to stay alive. But he had prayed to the Lord, and the Lord had answered him, in a most unexpected way.

Mackereth poured himself more whisky, relief pouring over him in a warm tide of satisfaction. He sipped the drink and crossed his legs and, suddenly aware of his masculinity, of the well-known, ever-recurring beat of blood in his loins, he rang the handbell for his manservant.

He would find a boy tonight and teach him the blessings of Christianity, and the wonder-working power of the Lord.

IN WHICH DR GUNN TAKES LEAVE

The captain's cabin in *Trelawney* had a low, white-painted ceiling, against which the dappled reflection of the yellow rushing river played like sun on a cornfield.

The captain stood now at one side of his table, hands behind his back, his face corrugated with worry.

'We've searched everywhere we're allowed to, sir,' Griggs was saying. 'But none of the people in any of the factories have seen Dr Gunn. I am afraid, sir, he must have been done away with.'

'What am I to tell his parents, or the owners?' asked the captain, almost speaking to himself. 'Gunn seemed a sensible young fellow; I can't understand why anyone should wish to harm him.'

'All I can remember, sir, is that we were having a meal, and a fight started. Dr Gunn stood against one wall to keep out of trouble. Then I got hit on the head myself. When I came round I was the only European left in the place. I couldn't make any of the Chinks understand my friend was missing.'

'It seems -then that this extraordinary city has claimed another victim. I will make my report in the log accordingly. In the meantime, Griggs, every officer who visits Canton is to ask every other European they meet whether they have seen the doctor. It is just possible he may have been kidnapped and robbed and then turned loose naked, or even put in Chinese clothes. Now — how's the loading going?'

'Last bales of tea and silk are promised for noon tomorrow, sir. We can catch the afternoon tide.'

'Good.'

The captain nodded a dismissal; Griggs went out on the deck. What the devil could have happened to Gunn? The current was swift and the river strong. Maybe Gunn's body was already out at sea?

Despite the heat, Griggs shuddered at the thought. But then, unless you looked after yourself in the East, no-one else looked after you. You had to stand on your own two feet — or others would carry you out to your grave on theirs.

The British frigate *Andromache* swung into Macao Roads, and anchor chains went out and down with a rusty roar. High in the old forts above the Praya Grande at the base of the blue mountains, the ancient Portuguese guns fired their ritual salute.

These bronze cannon, barrels decorated with leaves and fierce faces, had originally been installed by early Portuguese settlers to ward off pirates and marauders. Now they were used exclusively to fire salutes at the arrival and departure of any important personage. And surely there could be no more important British personage to arrive than Lord Napier, the Prime Minister's personal representative, a tall, thin figure with sandy hair, face reddened by the months of sea voyage, now being rowed ashore energetically in the naval longboat?

The guns died, white smoke blew away from their mouths, and the sea-birds settled. The Praya Grande, facing the glittering sea, was crowded with British and Portuguese merchants and their families eager to see the new arrival. The boat bumped against the quay, sailors expertly threw ropes to men ashore, and Napier began to climb up the stone steps, eyes narrowed against the blaze of sun. The local manager of Jardine, Matheson stepped forward to meet him.

'Welcome to the East, your lordship,' he said gravely, taking off his top hat and bowing from the waist.

'Thank you,' replied Napier. He had a pleasant voice, with a Scots accent. 'I am glad to be here.'

He looked about him with interest, nodding at the crowds, wondering who they all were, what they all did.

'I am sorry that both Dr Jardine and Mr Matheson are in Canton, your lordship,' the manager went on. 'They did not know the date of your arrival, otherwise they would most certainly have been here to greet you personally.'

'I'm sure they would,' agreed Lord Napier. 'But we will meet soon — here or there.'

'We have placed a house at your disposal here, my lord. Until you make your own plans.'

'Good.'

Lord Napier climbed into a palanquin; his wife was helped into a second, and his two daughters jumped into a third. At a quick jog-trot, the bearers set off up the hill. Tropical flowers blazed bright with colours as a painter's palette; orange and lemon and peach trees added their fragrance to the air.

The house overlooked the waterfront, leaning over redtiled roofs as though eager to be closer to the sea. The rooms inside were cool, scented from sprays of flowers in blue china vases. Such was the change from being cramped in the frigate, even though they had been given the captain's quarters, that Napier's daughters cried out in delight and surprise.

'You see,' said Napier happily, 'we *shall* be quite comfortable here. I am sorry.to bring you all so far from home, but it is in the cause of duty, and we will be able to do a great work for our country. And then, after perhaps a year, maybe less, back to Scotland. This time, for good.'

Napier was a kind man, who had recently inherited a great estate in Selkirkshire, and who counted every day he was absent from it as one wasted beyond recall. He had served in the Navy as a mid-shipman at Trafalgar, then as a lieutenant, and had retired from the service to marry.

He had been elected a fellow of the Royal Society of Edinburgh, an honour of which he was extremely proud, and as a countryman, his ambition was to breed the finest sheep in the world. He believed that to produce them his workers should also share his interest, and this they could not do fully if they had to live in the usual bothies or stone hovels generally considered good enough for Scottish farm labourers.

So he modernized their cottages and built roads through his estates so that it was possible to drive by carriage to the most remote farm. But before he could gather the advantage of these expensive improvements, he had received a personal letter from Lord Palmerston, the Foreign Secretary, requesting his presence most urgently in London.

Standing now, looking out through the windows set in walls three feet thick to withstand the heat of the hottest day, Napier recalled that interview.

Palmerston, a huge man, wearing his favourite clothes of blue coat over green trousers, his whiskers black and bushy, had received him in his room in the Foreign Office.

'I wanted to see you,' he began immediately, 'about a new appointment in the Far East.'

'To do what, Foreign Secretary?' asked Napier cautiously. He had retired from the Navy; he had no wish to sail anywhere again; he had infinitely more agreeable work in Scotland claiming his attention.

'A very good question, Napier, because I see this as possibly the most crucial overseas appointment this Government has yet had to make. You will have the title of Chief Superintendent of Trade. I refer to the China trade.'

'*If* I accept the appointment, you mean, Foreign Secretary,' said Napier quickly.

Palmerston looked at him in pained surprise, his eyebrows two disapproving question-marks.

'You would not think of declining such a signal honour, Napier?'

'I would far rather stay in Scotland.'

'Hm. No doubt most of us could sometimes find occupations we would far rather follow than the sometimes onerous tasks we are called upon to carry out in the furtherance of our country's interests. Now, to proceed. As you know, the Government has terminated the East India Company's monopoly of trade with China. We felt it proper to introduce competition, both for the products of China and for our own.

'When John Company had this monopoly, they worked with what they called a Select Committee to make sure no-one exceeded his brief. For it is with trade, Napier, as with so many other matters, that the people principally involved become too easily convinced of their own paramount importance.

'Agreed, these merchants bring vast sums into India and Britain. We can do many things with that money, but we must maintain some kind of surveillance on their activities.

'The trouble is, the Chinese Emperor will not accept a British ambassador at his court. British governments have pressed for generations to have ambassadors in Peking, but always without success. The Emperor believes that if he allows us an ambassador, then we will seek other privileges. They fear we will end up by taking over their whole country, as we have done in India, as we are doing in Burma and Malaya.

'I need not dwell on this further, for you know it is absurd. Our Empire is complete. We have no territorial ambitions anywhere else in all the world. But we have trading ambitions — and there are three hundred million people in China. We have a lot we *could* sell them. They, in return, could no doubt sell us much more apart from tea and silk. It will be your commission, as Superintendent, to act as go-between with the merchants, both British and the Chinese counterparts, and of course, with the Emperor himself.

'The Chinese Viceroy at Canton has expressed a readiness to accept some such person as yourself, and after very long deliberations, I have selected you.'

'But why did you choose me, Foreign Secretary? I have no

ambitions whatever in the world of commerce, and I am not a politician. I have served in the Navy for a number of years, in many different appointments. I am forty-eight now and I wish to devote my days to the welfare of my estate, and to my family responsibilities.'

'I fully sympathize with you. Fully. But all of us are servants of the State and servants of His Majesty. Also, apart from your qualities of administration and courage, both of which you have demonstrated in the Navy, you are .a Peer of the Realm. That was one reason I chose you. It is essential to have a Superintendent known to be socially above the mercantile classes, and beyond all taint of bribery.

'Secondly, our relations with China cannot proceed at their present slow pace. Sailors from our merchant ships have been seized, strangled, robbed. Ships have been impounded until we paid grotesque fines. Iniquitous duties are levied at the whim of some petty local Chinese official.

'It is not impossible, although I hope that this will never come to pass, that the Navy *may* have to extend its presence into Chinese coastal waters. If that unhappy and unlooked for eventuality should arise, then you, sir, are the only British peer who has known active service afloat in His Majesty's ships.

'Third, there is the difficult question of the Coast Trade.'

Palmerston paused.

'What precisely do you mean by that, Foreign Secretary?' asked Napier.

'The Coast Trade elsewhere would be called opium smuggling. It is not desirable that you, in your official capacity, should encourage such adventures. But you must also never lose sight of the fact that you have no authority to interfere with them or prevent them. British subjects who are engaged in transporting opium and selling it are entitled to the same privileges as others of British birth. No more. But, equally, no less.

'You must remember that an increasing proportion of the

total. six million pounds revenue coming into India every year through the East India Company's overseas trading operations, stems from the sale of opium to Chinese natives, against the direct orders of their rulers.'

'Even so, sir, it is not a trade of which I feel we should be very proud in this country,' ventured Napier.

There seemed something degrading about smuggling prohibited drugs into a far-off heathen country, no matter how profitable this, might be.

'There's nothing much to be proud of in *any* mercantile operation Napier, if you look closely enough. Merchants are merchants .the world over. As Anacharsis put it, "The market is a place set apart where men may deceive each other."

'But opium has a great value — so do not deceive yourself about that — and if we do not supply this commodity, then other countries will.

'The Americans are already our competitors. They buy it from the Turks who have been growing the poppies for generations. The Chinese used to grow poppies themselves, of course, but their soil is poor and no-one can approach the superior quality of our product, produced in Bengal and Madras.

'As to the basic charges for your commission, in essence, we wish to establish friendly relations with China and the Emperor, with eventually an exchange of ambassadors. He still refuses to entertain this possibility. I hope, and my colleagues in the Government join me in the hope, that you will be able to reverse this negative policy. To do this, of course, you will have to take up residence in Canton. Proceed first to Macao, then to Canton, where you will present your credentials as Superintendent of Trade to the local Viceroy, who will pass them on to the Emperor.

'At no time are you to adopt any tone of threat or menace to the Chinese. I am told that certain of the mercantile community, including Dr Jardine — who is one of our most successful merchants — are men of some choler, and possibly not diplomatic in dealing with others of different nationality or colour. So at all times be moderate and respect the laws of the country.'

'So I *must* go then, Foreign Secretary?' Napier's questions sounded wistful; Scotland had never seemed more inviting.

'You *are* at liberty to refuse, Napier. But I do not think you will. I most earnestly trust you will undertake the commission.'

It was only afterwards, when Napier was walking down the corridor behind the Foreign Office butler to his carriage, that he realized Palmerston had not really discussed the intricacies of the posting with him. The brief was wide and vague as a Highland mist. This was, no doubt, to absolve the Government of any blame should he fail in his mission. The market was not the only place where men deceived each other.

How far away Palmerston's office seemed now, in this blinding eye-aching heat of Macao! Firecrackers, were exploding like gunfire along the beach; a ceremony of some kind was in progress. A band of brass instruments and huge drums was marching out of step -and barefoot along the dusty road on the edge of a sea that glowed like melted blue glass. Well, he would have to do his best; there was nothing else he could do. And the sooner he began, the sooner he could return.

'What is the earliest date I can sail for Canton?', he asked the manager.

'When we hear from Dr Jardine that arrangements have been made for you to land there. I will send a letter by fast cutter tonight, your lordship, which will be in Dr Jardine's hands tomorrow.'

'What arrangements do you mean? All I require is a house and an office.'

'It is not as simple as that, your lordship. You also require what is called a Red Pass, issued by the Chinese authorities. They regard us all as Barbarians, and we are expected to carry these passes.'

'Can you obtain one here?'

'Regrettably that is impossible, your lordship. The Chinese control this island, in collaboration with the Portuguese, but no-one has authority to issue such a pass.'

'Who has. authority, then?'

'Only the Emperor.'

'The Emperor? But he's in Peking, fifteen hundred miles away. How long will it take for a message to reach him and for him to reply?'

'Possibly three months. Maybe longer if there are floods.'

"Three *months?* Are there no quicker means of communication between Canton and Peking?'

'The Chinese do have an express service, with relays of horsemen who, between them, can cover a hundred and fifty miles a day. But we would still have to wait weeks, perhaps months, before the Emperor replies.'

'But why? I am not some merchant who seeks permission to do some petty thing. I am His Majesty's plenipotentiary — his ambassador, all but in name.'

'Your lordship, the Chinese authorities do not wish to receive a British ambassador.'

'Well damn it, I have not come all this way against my own inclinations, spending months at sea, just to wait here indefinitely. We will have to sail to Canton without this pass. There must be someone in authority there who will appreciate the situation. The Chinese Viceroy or Governor, for example. He must have *some* authority, surely?'

'Not to allow you to land, your lordship.'

'Well, maybe I do not need permission as I am a diplomat, and not a trader. Pray be so good as to inform Dr Jardine of my intentions.'

The manager bowed. Things were going to be difficult; he could see that. First, Lord Napier with his raw red skin and sandy hair was the epitome of everything the Chinese, with their sallow complexions and black oily hair, hated and despised. He might have been a living caricature of a Red-Bristled Barbarian.

If he foolishly persisted in going to Canton without a proper pass, the manager could also foresee certain inevitable consequences. First, the Viceroy would have to report his un-invited arrival to the Emperor. Then knowing he would incur His Majesty's severe displeasure for allowing the Barbarian to land, yet being unable to prevent him physically because of the Barbarian's gunboat, the Viceroy would demand an imme-diate levy from the Hong merchants against any financial de-mands from Peking.

The merchants, in turn, would show their disapproval of the situation by withdrawing all local labour from the quay, and possibly even impounding cargoes and ships. The British merchants would have to pay them further enormous bribes, with tens of thousands of pounds of profit lost — and all be-cause the Government in London had sent out this emissary who seemed intent on going the wrong way about things.

Well, he was only the local manager; he owned no shares in the company. But now he pitied those who did.

Lord Napier's arrival in a British man-of-war had, of course, been signalled from fort to fort along the banks of the Pearl River, and even as Napier was declaring what he would do, the Chinese Viceroy of Canton was examining these reports.

Viceroy Lu Ku'un was a plump man in middle life, who had only recently succeeded the unfortunate official who had failed to subdue the revolt of the self-styled Golden Dragon King. Lu had no intention of also making the journey back to Peking in chains, but unless he handled this new Barbarian carefully, that could conceivably happen, The Emperor never deigned to travel to Canton; he therefore had no idea of local conditions, and relied for information on all kinds of corres-pondents, who coloured their reports according to their own relations with the Viceroy.

Lu's spies in Macao sped to Canton in swift boats, called

centipedes because of the number of their oars, with the grievous news that Lord Napier intended to land in Canton without official permission.

Lu had taken years to climb up the ladder of preferment. A word of fulsome praise for a superior here; a judicious bribe there; a calculated betrayal elsewhere had all contributed to his promotion. If he maintained the Emperor's confidence and survived as Viceroy, he would soon be very rich. For this wealth, of course, Lu would have to rely on the Coast Trade, because he was in supreme charge of the area; and as such he received the largest share of the bribes that the Barbarians paid.

He must therefore deal swiftly with the matter, but delicately, for he did not wish a direct confrontation with the British frigate. The ancient defensive forts along the river possessed crumbling guns that could neither be traversed nor raised nor lowered, but could only hurl their iron balls at set points in the river. They were thus useless against any enemy who could manoeuvre.

Under the command of a Chinese admiral who preferred to stay in port painting delicate faces on fans, Lu could call on a fleet of sampans and war junks. But if he antagonized Napier, then the *Andromache* might rampage up and down the river, and do as much harm to his reputation as to the war junks and sampans it encountered.

He would tread a middle course warily, like a walker on a tightrope. Accordingly, he called for tea, then for hot damp towels, which servants held expertly to his brow. Thus refreshed, he sent for his principal secretary, who arrived, writing brush in hand. Lu began to dictate a message to the Hong merchants. If they took their share of the good things in trading with the Barbarians, then they must also bear their quota of the bad.

First, he told them of the arrival of a Western official who was not a merchant. The ideograph for this perplexed the secretary, until he decided that the official was obviously a Barbarian and come to see what he could. So he referred to Napier as the Barbarian Eye.

'When this Order is received by the said Hong merchants,' Lu intoned in his official and impressive voice, 'let them immediately go into Macao and ascertain clearly from the Barbarian Eye why he has come to Canton province.

'And let them authoritatively enjoin upon him the laws of the Celestial Empire, to wit that, with the exception of the merchants and the *taipans,* their heads, *no* other Barbarian can be permitted to enter Canton, save after a report has been made and an Imperial Mandate received.

'The said Barbarian Eye, if he wishes to come to Canton, must inform the said Hong merchants, so that they may petition me, the Viceroy, and I will by express messenger send a memorial, and all must respectfully wait until His Majesty deigns to send a_ Mandate. Then orders will be issued requiring obedience. Oppose not! A special order!

'Now,' Lu told the secretary in his usual speaking voice, 'post up copies where they may be seen — and speedily.'

The secretary fled away, impressed by the obvious urgency of his orders. The Hong merchants, crowding round the copies as they were nailed up on public notice boards, acted even more swiftly. Half a dozen of the most senior immediately dropped all other work and set off for Macao in the fastest boat they could command. This sailed through inner creeks and swampy passages which no Westerner knew, for it was imperative, that they should reach Macao before this Barbarian Eye, acting perhaps in ignorance or folly or maybe (might heaven and their ancestors forbid) in malevolence, set sail for Canton.

Should he land there without the necessary permission, then great would be their distress. The Viceroy would use the Barbarian's disobedience to his command as another lever to squeeze out more money from them in case he was to be punished himself.-

As their boat, with its naked sweating rowers, under its clouds of billowing canvas, approached Macao, they saw with alarm that the quay was empty of large craft. A few sampans bobbed against the slime-encrusted steps, but there were no vessels of consequence, and no sign of any British man-of-war. The Barbarian Eye had gone, and with him an enormous part of their fortune.

As the prow of their vessel scraped uselessly against the steps, and one of the crew made fast, the bells of the twelve churches in Macao began to strike three o'clock, the Hour of the Horse. Some bells boomed, others were flat and cracked. But so far as the worried merchants were concerned, all sounded a dirge; a knell for a lost chance, a lost fortune.

The Parsee stood, as he always stood in the morning, looking out to sea, watching, his ships carrying his cargoes. His treasure sailed in. their deep holds, and his heart travelled with it.

A merchantman was coming up the Roads, tacking from side to side against the summer wind. She sped gracefully over the water like a huge sea bird, white wings extended.

The Parsee sipped tea thoughtfully from an oval cup without a handle. Behind him, a little to one side, as was fitting for an inferior, waited a man of much darker skin. Although his *dhoti* was well cut and his sandals correctly curled at the toes, a-glitter with semi-precious jewels sewn into the leather, he had the obsequiousness of a hireling.

:'So you have examined my daughter,' said the Parsee at last. 'And what do you find?'

'I find sir,' replied the' other man in the curious sing-song voice of an educated Indian, 'that, without any doubt, she is now with child.'

'As a doctor, you are certain?'

'As God will judge me, sir, I am certain.'

'I have heard of women who miss their monthly flow and swell up as though with child, but it is imagination, a trick of their mind. They imagine the child they desire is within them. Could this have happened to my daughter?'

'I have treated cases such as you mention, sir, but never one so healthy and young and vigorous as your daughter. I have made my tests. Your daughter is with child.'

'It is good,' said the Parsee, satisfied. 'See my secretaries on your way out. They will pay your fee. Truly, when he returns, my son-in-law will be pleased to know that his union has been blessed.'

The Indian doctor bowed his agreement, then folded his hands, dry and scaly as the claws of a predatory bird, and backed away towards the door. The Parsee gave him five minutes to be out of the way and pulled the bell tassel. The servant who had conducted Gunn to his room appeared in the doorway. 'Send the English doctor to me,' the Parsee commanded.

'He is asleep,' said the servant.

'I do not doubt he sleeps well, after his exertions,' said the Parsee dryly. 'Were I younger, I might envy him. I am sure they have both done their best to earn him his money. Awaken him and send him here.'

'As you say, my master.'

He was back within ten minutes with Gunn, wearing his uniform, which had been laundered and pressed, his shoes polished. Gunn felt oddly relaxed with the Parsee now, not ill at ease. He also felt infinitely more mature than when he, had first met the man. Maybe this was because he had learned much that he had never imagined before about women, not only physically but mentally; and perhaps he had taught the girl something, too.

He had grown so accustomed to being a prisoner of desire, sleeping naked with this warm, delightful, passionate woman whose body enfolded his, who was always eager for the act of love, that the world outside their four walls had grown farther away and correspondingly less important. What could her father possibly want with him now that meant he had to be awakened and brought here?

The Parsee poured out a cup of tea for Gunn, another for himself.

'I am pleased to inform you that your endeavours with my daughter have been successful.'

'You mean ... ?' began Gunn, surprised.

'I mean, she is with child by you. I have also just received intelligence that her husband is due here very soon. He left Calcutta fourteen days ago. If the winds had been in his favour, he should have been here now. I have just been watching a ship coming up the Roads. If he is not aboard that, they will at least have news of him. You will have to go, Dr Gunn.'

'Go?' Gunn repeated the word. It held a sudden horror, a sudden emptiness, echoing like a well. *'Go?'*

'There is no reason for you to stay here any longer, doctor.' said the Parsee gently. 'It is time for you to leave.'

'But I've grown *used* to life here,' said Gunn, amazed he was uttering such words; and that they were completely true.

'You pay my humble hospitality great honour, but you have done that for which you were hired. You *must* go.'

'But where? And what will I do?'

'There is a schooner returning to Canton. You will travel in her. I understand that the *Trelawney* is expected soon at Whampoa. Boats ply regularly between Canton and that island. I leave what explanation you give your captain to your own ingenuity.'

'But what will your daughter think?'

It seemed astonishing that, after weeks of total intimacy, Gunn still did not know her name, had never even asked it; and she had never told him. Truly, the East was strange and wonderful.

'Sentimental farewells are things of the English mind, doctor. They belong to a cold country. In the East we believe that our days, our nights, our loves and our losses are all part of the great celestial equation that forms our whole life. And life is a continuing journey. We meet people, we part from them. We carry their memories in our minds. And, in your case, my daughter carries something stronger than .any memory in her body. Go now, Englishman.'

'But *I must* say goodbye.'

'I do not repeat myself, doctor. My servant will escort you to the schooner.'

'Wait,' said Gunn. 'I *can't* go.'

The Parsee smiled. "

'You are young, Englishman. When you are as old as me you will know that all women are much alike. At first, they seem sweet as the distant scent of the lemon tree. But if you taste the fruit too long, it grows bitter on the tongue.'

'But I cannot return to *Trelawney.*'

To be stuck in that ship, battling up against the wind for months on end, with hard tack, salt pork, a barrel of limes or apples? No. Not again. Not after this. Never again.

'That is your life, doctor. You chose it.'

'I chose it because I needed a profession. I had no money to start in trade, no land or business to inherit But you have paid me money. I am poor no more.'

'I would not say you were *rich,* Englishman.'

'No, sir. Not rich, as you count, wealth. But is there no work I could do here? As your physician, perhaps?'

'No. My daughter will be returning with her husband to Bombay as soon as his ship turns round. You would then be just as lonely here as in your own vessel, or in your own country. There is nothing for you here.'

'What about one of these opium boats? Smuggling? People might get wounded. I could help.'

'You are most foolishly trying to cling to the past. That is something no-one can ever do. Take your cheque, and when you call at Calcutta, cash it. Gold speaks with a louder voice than paper money. And both are stronger than dreams.'

Gunn bowed his head. What the older man said was true. This had been an episode in his life, but was not his whole life, only part of it. Yet like one tiny crystal of potassium permanganate dropped in a bowl of clear water, it had coloured all that came after, like the petals of a rose. He had absorbed an experience into his blood, his brain, his bone: but what the Parsee said was still true. He must go.

He stretched out his hand.

'Perhaps we will meet again,' he said hopefully, still clinging to his dream. 'All three of us?'

'Perhaps,' agreed the Parsee. 'Perhaps, indeed.'

He turned back to his view of the Praya. The merchantman was coming into harbour now, her sails flapping loosely like huge white sheets above the scrubbed decks. It would be interesting to learn whether his son-in-law was aboard, and even more interesting to discover how he would take the fact of his wife's pregnancy. There might be some little difficulty in explaining its length; but men were notoriously vain and gullible over such matters. He did not foresee much trouble.

Gunn went out, along the corridor, down stone steps into a formal garden where fountains threw up long water sprays, and yellow-plumaged birds called to each other in a giant aviary made of bamboo slats. The air felt sharp and clear, rinsed with the scent of orange trees.

He looked back at the house. The grey shutters had faded in years of almost perpetual summer; the walls were of yellowish stone, in the seventeenth-century style, when the Portuguese and Spanish stars had been rising, before their empires in the East and South America had began to crumble: How fortunate he was to be British, with Britain's vast possessions all around the globe, so that if the sun went down on one, it was already rising on another!

In silence, Gunn followed the servant along the quay, turning over in his mind what he would do, what he would say when he returned to *Trelawney.* He had been kidnapped, held for some kind of ransom, and then quite inexplicably released. Then he had caught the first boat back to Canton.

The captain should be pleased to see him. Griggs would question him closely, of course, but there was nothing he could not adequately explain. Suddenly, the servant turned to him and stopped.

'What's the matter?' asked Gunn, still absorbed in his own thoughts.

'You asked my master about an opium boat, yes?'

'I did.'

'There is such a boat, a clipper, due to sail soon. -The *Hesperides*. An American missionary is aboard who speaks Chinese.'

'What about it?.'

'I think their trip will be successful. Why do you not see the captain?'

'Is he English?'

'Goanese. Part Portuguese, part Indian. But he speaks English.'

'Does he need a ship's surgeon?'

'You should ask him.'

Odd, Gunn thought, how he was treating this man almost as a friend and equal, not as a servant; but there was something about the East that seemed to melt- all pre-established strata of rank and authority. You were who you were, because of what you could do; by reason of your wit or your courage or your cunning. These things were more important here than where and to whom you had been born; and it was right that they were.

'What about your master?'

'He need never know.'

'Where is this clipper?'

'I will show you.'

It was much hotter now in the sun; Gunn could feel sweat trickle down between his shoulder blades. They came to a.

clipper moored fore and aft against the quay: black hull, white superstructure; spars, masts and bowsprit newly varnished; the sails furled, not neatly, but adequately.

'Here she is,' said the servant. 'The *Hesperides.*'

'Come aboard with me.'

'It is not right that I should do so. I might be seen and my master told.'

'Would he punish you?'

'Any master punishes a servant who disobeys his orders. My orders were to take you to another vessel.'

'Where is she?'

'Two hundred metres down the quay.'

Gunn could see a schooner ahead of them, preparing to sail. A handful of men were on the quayside, coiling ropes.

'Thank you,' he said. The servant bowed and turned, and within seconds he was lost in the crowd of coolies and strollers and beggars. But as soon as he was out of Gunn's sight, he climbed on a bale of silk. and stood looking back at the clipper. He watched Gunn go up the gangway, waited for twenty minutes in case he came down, and then went back obediently to his master.

The Parsee was standing where he had left him, looking out to sea. The servant entered the room, and the Parsee turned, eyebrows raised questioningly.

'He went aboard the clipper, master,' said the servant.

'I thought he would. It is strange that when the English, the Americans and the French, and others from colder climates, come East, so often the heat goes to their heads like strong wine. They lose all wish to go home. They hang on here even if they have no reason to do so. The East for them is like an incurable disease. They cannot get it out of their blood. Tell me, have the other arrangements been made?'

'Yes, master.'

'Good.'

The Parsee nodded his dismissal, and stood, hands behind

his back, thinking about Gunn. Ah, to be so naive that you genuinely believed you would receive the equivalent of three thousand pounds for the act of love, and then return to tell others about it!

Even so, he felt a certain sadness in his heart; the boy had spirit. And he would let no hint of what he had ordered reach his daughter, for she was still in tears at Gunn's precipitate departure. She would have to dry her eyes before her husband arrived. But perhaps he would believe that she was weeping for joy at his return? Truly the gullibility of men was only equalled by the fathomless duplicity of women.

IN WHICH THE HESPERIDES SAILS NORTH AND NEW CONTACTS ARE MADE

'Anyone on board?' Gunn called as he came up the gangway.

Four Lascars, brown arms blue with tattoos, naked save for loincloths, were sponging the deck with huge 'squeegees.

'Do you speak English?' Gunn asked one of them.

The man shook his head. The others paid no attention to him. Gunn walked up the companionway into a deck cabin. A dark-skinned man was reading a Portuguese newspaper. He wore a dirty white duck uniform, cap pushed to the back of his head, and white canvas shoes with a hole cut to ease a bunion on his left big toe.

'Can I see the captain?' asked Gunn.

'I am the captain,' the man replied in English. What is it you want?'

It was no good lying; no good making up some story that could easily be broken down. He had better tell the truth.

'I am an English doctor,' said Gunn. 'I want a job.'

'How do I know you're a doctor?'

'You will have to take my word for it. But if you have any

case of illness aboard I can treat it.'

'What with? Where are your medicines and your instruments?'

'They are not with me,' Gunn admitted.

'Where are they, then?'

'I was a ship's doctor. I became involved in a fight at Canton and was brought here. Now I do not wish to return.'

'Why should I need a doctor with a healthy crew?'

'No-one is healthy for ever. If we were, we should all live for ever.'

'That is true. But we do not.'

He threw the paper to one side, and stood up, stopped, bent his body and broke wind.

'I am not healthy,' he announced. 'I have an ache in my guts all the time. What is causing that?'

'I would have to examine you,' said Gunn.

'Then you shall,' announced the captain. 'Follow me.'

He went down a companionway, took a key from his jacket pocket and opened a cabin door. It contained a porthole, a bunk with a stained wood side, and a stained wooden chest bolted to the floor.

The captain took out another key, and unlocked the chest. It was filled with drugs in glass bottles, each labelled in black and gold by its Latin name.

'*Now* cure my gut,' he commanded.

'Take off your jacket.'

The man peeled it from his shoulders. His body stank with sour sweat. His stomach was like a huge soft pale bubble.

Gunn placed his hand over his heart to feel the beat, moved his fingers about the man's stomach. The captain stood there, watching him suspiciously.

'Have you ever had treatment for this pain?'

'Grog is my treatment, doctor.'

'I see.'

Gunn took out three of the glass bottles, removed the

ground-glass stoppers, sniffed cautiously at the contents to make sure they were not adulterated, then measured out a small amount from each and shook it into a glass.

He crossed to the basin.

'Is this water drinkable?' he asked.

'I drink it,' replied the captain stiffly.

Gunn poured some on to the powder and stirred it.

'Drink that,' he said, and glanced at his watch: five o'clock in the afternoon.

'You will need another dose at nine tonight, and every four hours tomorrow. By the next day you should be feeling better. If not, you will be dead.'

'You speak with certainty,' said the captain, impressed and uneasy. What if the second prognosis, was the right one?

'I have had several years' training,' Gunn explained grandly. 'I have also seen a number of men who drink too much, take too little exercise, and are worried. I am looking at another now.'

The captain said nothing. He swallowed the drink, tipped the glass upside down on the board by the sink and put on his jacket.

'You can sail with us,' he said shortly.

'What's the pay?'

'Twenty dollars a week. Spanish dollars, which are the currency here, worth five English shillings each in the market, a bit less in the banks. Paid in Chinese silver. And your keep.'

'How long is the voyage?'

'Impossible to say.'

'What's the cargo?'

'Dirt. Foreign mud.'

'You mean — opium?'

'I mean nothing else. We're sailing three hundred miles north to try new markets, and there may be trouble. Sometimes the Chinese put on a great show of anger, but they don't generally mean any harm. It's only because a new official is in the area — maybe someone from Peking to check that the local authorities really are trying to stop the trade.

'They fire guns, send out a few junks or fire-ships piled up with burning straw to catch our sails alight. Sometimes they even chase us, but not very hard. But just occasionally, *very* occasionally, we do meet an incorruptible official. Then you might be useful. People could get hurt.'

'When do you sail?' asked Gunn.

'We're still taking on fresh water. The tide will be right in about two hours.'

'I'll be with you,' said Gunn.

He held out his hand.

'I never shake hands,' said the captain shortly. 'It's unlucky.'

He turned away for a moment, so that Gunn could not see his eyes. It was one thing to take a man to almost certain death, but you could not shake hands with him. You could not allow yourself to become friendly towards him, even though he had been friendly to you. That was against his code of conduct, and he prided himself on the strictness of his code. He had been a Catholic once.

'How many crew do you carry?'

'Twenty.'

'Who are they?'

'Some are like me, Goanese. Other are Lascars or Madrassis. And we've an American interpreter.'

'Who owns the boat?'

'An Englishman, Mr Crutchley.'

'Who's he?'

'He has a company like Jardine, Matheson, called Crutchley and Company. It is not a big company yet. But it will be if he lives.'

'Shouldn't he live?'

'He drinks even more than me.'

'What is your name?'

'Fernandes. Juan Fernandes.'

'I am Robert Gunn. Your doctor.'

'So it seems,' said Fernandes, and went out and up on deck.

Crutchley poured himself five fingers of rum, drank them all, and then poured himself another hand! He was six foot four, broad at the shoulders, with a huge gut on him as though he had swallowed a giant cannonball. He wore a loose shirt without a collar and blue duck trousers and high-button, soft leather boots.

He stood now in his cabin, listening to Fernandes' orders, being shouted and repeated, and the 'Aye, aye, sirs,' the scream of the anchor chain as it came up slowly, and the slap as the bo'sun smacked it with a fat wet hand.

The deck creaked and moved under his feet and he braced himself automatically to meet the roll of the current. He was carrying some idiot aboard who had to be dropped off. He wasn't sure why, but he'd told Fernandes to engage him in any capacity he wanted.

The Parsee was very rich and, under another name, he owned a share in the schooner. Like Jardine and Matheson and all the rest of the *taipans,* he owned shares in so many enter-prises, so many ships, so many dreams, one would think he must, lose count of them all, but he didn't. He never forgot anything.

The Parsee could also say whether Crutchley or Fernandes worked again, or whether they went hungry; or whether their usefulness was at an, end and they were simply to be tossed, throats cut, into the Roads. Crutchley was a big man, but he was soft inside, like melting butter, and his stomach ran when he thought of the ruthlessness of the rich. They could buy any-thing and. anyone, and they did, whenever they wanted. Well, he'd be one of them soon. And this voyage would help. They were carrying five hundred chests of opium, valued at a hun-dred and fifty thousand Spanish dollars. At four dollars to the English pound, this was thirty-nine thousand pounds. Much of that would be profit. There was a risk, of course, but life was full of risks. You could be knocked down by a carriage in the street and die; and the risk on this run was slight.

Crutchley poured out a third rum and wiped his thick lips with the back of his right hand. Five thousand pounds of the profit would be his, buttoned down in his back pocket, with no deductions. He already had nearly four thousand pounds in coin stored in the room he rented in Macao, where he kept four locks on the door because he could not trust the bank.

He was making a lot of money. But the trouble with money was that you either had none, or you didn't have enough; you could *never* have enough. Even the Parsee and Jardine and Matheson hadn't enough, and they must have several hundred times more than he had.

But why should he grumble? He was making more in a single voyage than he could make in ten years in any other job. He had been a grocer's assistant in England, and then had tried his luck with the East India Company in Calcutta. Then he had sailed farther east in the galley of a merchantman, and at Singapore the cook had gone mad and blown out his brains and Crutchley had taken over. He discovered that the cook had been buying the cheapest provisions, but prudently putting the highest prices on his tally. So Crutchley had taken over this arrangement, too, and adulterated the sugar and weakened the coffee and, by the time he had served for six months, he had made a few hundred pounds for himself. And all the while the East had lured him on because of the stories he heard about other men's quick fortunes.

In Whampoa he started as a cook in one of Jardine's ships, and then crossed over to a rival firm, Dent & Company, and then returned. Now, four years later, he had a clipper of his own. Well, not quite his own; not yet; but at least he had a share in its profits.

He went up on deck unsteadily, suddenly eager to feel the cool breeze on his huge, soft, pustuled body. The other Englishman was there. He nodded to him distantly.

'I'm Gunn,' said the new arrival. 'Dr Gunn. And you, sir?'

'Crutchley's the name!'

'You own this vessel?'

'My company does.'

'But you are the company?'

'There are other shareholders.' There always were; like the Parsee and Jardine. The Chinese called Jardine the Iron Headed Old Rat, because once he had .taken some petition to the Canton City gate to hand to the local mandarin. There, Chinese police or thugs — you. gave them one name or the other, according to whether you were Chinese or European — had set on him, and beaten him about the head with sticks and bamboo staves. But they hadn't hurt him at all. He had been quite unharmed, even unalarmed, and had just stood calmly smoothing back his thick black hair with one hand and presenting his petition with the other.

Well, one day, Crutchley would own *every* share of his company. Then by God, he'd cut down on all expenditure and squeeze a fortune out of each run. Soon, too; very soon.

'Where is the voyage taking us, Mr Crutchley?' asked Gunn.

'Too bloody far,' said Crutchley shortly. 'The names won't mean much to you if you're new here. Are you?'

'Fairly.'

'Right. Well, we've two objects. We've got to hand over some mud to buyers at Namoa Island, in the Bay of Swatow, up north. We're picking it up first at Lin-tin. And then on up the coast. We've got so much mud, we can't shift it fast enough.'

The ship surged through the green sea, and the bows ducked and the figurehead pointed her wooden breasts at the water and raised them again, and her sightless wooden eyes peered ahead and saw nothing. But Gunn saw Lintin Island grow larger, and then they swung beneath the shadow of the mountains into the Roads. Half a dozen other ships already lay in the bay, anchored fore and aft. They were barque-rigged, with shining decks, twenty gun-ports, and big heads of sail, all furled. They seemed a curious cross between warship and trader, clearly built for speed rather than for carrying the maximum amount of cargo or passengers. He guessed these were the opium clippers, built in Calcutta, copies of American gun-runners, and capable of such speed that nothing under sail — or even with the new steam engines — could catch them.

On the way out, he had heard how a steam tug in Calcutta had attempted to race one of these clippers for a few miles, but all that had happened was that the clipper had drawn steadily and gracefully ahead, while the crew of the tug poured into the roaring furnace all the coal they carried, and then fell farther behind until, finally humiliated, they had to turn back to port.

The anchor chains ran out, and Gunn saw they were near one of three tarred mastless floating hulks with decks walled in by planks and roofed over. They could be prison ships, and although they appeared deserted, almost derelict, people were obviously living in them, for they had chimneys and small windows and even verandahs with flowers in earthenware pots.

Double anchor chains fore and aft held them firm against winds and tides and currents. They looked sinister and evil and he wondered what they were. He heard a movement, and Fernandes came alongside him, and leaned on the rail.

'That's where we take on the cargo,' he explained. 'From these floating warehouses, packed to the rafters with mud. The Chinese have boats with fifty oars — we call 'em centipedes or scrambling dragons — and they run supplies ashore from these hulks to make some money for themselves. We have to load up with chests, which is a bit more difficult.'

'What about the clippers?' asked Gunn.

'They'll sail right up the coast for several hundred miles. They bring them down from Calcutta, and nothing can catch them — or harm them. Look at those swivel guns. They're better than you'll find on many British men-o'-war. Even the crew are armed with muskets. They're pretty tough to touch, those.'

'Do the Chinese ever try?'

'Not often,' admitted Fernandes. 'The bribes are too high. Every now and then, of course, as I said, when there's a new Viceroy or some local mandarin who feels he should send a. report that the Foreign Devils have been driven off by the loyal Chinese, they indulge in a bit of play acting.

'They wait until one of the clippers is going to leave and, once she's under way, they follow her. The clipper captain enters into the joke. He doesn't hoist all his sail. He lets the Chinese nearly come up with him, but if they draw too close, they'll fall back themselves to give him a chance.

'This goes on for a while, but once he's out of range they'll shoot every round they've got after him, including arrows. But, of course, they never hit anything. They don't mean to. Why *should* they hit their own livelihood? They receive more from the captain for allowing one visit ashore than they make in a year from the celestial Son of Heaven, or whatever the Emperor calls himself.

'But they've done their duty. They've put up a show. Everyone reports that the Foreign Devils fled away and, of course, a memorial to this effect is written out laboriously and sent over the mountains to Peking. And, if the Emperor ever reads it, he sends back his thanks in vermilion ink, which is the highest praise any Chink ever gets. Vermilion bloody ink!'

'You take a cynical view of these proceedings?' suggested Gunn.

'Not cynical, doctor. Realistic."

As he spoke, small boats were butting alongside the vessel and men were shouting in high sing-song voices. Oddly shaped bundles, wrapped in sacking and bound with thin ropes, were being handed up; the opium was coming aboard. Within two hours, the holds were full. Up came the anchors and the ship turned north; Lintin's rock finger shrank on the southern horizon.

Gunn went down to his cabin, kicked off his shoes and lay on his bunk. So he had achieved what he wanted: a place in an opium runner. Now what he made of his chance was entirely up to him. He thought of the Parsee girl with her round breasts, and the big nipples with wide, brown aureoles and her warm, firm thighs. He felt her legs gripping him, the inside of her knees against the small of his back, and he wanted her. Or was he only trying to convince himself that he did?

It was a passing need, and he knew that with every day, her attraction, and then her memory, would fade, just as Marion was only a name now to him, nothing more. There would be other days and nights and he would find other women to fill them. He fell asleep, and when he awoke, it was five o'clock in the morning and he was cold. He took off his clothes crawled under the sheets, and slept until eight.

A steward brought him tea. He drank it, washed and shaved and went up on deck. The open sea stretched on their right, endless and blue as cobalt. On the left, lay the coast, a dim green smudge, lined with orange and lemon trees. Mackereth came up behind him silently.

'Good morning,' he said. 'Blowing hard for this time of year.'

Gunn looked at him; this must be the missionary interpreter. Mackereth's head seemed big for his body; he appeared squat as a toad in white linen trousers, a black jacket, a greasy cravat, and he had cut himself while shaving; beads of blood had dried brown on the soiled silk.

'We haven't met,' said Gunn, and introduced himself.

'I am a missionary, a traveller in the service of Our Lord,' replied Mackereth proudly. 'Do you, as a physician, also hope to help the heathen natives?'

'No. Only the crew, if they need me. Are you planning to go ashore?'

'This is my first trip so far up the coast,' said Mackereth, leaning on the rail and breathing the salt air deeply. Only the first, I hope, of many. The harvest truly is plenteous, but the labourers are few. Matthew nine, verse thirty-seven. Certainly, if the Lord wills, I will go into the vineyard.'

'How do you know if He wills it, or not?' asked Gunn.

'I feel it here.'

Mackereth tapped his chest in the general region of his heart.

'I am travelling now largely as an interpreter, for it is difficult even to understand pidgin English up the coast, so they say. I speak several dialects.'

'That is a very rare accomplishment.'

'It sure is. Any Chinese found teaching a Foreign Devil his language faces the death penalty.'

'That explains how, when we stopped at Singapore, I was told that although three hundred thousand Chinese lived on that island, yet not *one* Britisher spoke any of their lingo.'

'I am not a Britisher,' said Mackereth shortly. 'I am American.'

'I am sorry,' said Gunn. 'No offence meant. Do you attend to the crew here, spiritually?'

'If they wish to receive the message, I will gladly preach the wonder-working power of God to them. But so far I have not had words with them. Apart, of course, from the captain.'

'How long do you think the voyage will take us?'

'It depends on the business they do. It could be weeks or months. There's a timelessness in the East, Dr Gunn, that personally I find attractive. In America, as in Europe, all is hustle and bustle and rush. And for what purpose? Here, we can apply ourselves to the things that really matter. We can enjoy the passing moments - like now - and God's beautiful handiwork on every side. The sun, the sea, the distant coast.'

'You are a philosopher?'

'Not really,' said Mackereth, pleased at the suggestion. 'But I like to make the most of each day, each minute. Remember, Dr Gunn, life is a journey without return. We shall never pass

this way again. Let us, therefore, make good use of all our opportunities as we see them. Now, I will bid you good morning.
I have prayers to make.'

'Of course,' said Gunn. He watched Mackereth go down the
companionway. An. odd character, a bit too oily for his taste,
but there was no doubt that what he said was true. And Gunn
was determined to follow his advice about opportunities.
Mackereth had a ready convert there.

They were running in closer to shore now. The countryside
stretched green and flat, with patches of cabbage, then Indian
corn and millet. He could see the brick walls of a small town:
a pagoda, built on a hill because demons and devils could not
run uphill; a pyramid of sacks of salt covered by mats; huts
built of half-burned bricks thatched with rushes, some with
blue and yellow ribbons flying from their eaves as an insurance against evil spirits.

It was warm, but not as hot as in Macao, and a cool breeze
blew in from the ocean. Fernandes came up alongside him and
slapped him familiarly on the back.

'How's the stomach?' asked Gunn.

'Better,' he admitted. 'Easier in every way.'

'You should be taking your next dose of physic soon,' said
Gunn.

'I will do that, doctor. But first we have work. Mud to sell.'

'How do we offload it?'

'We don't. Natives come out in boats.'

'Isn't it risky, trading in opium in broad daylight?'

'Even if we did it by night, they'd still know wouldn't they?
Our company will have made its dispositions. The local mandarin will have received a huge fee. Doubtless he will pass on
money to others whose duty is to watch us. If he has given
enough, we will be all right.'

'I hope so.'

'Do not worry, doctor. This is the easiest way of making
money, apart from printing your own banknotes. Mr Crutch-

ley would not be concerned in it otherwise, I assure you.'

They were now about half a mile out from shore. Ahead lay several sampans and man-of-war junks, with high sterns and tiny thin guns, poking like porcupine quills from their sides. One flew a strange multi-coloured flag with two long tongues.

'That's the local commodore of the Chinese navy,' explained Fernandes. 'He'll have to be taken care of, too.'

A ship's officer was shouting orders; the sails fell slack and empty of wind, whackering away at the spars. The clipper slowed and rocked on the oily, burnished water, turning slightly with the tide, pointing to the shore. The loose sails beat above their heads like great drums.

A small boat, known as a fast crab, had left the nearest junk and was heading towards them; painted oars dipped rhythmically into the sea. In the stern, beneath a huge scarlet silk umbrella, embroidered with designs of flowers and birds, a fat man sat in a wicker armchair smoking a long clay pipe. His hat was ornamented with a mandarin's red button. Three servants stood — one behind, one on either side — and fanned him with painted paper fans.

Close to the mandarin, heads bowed, hands folded, stood several officials in grass-cloth robes and rattan hats, bound with red silk cords.

'Who's this fellow?' asked Gunn.

Crutchley came up to one side.

'He runs the port here,' he replied. His voice was thick with rum, his eyes red-rimmed as though they had been sandpapered.

'Does he know what we're carrying?'

' 'Course he bloody does. He wants his fee, that's why he's coming out. He'll be watched by others on the shore. So he must go through the motions of enquiring what cargo we carry. That's his job. Then we'll sell him our mud. That's *our* job. And. the quicker we start, the better.'

A gangway was run down, and Crutchley saluted the mandarin as he came slowly up the steps, followed by one servant carrying a fan. The mandarin bowed to Crutchley and then to Gunn. He had a bland, expressionless face, long waxed moustaches and a pigtail that reached down to his calves. He sat down in a chair that had been brought up for him. Everyone else remained standing.

'Where's that preacher?' asked Crutchley suddenly. 'This fellow no speak pidgin.'

'He's praying,' said Gunn.

'Get him off his knees and up here,' ordered Crutchley. 'He's paid to interpret, not to pray. He can pray in his own time.'

A cabin boy ran down for Mackereth, who came up, wiping his mouth with the back of his hand. His face was flushed; he had been at the whisky again.

'Do your stuff with this Chink,' ordered Crutchley, nodding towards the mandarin. Mackereth cleared his throat and began to speak in a high-pitched voice, now and then inclining his head to one side or the other, or nodding vigorously, pursing up his face like an actor. Finally, he turned to Crutchley.

'I have told His Excellency that we would not have dared to come so close to shore had not contrary winds and strong hostile currents driven us from our appointed course, which was from Singapore to Canton by way of Whampoa.

'Unfortunately, through being driven so fair out of our course, we have run short of water, and therefore it is necessary to seek this pleasant spot in order to replenish both water and provisions.'

'Never mind what you've said,' said Crutchley. 'What does *he* say?'

'He says they are pleased to supply what we need. But he insists that as soon as water and victuals have been delivered, we must depart at once for Canton. By Imperial Decree, no loitering is permitted. Is that understood?'

'Of course it's bloody understood,' said Crutchley angrily. 'Cut out all this rubbish, and let's get down to the object of the visit. How much mud is he going to buy? And what is he going to pay?'

'It is impossible to do this so crudely,' retorted Mackereth, angry in his turn, whisky firing his blood. 'You've asked me up here to interpret. There's a certain etiquette we have to follow. No wonder they call us Barbarians!'

'Get on with it,' said Crutchley sullenly.

Mackereth began to speak again. Then the mandarin nodded and, putting down his hand, pulled out a long tube of parchment from the top of his right boot. He handed this to Mackereth who unrolled it and began to read.

'True copy of Imperial Edict. His Majesty, being ever desirous that his compassion be made manifest, even to the least deserving, even to Barbarians from the outer seas, cannot deny to such, who are in distress from lack of food, through adverse seas and currents, the necessary means of continuing their voyage. When supplied they must not linger, but put to sea again immediately. Respect this!'

Mackereth nodded and rolled up the Edict and handed it back to the mandarin, who replaced it in his boot. Then the man stood up and said something in a low voice. Mackereth turned to Crutchley.

'Where's the wine? It's courtesy to offer them a drink, you know.'

'Get on with it, man,' said Crutchley irritably. 'I'm trying to trade, not run a bloody tap-room.'

But he nodded to the cabin boy, who sprinted below decks again, and returned with, a tray, a bottle of red wine and four glasses. Crutchley filled the glasses and handed them round, and then raised his in a form of toast. The mandarin emptied his glass and immediately held it out to be refilled. Then he spoke; Mackereth interpreted.

'He asks how many chests of foreign mud we have aboard.'

'Tell him five hundred.'

'Are they all destined for Namoa?'

'Some are. We'd like to try the ground around here. See if we can find any buyers.'

'He says you are wise to stay in this area. Farther north, along the coast, a new set of customs officers are exceedingly strict. At Amoy they recently decapitated a number of smugglers. Their heads are on pikes around the town.'

'Tell him we're not going to Amoy.'

'He repeats that you are wise. He wishes to assume that you are landing some chests here.'

'Obviously we bloody are. Why else have we come here?'

'I will tell him,' said Mackereth icily, 'that with His Excellency's permission, such is our intention.'

More head shaking, more talk.

'He says his permission depends on how much you are going to offer him,' said Mackereth.

'Tell him the same as before.'

The mandarin nodded.

'All same custom,' said Crutchley, too impatient to wait for Mackereth to translate. 'Just like lastee time. All-light, number one top flight pickings, yes?'

'All same custom,' the mandarin repeated like a parrot.

'Don't know why you're here at all,' Crutchley told Mackereth. 'I've done the deal myself. Same terms as last time. Ten per cent flat on the middle price. I even had the bloody coins counted out in advance. All your bloody palaver.'

A sailor handed him a small leather bag. Crutchley dumped it on the table. It chinked with money. The mandarin picked up the bag and held it out at arm's length. From long experience, he knew the value of its contents by its weight. He bowed his thanks and handed the pouch to his servant, who concealed it in his robes. Immediately, his oarsmen sat upright, blades held out horizontally over the shining sea.

'He says he announces his departure,' said Mackereth.

'Not before time, either,' said Crutchley. 'Tell him to hurry his men out in their sampans for the mud. We don't want to miss the wind.'

The mandarin went down the companionway, into his crab and, without a backward glance, was rowed across to the largest junk. As he reached it, five sampans struck out towards the clipper from the shore.

'You speak the language well,' Gunn told Mackereth.

'You wouldn't think that was important if you listened to Mr Crutchley. You *can* get by with pidgin in many places, of course. But not for very delicate matters. And not at all farther up the coast.'

'Are you going ashore here?'

'There is really no need. Our stay will be very brief.'

'I wouldn't mind seeing the place,' said Gunn.

'As you don't speak the language, I think that would be most unwise. Now I must return to my devotions.'

Mackereth bowed and went below decks to his cabin. He locked the door and poured five fingers of whisky into a tooth glass, and stood looking through the open porthole at the blinding reflection of sun on sea.

He had done well in his interpretation, despite the crudeness of that vile drunken fellow Crutchley. But Crutchley did not count. Only Jardine and Matheson really counted. And Jardine would not have come to see him unless he needed him. The Iron Headed Old Rat did not waste time or money. He knew his value all right. He would give him other trips, other fees. How strange if he won back all the fortune he had lost! Or rather, to be more honest about it, if the Lord, in His infinite wisdom and compassion, had given him the gift of the strange Chinese tongue, so that he *could* win back his money. Truly the ways of the Lord were sometimes mysterious, but they worked in a very powerful fashion. I will say of the Lord, He is my refuge and my fortress: my God; in him. I trust. Psalm ninety-one, verse two. Mackereth poured another hand so that he could consider the ways of the Lord more closely.

Up on deck, Crutchley leaned over the rail idly for a few

moments, spitting in the sea. He had done well to sell at the middle price; he had been ready to come down, for he had heard that some buyers were holding off; they feared new penalties for trading in opium. He turned as though to go to his own cabin, and looked quickly around the deck. Only Gunn was near, his back to him. Crutchley pulled a small soft leather pouch from his trouser pocket.

'That bloody mandarin's left his wallet here,' he said in irritation.

'I thought he gave it to a servant,' said Gunn.

'He did. The fool must have dropped it, damn his eyes. We will have to return it to him as a matter of courtesy, otherwise he will think we have stolen it.'

'How will you get it to him?'

'In any normal country we would send a boat over with a couple of seamen and hand it back. But here, because he is a mandarin of high rank — you saw the colour of his button — an officer has to take it to him. It means a lot of rubbish, bowing and scraping. *Kow-towing,* they call it. Trouble is, I have no-one I can spare.'

'I'll take it,' said Gunn quickly.

'You mean that?' Crutchley looked at him with a new awareness, his manner suddenly conciliatory. 'I did not like to ask you.'

'I would be pleased to go.'

'Well, put on a hat because the sun is hotter than you think. I'll have a boat lowered for you. By the way, it's against all custom and etiquette to try to board a Chinese vessel, so do not approach that junk he came from. They might think we were going to seize it, or something. You will have to take the purse ashore.'

'But I don't speak the lingo.'

'You won't need to. They'll see you arrive, and send a secretary to meet you. We've landed here before. I'll get Mackereth to write a note in Chinese characters. Just give it to him with the purse.'

Gunn went down to his cabin. He put on a straw hat, and a new silk handkerchief in his breast pocket, and on the impulse, he slid his loose notes and the Parsee's cheque into his wallet and buttoned it in the inside pocket: of his jacket. Then he picked up a pair of spectacles with tinted glass against the sun, and came back on deck.

A small boat, with two Lascar sailors at the oars, had already been lowered and was bumping against the gangway. Crutchley handed him the pouch and a folded piece of paper, the ink still wet on vertical rows of Chinese characters.

'Where exactly do I land?' Gunn asked him.

Crutchley pointed towards the shore.

'You see that pagoda on the right? Just by there. We'll wait for you here, then it's up anchors and away to the north.'

Gunn climbed down the companion way, buttoned the paper and the pouch in the right hand pocket of his jacket, and climbed into the little rowing boat.

'Cast off,' Crutchley called to the sailors, and the little craft creaked against their straining oars. Slowly, the clipper shrank behind them until it was only a toy boat on a painted sea. They had anchored farther out than Gunn had imagined; distances over water are invariably deceptive.

Gunn settled back comfortably in the stern and trailed his hand into the salt, warm sea. Gradually, houses and the pagoda and the junks grew larger. Then he could see fish swimming in clear water beneath him, and formations of rock and weeds like long green beards on the sandy seabed.

The two sailors, trousers rolled over their knees, jumped out and pulled the boat up the shore so that he would not wet his feet.

He climbed out on the white sand. It stretched back for about twelve feet, and then degenerated into scrub and marshy grass and thick high bushes. The pagoda was of pinkish bricks, dilapidated and fading. The beach was quite empty.

'Where is the secretary, do you think?' Gunn asked the two Lascars. Neither spoke English, but one pointed to the pagoda, as though Gunn should go inside. Gunn nodded and walked up the beach. His feet sank in the soft sand over the tops of his shoes with every step. He pushed open a wooden door in the side of the pagoda. Inside, it was dark and smelled of cats' urine. He walked in, sniffing the foul air, nose wrinkled in distaste. As his eyes grew accustomed to the gloom, he could see rafters above his head hung with bats; a plump gilded image of Buddha smiled against the far wall, with some wilting flowers in glass jars at its feet.

He came out into the sun, not wishing to become involved with any native heathen rites of worship in case this might cause hostility. Where the deuce was the mandarin's secretary? He turned towards the sea. To his astonishment, the Lascars were already rowing hard out towards the clipper.

'Hey, wait a minute!' Gunn shouted.

Stupid fools! He ran down to the sea through the soft sand and shouted after them.

'Stop! Stop!'

They paid no attention to him. Of course, they did not understand his lingo. But surely they understood they were to ferry him back to the clipper? Crutchley or Fernandes would send them back as soon as they reached it, but what a ridiculous misunderstanding!

Gunn shaded his eyes to look along the beach; there might just be some other boat he could hail, but distances seemed much greater than from the clipper. From the sea, the town had appeared compact. In fact; the nearest houses were several hundred yards away, and, from them, twenty or thirty Chinese men were now walking towards him across the beach.

There was something sinister and menacing about their steady, slow purposeful pace, up to their ankles in sand, each man carrying a thick bamboo club. Gunn's heart fluttered in his throat like a bird.

These were no friendly peasants, nor any mandarin's secretary. They were coming to catch him, maybe to kill him, certainly to beat him as a Barbarian for having the temerity to land on China's celestial soil.

He turned, but there was nowhere he could run. The beach petered out in some huge boulders and other rocks too large to climb. He thought for a moment of running back into the sea and swimming towards the boat, but it was already too far off, and there were bound to be sharks.

It was no good trying to speak to these heathen either, or to reason with them: they would not understand a word he said. He ran up the beach, past the pagoda, into the jungle. He would only have an hour or two to wait at the most, until Crutchley or Fernandes sent back the oarsmen, and until they returned he would have to hide here.

The trees stood close together. Their leaves were thick as fans and fleshy and soft, shutting out the sun, so that-he was almost instantly engulfed in a green twilight. The ground beneath his feet felt soft with moss, and marshy; his feet sank into unexpectedly cold mud. Once, he lost his left shoe and had to scramble about for it on his knees, sobbing for breath, listening for his pursuers crashing through branches after him. He ran on again, and paused to get his breath and listen, and then ran on farther into the forest. Finally, he stopped running, convinced no-one was still following him. He looked behind him, but the trees and the bushes had closed up over the hurried path he had forced through them, and it was impossible to say from which direction he had come, or where the sea lay. Was he running inland or sideways — or back towards the beach?

Gunn's heart beat like a drum beneath his jacket,, and as he stood, sweat streaming down his back, soaking his clothes, running into his eyes and making them smart, he heard jungle birds begin to laugh. And he realized they were not laughing at each other; they were laughing at him.

IN WHICH THE SON OF HEAVEN MAKES AN IMPORTANT DECISION

The Emperor sat beneath a parasol on a promontory in the flower garden of his country' palace at Jehol, some miles from the Great Wall, on the road to Inner Mongolia. A table had been set before him with a crystal, bowl containing three golden fish should he weary of the sight of flowers and trees.

His predecessors had built this palace, to which the court retreated every, year in the hot weather, and the gardens were so beautiful that poets called them The Paradise of Countless Trees. Here were planted rows of apple-trees and apricots and pears, and corianders and walnuts. Clusters of willow trees trailed thin green branches by the shores of a wide lake covered with lotus blossoms and water lilies, and fish darted like arrows through the clear water.

Summer houses dotted artificial hills, and streams were cunningly routed to pour over small waterfalls, under bridges and between porcelain lions. Two roads led to this scented garden. One only the Emperor used when he travelled from his palace in the Forbidden City. The other was used by men of lower birth; by visitors, such as mandarins and local governors, and by messengers bringing tribute and news. At The Hour of the Snake, nine o'clock in the morning as the Barbar-

119

ians counted time, the Emperor, seated on the small hill to which both these roads led, looked down them towards the south. Now that rain had replenished the rivers and the lakes he felt relaxed and at ease, and an infinity away from the stinking streets of Peking, inches deep in dung, and blue with flies.

Tao was thinking of a couplet he might compose to mark the felicity of this pleasing place, and raising his eyes to heaven for inspiration, his attention was caught by a faint, cloud of dust some miles down the common road. This was too small to mean an approach of important visitors; it must be a single messenger. His heart immediately sank at the prospect, and some of his pleasure drained from the day. How sad and also how significant that, now, whenever anyone brought news, one assumed in advance that the tidings must be bad: some new insurrection, a flood, a drought!

As the rider approached the outer gatehouse of the palace, guards with whips and bamboos went out to him. He flung himself from his horse and almost collapsed. The animal stood exhausted, head down, mouth foaming, flanks going in and out like bellows.

'We bring from the illustrious Viceroy at Canton, to the all-supreme, most high, his most puissant Majesty, the Son of Heaven, Greetings and Intelligence,' announced the rider.

He was a young man of high birth, proud at being selected for such a fearful journey of fifteen hundred miles through hard and sometimes hostile country. His face was caked with dust and sweat, his eyes red from staring into the sun. Royal servants led him into a bath-house, where he bathed, dried himself with warm towels, put on a white robe, and then barefoot, as a mark of humility, he was led into the presence of the Emperor.

The young man flung himself prostrate in front of Tao, and even when the Emperor graciously commanded him to rise, he remained on his knees as he handed over the roll of vellum on which was painted the Viceroy's account of Lord Napier's intentions.

The Emperor skimmed through it. Canton was a long way off and, in the scented groves of Jehol, what happened there the endless sordid wranglings with Barbarian traders from beyond the Outer Seas seemed even more remote and unimportant. But Lu was a sound man; he would not have sent a special messenger unless he had something important to impart.

Tao read on. Some Barbarian Eye seeking to land without Royal permission? But of course these Barbarians knew nothing of civilized conduct, otherwise they would have followed the Confucian rule; when you seek to enter the frontiers of a country, you enquire respecting its prohibitions and laws.

This Barbarian Eye, to whom Lu's secretary had so aptly and amusingly given the ideograph of Laboriously Vile, was seeking to enter the frontiers of the Celestial Empire as an uninvited person, like a thief. It was meaningless for him to claim to be an official and not a merchant. In any case, the Emperor had no wish to see any British officials or ambassadors. For generations, his forebears had tried to make this clear, but even so, like blunt-nosed hogs, the Barbarians butted their bristled bodies against his rules. They would have to be taught a lesson.

He called for a' Secretary and dictated a quick reply.

'Whereas Barbarian merchants of all nations' are graciously permitted to trade without suspicion or anxiety, this man must be cut off from the Celestial Empire. Let all with trembling awe obey! Oppose not!'

He nodded agreeably to the young man, who reminded him slightly of one of his own sons; upstanding, vigorous, ready to do some great thing if only he knew what it was. But then, were not the saddest words in the world, if only? How pleasant Jehol would be if only its peace was not penetrated by news such as this. Maybe he could involve some such thought in his couplet? But meanwhile, he would speak with this youth, and draw news from him as one draws milk from a coconut.

'Tell me,' he began, 'what do you *know* of the Barbarian? Have *you* seen this Eye?'

'No, Your Most Celestial Majesty. It has not been permitted for my humble eyes to gaze, upon his horrific countenance. But I have heard his hair is red, his skin is raw, his body long and thin. Truly he typifies and embodies all that is detestable about the subject barbarian peoples beyond the farther seas.'

'You speak well, my son,' said the Emperor. 'We know little of these people. We hear facts as small as grains of sand. It is said that American men take only one wife each. We have learned, with surprise and astonishment, that they also have surnames, and respect such family distinctions as father and brother and wife. In short, We understand that they and the English do not live like brute cattle, as one could easily assume from their habits and behaviour.

'We have heard it said that in a battle, when the English take prisoners, they eventually repatriate them, instead of keeping them as slaves, as we do.

'They wear armour of what we call elephant skin, but which comes from trees and plantations as some kind of gum. A sword cannot wound them through this coat. They wear strange clothes for our climate, so heavy, so tight, that we have heard it said when their soldiers fall down they cannot rise again.

'And in the English capital city of London, which.is only a huge emporium, we hear that three bridges span the main river, and water pipes bring clear drinking water to all the inhabitants: They have there, as everywhere, prostitutes, but illegitimate children are reared and fed and clothed and housed, and not destroyed as ours are. Men and women wear white clothes on happy occasions and black for mourning.

'When their trading junks go overseas and meet a vessel in distress, they send out boats to succour it, and feed the survivors and even return them to their countries under penalties of law. So they have some, merits of civilization.'

'What of America, Your Majesty?'

'That is another small island, ten days sailing to the west of England. The English once owned it, but there was a war. The Americans are chiefly distinguished by their mechanical ingenuity. They have ships that need no sails. They claim they are driven by great fires that cause water to boil and wheels to turn, but our admirals disbelieve this, and say their paddle wheels turn through teams of oxen below decks.

'When either of these races meet others of their kind they remove their hats and shake their hands. We believe this last custom is to show that their hands are empty, that they carry no weapons. Now they seek like serpents to enter the confines of Our Kingdom under the guise of trade, or as ambassadors, or tribute-bearers. But once inside, we will never see them out.

'Ride, young man. Remember what you have heard. It is Our pleasure that you will bring Us despatches from the Viceroy in future! Proceed! Delay not! An Imperial edict!'

He bowed dismissal. The young man backed out of his presence.

The gold fishes swam round, and round in their bowl, and Tao. sat looking at them. Not for the first time, he thought, their existence was curiously symbolic of human life, endlessly seeking after something they would never find; something they would never know.

He sat down at the table and called for his parchment, his brush and his vermilion Imperial ink. But the muse had left him; his thoughts had fluttered like a flight of starlings. He was worried about this news from Canton. Lu was sound enough, but he was not a hard man, and what was needed there was a man like a hammer who could beat down Laboriously Vile and his upstart underlings and, at the same time, show the Hong merchants and any bribeable officials that death awaited all who opposed the Emperor's wish. But who could he send, who could he trust? He sat, thinking. Then the gods helped him, the shades of his ancestors came graciously to his aid. He remembered the name of the one man he knew in his bones and blood was above and. beyond all temptations of money and women and power, Lin Tse-Lsu, the Governor-General of: the important provinces, Hupeh and Hunan. And as he thought of him, the Emperor's contentment returned, and once more the day seemed sweet as scented honey.

He called for his chief counsellor.

'The Imperial wish,' he said briefly, 'is that Lin be brought to Us with all speed. Obey! Instantly obey!'

Mackereth leaned on - the rail and watched the rowing boat return.

'What has happened to Gunn? He isn't in the boat,' he called to Fernandes, but Fernandes was busy in the wheel-house.

'I didn't even know he was going ashore,' he said; his gut was hurting him again, and so was the knowledge that he had known Gunn was to be put ashore, and had done nothing to oppose the plan.

Mackereth hurried into Crutchley's cabin. Crutchley lay on his bunk, shoes kicked off, trousers loosened at the belt, his shirt open at the neck. He was sweating; the cabin smelled sour with the stench of his unwashed body. A glass of rum, brown as. creosote, was by his hand. He looked, thought Mackereth with distaste, like a long bloated pig.

'The boat's back, Mr Crutchley,' he reported. 'But there's no sign of the doctor.'

'Perhaps the mandarin is giving him hospitality. He can afford to with the money we paid him, the slit-eyed swine.'

'Gunn's never been ashore before.'

'Well, he's bloody ashore now, isn't he? There's a first time for everything. And whether he's here or there, we're sailing.'

'But how can he get back to the ship?'

Crutchley swung himself up, belched and stood in his stocking feet, towering over Mackereth.

'That's his problem. Perhaps he doesn't want to come back to the ship.'

'Don't be ridiculous,' replied Mackereth. 'We can't leave him ashore, on his own, in what is almost certainly a hostile place. You're drunk, man.' Crutchley seized Mackereth by the cravat.

'Don't call me *man*. And I'm *never* drunk,' he said between clenched teeth. 'If I didn't need you as an interpreter I'd have you flogged and put in irons.'

'Get your foul hands off me,' shouted Mackereth, backing away. Crutchley lowered his huge hands.

'When we return to Macao I'll tell Dr Jardine of this disgusting behaviour,' Mackereth went on. 'I *demand* that a boat goes back to pick up the doctor.'

'You can demand what you like. But you'll get nothing. He'll be quite safe there.'

'How do you mean, *quite safe?* He doesn't know anybody, he doesn't speak a word of the lingo. They'll cut him to pieces instantly as a Barbarian who has landed without permission.'

'Rubbish!'

Crutchley swayed on his feet, picked up the glass and drained it.

'This is my ship and my company. I say what you do. And I say we sail within the hour.'

'You only own a share of this company. Dr Jardine and the Parsee own the rest. We'll see what *they* say.'

'I'll tell you what they'll say,' said Crutchley bending down to Mackereth, so that the priest could smell his foul, rum-heavy breath, like a whiff from a distillery. 'At least I know what the Parsee'll say. For he *told* me to leave him there. Or, rather, he *asked* me. No-one gives me orders. It's part of his plan.'

'What plan?'

'There are more plans in heaven and earth than are dreamed of in your philosophy, Mackereth. I am not beholden to answer your questions. Suffice it that I am sure Dr Gunn will be taken care of.'

As Crutchley said the words, a sudden thought of how Gunn would be taken care of struck an icy shaft of fear at his heart.

He could imagine the cudgelling by bamboo clubs, then the sharp slivers of bamboo being pressed into Gunn's testicles like darts, until he was delirious with pain and fear. Then his tormentors would bind his neck with iron chains, and slowly and ceremoniously tighten them until Gunn's eyes bulged in his head like giant onions, and his face went black. Then, mercifully, he would die on the hot sand, maybe even within sight of the clipper sailing away.

How would *he* fare in such a situation? Could he possibly survive? That was a terrible thought, and he hated this snivelling fool Mackereth for making him think it.

'Get out of my cabin!' he shouted. 'Go back to your little bum boys! And if I catch you up the arse of anyone in this ship, I'll have you flogged with a hundred -lashes. You're no more a man of God than I am. But then I don't pretend to be. You're not even a *man.* . You're a thing, a half-man! A hermaphrodite, a pederast!'

'Never have I been spoken to in my life like this,' said Mackereth, with surprising dignity. 'I will remember every syllable of our conversation. I will communicate much of it to Captain Fernandes now, so if you imagine you can get rid of me in the way you appear to have got rid of Dr Gunn, you are mistaken. Good day to you, Mr Crutchley.'

Mackereth walked out, along the creaking deck, to his own cabin, and sat down on the bunk, head in his hands. In this confounded heat, and being confined in this wretched vessel with this animal Crutchley, he felt trapped and terrified. He hated himself for being in this situation, where his only consolations were whisky and the Lord. How differently, how deferentially had he been treated when he was rich!

He poured himself some whisky, and the neck of the bottle rattled on the edge of the glass. This vile country, this terrible trade. Yet he needed the money, for how could he spread the word of God without money?

The fear of the Lord is the beginning of wisdom, Psalm one

hundred and eleven, verse ten. The love of money is the root of all evil, the first Epistle of Paul to Timothy, chapter six, verse ten.

Mackereth heard the rattle of the anchor chains corning up and the shouts of officers and crew as the sails were unfurled, and he stood up and saw the shore pivot through, the circle of his porthole. They were sailing away, as Crutchley had said they would. And they had left one of their number behind to almost, certain death. Overcome by whisky and hatred at his own weakness, Mackereth dropped on his knees beside his bunk.

'O, God,' he prayed, 'who art the author of all impulses of good, who fighteth the evil that is in every man's heart, I beg and beseech you to look down in mercy on thy subject, Robert Gunn, wherever he is.

'Guard him, I pray you, with your angel hosts. Succour him and bring him back safely. I ask this in the name of the Father and the Son and the Holy Ghost, for Whom all things are possible, to Whom all things are known. Amen.'

Mackereth stood up, finished the glass, and looked out of the porthole. The clipper had turned completely now. There was nothing but the sea; they were heading north. He sat down on the bunk, put his head in his hands again, and wept.

Gunn stopped running and stood, back against a tree, listening for any pursuers. But he could hear nothing except the harmless cackling of strange birds, the creak of branches, the distant chatter of monkeys.

So far as he knew, the shore was behind him, but since he could not see the sun, he was not certain. Near his feet he saw a sudden silver glitter of scales; a serpent slid silently over the moss.

Why hadn't the Lascars waited for him? And what had happened to the mandarin's secretary? Unease spread through him. He put a hand in his pocket and took out the sheet of paper Crutchley had given him. It was covered in what seemed to be crude Chinese characters, but they meant nothing to him; they could be true or false. He opened the pouch and shook out the coins into his palm. They were all copper pennies.

So he had been sent on a fool's errand. The mandarin's servant had not dropped his purse. Crutchley had simply wanted rid of Gunn. But why?

He put the pouch and the paper back in his pocket, and his fingers touched another piece of paper: the Parsee's cheque.

Of course. The Parsee had given him a cheque, but owning a share in the *Hesperides,* was it not possible that he had told Crutchley to be rid of Gunn as soon as he could safely do so? An uncashed cheque was no debit on any account. By sending Gunn ashore alone on a hostile coast, the Parsee was not only saving his money, he was guaranteeing Gunn's silence.

He had been tricked by someone he had trusted, by someone he had been naive enough to imagine would keep his word. He could hear the Parsee's voice again. *I am a man of my word and my family's honour . . . broken promises mean broken friendships . . .'*

Well, he would confound them all: he would survive, and he would return — and cash the Parsee's cheque. Anger had ousted unease. He would show himself a match for these rogues. Then, if necessary, he would seek out Dr Jardine and tell him, as one medical man to another, how he had been tricked.

For he had learned one thing; he would never- be tricked again.

Gunn looked around the jungle, steamy as a hothouse. Trunks entwined with each other; tendrils hung down from branches; plump, pale-green leaves, some sharp-edged like the blades of strange swords, others pulpy as human flesh, kept out air and light. He began to be aware of a twittering of insects, the whine of mosquitoes, the croak and tuck-too of frogs. These were the sounds of evening; soon it would be night.

He felt surrounded by dangers he did not know and would never recognize. But most dangerous of all were the Chinese predators who might still be stalking him. He must find his way back to the coast and travel along the edge of the sea. Then, if he walked far enough, surely he would reach some village where he could bluff a fisherman with his bag of copper coins into taking him to Macao? But first he had to find his bearings.

He took out his pocket-knife and carved a crude cross on an overhanging branch. He had read that people in jungles often walked in circles, so at least he would know where he had been, even if he wasn't sure where he was going:

Then he took off his hat, wiped the sweat from his forehead and hair and set out through the easiest way between the trees. He would walk until darkness and then hole up somewhere, and after a few hours' sleep, when the moon rose, he would start walking again. It would be safer to move by night.

Gunn set off briskly enough, but the humidity and heat were greater than he had realized. Within minutes, he was soaking with sweat. His collar rasped against his neck, and his tongue swelled like a dried sponge. He sat down against the trunk of a tree, but almost instantly was on his feet. He had sat upon a nest of red ants, and they were burrowing through his. trousers, crawling up above his socks, biting his flesh.

He beat his body with his hands to try to kill them, and started off again, while they bored through the sweaty folds of skin about his buttocks.

He looked at his watch. He must have spent longer resting than he had realized. The hands now pointed to six-thirty. All the time, as he walked, he seemed to be passing the same trees. The only signs of life were bright-plumaged birds that took off unexpectedly in almost vertical flight. Now and then, monkeys swung above his head, gibbering and throwing down nut kernels at him.

Seven o'clock. Gunn had no idea now in which direction he was heading. The tops of the trees were dark and he could only see the trunks as deeper shadows. He felt panic grow like another tree within him. He was afraid to stop, and yet what progress was he making? He glanced at his watch again. Still seven o'clock. It had stopped. Either his sweat had seeped into the case, or he had banged it somewhere, blundering into a tree-trunk.

He came to a small clearing. The ground was soft and marshy, with a putrid smell of decay. He sat down, back against a tree, then stretched out at its base. He must have slept, for he was suddenly wide awake and surprisingly cold. His sweat was clammy and chill, and his feet had swelled painfully in his boots. Through the first gap he had seen between the tree tops, a few stars glittered.

His face and hands were puffy and stiff with insect bites, but he lay still, not moving, wondering why he had awakened, every nerve tense as a violin string.

Something whistled above his head and twanged into the tree trunk four or five feet above him. Against the dim sky, he could see an arrow quivering; then a second, and a third. Each one came a little lower, a little nearer to him. Some archer was shooting at him; taking his time, amusing himself.

Gunn rolled to one side, stood up and began to run. He took three paces and fell flat on his face.

A rope, or length of jungle creeper, had been tied between two trees about a foot from the ground, and he had not seen it. Painfully, he dragged himself up. He heard chattering behind the trees, but he still could not see anyone. The Chinese must have trailed him like a wild animal from the beach, keeping him in sight all the time. Now they had come in for the kill.

Gunn paused, irresolute, his body one huge bruise, his muscles aching. Then, with a great roar, part rage, part fear, he started to run, crashing through the undergrowth like a beast. Thorns plucked at him and scratched his face. He thought he heard others running, too, but whether after him or away, he could not be sure. He had no idea where he was going; he just had to escape or die.

He blundered on, and gradually the forest grew lighter. Dawn was coming up. The sun was filtering through the trees, and now he could see their trunks, grey and ghostly, and the hanging tendrils of creeper.' His run slowed to a walk. He felt terribly tired. Breath rattled like stones in his throat; hammers beat in his head, and when he shut his eyes, all he could see was a dim redness. His mouth was dry as powdered sand.

He stumbled on for a few more paces and then paused, resting against the branch of a tree over which he could throw his arms. Then he straightened up and tried to walk. And all the while, on either side, soundless feet were following him. Unseen eyes watched him between thick leaves and twisted tree trunks. And, finally, when Gunn could walk no more, when he collapsed, sobbing for air, every breath burning his throat like the blast from a furnace door, when the red ants scurried busily over his hands and his face and his sweaty neck, and he lacked even the strength to brush them away, these hidden watchers moved in on him.

Quickly, they tied his wrists behind his back, then his knees and his ankles. One of them cut down a long bamboo pole, and they bound his whole body to this so that, head drooping, they carried him away in triumph through the secret paths of the forest.

Gunn could see nothing but the ground receding or growing nearer with every jolting step they took. He tried to speak, but he had no voice left, and his swollen throat would not fashion any words, so he let his head fall and shut his eyes and prayed the end would be quick.

Presently, their pace slowed. He raised his head as much as he could and opened his eyes. He was in a clearing of some kind, with a few huts made of wattle, thatched with straw and plantain leaves.

His captors lowered him to the ground. Someone cut his bonds and brought him a big shell, with water in it. He seized it greedily, and then forced himself to sip slowly because he knew the dangers of drinking too fast in his exhausted condition.

Half a dozen Chinese men in loincloths, some with bows and arrows, others wearing short swords, squatted on their hams, looking at him. Some lit cigars made from single rolled black leaves; the smell of the smoke was pungent and not displeasing. Gunn saw they were looking behind him, and he turned to see why.

A man, much taller and fatter than airy of the Chinese, had entered the clearing from one of the huts. Gunn struggled to his feet. The man held out his hand.

'It's a bloody fine thing,' he said in English, 'when we've got to bring you in trussed like a chicken before you'll sit down to dinner with us.'

'Who are you?' Gunn asked him hoarsely.

'The name's MacPherson,' said the man; he had a Scottish accent, and was about fifty years old. His body was brown, his arms tattooed with daggers and foxes' heads and the words 'Death before Dishonour.'

'I was a sailor in a British ship once,' he explained.

'I was in a ship, too,' said Gunn.

'You chose a bad place to come ashore,' said MacPherson. 'But now you're here, we'll try and make you as welcome as we would if we were back in my home town, Coupar Angus, in Scotland.'

'I was at St Andrews University,' said Gunn. 'I am a doctor.'

'Are you now?' asked MacPherson with interest. 'Well, then, you can do some treatment on some of us here. Me, for a start. I'll tell you frankly, doctor, it's the pox I think I have.'

IN WHICH LABORIOUSLY VILE LOSES FACE AND DR GUNN FINDS AN ANSWER

Lord Napier sat back in his chair in the dining-room over-looking the river inside the English factory at Canton.

On the table were the remains of breakfast he had just eaten with William Jardine and Captain Charles Elliot, a former naval officer in his late thirties, and now attached to his staff.

The room was wide and airy; a life-sized portrait by Lawrence of King George IV in his royal robes, looked down on them superciliously from one wall. It had been hung there by Lord Amherst, a nephew of the Lord Amherst who had commanded the British forces in North America during the Seven Years War, and who had advised headquarters in the American War of Independence.

The British Government had sent this young man to Peking some years previously, in the hope that the Emperor would allow him to stay as British Ambassador. Among his gifts, he had brought this picture of his King. But the Emperor had rejected both his presence and his present, and finally the portrait had been brought back to Canton and given to the English factory.

'Well, gentlemen,' said Napier. 'We've landed, we've slept the night, we've breakfasted, and we've had no trouble whatever. Nothing. I tell you, Jardine is right. What these Chinese need is firmness. Civility, too, of course, but firmness of purpose first.'

'I am glad you agree with me, my lord,' Jardine replied in his clipped way. 'The trouble is, we're all far too eager to agree to any kind of extortion they suggest. But that's like Danegeld. You can keep on paying the money, but you will never get rid of the Dane. It's high time we took a stand here. So far and no farther, is my motto.'

'I wouldn't entirely agree,' said Captain Elliot. 'I would rather handle this in a more diplomatic way.'

'That's because your-father was a diplomat for so long, Elliot. Times have changed — and remember, we're not dealing with Europeans here but Chinese.'

'Most people react better to reason than to rudeness. At least, that is my experience.'

But what *was* Elliot's experience? Jardine thought irritably. He-knew he had entered the Navy at thirteen as a first-class volunteer on board the *Leviathan,* and served in the East and West Indies, where he had reached the rank of captain, and then the government had seconded him to British Guiana with the quaint title of Protector of Slaves.

The very nature of this title was naturally obnoxious to the sugar planters, who were understandably less interested in protecting slaves than in getting the most work out of them. But Elliot, partly because of his patrician manner — the fact that his uncle was the Earl of Minto meant that he was not forced to endure the heat and humidity of Guiana for commercial profit — helped to secure better working conditions for the blacks.

He had persuaded the owners to allow them free time from sunset every Saturday to sunrise on the Monday. And the hours they could work in the fields were limited from six in the morning to six in the evening, with two hours break. No overseer could carry a whip in the field, and no women could be whipped. Owners had to keep records of all punishments, and, under Elliot, slaves were granted the privilege of marriage. He even arranged for them to be allowed to buy property, and to save their wages to buy their own freedom.

Elliot knew more about subject peoples than either Napier or Jardine, and he watched the two men now with a certain cool detachment.

Napier he trusted, because of his background, which made him above bribery or the love or need of money. He would do all he could, as well as he could, and as quickly as he could because he wanted to go home.

Jardine was an animal of a different kind. An apothecary was hardly a gentleman, and certainly his insistence on driving as hard a bargain as he could with the Chinese was not to Elliot's liking. He might be clever and brave and rich, but he lacked sympathy, and in dealing with Eastern peoples, this quality was essential.

Elliot turned to Napier.

'What will you do now, sir?' he asked.

'Send for the interpreter, and write a personal letter to the Viceroy, explaining why I'm here. He can pass this on to his Emperor if he so wishes, and then we can meet and discuss this whole matter, speedily and harmoniously.'

'It is not so simple as that, I'm certain,' replied Elliot. 'With respect, sir, these Chinese have their own way of going about things.'

'Well, we'll teach them *our* way. They've been stuck out here, behind their Great Wall, for so long they simply don't know what's going on outside in the world. Damn it, I didn't come here to try to *annexe* their wretched country. I want to open it up for the good of the Chinese, as much as for our own. Can't they *see* that?'

'They'll see nothing, sir,' said Jardine.

'Maybe,' agreed Elliot. 'But they are still the indigenous aboriginals of this country, and we are the strangers. I think we should proceed cautiously. Gain their confidence first.'

'We'll do as *I* say,' retorted Napier shortly and rang the bell for his interpreter. As he began dictation, one of his staff knocked at the door.

'What do you want?' asked Napier irritably. The heat was very trying, and since his arrival in Canton he had been feeling feverish and short-tempered.

'Two Chinese Hong merchants are here to see you, my lord.'

'I do not wish to see them. I am dealing direct with the Viceroy.'

'With your permission, my lord. They say they tried to see you earlier in Macao, but you had left. They have an urgent letter to lay before you.'

'Thank them, but explain that I am communicating with the Viceroy in a manner befitting His Britannic Majesty and the honour of the British nation. You may go.'

The servant bowed and withdrew.

The two Hong merchants stood, hands folded, faces impassive as this reply was relayed to them. Then they called for their litters and hurried back to Viceroy Lu.

Over cups of milkless tea, with hot damp towels pressed comfortingly against their foreheads, the three men considered the situation. All admitted its gravity, for when Barbarians behaved badly in terms of Chinese etiquette, then, after being fined heavily, the threat of being beaten with bamboos on the Emperor's orders — or, worse still, being taken on foot in iron chains to Peking — loomed unpleasantly near.

In Peking they would be 'unbuttoned' — which meant losing this Oriental emblem of rank and wealth — and sentenced to exile in the Colo, the cold, snowy border country. The best they could hope for there would be some tedious job, such as a sweeper in a temple, and death would generally be their only release from disgrace.

The knowledge they could do nothing to influence this foolish, uninvited envoy Laboriously Vile made their fears even more grievous. The warmest towels on their faces could not melt the chill in their hearts.

As soon as Napier had finished his letter, he had it translated, and his private secretary took it to the Petition Gate, where, by long custom, important missives intended for the Viceroy personally had to be delivered. Here a mandarin would normally accept it, and convey it personally to the Viceroy's office.

But at the Gate, although the mandarin was waiting, he refused to take the letter.

'What's the matter with the man?' the secretary asked his interpreter. 'It's addressed to the Viceroy. Explain he *must* take it.'

'I must tell you, sir,' the interpreter replied haltingly. 'Honourable mandarin says the letter is headed with the ideograph that means *Letter.*'

'What else does he expect a letter to be headed with?'

'It should be headed with the character *Pin* for Petition, sir.'

'To the devil with Pin and Petition. This is a personal letter, not a petition. I'm not petitioning to set someone free, or asking a favour. This is a letter from His Majesty's representative here in Canton to the Viceroy. We're not *asking* anything. We're *saying* something.'

'I am sorry, sir, He will not accept it.'

By now a crowd of Chinese had gathered around the gate, amused at the discomfiture of the Englishman. Some began to make chopping motions with the edge of their hands, as though cutting off invisible heads.

'This is ridiculous,' said the secretary. 'Find someone else to accept it.'

'There is no-one else, sir.'

'There *must* be. Explain I am not leaving this Gate until I have delivered this letter. Find a military officer if this fool won't take it.'

He stood sweating in the heat, in the stinking, dung-heavy air. It never occurred to him to be frightened; although he was surrounded by hundreds of increasingly hostile Chinese, some with bamboo staves, others with swords, who could cut him down as easily as he would swat a fly. He was English and so above all these heathen races with their filthy habits and cringing unmanly ways, bowing down to stone gods and spirits in rivers and the sea.

Finally, a general arrived with a junior officer at his side. The secretary handed the letter to the young man, who bowed politely but refused to accept it.

'Explain to him, man,' the secretary shouted to the interpreter, who jabbered away hastily. The young man smiled, but still would not take the letter in his hand. The crowd were jeering now, shouting at the secretary, mimicking his annoyance. Then the secretary saw one of the Hong merchants, who had called that morning, and who spoke a little English.

'Can you help me?' he asked him, as calmly as he could.

The merchant bowed, his hands concealed in the wide, loose sleeves of his robe.

'His honour the general is infinitely distressed that you should have come all this way in vain,' he explained, 'but there are obstacles — as I am sure you appreciate — in the way of him *personally* handling this *petition*. Strong gales do not make smooth seas. Nevertheless I will take it from you, and we will both lay it before the Viceroy.'

'No,' said the secretary. 'We could have given it to you this morning if we had wanted you to take it. And it is *not* a petition. It's a letter.'

'In that case, I am very exceedingly sorry, sir, but nothing I can do will help you.'

And the merchant, the general and the mandarin bowed, and turned and slowly walked away.

'The swine!' said the secretary furiously. 'The insulting

swine.'

Now the crowd began to hoot. Some threw up their round hats in the air, and jostled him, coming so close that he could smell their filthy breath. He put up his fists to defend himself, and for the first time he realized the danger of his own position. He turned and walked back to the factory, not hurrying or looking over his shoulder, although hundreds ran behind him on their bare feet, all but beating him on the back with their sticks, yet not quite daring to touch him for fear that, although ludicrously outnumbered, he still might harm them in some magical western way.

The Hong merchant hastened to report his meeting to the Viceroy.

'You will tell this Barbarian Eye, this Laboriously Vile,' Lu ordered him, 'that he must *immediately* return to Macao, nor presume to return here without permission.

'It is the most established of all our rules that a traveller from devildom must *always* obtain a Red Pass before he enters the celestial regions. And no such pass is ever issued without reference to the Emperor.

'Every nation has its laws; even England, and how much more so in this Heavenly Realm? Subject to its soothing care lie ten thousand kingdoms. The four oceans of the world rest within its shelter. This said Barbarian Eye, having come a myriad leagues over the sea, must know that I, the Viceroy, administer the Imperial Wish by cherishing with tenderness such men who come from a distance.

'I do not wish to treat the outer Barbarians slightingly, but national laws are strict. Let him return. Should he oppose or disobey, it will be because *you* and the other Hong merchants have mismanaged the affair, and the law will instantly be brought down on you in all its utmost force and severity.'

'You mean there could be death for some of us, Your Excellency?' asked the merchant nervously.

'I mean that,' agreed Lu. 'As wheels revolve, so sloth and

insolence are punished. I will pick out the worst offenders among you and deal with them publicly so that others can learn from their folly. I have no power nor even the faintest wish to modify Imperial Edicts. You know that.'

'I do indeed know that, Your Excellency, and the knowledge weighs like rocks upon my heart. And unless the gods and our ancestors come speedily to our aid, then truly our troubles will be as the waves of the sea, without number and without end.'

Napier paced up and down the library of the British factory, looking out across the river. Next door, in the billiards room, a game was in progress; he could hear the click of the balls. The sound was faintly irritating; maybe because it seemed frivolous when great issues were at risk; or maybe because he still felt unwell.

'I just *cannot* understand the way these peoples' minds work,' he said, baffled. 'In any other country in the world an ambassador — which I am in all save name — would be treated with courtesy and civility. He delivers a letter, he receives a reply.'

'China is like *no* other country, sir,' replied Jardine. 'Hundreds die every week in Canton. They die in the streets — anywhere. They've even got a courtyard in a western suburb where the poor devils are supposed to drag themselves so they can die at the least inconvenience to their fellow men. You will not find that attitude in any other country I have heard of.

'If a child is ill or unwanted, the parents simply put it out to die with a mat over its body. There's a curious kind of poor law whereby anyone can go into a shop carrying a couple of pieces of bamboo, and bang these together until the shopkeeper gives them money to clear out.'

'How much money?'

'Cash,' said Jardine. 'The smallest coin in use. The tenth part of a ha'penny. They use up so much energy going from shop to shop beating their bamboos that it's never worth their while to do it instead of working!'

'I have never heard of such customs in any other country,' agreed Napier. 'Never.'

'We either deal with them under their strange regulations, or we don't deal at all.'

'Rubbish, Elliot. You can't mean that.'

'I do, sir. I've been here for quite a time.'

'Nothing like so long as I have,' interrupted Jardine. 'And every time I've tried to increase trade I've been told by someone or other that we've got to respect this Chinese rule or that, whatever it may be. But I've always ignored them all, and gone my own way — and look at me now.

'I started at eighteen as a doctor in a ship with nothing except my pay. And now, gentlemen, James Matheson and I control possibly the most prosperous trading company east of Suez.'

'There may be a price for such an achievement, Dr Jardine, that others may be asked to pay in the future,' said Elliot.

'I'm not concerned with what others *may* be asked to pay in the future. I'm concerned with what I have to pay now, what *I* am doing *now.*'

Jardine lit a cheroot.

'So you know all about opium then, do you?' he went on challengingly.

Elliot shook his head.

'Not all,' he said. 'Just a little. I've been in India, too. I've seen it grow.'

He suddenly remembered fields as far as his eye could stretch, some red like new-shed blood with poppy blooms, others like snow with white poppies. In between the rows, each planted a foot apart, natives in loincloths and wearing white turbans against the heat, carried glistening hogskins of water, pausing to give each poppy a drink, and then going on.

'These plants are far better looked after than humans out here,' Elliot had said to the East India Company manager, with whom he was staying.

'Of course they are,' the manager agreed. 'They are also more expensive and far more productive. And I'll tell you this. We are producing one pound of opium in India for every ounce that our nearest rival, Turkey, can extract. Our quality's better, too. The Americans have to take the Turkish stuff for their China trade, but the Chinese like ours better. Here's the proof. Twenty years ago, here in Bihar, we had less than six and a half thousand acres under poppies. We've now twice that amount.'

'What's the difference in profit — if you sowed this acreage with grain, for instance?' asked Elliot.

'There is just no comparison. You'd get barely enough grain out of this poor soil to feed the fellows who grow it, and give them the strength to go back and grow some more. And that's not how anyone gets rich, Elliot. My God, no.'

'What do these chaps earn a week growing poppies?'

'During harvest we pay them the equivalent of three pence a day.'

'And how long does the harvest last?'

'A fortnight.'

'But what about the rest of the year?'

The manager shrugged; how natives lived then was their concern, not his. If they did not want work they could go elsewhere. If there was no other work, then they could squat on their haunches in the dust in the sun, and cast dice or smoke rolled-up leaves and wait for better times.

'On average, over twelve months, they get around thirteen shillings a year. That's if their wife is working, too, of course, and they have a couple of kids who can help crop the stuff.'

'What's the sequence of events?'

'We plough up the soil three times with oxen, or men sometimes — they're cheaper than oxen. Then we scratch out the troughs where we mean to plant the poppies, and if there's any water we dig irrigation dykes as well.

'We sow the poppy seeds in November and by March the petals have dropped and we're ready to cut. We send the fellows down for these seed cases. I'll show you one.'

The manager leaned over and pulled the head from a poppy. Under the stamen Elliot saw a bulbous growth, green and fleshy. The manager took a knife with a hooked blade, and slit this with four vertical cuts. Almost at once, white juice began to bleed from the wounds.

'If the farmers — the fellows we use — can't afford to buy their own knives or won't steal them, they'll sharpen up a freshwater mussel shell and use that. They're very skilful, I can tell you.

'We try to cut the stuff in, the afternoon, then it oozes out all night, and next day the sun hardens it into a black sticky gum. That is your raw opium. Another set of fellows scoop it off with a sort of iron spoon, like the trowels gardeners use back home.'

'Does that take long?'

'A deuce of a time. A fellow can work all day and collect barely an ounce. You can't hurry it, you know. Come on, I'll show you the depot where we do the processing.'

They walked down a hard, trodden path to a wooden building, sixty or seventy feet tall. From inside came the sound of singing and chanting; all around it the air hung with the dreadful sweetness of poisoned honey.

The manager pushed open a door. Pyramids of opium balls wrapped in poppy leaves stood at one end of the vast floor, and Indian children were carrying two at a time, each as big as their head, to the far end where sliding ladders had been set up against racks that reached up to the roof. These balls were carefully handed up from one worker to another, until all the spaces were filled. They sang as they worked, endless repetitive ditties.

The building looked like some grotesque library, with shelves' packed not with books, but opium balls to give more deadly pleasure to the people who used them than any book could ever do.

'We've got it well organized here,' said the manager proudly. 'At one end, as you can see, they're rolling the stuff into balls. They're so expert that each one weighs almost exactly two pounds. Then we measure 'em on those scales and pare 'em down a bit or add a bit. Then we wrap 'em in leaves and store 'em until they're wanted.

'When they get the hang of things, these young 'uns can produce a hundred balls of opium a day. There's a fortune under this roof. Maybe half a million pounds of mud.'

'Won't the opium rot if it is' not used?'

'Oh, we've got fellows up there, agile as monkeys to stop that lark. They turn those opium balls round every day and dust them with crushed poppy petals. That keeps away the insects and mildew and moths.'

'What happens after this?'

'We pack the mud balls in chests of mango wood, because it's sweet. We fit about seventy to a chest, which is enough to supply six-fifty or seven hundred addicts for a year.'

'How much will an addict smoke a day?'

'It depends how far gone he is. Ten grains to start with. Up to forty when they are really caught. They're not much use after that, you know. They just sit and dream, whether they're smoking or not. That is why the East India Company forbids *any* smoking here. Absolutely most rigorously.'

'Yet their directors don't mind exporting the stuff?'

'Well, *they* don't export it. Someone else does. A few years ago we only pushed out about a thousand chests from Calcutta. This last year, we're selling fourteen thousand. But we sell it to others who ship it. That is not our affair.'

'Do you grow it all here?'

'No. Some we move out through Bombay. That's been grown in Malwa, in the north. The Company don't have anything to do with that area, but it's got to cross Company land, so the directors slapped a transit tax on it thirty years ago.'

'What do you make out of *that* a year?'

'Me personally, nothing, more's the pity. But I tell you, the Company made nearly a third of a million pounds last year. Just out of the tax!'

'What's the profit on this stuff?'

'We make between four and five hundred per cent net, when everything's taken off. The dealers on the coast will make several hundred per cent on what *they* shift, and the buyers, I don't know, maybe two or three hundred per cent, because they often adulterate it to make it go further. Add sugar or molasses or even cow-dung. There's a fortune in opium for everyone involved.'

'Not everyone,' said Elliot dryly. 'Not for those men out there with their wives and families, slitting the pods, gathering it in at an ounce a day for about a shilling a month pay between them. Or for the others who finally pay what they can't afford for a few hours oblivion. They do not draw much benefit from any of these processes or transactions — yet without them there would be no Coast Trade at all!'

'Come, come, captain. You can't look at everything in terms like that. We have to make a profit or no-one could stay in business doing anything. A lot of money we make from this goes to the shareholders. We plough more back into works in India. So it helps everybody in the end.'

The old argument that if the British did not grow the stuff, then others would, was very convincing. But to be convincing was not always the same as being right; and sitting now in the factory at Canton, with Jardine looking at him belligerently, Elliot once more experienced that same sense of depression he had felt in the poppy fields of Bihar.

'I can't believe there, is any lasting virtue in a trade like this,' he said. 'No matter how many people it makes rich. We're undermining the whole fibre of the workmen in the country.'

'There are hundreds of thousands who never smoke the stuff,' retorted Jardine. 'It would take centuries to undermine them all. They're dam' glad to be undermined, too, I'll tell you.

'What with their living conditions, I look upon myself as a merchant who does not only deal in the obvious commodities like tea and silk and British machinery. I'm a merchant of dreams, a pedlar of oblivion.

'Look at our own country. Drunk for a penny, dead drunk for tuppence — you know the slogan, don't you? How many mothers have I seen feed a little child a spoonful of gin or some elixir that contained opium because they could not afford food, nor could they bear to hear the hungry child cry any longer!'

'I would prefer to increase our legitimate trade, as opposed to this dealing in mud.'

'That is why I am so anxious to get the country opened up,' agreed Jardine. 'Once we have an ambassador in Peking, and the Chinese send an ambassador to London on a proper basis, there will be no need to go scuttling up the coast, bribing all these people, wondering who can be trusted, who can't. We would trade in an open way. We've got the navy; we've got the merchant fleet; we've nothing to beat — except these iron-headed Chinese. They call me the Iron-Headed Old Rat. Did you know?'

'I had heard.'

'But they're the ones themselves with the stupid iron heads. They can't see any new idea. They think they can go on sheltering behind their Great Wall, as - they have done for thousands of years, ignoring all the inventions, all the progress of the nineteenth century. Well, they'll have to change one day, and we're in a position to make them do it. But we don't want to. The War of the Iron Rats. That's going on all the time. Has been, I suppose, ever since Marco Polo landed. East against West. Privilege against progress, yellow against white. Yet I like the people. Although they are so stupidly advised, they are courteous and industrious and honest. Who would be the victor in a war against such a reluctant enemy?'

'Who indeed?' echoed Elliot. 'Who indeed?'

'Even so,' said Jardine. 'All this soft talk we hear about humouring the Chinese, abiding by their rules and regulations, is quite the wrong tack to take. Next thing, we'll have them here telling us we've got to get out.'

'They have already *been* here,' replied Napier. 'They came with three Edicts. I have had them translated.'

He opened a drawer in a table.

'Say not that you are not forewarned,' he read dramatically. 'Tremble here at. A special Order. Four English devils ...' — actually there are only three of us — '... have been observed landing and clandestinely entering the British factory.

'This could only have happened with the knowledge and connivance and help of the Hong merchants. The Barbarian Eye must go, or else the merchants will be punished. These are the orders. Tremble here at! Intensely tremble!'

He put the papers down on the desk and smiled.

'We received these copies from a friend,' said Elliot. 'One of the Hong merchants.'

'What do *they* think about it?' asked Napier.

'They wish you would go, sir. They know they're going to be squeezed for enormous indemnities until you do. And I do not think we will achieve anything by staying here without the proper permission.'

'Maybe. Maybe not. But we'll certainly achieve nothing by returning to Macao,' said Jardine irritably. 'We've got to show we're not some subject face like Turks or Portugooses, people like that. We're *British.*

'Better to have a showdown and know where we stand than just wait here being made fools of by men in pigtails.'

'Jardine's right,' said Napier. 'I've been East before, too, and out here face is everything. We lost face when these fellows wouldn't take my letter. We've *got* to get it back. The questions is — how?'

'What do you mean, *pox?*' asked Gunn wearily.

He was convinced that he must be delirious with some

fierce, unknown fever and so imagining this Scotsman, and even the fact that he appeared friendly.

'What do I mean by pox?' repeated MacPherson. 'I'll *show* you what I mean.' He put down his hand to his groin; Gunn saw his phallus, swollen and raw.

'That may not be pox at all,' said Gunn. 'But in any event, I can't cure you here. I have no medicines. They're back on board.'

'But you *could* cure me, if you had your physic?'

'Of course.'

'Good. Well, what is your ship?'

'I'm surgeon in the *Hesperides*. Crutchley & Company. Captain Fernandes.'

'What are you doing here, then? The *Hesperides* is due to call within a week in any case, so my people tell me. You're lucky you've not been caught and tortured as a bloody Barbarian.'

'Yes.'

'Can you walk?' MacPherson asked.

'Slowly.'

'Slowly does it then.'

Two Chinese stepped forward, and linked their arms behind Gunn's back and helped him into the nearest hut. He lay down thankfully on a rush mat. One of the men filled an earthenware cup with water and held this up to Gunn's lips. MacPherson came to the mouth of the tent, his thumbs hooked in his loincloth.

'Is Crutchley aboard? Tall fellow with a foul mouth?'

'Yes. He's aboard,' replied Gunn. 'We anchored down the coast. The mandarin came out to fix terms, and when he left the ship Crutchley told me he had left his purse of coins behind. Apparently, only an officer could return it. I volunteered. But as soon as I stepped ashore, the Lascars rowed off. A crowd of Chinese chased me, and I escaped into the forest.'

'Crutchley meant to maroon you, of course.'

'I couldn't believe that at first. But I do now. The money purse he gave me was full of pennies. But why should he *want* to maroon me?'

'Someone told him to, probably. Someone powerful. Had any dealings in Macao?'

'Only one. With a Parsee.'

'There are dozens there. What's his name? Sodawaterwallah? Bobbajee? Chatterjee?'

'I never heard his name. He had a married daughter. Lived in a large house overlooking the bay. Had a room from which he could watch all the ships?'

'I know him. Or, rather, I know of him. He controls Crutchley's company. Crutchley just supplies the English name, with a few shares, I suppose. Jardine owns a few, too. But the Parsee has the muscle. You did a deal with him?'

'Of a sort.'

'He paid you?'

'By cheque. Three thousand sovereigns.'

'You didn't expect to live to cash a *cheque* for that amount here, did you? If he'd given you gold, he'd probably have had you clubbed down. But to accept a cheque! When he wrote that, doctor, he was writing your death warrant.'

'You really mean that?'

'Of course I mean it. You'd given him three thousand sound reasons for wanting you out of the way.'

'Who are *you*, anyway?' Gunn asked him. 'And how are you living here? I thought no foreigners were allowed to live in China?'

'They bloody well aren't, mate. But I've been here a good few years now. I'm accepted. I'm not a red-bristle-arsed Barbarian anymore. Nor even a Scot with a skin full of whisky and haggis. They think I am a child of Han in disguise! Some child — some disguise! I speak their lingo, that's the reason. Learned it in Singapore when I was a lad. Who's interpreting in the Hesperides?'

'An American. Missionary called Mackereth.'

'Never heard of him. He's probably like that fellow Gutzlaff Jardine uses so much, who peddles mud with his left hand and religion with his right. Somehow he balances his books and his conscience. I do not trust him, though. He *uses* Chinks. I don't. I let them use *me* to help *them.* When the opium boats come in and there's an argy-bargy about prices, and everyone's speaking pidgin, I get within earshot and tell the Chinks whether they're being swindled or not.'

'But you weren't up the coast when we came in?'

'Of course not. There was no need to be. The mandarin there controls that trade. But an awful lot of trade, boy, is done up here. Pirate ships. Some of Jardine's captains making money on the side. Some of the Parsee's lads doing likewise.'

'How did you get here?' asked Gunn.

'Like you, or nearly like you. Off a ship. I was in the *Black Boy,* a clipper out from Sydney to Singapore. One day we came across two junks, part burnt but, sails gone, wood still smouldering, people shouting for help — or so we thought. We hove to, and before we knew where the devil we were, they'd grappling irons out and were on deck slitting our bloody throats. It was a trap. And we jumped right into it.'

'But you survived?'

'Of course I survived. I wouldn't be here otherwise, would I? I was second mate. Captain went down. So did the first mate and nearly all the rest. They're cunning swine, Chinese pirates. When they capture a foreign ship, they always leave *some* crew alive to work her, for their method of seamanship isn't ours. So they spared me to run the vessel. We were carrying grain, with hatches open because of the heat. They battened down all hatches — and the grain caught fire. Ship burned out half a mile off shore.

'We jumped into the sea, and the tide carried us in. Some of the pirates also reached the shore. They were going to kill me at first. Then they decided not to. They weren't all that certain, how the locals would treat them, for pirates are out-laws here. When they knew I spoke English *and* dialect they thought I might be more useful to them alive than dead. Maybe they could ransom me.

'We had a bit of trouble with the locals at first, then some Americans came, trying to sell a cargo of Turkish mud. They spoke pidgin, but the natives here couldn't understand them. I did. I became the go-between. And that's what I've been ever since, the man in the middle. No doubt, I'll die in bed like all good sailors. Whose bed, though, is a different matter.'

'Possibly. But now you need treatment'

'How can you get your physic?'

'When the *Hesperides* comes in, I will go back on board.'

'Don't be a fool. Crutchley will have you over the side as soon as it is dark.'

'You think so?'

'I *know* so.'

'Tell me, then, are *you* content to stay on here?' asked Gunn slowly, an idea forming in his mind.

'What else am I offered? And how the devil could I get away? These Chinks wouldn't let me go, for they need me. And I rather like the life. I've got a Chink woman and I puff a pipe of opium when I want to.'

'But would you go home — if you could?'

'Where's home?' asked MacPherson, 'I haven't been back to Scotland for twelve years. They must have given me up for dead long since.'

'But you speak the dialects. You could be useful to merchants in Macao or Canton.'

'As useful to them as *you* were useful to the Parsee, eh? They'd use me — and then get rid of me.'

'Not if you went back in a position of power.'

'What are you talking about?'

'Listen,' said Gunn earnestly, 'when the *Hesperides* arrives, let's *both* go aboard.'

'I couldn't leave Ling Fai, my woman.'

'Take her with you.'

'You don't know what you're talking about. How *could* I take her? I have no money. In any case, the *Hesperides* is not a passenger vessel.'

'If we took over the *Hesperides,* we could sail where we wanted, with whom we wanted.'

'Take her over? You've been touched by the sun, I think, doctor. You need treatment more than me!'

'Give me something to eat,' said Gunn. 'And I'll tell you what I have in mind.'

MacPherson clapped his hands, and spoke rapidly in a high-pitched, sing-song voice. A girl carried in a bamboo tray with a coconut split in two. Gunn drank the sharp, fresh juice gratefully. Another girl brought in a bowl of steaming rice overlaid with thin strips of boiled fish. Gunn ate with his fingers. With every mouthful, he felt strength return, and with his strength a strange cold determination he had never experienced before.

He thought of the Parsee and his talk of a promise being a debt; of Crutchley and the purse of pennies. He remembered his shock at seeing the Lascars row hastily out to sea, and the Chinese with their bamboo clubs walking slowly along the beach towards him. He thought of all these people and knew what he had to do.

'When the *Hesperides* puts in here, we're going aboard,' he told MacPherson, 'Both of us. They'll send a boat ashore, first. Maybe with Mackereth, or if he is too timid, someone who speaks a bit of pidgin, to see what the reception's like.

'You brief one of your Chinks to tell them that the local mandarin has discovered something more precious than opium here. Gold or rubies, jade — anything. But they will need, as many men as possible to carry it back. Crutchley will denude his ship, but he won't come himself. You lead the crew into the forest — and we'll bind them up. Then we take some of your fellows — put on Chink clothes ourselves — and we will row back.'

'And then what?'

'Leave that to me,' said Gunn. 'I have a debt to pay to Crutchley.'

'This is mutiny.'

'What Crutchley did to me was nearly murder. And who will know exactly what happened — after it's happened?'

'What about the Parsee and Jardine? They're very influential. They won't stand for that.'

'They are both several hundred miles away. We will see what they'll stand for — or what they won't — in our own time.'

'You'll never get away with this.'

'What is the alternative? To stay here in the jungle — you rotting with what you think is pox, and the Chinks along the coast still after me?'

'It's an idea,' allowed MacPherson slowly.

'It's a certainty. We'll keep Captain Fernandes as a hostage. He'll testify to anything we tell him to.'

As Gunn spoke, he remembered how Fernandes had refused to shake hands with him; maybe he knew even then what Crutchley planned to do?

'What about Crutchley, doctor?'

'I have told you. I will deal with him.'

'And the Parsee? He'll not sit by if you seize his ship.'

'How can he stop us from a distance? And, remember, we can sail under several flags, if need be.'

'You're bloody right,' agreed MacPherson. 'Matheson is the Danish Consul, and every now and then he hoists the Danish flag on his boats and none of the Company ships or even the Navy can lay a finger on him.'

'The *Hesperides* will have a flag locker, too.'

'And to think I have been here for years, and it needed you to come with a plan of escape,' said MacPherson slowly.

'You're wrong,' said Gunn. 'It doesn't need me. It needs *both* of us. We are like elements in science — inadequate on their own, but joined together they produce an explosion — or a new metal. And the new metal we will discover together, MacPherson, is very precious. Gold!'

He put out his hand; MacPherson shook it firmly.

'I'll find you some Chink clothes,' he said. 'There's a stream I wash in, the other side of the clearing. I bought a dozen bars of soap from the last boat that called.'

He paused, suddenly nervous at the prospect before them.

'Are you *certain* you can do it, doctor?'

'No,' admitted Gunn. 'Nothing in life is certain — except that one day we'll all be required to leave it. But if you want to succeed, or even to survive, you don't ask questions. Can I do this? *Shall* I do the other? — you dam' well *do* them. This thing, MacPherson, we'll do together.'

As he watched the other man go off happily, his doubts removed, Gunn realized that his experience had increased another ability he had not known he possessed; the gift of persuasion. For in persuading MacPherson that he could carry out what he had originally only mentioned as a passing thought, he had also persuaded himself.

IN WHICH MR CRUTCHLEY IS PERSUADED TO MAKE A MOVE

Captain Fernandes smoothed back his thick curly hair, put on his white cap and went in to see Crutchley. He was frightened of the man, not only because of his physical size, but because of his moods. One day Crutchley would offer him a glass of rum; the next, smash the glass out of his hand, shouting that Fernandes was drunk or insulting.

Fernandes knew that Crutchley had just marooned Gunn, which was virtually murder by a gentler name. And he feared for his own safety, his own future. Without money or character or influence in the East, you lacked the power to maintain even a basic human dignity. Fernandes realized that Crutchley would just as easily be rid of him; he was also expendable.

'Landfall on the port bow, sir,' he announced briskly, keeping fear out of his voice.

'Don't be a bloody fool.' said Crutchley thickly, a glass of rum in his hand. 'We've not been out of sight of land since we left Namoa. Do you mean we've reached our compass bearing?'

'Yes, sir.'

'Well, turn the clipper in. Go as close as you can. We have no charts for this coast?'

'Not with depth markings, sir.'

'Well, for God's sake don't run aground or hole the bottom. Stand off at a half a mile, if it's shallow. Take that interpreter fellow, Mackereth, and six Lascars with pistols and staves in the longboat, and see what sort of reception the locals give you.'

'You mean you want *me* to go ashore, sir?'

'And why ever not?'

'I don't like leaving the ship, sir. A captain should remain in command at all times.'

'You mean you're bloody frightened, you dago. Get in that longboat and do as I tell you. *I'm* in command. Find out the going price for the mud, and how much they will take, and then report back to me.'

Fernandes swallowed. Who could stand up for rules against Crutchley? His gut began to burn with the fire of humiliation. He saluted, and went out to give his orders.

Mackereth came up on deck as the bows swung in towards the opalescent greenness of the shore. He could see a thin rim of waves breaking like a wide white smile. The air felt very hot and still; seabirds were calling and diving in their wake. The rusty anchor chains screamed out, davits swung like hinged fingers, and the longboat went slowly into the water.

'I want you to come with us,' Fernandes told Mackereth. 'I can speak pidgin, but these fellows may not understand it.'

The beach was empty as a dead man's eyes, the sand white as a skull picked of all flesh. Mackereth did not like the look of it.

'You're coming yourself?' he asked hopefully.

Fernandes nodded.

'Good.' Mackereth felt relieved; he would not be left behind, like Gunn. He went down to his cabin; it seemed suddenly very friendly. He looked for reassurance at the brass crucifix on the locker by his bunk; the figure on the cross looked back at him.

'Oh, God,' he prayed, 'under whose rule we all serve, let us come to no harm in this journey we make in thy name.' Of course, it was hardly in God's name; but at least God should benefit if Mackereth made enough money to allow tracts to be translated and distributed. God would understand.

Mackereth poured himself some whisky. It was bad to drink in this heat, but he felt hollow and frightened, and the drink drove out the fear; or some of it. Then he came up on deck and climbed over the rail, and went down the swinging rope ladder into the boat. The coxswain nodded to the oarsmen; oars flicked like silver fish in the cobalt sea.

Fernandes scanned the beach. It was still deserted, but as they approached within thirty yards, three figures walked out of the bushes and stood, watching them. They were dark-skinned natives, with grass-cloth drawers and rattan hats against the fierce blaze of the sun.

'Easy all!' shouted Fernandes. The sailors shipped their oars, and the boat drifted on through the chuckling, glittering water. White waves flung themselves uselessly against the shore, and soaked back in a flurry of foam.

'All wantee number one Chinese man! All chop, quickly run! Make muchee Chinese silver topside!' Fernandes shouted. His voice sounded high and nervous. The men on the shore still stood in silence, watching them.

'They don't understand,' said Fernandes. 'You tell them in their lingo.'

Mackereth cupped his hands around his mouth and began to shout in Cantonese, then in dialect. One of the men called back.

'He welcomes us ashore,' Mackereth said.

'Row in,' ordered Fernandes.

As the bows grated on loose shingle, they jumped out into the shallow water and waded ashore. The six Lascars walked behind them, pistols in their belts. The first Chinese man began to gabble away, head on one side. Mackereth questioned him closely; then turned to Fernandes.

'They want to buy,' he said, smiling with relief.

'What price?'

'The going rate. Eight hundred dollars a chest.'

'A fair price,' agreed Fernandes.

'There's another thing,' said Mackereth, and his voice was suddenly hoarse. 'They want to pay in gold.'

This was most unusual; it was the custom for the Chinese to pay in silver coins.

'Let's see it, then.'

The first man put his hand in the folds of his loincloth and pulled out a handful of gold coins: Mackereth picked out one and examined it.

'They're Portuguese guineas.'

'Do they know their value?' asked Fernandes. 'Tell them they're not as good as silver.'

'I have done so.' said Mackereth. 'They say the mandarin has four chests of golden guineas inland. Taken from some boat that went down. But they do not realize its value in trade. They think it is inferior to silver.'

'My God!' said Fernandes. 'We could make our fortune.'

'They want us to inspect them. They're only about fifty yards away — in the jungle.'

'Is it safe?'

'I would think so.'

'Wait,' said Fernandes, always cautious. He turned to the Lascars.

'Beach the boat,' he ordered. 'Then ship your oars and come with us.'

'Follow me;' said Mackereth, relishing the unlikely role of leader. In single file, they followed the three Chinese into the jungle. Under the thick bamboos, it was much darker and hotter than any of them had imagined. Sweat glistened on their bodies like glass. They reached a clearing; another Chinese man was standing outside a thatched hut. He bowed to them and said something to Mackereth.

'He wants us to rest awhile and drink some rice wine with him. I think we should. We have to go at these people's pace.

It's no good rushing them.'

'Make it as quick as you can then. I think we've come more than fifty yards.'

'Distance is deceptive in the heat,' said Mackereth reassuringly.

The Chinese cupped his hands; three girls came out of the hut carrying bamboo trays with oval Chinese cups and jugs. They filled the cups and took them round to the Lascars.

'What about us?' asked Fernandes.

'Wait,' said Mackereth. 'The leader has explained it is the custom to give drink to the servants first, and to the quality afterwards.'

'As you say,' said Fernandes, but he hated being surrounded by a solid green wall of trees. It seemed to him that he was being watched and fear ran cold fingers down his back. The Lascars drank greedily and held out the little cups for more.

Another girl brought out two slightly larger cups containing pale wine. It tasted sweet and was very cold. A noise made Fernandes turn, glass half empty. One of the Lascars was down on his knees. Then he pitched forward on the ground. - 'What's the matter with him?'

'Probably the heat.'

'No!' cried Fernandes in terror, for suddenly other Lascars were falling and the rest were staggering about, hands in front of them like blind men.

'It's a trap! They've been drugged. Come on! Back to the boat!'

He turned to run, and a hard voice called out from the jungle: 'Stand where you are, captain. Put your hands on your head. And you, Mr Mackereth.'

'My God,' said Fernandes hoarsely.

'You do well to call upon your Maker,' said MacPherson, coming out of the trees, a sabre in his right hand. 'But you should remember, the gods help those who help themselves.'

'Who are you?' asked Fernandes, some slight courage returning. After all, this man spoke English.

As he spoke, other men ran out of the hut to the Lascars who lay inert or writhed feebly on the ground, like sleepers overcome by evil dreams? They relieved them of their pistols, stripped off their clothes, and bound their wrists and ankles with jungle creeper.

'What is the meaning of this attack?' asked Mackereth.

'We are going back with you to the *Hesperides*,' replied MacPherson.

'We?' repeated Fernandes.

'Yes,' said Gunn. 'We.'

He had come up behind them quietly.

'My God, you are still alive!'

'You didn't expect that, did you?'

'It's a miracle,' said Mackereth. 'My prayers have been answered.'

'Shut up,' said MacPherson. He took a pistol from one of his men and pointed it towards Mackereth and Fernandes.

'The name's MacPherson, in case you want to know. We are going to take over the *Hesperides.*'

'This is mutiny,' whispered Fernandes. 'I never meant any harm to Gunn. I swear I didn't.'

'You didn't mean any good to me, either,' said Gunn. 'Now it is my turn.'

They walked back through the trees to the beach. MacPherson's men now wearing the Lascars' clothes, had already launched the longboat.

'What will you do with us?' asked Fernandes fearfully.

'That depends,' said MacPherson casually. 'On what?'

'On how you behave. Turn about, and sit facing the stern. And if either of you shout or give any warning to Crutchley, I'll shoot you both out of hand.'

He turned to Mackereth.

'If you wish to spread the word of God, you must stay alive to do it.'

'I have never done any harm to Gunn. I prayed for his safety.'

'Then I'm sure he'll pray for yours now.'

The boat slid out through the thrash of breaking waves.

'When we draw near to the *Hesperides,* Crutchley or some-one else may ask who we are,' MacPherson told Fernandes. 'You say we are from the mandarin, and we have to come aboard.'

'He'll see you are not Chinese.'

'We've got these,' said MacPherson, tapping his rattan hat. 'He won't see our faces until we *are* aboard. That is unless you intend to warn him?'

'I'll say nothing,' said Fernandes quickly. 'I swear it.'

'How near are we?' asked Gunn, facing the stern.

'Twenty yards.'

'Is Crutchley on deck?'

'Yes,' replied Fernandes.

'Give the command to the crew,' said MacPherson.

He pushed back the hammer on the pistol and sat with it between his knees aiming at Fernandes' groin, a yard away.

Fernandes shouted: 'Prepare to pull alongside! Easy, port side. Hard over, starboard side. All together — *row!*'

Crutchley bellowed from the rail: 'Who's with you?'

'The mandarin's representatives, sir.'

'What are they coming out here for?'

They have to discuss the price. They have gold instead of silver.'

'Gold,' repeated Crutchley in a more reverent voice. 'Let them both come up.'

The longboat bumped against the tarred hull. MacPherson gripped the rope ladder, keeping his face down so that anyone on the high deck would only see the top of his head. He swung up easily hand over hand and on to the deck.

'You speakee pidgin?' Crutchley asked.

'Much speakee. Plenty gold from mandarin. You likee, yes? No trub at all. All easy going,' said MacPherson, head still down as he climbed over the rail. Gunn swarmed up after him, and then came two Chinese.

'You!' said Crutchley in amazement, as he stared at Gunn. 'I thought you were dead.'

Bemused with drink and heat and surprise, Crutchley put up one hand to his eyes to shut out the blinding light, to try and force himself to focus his thoughts. Then he shouted to Captain Fernandes, 'Send up all the Lascars!'

'They are still ashore,' replied Gunn.

'Then who are these?'

'My men,' said MacPherson.

'Who the hell are you?'

'Name of 'MacPherson. Lately mate of the *Black Boy*.'

'Where have you both come from? I don't understand.'

'You don't have to,' said Gunn. 'We are taking over.'

'You dam' well aren't,' shouted Crutchley, and jumped at him. . .

MacPherson thrust out his right foot. Crutchley tripped and as he went down, Gunn brought up his right knee into his face. Crutchley rolled uselessly on the deck, doubled up with pain. Then he slowly staggered to his feet. In his right hand, he held a knife.

'Shall I shoot him?' asked MacPherson.

'No,' said Gunn. 'I'll deal with him.'

'How?'

'I am going to give him a chance.'

'You're mad,' said MacPherson.

'Possibly. But *he* gave me a chance, and I lived. He can have the same opportunity. On my terms. First, drop your knife or I will shoot your hand off.'

Crutchley straightened up, his eyes like live coals in his head. Slowly, his fingers opened. The knife clattered down on the deck.

'Get up forrard,' ordered Gunn, jerking his pistol at him. 'And keep your hands on top of your head.'

They walked up the gently sloping deck under the giant mast. Water chuckled at a secret joke beneath the bows; the huge painted figurehead stared at the shore and saw nothing.

'Turn around,' said Gunn. 'Now, no argument, and no discussion. You either accept my terms, or you don't. If you don't, I'll shoot you here, where there are no witnesses, and say it was in self-defence.'

He put his left hand in his pocket, separated his father's letter from the envelope, took out the envelope and a stub of pencil.

'I will put these down on the deck between us,' he said, 'and then I will back away six paces. You will pick them up and write what I tell you.'

'What will you do then?' asked Crutchley. 'Shoot me?'

'No. I will put you in the longboat, and you can row ashore. Your Lascars are already there. You will not be alone, like me.'

Crutchley crouched on the deck, and picked up the pencil.

'Now write this,' ordered Gunn. 'I, Richard Crutchley, hereby give and bequeath to Dr Robert Gunn my entire shareholding in Crutchley & Company. Signed freely this day, July 11th, 1833. Richard Crutchley. Witness — Leave a space for that, Fernandes will witness it.'

'You are ruining me,' said Crutchley in a small protesting voice, as he wrote.

'I could have killed you,' Gunn reminded him, as he picked up the envelope and the pencil. They walked back in silence to the others. Gunn handed the paper to Fernandes.

'Sign that,' he told him.

Fernandes signed with a trembling hand.

'Now go down the ladder to the longboat,' Gunn told Crutchley.

'This is mutiny,' said Crutchley bitterly. 'Mutiny and armed robbery. The Parsee will never allow this. You'll hang for this, Gunn.'

Gunn said nothing; Crutchley went down the ladder and

then, reluctantly, he picked up the oars and began to row.

Mackereth leaned on the rail, watching him. How are the mighty, fallen! Second Samuel, chapter one, verse nineteen.

'Who is this man?' he asked Gunn, nodding towards MacPherson.

'A friend,' said Gunn. 'As I hope you are.'

'I am,' said Mackereth earnestly. 'I assure you I am. A most loyal friend. I begged Crutchley to send the boat back for you at Namoa, but he refused. Captain Fernandes knows that, don't you, captain?'

Fernandes nodded.

'Yes, I know that. It is true, Dr Gunn.'

'I am pleased to hear it. Now you, captain, should be pleased to hear that for the time being I am leaving you to command this vessel. I did not cure your stomach pains for nothing. We are going on up the coast as Mr Crutchley intended. We will sell our mud, then we shall return to Macao.'

'Very good, doctor.'

Fernandes climbed up to the wheelhouse and began to shout orders. The sails unfurled, and the breeze filled them. The tall ship bent slightly as she slid through the shining sea. Behind them, the longboat shrank in the distance to a toy.

'Now,' said MacPherson to Gunn. 'What about that treatment you promised me? And I've got a confession to make. I have brought my woman Ling Fai aboard.'

'How?'

'She was rowing number three in the longboat. And you never saw her?'

MacPherson smiled.

'Come here, Ling,' he said gently.

A figure moved from behind a lifeboat.

Gunn saw Ling Fai's face for the first time, and it was beautiful; an almond-coloured skin, a nervous shy smile around her mouth, her eyes dark and surprisingly wide, like sloes. She had an air of fresh innocence and laughter about her that was strangely appealing. Gunn could see the outline of her small breasts and the pointed nipples beneath the thin material of her shirt; he thought suddenly of the Parsee's daughter.

'You've not given *her* what you think you have?' he asked MacPherson anxiously.

'I have not,' replied the Scot indignantly. 'I've not lain with her since my member grew inflamed.'

'Does she know you think you are infected?'

'No. She just thinks I do not want her.'

'Then I'll keep your secret,' said Gunn. 'You will have your treatment. But first let us examine our cargo. I'm a merchant first now and a physician second.'

MacPherson ordered the crew to open the first hatch, and they peered, down through the square opening at the piles of boxes of light mango-wood,_ each branded, 'Patna Opium' and the trademark of a heart divided into four, bearing the letters U.E.I.C. These initials stood for United East India Company, a mark so highly regarded that it was a guarantee of high quality. No merchant would bother to examine or query any package that bore it.

'Where shall we try for our first customers?' asked Gunn.

'We're asking for trouble if we stay close,' said MacPherson. 'I hear a new local governor has just taken over in Whang-pi, about fifty miles north. He should be willing to trade, for his appointment will have cost him a fortune to purchase.'

'I overheard Crutchley say that one of Jardine's clippers was already visiting him for that same purpose,' warned Mackereth.

'Then that confirms our good judgment,' replied Gunn.

'What if Jardine and Matheson object?

'Never mind them,' said Gunn airily. 'What if *I* object to *them* being there?'

Mackereth opened his mouth to speak, and then swallowed his words. Events were happening too quickly for him, and he felt fear's teeth gnaw his stomach. He went below to his cabin, and poured a comforting five fingers of Queen Anne. Truly the ways of the Lord were wonderful to behold, he told himself. They that go down to the sea in ships, that do business in great waters: these see the works of the Lord, and his wonders in the deep. Psalm One hundred and seven, verse twenty-three.

Gunn, who h ~had believed to be dead, had come back from the grave. And likewise Crutchley, his tormentor, had been removed. He closed his eyes and mouthed a hoarse prayer of thanks to God. Then he poured another whisky, and a third after that.

The *Hesperides* sailed on. It was early morning when they sighted the other clipper. She was much larger than the *Hesperides,* her black hull freshly tarred, three masts sharply raked, varnish gleaming like glass, white sails neatly furled. A gaggle of local boats bobbed busily around her. Fernandes lowered his glasses and turned to Gunn.

'The *Bosphorus,*' he announced. 'One of Jardine's fleet, as Mackereth said. Captain Ferguson commanding.'

'Is she armed?' asked Gunn.

'Yes. A single row of cannon on either side.'

'Will they use them?'

'Not while they think this is still Crutchley's ship.'

Gunn glanced up at the flag. Just for a moment, he was tempted to haul it down and hoist the Stars and Stripes, or the Danish white cross on a red back. Then he dismissed the idea; they would start as he meant, to continue.

'We'll go in under the Jack' he said. 'Bring her alongside within hailing distance. Anchor her fore and aft, and leave the rest to me.'

He turned to MacPherson.

'Any trouble, and you take over. You understand, Fernandes? You don't want to go ashore like Crutchley, do you?'

'No, doctor,' said Fernandes fearfully. 'I do not.'

The sampans scattered as the huge bowsprit pointed its long finger above them, and the anchor chains rattled out.

'Open all hatches,' bellowed MacPherson. The Chinese leapt to their task. Rope ladders dropped on either side. The *Hesperides* now pointed towards the shore, thirty feet from the *Bosphorus.*

'What is the usual procedure?' Gunn asked MacPherson in a low voice.

'Generally, the ship waits until the Chinese send out someone to see what price we are asking.'

Gunn remembered the wine Crutchley had served to the mandarin, and ordered a cabin boy to bring up two bottles of claret, and half a dozen glasses.

A Scottish voice hailed them from the *Bosphorus.*

'Captain Ferguson speaking. We're trading here already. You have trouble and wish our aid?'

Gunn cupped his hands around his mouth.

'No trouble,' he said. 'But thank you kindly for your enquiry. We are also trading here.'

'I think not. If you do you will ruin the market for both of us. We have paid our *cumsha*— our bribes. Why not go farther up the coast?'

'Because I want to stay here.'

'Who are *you,* sir? Where's Captain Fernandes? And Mr Crutchley?'

'Captain Fernandes is in the wheelhouse. And Mr Crutchley has made over the shares in his company to me. My name is Gunn. Dr Gunn.'

'Where is Mr Crutchley?'

'He has decided to take a holiday ashore.'

'A holiday ashore?' Captain Ferguson's speaking trumpet magnified his amazement. 'What exactly do you mean, sir?'

'I repeat. Crutchley decided to take a holiday ashore. He had his reasons, I am sure.'

Captain Ferguson lowered his speaking trumpet and turned to one of his officers, who focused his glass on the *Hesperides.*

'A sampan with a mandarin coming up on the port side,'

MacPherson called to Gun. 'A red button man.'

'Show him all courtesy.'

'You are deliberately interfering with our trade!' shouted Captain Ferguson angrily. 'Why, sir? What is your object?'

Gunn did not reply, but went down to meet the mandarin, a fat man with hands folded in his loose sleeves, eyes like slits in a bladder of white lard, waxed black moustachios reaching down below his chin.

'Speak to him in his lingo,' Gunn told Mackereth. As he began to talk in a high-pitched chatter, the mandarin bowed and answered. Mackereth translated.

'He says they are paying ten dollars a pound for mud from the *Bosphorus*.'

'Tell him it's our pleasure to sell it to him at nine dollars.'

'He will take twenty chests. But he does not wish to spoil relations with the *Bosphorus*.'

'Tell him that he will make friends with us. That whatever the *Bosphorus* charges, we will always charge less. Then let him put his money on the deck, and get the chests out of the hold.'

More sampans bumped frail bows against the tarred hull of the *Hesperides*. Out came ropes on swinging wooden cranes; down into the sampans went the boxes. Ten minutes later, Captain Ferguson of the *Bosphorus* shouted again.

'You're undercutting us, sir. Don't you know the agreed price is ten?'

'*Your* agreed price. Not mine.'

Gunn poured out glasses of wine for the mandarin, then for Mackereth and MacPherson and for himself.

They drank a toast to their future business relationship. He was enjoying himself; he felt fulfilled, relaxed, content.

It was as though he had been searching blindly all his life for such a situation, and now he wanted to savour every separate second: the glittering sea, the shouting coolies, the bowing blandness of the mandarin, the flag whackering away at the masthead, the annoyance of the other captain; especially the annoyance of the other captain. Ferguson was shouting again now.

'We have specific orders to trade here, to make new contacts and I am going to carry them out, whatever you may do. We are lowering our price to eight dollars.'

'Tell the mandarin he can have another twenty crates at seven,' Gunn told Mackereth quickly. 'And if he takes forty, well give him the lot at six and a half dollars, last price.'

Mackereth translated; the mandarin nodded his head. More boxes were lowered into the sampans. Gunn waited until this news percolated back to Captain Ferguson, a process that only took a few minutes.

'I demand that you desist from this ruinous behaviour,' Ferguson shouted angrily.

MacPherson handed Gunn a speaking trumpet.

'You can *demand* what you like,' he called back, but only from inferiors, never from an equal or superior. So, Captain Ferguson, I will sell at any price I like. That, I believe, is Dr Jardine's business philosophy, and it is also mine. And I stay here until we have sold every box — even if we come down to a dollar a time. You can stay with us, or pull up your anchors and sail away. The choice is yours, captain. I wish you no harm, but I state my case.'

They waited for five minutes, and then they heard shouts of command from the *Bosphorus*. Up came the anchors, down clattered the great canvas sails. The clipper began to move.

'You will hear about this in Macao. We will be there before you. Jardine will not like this, and he is a very powerful man. Also, he owns shares in your company.'

'He is not the majority shareholder,' shouted Gunn. 'I will outvote him.'

'I do not wish to argue and quarrel in front of natives,' retorted Ferguson. 'I find your behaviour most suspicious. I believe you have done away with Mr Crutchley in some way. If you have, I will see to it that you are hanged! All of you.'

Then the *Bosphorus* was past them, sailing slowly out to sea.

Gunn turned to MacPherson.

'We've done it!' he said triumphantly. 'We've *done* it!'

'We still have to meet them back in Macao,' replied MacPherson in a worried tone.

'As a shareholder in Crutchley & Company, you can leave that to me. There's another thing I must do when we dock, and that is change the name of the company. Crutchley is out of it for good. He belongs to the past. What shall we call it now?'

'What about Gunn-MacPherson or MacPherson-Gunn?'

'No. I do not wish to use our names, because if one of us left, we would have to change it again. There would be no continuity, and continuity is important It is good for trade.

'I'll tell you what. We seized this clipper by claiming that a mandarin who doesn't exist had found gold that wasn't there. Well, it's going to be there from now on for both of us. Well call our company Mandarin-Gold. Everyone knows a mandarin is powerful, and that the whole world turns on a golden axle. That's our name, MacPherson. One day it will be known not only along the China coast, but round the world. Now, come below deck. You tell me I have a patient to treat.'

Jardine lit a long cigar, blew out the lucifer and turned to his partner, Matheson. They were seated in an upper room of Creek Factory. The hour was evening, with candles lit; the river's shining floor reflected the coloured paper lanterns on the quay. Through the window, they could see the clock on the chapel spire of the English factory. This was the only public clock in Canton; everyone regulated his watch as- they passed it; Jardine did so now, out of habit.

'If you ask me, we're making damned fools of ourselves,' he said slowly. 'Our views must carry weight, and the Americans also agree we simply cannot allow this situation to continue.

'We're just specking away along the coast of China, when if we could only secure diplomatic representation at Peking, we could open up the whole country, with corresponding benefits to the whole community here as well as to our own companies.'

'You heard what happened today with Napier?' asked Matheson.

'Yes,' agreed Jardine shortly. 'I heard.'

He hated to think of the supine way in which the British were conducting their negotiations, when a couple of gunboats up the river, with maybe the despatch of some troops ashore, could instantly transform the absurd pretensions of the Chinese. He had seen Napier's despatch to the government in London in which his lordship had expressed a similar opinion: 'Three or four frigates or brigs, with a few steady British troops, not sepoys, would settle the thing in an inconceivably short time. It would have brilliant consequences for the British firms in China and the American contemporaries, and for the other European merchants as well.'

It could be done so easily, too, Napier had added, 'with a facility unknown, even in the capture of a paltry West Indian island.' But these were only words, not deeds. Everyone knew that the Chinese army had arrows and pikes and shields and swords, but little else. They were badly disciplined, and their guns were useless. The shore batteries along the Bogue were contemptible, and capable of lobbing shots into the water and nothing, more. Why, the gunners had sold so much of their gunpowder to British opium ships for their armament that they had to adulterate their remaining stocks with one measure of sand for every two of powder.

Yet despite these ludicrous weaknesses, the Chinese still possessed inexplicable confidence in their own superiority. This had been evidenced when Lu had quite unexpectedly asked for Lord Napier to arrange a. meeting at eleven o'clock one morning recently in the English factory. Three mandarins desired to attend. Optimism among Lord Napier's party was high; no doubt they wished to conclude some kind of agreement.

In China, the direction in which authority traditionally faced was always south. Thus the Chinese interpreters set out three chairs for the mandarins in a semi-circle facing south. The chairs for the British were on the east and west sides of the hall.

'But where's Lord Napier going to sit?' asked Elliot, for no chair whatever had been allocated to him.

'Possibly he will stand,' suggested the head interpreter, indifferent to the question.

'But this is ridiculous,' Elliot protested. 'You must bring a seat. He cannot be expected to stand.'

Napier agreed; on no account would he stand while inferiors sat. In any case, one row of chairs had their backs to the portrait of George IV, and this, surely, was insulting to the Sovereign? He had already been insulted when the Emperor had refused to accept the picture as a gift. A further slight would be insupportable. Napier therefore ordered that all the chairs should be reversed so that no-one sat with their back to the King's picture, and he chose the centre seat for himself, with a mandarin on either side, and facing the third.

When the Hong merchants arrived to check arrangements for the meeting, they immediately begged Lord Napier to put the chairs back as they were. The mandarins would be offended beyond all apology if they did not face south. They would fine the Hong merchants heavily, and maybe even cause them to be beaten with bamboos, for they would be blamed for this calculated affront.

'I cannot alter anything now,' retorted Lord Napier when this was translated to him. 'This is *our* factory. They will sit as I say.'

Usually, he would have replied in a more conciliatory way, but something about Canton, the hot, humid climate and the endless prevarications of the Chinese to what he regarded as reasonable requests, with Jardine on one side demanding fierce and instant action, and Elliot on the other advising caution, provoked a mounting irritation about his assignment and its vague responsibilities.

He sent back his reports to London, but to receive any reply would take six months — assuming that the Foreign Secretary wrote immediately, which was unlikely. After all, European problems were infinitely more pressing than what did or did not happen on the other side of the world to a handful of British merchants and privateers, even allowing their vast financial contribution to the East India Company. And in any case the problem would have resolved itself, for good or bad, long before Napier received his Government's instructions. He had to make his own decisions — but how could he do so when the Chinese acted without any reference to realities? Also, he had not been feeling well for some weeks. Each night he would lie awake in his hot bedroom, shutters closed against the noxious fumes of night, listening to gongs and firecrackers and the high-pitched wailing that the Chinese called music, wondering how his wife and daughters were faring at Macao, how his estate in Scotland was being managed, whether his sheep were being given the care he could have given them were he home instead of in this nightmare, alien land.

At eleven o'clock precisely Napier sat down in the centre chair. He and his staff waited, but no mandarins arrived. Half-past eleven; twelve; one o'clock passed and still no mandarins. Then at a quarter past one they walked in, hands in their sleeves, smiling and bowing.

'You're late,' Napier greeted them through his interpreter. His head was aching and his eyes burned like hot ashes. He contained his anger with difficulty; how could *anyone* treat with these people?

'Were you not aware that the time was fixed, at your wish, for eleven o'clock?' he asked them, and without waiting for a reply, went on: 'This is an insult to His Britannic Majesty which cannot be overlooked a second time; Whereas, on previous occasions, you have only had to deal with the servants of a private company of merchants, you must understand that henceforth your communications will be held with officers appointed by His Britannic Majesty, who are by no means inclined to submit to such indignities!'

The mandarins sat impassive, as though they heard nothing and understood nothing. Napier was not aware that, under their own peculiar etiquette, they had purposely arrived two hours after the appointed time, for this was the accepted custom when calling upon inferior personages of lesser rank, such as Barbarians. Had they been invited by a person of superior rank for eleven, they would have arrived at nine.

Because the mandarins had smiled and bowed their heads when his message was translated, Napier assumed they had accepted his superiority and acknowledged their error. He did not realize how deeply he had insulted them.

Napier then asked the senior mandarin, the Prefect, why they wished to see him. The senior mandarin replied that Viceroy Lu had asked him to discover what Lord Napier was doing in Canton without official permission, and when he proposed to leave.

Napier explained that when the East India Company, which had previously conducted trade with the Hong merchants, had surrendered its monopoly in China, the Viceroy in Canton had specifically asked for some new person to represent the English merchants. He was that person. He would return to Macao when he wished to do so.

But you are *not* a merchant, the Prefect pointed out quickly, you are an official. This means that the King of England wishes to change the system. The correct procedure would have been for the King to inform the Viceroy of this desire, and then seek the orders of the Son of Heaven. Instead, he had simply sent Lord Napier, who, doubtless out of ignorance rather than ill will, had arrived in Canton intent on changing in a day a system of regulations that had existed for generations.

Once more, Napier produced his personal letter for the Viceroy, but they refused to accept it. The meeting ended with forced smiles and sweetmeats and wine, but nothing was agreed and nothing had changed.

Napier then drafted a notice which he had translated into Chinese and displayed on the factory walls. This claimed that 'thousands of industrious Chinese must suffer ruin simply through the perversity of their government, unless they opened their frontiers to trade,'

Lu replied with posters pasted on every vacant wall. They described Napier as 'a Lawless Foreign Slave, a Barbarian dog named Laboriously Vile,' and reminded him that it was a capital offence to incite the people against their rules. Anyone would therefore be justified in decapitating him and displaying his head on a pike as a warning to others.

Now, Jardine remembered Napier's astonishment when the translation was read out to him.

'But I don't understand it,' he said in a shocked voice. 'This is utterly ridiculous. We are trying to open up China for the good of the Chinese people as much as for our own profit. Cannot they *see* that?'

'There's worse to come, sir,' reported Elliot. 'The Viceroy is withdrawing all Chinese labour from our factories and the quay. All commercial transactions between Chinese merchants and everyone in the factory is coming to a standstill.'

'For how long?' asked Napier.

'Until you leave.'

'I'll *never* leave,' said Napier.

'Then it would appear, gentlemen,' said Elliot, 'that we have reached an impasse. The shopkeepers, I am told, are under penalty of death if they sell us any goods. We cannot trade, so the whole purpose of being here is nullified.'

'You are too defeatist,' replied Jardine. 'You should be in commerce like me. Then you'd have to find ways around difficulties, over them, under them. You don't just accept them and say we're at an impasse and there's nothing we can do. You break the impasse.'

'And how do you propose to do that, doctor?' asked Elliot sarcastically.

'I would tell you how I'd do it, if Lord Napier asked my opinion,' replied Jardine.

'I am asking you,' said Napier immediately. 'How *would* you do it?'

'First, I'd take the *Andromache,* and the frigate *Imogene,* that's just come over from India to relieve her, and I'd sail up this river and fire on their stone forts. Make the Chinese realize that they cannot go on as they are. They'd ask for terms — and our terms would include an Ambassador at Peking.'

'I disagree completely,' said Elliot. 'There are literally millions of Chinese and a handful of us. It's of no real concern to the Emperor in Peking what happens in this remote part of his kingdom.

'A few shells fired at some mud fort? The Emperor would not capitulate for that — and the Viceroy would not dare to, even if he wished he could.'

'You don't know the East like I do,' Jardine assured him earnestly. 'I know these people's minds. I have to, or I could not survive commercially. They're tortuous, but like anyone else, they respect success. They will bow down to the strongest man.' Napier turned to Elliot.

'There's sense in what he says,' he said. 'Damn it, we'll never make progress with this Viceroy pasting up messages all around the town.'

'But with respect, sir, *you* pasted up the first notice?

'Of course I did. Because it's only right and proper that the Chinese people should realize how they are being duped by their idiotic rulers. Basically, I am sure they are a simple and friendly people. But they believe what their leaders tell them for they have no yardstick to measure what is true and what is false.'

He turned to Jardine.

'Have you anyone who knows the river well?'

'Of course. I'll lend the *Andromache* my most experienced captain. He knows this river like the back of his hand.'

'Very good,' said Napier. 'Then let the ships sail as soon as possible.'

'We had better land some marines in Canton,' Jardine suggested. 'Just to show that all our power and prowess is not confined to the navy. That would take their stage army down a peg, eh?'

'If I may interrupt, sir,' said Elliot.

'You may not,' retorted Napier. 'It is agreed.'

The *Imogene* had aboard her a dozen Royal Marines, and they were ferried up through the night from the river mouth, fifty miles away. Unfortunately, the frigates could not follow them speedily, for there was no wind. When it. sprang up two days later, it came from the wrong direction, so they had to tack slowly and heavily past the first two forts, moving sluggishly against tide and wind.

The forts fired a few cannon balls at them, but all missed. Then the wind dropped suddenly, and with thirty, guns pointing out from each fort, the two ships were sitting targets. But the Chinese guns could not traverse and their cannon balls still splashed uselessly in the streaming tide. The frigates' guns hammered back at the forts; the sailors could see Chinese soldiers fleeing, clothes ablaze. Then mercifully the wind freshened, and the two ships sailed on slowly, crowded with sail, to the safety of Whampoa Island. One rating had been wounded and the *Imogene* reported a main shroud shot away.

Viceroy Lu, by now concerned about his own position should the ships reach Canton, and word of this Barbarian insolence travel to the ears of the Emperor, immediately sank a string of barges across the river between Whampoa and Canton. Then he ordered the Chinese Army to draw cables from bank to bank. Rows of sharpened stakes were dug into the shore near Canton to delay any invasion. Next, scores of sampans were loaded with wood, straw, sulphur, saltpetre and kegs of oil ready to float out as fireships against the frigates. Two thousand Chinese troops stood by with bows and arrows, muskets and sharpened swords.

Some of these fireboats had ingenious detonators, for the Chinese, as the discoverers of gunpowder, had also pioneered new ways to use it. Lu was proud of the clockwork mechanisms that, at any decided hour, could set off a flintlock and ignite a sampan. The leading boats, which he would expect to be sunk first, contained leather bellows, and if the boats submerged, water would rush into these bellows through a metal tube and inflate them. Their movement would activate a linkage to flintlocks which would fire and so explode gunpowder charges.

Lu had also arranged for a number of powder barrels to be sunk in the centre of the river, where one of the British ships would most probably attempt to pass. Each barrel contained a fine glass tube of sulphuric acid. If the barrel received even a glancing blow, this tube would break and the contents explode.

The two naval ships were powerless against these engines of defence. All the Europeans and Americans and, worse, all the Chinese in Canton and Macao knew this.

Napier had never visualized such a situation. He dictated a rambling message to the Viceroy: 'It is a very serious offence to fire upon or otherwise insult the British flag. I recommend the Viceroy to take warning in time. His Majesty will not permit such folly, wickedness and cruelty as he has been guilty of since my arrival here, to go unpunished. Therefore, tremble, Viceroy Loo! Intensely tremble.'

'You have spelt the name wrong, sir,' said Elliot as he wrote this down at Napier's dictation. 'It is *Lu*. L-U.'

'I have spelt it as I want. Loo. L-O-O. Transmit the message as it is.'

Napier's irritation had been exacerbated by his insidious illness; his skin was now hot and dry, his eyes ached, his lips were cracked and his breath burned in his throat. Now, he could, only walk with assistance, and the breakdown of his physical powers inflamed his mind and clouded his judgement.

'As you say, sir.'

And so it was sent. But Lu knew that he just had to sit and wait. Sooner than Lu had expected, Jardine sought a meeting With the Hong merchants.

'Lord Napier is seriously ill,' he explained. 'As a doctor I cannot be optimistic about his chances of recovery if he stays here. We seek the Viceroy's permission to move him.'

Back came the message from Lu: 'If the Barbarian Eye will speedily repent of his errors, if he will withdraw his ships of war and remain obedient to the old rules governing the conduct of the Barbarians and the citizens of the Celestial Kingdom, I will yet grant him some slight indulgence.'

'And if he does not?' parried Jardine.

'This is his last chance. If he does not learn from his previous errors and accept our offer, the celestial troops will drive him out.'

'I will tell him of your terms,' said Jardine. But Napier was now too ill to understand clearly what was happening. He lay in his small hot bedroom, and while the bright sun outside blazed on the water, he dreamed of the cool clear lochs of Scotland, and saw again in his mind's fevered eye trout streams and wood fires ringed in by the kindly purple hills of home.

Why was he here in this strange, hot, unfriendly place? What was he doing, what could he hope to achieve with these orientals who had no wish and no need for anything he could offer them? Questions sought answers in his tormented mind, and found neither comfort nor reply.

Lu was still concerned at losing face by the bombardment of his forts and determined that the British should lose an equal amount of face on their side. He insisted that Napier should not travel to Macao in a British ship, but in a Chinese vessel, and under a guard of Chinese soldiers.

So Napier and his party set off miserably and in darkness, which mercifully hid the full extent of their humiliation. The night was noisy and hot, and at a creek port twenty miles from, Macao they were detained for hours, while an officious Chinese customs man examined their papers. All around the ship crackers kept exploding and gongs booming in some interminable Chinese festival. Even the tides were against them; they took eighteen hours to cover the final twenty miles to Macao.

Lord Napier by then was too weak to walk and had to be carried ashore.

He lay for some weeks with a high temperature; his health steadily worsening. The frequent ringing of the bells from the twelve churches in Macao so disturbed his fevered sleep that, in the last days, the Portuguese priests stilled them. Thus when Lord Napier died, he died in a silence of bells.

And with him died Jardine's dreams for quickly opening up China's vast and secret kingdom to Western trade. Yet the benefits he believed would flow from its realization were too abundant to abandon easily. So he sat now, his cigar growing its ashy beard, looking at the dancing lights outside. Matheson was going back to England, accompanying Lady Napier and her two daughters. There he would see the Foreign Minister and then the Prime Minister to urge on them both some positive action in the East — to open up the area to trade and to teach China that British subjects could not be treated with such contempt.

A servant knocked on the door, and the sound scattered the thoughts of both men like birds at a gunshot.

'Come in,' called Jardine.

'There is a clipper captain to see you, sir. Captain Ferguson.'

'What does he want at this hour?'

'He wishes to see you urgently, sir.'

'Show him in, then.'

This could only mean more trouble. Ferguson was a Lowland Scot in his late forties; tough, honest and unimaginative. He would not seek an interview with his employer outside specified hours unless the matter was important. He came in awkwardly, holding his cap in both hands.

'Begging your pardon, gentlemen,' he began. 'I heard that Mr Matheson was going back to England with Lady Napier, and I thought you might be engaged tomorrow.'

'What's it about?' asked Jardine briefly.

'The *Hesperides,* sir.'

'Well?'

'We were trying the north coast trade, sir, as you suggested. And I understood from Captain Fernandes that he was also on the same tack, but in a different area. So I hailed the *Hesperides* when she came alongside. Some young feller replied — name of Gunn. Dr Gunn. I asked after Captain Fernandes and the young feller said he was too busy to talk.'

'What about Crutchley? Where was he?'

'This Dr Gunn said he wasn't on board, sir. Said he had decided to take a holiday ashore. His actual words. Then they started trading and deliberately undercut us. I told him to stop. He refused. I warned him you would not like this.'

'What did he say to that?'

'He said you were not the majority shareholder in his company.'

'Was he civil?' asked Matheson.

'Civil, yes, sir. But reserved. He seemed rather, well, almost *amused* at the whole thing. As though he were enjoying it.'

'Did he say why Crutchley had gone ashore? Was this his way of telling you he had gone native?'

'I don't know, sir. Mr Crutchley drank heavily, of course.'

There was nothing odd in that; you drank or had a half-caste mistress, or, if you were like Mackereth, a boy; but you always remembered who you were; you never let down your guard completely, unless the sun got at you and everything became too much to bear. Maybe this had happened to Crutchley?

'Who is this fellow Gunn? I've never heard of him before.'

'I've been making some enquiries, sir. I understand he disappeared in Canton some time back, off the *Trelawney*. Officers of the *Trelawney* were asking after him. They thought he might have been kidnapped.'

'Where's the *Trelawney* now?'

'On the homeward run.'

'It's odd that this Dr Gunn should suddenly turn up at Whang-pi. That's four hundred miles away from here. A *doctor*, you say? A *medical* doctor?'

'I assume so, sir.'

"Thank you very much, captain. Well, he has to come back either to Whampoa or Macao, and I'll make it my concern to see him and then we can sort this out between us.'

'I thought you would, sir,' said Ferguson, relief in his voice. He was a sharp one, was Jardine. It would take more than Gunn to upset him.

'Goodnight, gentlemen. I am sorry to have disturbed you.'

'What do you make of that?' asked Matheson, when they were alone.

'God knows,' said Jardine. 'But others have started up against us, too, remember. And we taught them all a lesson.'

How many times had they ordered their captains to pull alongside a rival and undercut him? If he was selling mud at ten dollars a pound, then you sold it at eight. When he came down to eight, you dropped to six. You could afford to lose a whole shipload because you had so many other interests, and he had nothing.

His whole future was bound up with one boat, while to you a ship was only a part of a vast mercantile equation, an unimportant fraction of your equity.

You were lending money; buying goods for other merchants; remitting returns in goods, bills and specie. Your name was enough to guarantee bonds and bills. You chartered ships of all kinds, and you handled freight. You collected debts, insured cargoes, borrowed money from Parsees and Jews in India at rates as high as twelve per cent, and then lent it out again to the Hong merchants at twenty or twenty-five, and often not even on a letter, but on your word, and a handshake. You were accepted, trusted, envied, copied and feared. You were Jardine and Matheson, and every merchant east of the Cape knew your credit was sound and your promise was your bond.

Other companies had admitted defeat, graciously or not, because they had to. One, Rona-Lloyd, with five or six ships, had capitulated only months before; now, it seemed, another upstart would have to be taught the same lessons. Jardine would instruct his captains accordingly. But first he would discover what he could about this man Gunn. He did not like to fight another doctor and the cheek of this young fellow commended itself to him. He stood up.

'I'm going to bed,' he said.

'Shall I ask the Parsee about Gunn?' asked Matheson. 'He has spies everywhere.'

'No. Say nothing of this to him,' replied Jardine. 'Gunn, after all, is one of us. Whatever we have to do, we'll do. Goodnight.'

He walked out of the room and along the corridor to his own quarters, and stood for a long time at the window overlooking the river. The lanterns were still alight; a lot of traffic was on the water for this hour.

Watching the familiar scene, the houseboats, the sampans, the junks, he felt an almost overwhelming sadness that he was where he was; all the fun had been in the journey, not the arrival.

Jardine even found himself, in a wry and quite inexplicable way, envying Gunn. Whoever he might be, he was only starting *his* journey; and now he would have to fight him. It was as though he was preparing to fight himself, as he had been, when he was beginning, years ago.

IN WHICH A NEWCOMER ARRIVES IN CANTON, AND THE PARSEE MAKES A PROPHECY

It was the Hour of the Hare, five o'clock on Sunday morning, as the Barbarians counted time and days, when Viceroy Lu's personal bodyguard parted the silken curtains of the Viceroy's bedchamber.

'My master,' he said breathlessly. 'I have urgent news.'

Lu stirred uneasily from his slumber and sat up on the silken couch. Through the parchment window, the Pearl River ran like liquid lead. The sun was not yet up; the junks and sampans showed no lights.

'An important procession has been sighted approaching Canton. We have sent out emissaries. They report it is Lin Tse-Lsu, the Governor General of Hupeh and Hunan.'

'I was not warned of any visit,' said Lu, flinging his legs out of bed, sleep forgotten. 'Why is he coming here unannounced?'

'The emissaries say he is travelling as the Emperor's Special Commissioner.'

'I see.'

Lu's voice was only a whisper. The room felt suddenly grey as the rushing river, and intensely cold. Only once or twice to his knowledge had a Chinese Emperor sent a Special Commissioner to an outlying province. When he did, it meant that the local Viceroy or Governor was this Commissioner's subordinate, that their past actions would be ruthlessly scrutinized for any sign of laxness or misdeeds.

Because of the Commissioner's long journey, and the fact that the Emperor was personally involved, the Viceroy concerned would almost certainly have to be shown to have been negligent in some way, and Lu knew that the Commissioner would not lack informants about his own involvement with, the Coast trade.

Lu had accepted enormous bribes to help what he held office to halt. Sometimes he had even used official barges and Chinese sailors to ferry mud ashore more quickly. When Lin arrived bluffs would be called and guilty consciences bruised. Mandarins would be arrested at random and their wealth confiscated; others would be draped in chains and beaten by bamboos. Some might even be put to death. Those who feared these unhappy attentions would be eager to incriminate others to diminish their own risk of punishment. He could not trust anyone to keep silence about his own involvement; fear would loosen their long tongues as a sharp knife loosens the cord around a bale of hay.

Lin.

The name rang in the cold room with all the harshness of a hollow gong. Their paths had crossed before, briefly, when Lin had dealt ruthlessly with salt smugglers, who sought to make fortunes for themselves by breaking the Government monopoly in that essential trade.

Lu had only been involved on the periphery of events, in pocketing a percentage for allowing illegal transactions to prosper, and he had not been discovered, although he wondered whether Lin suspected him.

Lin's success then had so impressed the Emperor that he asked him for his suggestions to suppress the forbidden opium trade. Lin had proposed an ingenious scheme to stem the frightening flow of Chinese silver overseas in the chests of the opium ships. The most common coins were of copper, called cash. These had holes in their centres and were frequently carried on a string around the owner's neck. For generations, one ounce of silver had equalled 1,000 cash.

Now the rarity value of silver had increased, so much that an ounce was worth 1,600 cash. Because many local taxes were collected in cash and paid to Peking in silver, the physical difficulty of carrying so many tiny copper coins so far now jeopardized the country's fiscal system.

Lin's proposal was that, instead of selling legitimate goods, such as rhubarb and tea, to foreign merchants at the prices commanded in China, the Barbarians should pay twice or even five times the local market price. In this way, more money would enter China than was leaving it. Yes, Lin was clever. Worse, he was incorruptible.

As the second of three sons of a poor scholar, born in the capital of Fuhkien, a province on the South East Coast, Lin had learned Manchu, the language of the conquering emperors of China, and by knowing their language he had assimilated their ways.

Now in his fifties, given to writing gentle poems and to decorating fans, he was always willing to help young men of ability from poor families to rise as he had risen. When the Emperor had summoned him and ordered him to proceed to Canton to investigate past affairs, as the Son of Heaven described the object of his visit, Lin realized that his visit could either mark the pinnacle of his career or its ruin. There would be no compromise, no half-success.

Lin had set out from Peking with six men-at-arms to protect him, an outrider, a cook and two kitchen men to prepare vegetables and to wash dishes: Because Lin was basically a simple man, and he felt it important to travel without ostentation, he made it known that none of his staff would ride far ahead to assure the best accommodation for each night, and none would stay behind to take bribes.

Out of his own salary, he paid twenty servants to bear the litter on which he lay, and he hired two wagons and a stretcher to carry the luggage. At Government rest houses, Lin would eat only the ordinary fare offered to all travellers. Never was he or any of his colleagues to ask for a special menu or an extravagant dish, like fried swallows' nests. And he forbade his bearers to accept the gratuities customarily offered by locals eager to ingratiate themselves with authority.

By such means, Lin intended to set an example of - frugality and incorruptibility. In previous years, officials had frequently travelled the countryside with hundreds of armed retainers, virtually private armies, looting and pillaging as they went, and forcing villages to feed and accommodate them all for nothing.

So Lin journeyed with few retainers, and observed the strict religious rites of each day. On board ship in the Yangtze, for instance, he set out his incense altar on the deck, *kowtowed* in the direction of the Emperor's Palace in Peking, wished him a Happy New Year, and bowed to the shades of his ancestors.

Nothing delayed him.

At Nan-Ch'ang freezing winds were so strongly against him that his ship's sails stiffened with ice, and he had to send into the town for labourers with ropes to pull him past the quay. Now, after three months' journey, by land, river and latterly by sea, he approached Canton.

Runners from Viceroy Lu spread the word of Lin's arrival, and the Hong merchants spent hours on their knees praying to the gods that their guilt might not be discovered. Their emissaries meanwhile sailed in swift centipedes to Macao to warn comrades there, for clearly this man Lin presented a grave threat to all their enterprises. A hush, such as usually proceeded some ritual sacrifice, fell upon the hundreds of people who crowded the Canton quayside as his procession of boats approached.

River police with staves beat humble sampans to one side. Bearers in freshly laundered clothes stood by a newly varnished sedan chair for Lin to use, and lictors cracked their whips to keep a proper and respectful distance between the bearers and the inquisitive mob.

Elliot, watching the scene from the verandah of the English factory, thought the merchants had little enough to fear; the legend of Lin's ruthlessness was doubtless like other delusions with which the Chinese loved to surround themselves. It belonged to the unreality of guns painted on the doors of unarmed forts, and all-seeing eyes on the bows of boats.

Lin, rowed the final few miles by oarsmen in new white uniforms trimmed with red, sat in the stern, his jaw set, looking neither to right nor left.

Viceroy Lu and a dozen other notables leapt ashore from their splendid craft to genuflect before him. He waved them away as though their antics irritated him, and the linkmen carried his chair at a steady jog-trot to the local school where he was to set up headquarters.

'What do you think will happen now?' Elliot asked Jardine's manager, as the crowds melted away.

'Nothing,' the manager replied shortly. 'We've had all sorts of mandarins here over the opium trade. They issue a few fierce edicts, send back reports about their plans — and then they settle down to take their bribes like the rest.

'I'll wager this fellow Lin is no different, although he may prove more expensive. We'll have to see what the Hong merchants say. They'll soon find out his weaknesses.'

Everyone waited for less than a week before Lin published his first edict to foreigners. It began: 'I, Lin, Imperial High Commissioner of the Court of Heaven, President of the Board of War and Viceroy of Hu- Kuang, issue these my commands to the Barbarians of every nation.

'Let the Barbarians deliver to me every particle of opium on board their store-ships. There must not be the smallest grain concealed or withheld. And at the same time let the said Barbarians enter into a bond never hereafter to bring opium in their ships and to submit, should any be brought, to the extreme penalty of the law against the parties involved.

'If the Barbarians obey, their past errors will be pardoned. I will inform the Dragon's Seat that they are penitent and humble, and they will be allowed to trade in legitimate merchandise.

'If they do *not* obey immediately, then the inexorable force of the Chinese army, and the strength of the glorious Chinese navy, will be brought to bear upon them. All trade will end *for ever.* There will be no further transactions between the East and West of any kind.

'I, Lin, the High Commissioner, will cause deep pits to be dug. They will be filled with burning oil, and all opium will be cast into them and utterly destroyed. All Barbarian ships in which other opium is found will also be set on fire, and all other cargo they may be carrying will inevitably be destroyed. They will thus not only make no profit, they will be ruined instead.

'The Barbarians have three days to make their decision. Do not indulge in idle expectations, or seek to postpone matters, deferring to repent until lateness renders repentance ineffectual. Take note! A special Edict! Forget not!'

Even as Elliot and Jardine's manager read this warning, Lin was addressing the Hong merchants on the same subject. Such was his personality that these merchants, millionaires to a man, dropped to their knees and beat the ground with their foreheads to show the extent of their awe and respect. Lin waited until the abject drumming of their skulls had ceased, and then addressed himself in language that left no room for comfort or doubt about his intentions.

'You have hitherto been too friendly with the Barbarians,' he told them. 'You should, from henceforth, cultivate severity of deportment. You should act with energy, *not* to accrue more fortunes from forbidden and distasteful trade. In the meantime, you will surrender all the opium stocks — *all*, I repeat — of which you have knowledge.

'As a measure of the severity in which I regard this matter, I, the High Commissioner, will forthwith solicit the Imperial death-warrant, and select for execution one or two of the most unworthy of you. Never say that you did not receive early notice. Oppose not! A special Edict!'

The Hong merchants again prostrated themselves at his words.

Other mandarins had spoken in like terms to them, but they had been men of clay, who could be fashioned and persuaded by bribes. Lin was a man of iron; and iron could not be moulded by man's hands. Iron was stronger than the hands of any man.

Under the heavy wind and against the endless, smiling waves, the timbers of the *Hesperides* creaked like a forest in a storm. Gunn lay awake in his bunk, the porthole open. The moon painted the cabin walls silver.

He heard soft movements that did not belong to the accustomed groan of a plank against plank, and was instantly alert, prepared for trouble. A shadow, deeper than the rest, detached itself from the door. He reached under the mattress for his pistol.

'It's me,' said Ling Fai.

'What do you want?' asked Gunn, putting his pistol away. 'What's the matter?'

'I muchee want see you, close up looking. I want to thank you most muchee.'

'What ever for?' Gunn asked, puzzled. He had hardly seen this waif since they set sail: once or twice on deck, another time with MacPherson. He had been so busy with so many problems that he had almost forgotten she was aboard. No, that was not quite true. She excited him with her slim body and small breasts and delicate hands. And he did not want to see too much of her in case he forgot she was MacPherson's woman.

'You treating MacPherson-San for some illness?'

'Yes.'

'I do not know why he ill. But since you come, he has no trub. All smiling fellah. Like he used to be. So I want thank you most muchee. Topline thank you.'

'My job is curing people,' said Gunn, and then thought: Not any more. My job now is making money, and this was something altogether different. 'You speak English well, Ling Fai.'

'MacPherson-San taught me say thank you English way. Now I say big thank you as Chinee woman thanks man.'

Suddenly, she was in the bunk beside Gunn, her clothes off and her body warm against his. He felt her mouth on his chest, and then she moved down on his stomach, and sought him out, soft as warm honey, taking his hardening phallus between her lips.

All restraint vanished, Gunn caressed her breasts, and then slowly drew her up so that she lay on him. For a time they lay silent thus, their ears filled with the drumming of their hearts and the roar of the sea beyond the hull. Then their bodies began to move.

Afterwards — how long afterwards Gunn did not begin to guess — he was alone and the bunk seemed empty and altogether too large. He pushed back the sheet, climbed out, lit the oil lamp, and stood looking at himself in the mirror above the zinc washbasin. How long ago it seemed that he had looked at his reflection in his cabin in the *Trelawney* after he had heard that Marion had run off with Cartwright!

Since then he had been paid to get a native woman with child. He had been marooned and left for dead. In turn, he had bullied another man out of his company as the Parsee had sought to swindle him, and for a far greater sum. Then he had marooned this man, and seized his ship.

Most important of all, most despicable of all, he had rewarded MacPherson — who had saved his life — by lying with MacPherson's woman, two, three, four times in a night. And he would do the same again if he had the chance; and he knew he would be offered the chance.

Gunn leaned on his fists, and hated himself for he realized, deep inside him, that this was not the end of these terrible things; this was only the beginning. He would betray other, men, and seduce other women, break other promises and friendships if doing these things furthered his own fortunes. For the aim now was money. And then more money; and with more money, more power; and with enough power, the strength of cruelty, the knowledge you could do what you wanted, anywhere, at any time. And eventually you were so rich and so strong that no-one in all the world could stand against you. And then — what?

Outside the porthole, under the dying moon, the silver sea streamed past him.

The Parsee was standing as usual in the wide window of his house, telescope in his hand, watching the boats in the bay. He saw the *Hesperides* when she was still a mile off and raked the decks with his glass, trying to pick out Crutchley, but the distance was too great and the light from the sea was blinding.

He called for his servant.

'The *Hesperides* will dock by dusk,' he told him. 'Address yourself to it and inform Mr Crutchley that I will see him here immediately his ship is made fast.'

The servant bowed and went out into the waning, afternoon, down between the crumbling walls of the ancient houses to the quay. The boom of the church bells striking the hour drove out flocks of birds above him.

A berth had already been cleared, but the vessel came in as slowly as a blind man without a guide. Fernandes was a careful captain, and when the hull brushed against the thick rope buffers with a gentle creaking of timbers, not one fleck of tar or paint was displaced.

The servant walked up the gangway to Crutchley's cabin. Another man was standing in the doorway; fatter, older, tougher than Crutchley, with grey grizzled hair and a huge stomach. He was smoking a cheroot. MacPherson looked down at the servant without interest or recognition, although Gunn had warned him who he was when he saw him waiting on the quay.

'Where number one Clutchley? Parsee want see him topside,' the servant said in pidgin. He always used pidgin to the crews; everyone understood it.

'Mr. Crutchley is with us no longer,' MacPherson replied in Cantonese, turning bloodshot eyes to the darkening heavens. He crossed himself; these heathen always associated the delineation of the cross with death.

'What has happened Clutchley, eh?' asked the servant, fear tightening his throat like a vice. Danger gongs beat in his servile mind.

'It is too terrible to tell you. The Parsee would only punish you if you brought bad news to him.'

'*You* come tell him then,' said the servant quickly. He had not risen to his position as the Parsee's confidant by being slow in passing a chance of punishment to others.

'I dare not leave the vessel,' replied MacPherson earnestly, 'for there is something else. Plague. Do not approach too close to me.'

'Why for you not warn me, eh?' asked the servant nervously, plucking at his sleeves.

'I do so now. Let the Parsee come here so that I can explain to him what has happened. Then we must stand out off shore until the fever has burned itself out.'

'Parsee never comes to quay.'

'Let his son come down, then.'

'He has no son. Only daughter. And she hopes soon-time have child. Parsee got son-in-law, Mister Bonnarjee.'

'Then let Mr Bonnarjee come. But hurry, man. We must be off before dusk. Hurry, I say!'

The servant padded off back through the alleyways up to his master's house, fear prodding spurs on his heels. The Parsee listened to him in silence.

'Who is this man?' he asked when the servant had finished.

'I did not ask his name.'

'You should have done. You say they have the plague? Did they sell their mud first?'

'I did not ask, master. I was told to come swiftly and I did his bidding.'

'Did you see anyone else? Mr Crutchley? The American, Mackereth? Captain Fernandes?'

'No-one save this fat man in Mr Clutchley's doorway.'

The Parsee chewed his lips, thinking. Plague and other terrible fevers sometimes swept like fire through ships, and even decimated towns and islands. But so far his crews had not suffered from them. Maybe this infection came from trading along an unknown shore?

He would request his son-in-law to discover the truth of the matter, and with him he would send six servants with staves in case there was some infamy aboard. The thought of this other unknown nameless man in the *Hesperides* troubled him. And what ship had he left — and why?

Mr Bonnarjee, the Parsee's son-in-law, was a plump man in his late twenties, with soft breasts and a smooth skin, fleshy as a capon's wing. His muscles were clothed with fat, and when he walked he walked slowly, because to hurry made him breathless. He smelled of sweet scent and jasmine oil, and his hair was thick and black. Four bearers carried him in his sedan down to the docks and two more trotted behind him, carrying six long bamboos.

Bonnarjee could see no movement aboard the *Hesperides;*

no smoke from the galley; no face at a porthole; no snatch of song from the fo'c'sle. Then he saw MacPherson's head in Crutchley's doorway.

'Who are you?' he called in English.

'MacPherson's the name, and who are you, my fine plump friend?'

'I am Mr Bonnarjee. The son-in-law of the Parsee. I hear you have plague and great trouble aboard?'

'You hear truth,' agreed MacPherson. 'But come aboard. I must speak to you privately.'

'Is it *safe* to come aboard?'

'Of course it's safe,' replied MacPherson. 'Do not believe lies that servants and inferior people may tell you. There is far greater danger from those with long ears on the quay.'

Bonnarjee nodded to his servants, who lowered his chair and then waited at the base of the gangway. He climbed slowly up on deck.

'Come into the cabin,' said MacPherson.

'But will I not catch the plague?'

'No,' said Gunn from behind the door. 'I am a doctor, and I personally guarantee you will not.' Then he closed the door behind Bonnarjee and turned the key in the lock.

'Who are you both? Where is Captain Fernandes?' asked Bonnarjee, puzzled. He suddenly felt nervous. He was on his own in a locked cabin with two men who were, of course, his inferiors in breeding and wealth; and yet he feared them in an animal way. And even through the heavy scent he wore he smelled the sharp sweat of his own alarm.

'The captain is in his quarters.'

'And Mr Mackereth?'

'Praying,' said MacPherson. 'For all of us, I trust. Even for the unbaptized, like you, Mr Bonnarjee.'

'What has happened to Mr Crutchley? Is he dead of the plague?'

'He decided to leave the ship and go ashore,' explained Gunn. 'I think, possibly, some events had proved too much for him.'

'But what about the mud? My father-in-law desires to know. Have you sold it?'

'Of course. Every pound.'

'Ah!' said Bonnarjee in relief. The knowledge of profit expelled all thought of fear; the drum of his heart slowed immediately. 'Then the only casualties from the plague have been Lascars?'

'We have lost some of the original crew,' admitted Gunn.

'Who are *you*, anyway?' asked Bonnarjee.

'I am a snip's surgeon. And I think I had better give you some protection against the plague. It *can* be carried on the air, you know. But modern medical science has made great discoveries to combat it.'

As Gunn spoke, he opened his trunk, took out a scalpel, wiped the blade on cotton wool, dipped it in a small jar of greasy ointment, and holding out his hand, seized Bonnarjee's left wrist. Before the man could protest, he nicked the flesh, slightly, and then held the ointment on the blade against the cut.

Bonnarjee watched the little bead of blood trickle down his brown flesh so intently that he did not notice MacPherson's hand as he raised it to strike him across the back of his neck. Then the floor rippled beneath his feet like a shallow sea, the walls dissolved, and darkness swallowed him.

'Get him on the bed,' said Gunn quickly, tossing away the scalpel and the ointment. 'Gag him and tie his wrists and his ankles. He will come round soon, and if I'm not back here in one hour make him write a note — my life for his — and send one of the crew up to the Parsee's house with it. Meanwhile, stand off five hundred yards into the harbour, and observe my instructions!'

'My God, it's risky,' said MacPherson nervously. 'The Parsee is a dangerous man.'

'The world is full of dangerous men,' retorted Gunn. 'But we are most dangerous of all because we have so little to lose.'

He put a hand under the folds of Bonnarjee's robe, found a scented red silk handkerchief, pushed it in his right-hand trouser pocket, and walked down the gangway. The Parsee's six men waited patiently by the sedan. They raised their bamboos ready to club him if the senior servant gave the word. Gunn pushed them aside and spoke to him over their inferior heads.

'Take me to the Parsee!' he commanded. 'Immediately.'

The servant bowed, recognizing him. Gunn climbed into Bonnarjee's sedan, the bearers lifted the poles, and trotted obediently back up the hill. The servant led him into the house, along tiled corridors to the familiar room overlooking the sea. The Parsee turned from the window, and his face puckered with surprise, but only momentarily.

'Dr Gunn,' he said, holding out both hands, smiling a welcome. 'What a pleasure to see you back so soon! And I thought you were aboard the *Trelawney,* possibly at Singapore, or even in Calcutta by now?'

'You thought nothing of the kind,' replied Gunn shortly, ignoring the outstretched hands. The Parsee nodded dismissal to the servant. The double doors shut silently.

'You knew quite well that I did not return to the *Trelawney,*' Gunn continued as soon as they were alone. 'Your man here, no doubt on your instructions, suggested I join the *Hesperides* — so conveniently owned by you and your creature, Crutchley, who marooned me.

'You thought by doing this that I would lose my life. Then you would keep your three thousand pounds *and* your secret. And, despite all this, you still can — under certain conditions. *My* conditions.'

'I do not understand what you are talking about,' the Parsee replied in a puzzled voice.

'Then I will endeavour to make myself clearer to you. I

rejoined the *Hesperides* through the help of a Scot, MacPherson. He is aboard her now, out in the harbour. Crutchley is no longer involved.'

'What do you mean?'

The room was suddenly quiet.

'I mean that Crutchley decided to go ashore instead of me. He took my place, in a manner of speaking, and before he left he signed over his shares in the company to me.'

'You have proof of this?'

'I have,' said Gunn. 'But I only brought a copy of the document, which Captain Fernandes has witnessed. The original is in a safer place than on my person, since you and your servants outnumber me.'

He handed a piece of paper to the Parsee, who read it, then placed it under a quartz paperweight on his desk.

'You were saying?' he said quietly.

'I was saying that you could still keep your secret — *our* secret — under certain conditions. These are that you make over to me — on consideration of your cheque for three thousand pounds, which I will return to you — your controlling shares in Crutchley & Company.'

'Why should I do that?' asked the Parsee, smiling at the absurdity of the proposal. 'You speak like a fool or a dreamer. And yet I cannot believe you are either. You are trained as a man of science.'

'I am also a man of my word,' said Gunn. 'And you will do as I say, because your son-in-law is aboard the *Hesperides*.'

'You mean you have taken him prisoner? He is a hostage?'

'Not at all. He is simply asleep in my cabin.'

'Then I will send men to bring him back.'

'To do that, you would have to sail out into the bay. The ship, as you can see from your window, has now anchored off shore. Any attempt to board her by force will be met by force, and she carries twenty cannon. In such circumstances, my colleague, Mr MacPherson, would open a sealed envelope I have left in his keeping. It is an account of our transaction — your secret. How many of your enemies would rejoice in such an opportunity to ridicule your family name — and Mr Bonnarjee's virility?

'Also remember that your son-in-law is asleep. I have drugged him. If I do not return, he will quite simply never wake up again. It is useless torturing me to tell you the name of the drug because, although I would no doubt do so, that would not help Mr Bonnarjee. Unless *I* return to administer the antidote, which is not readily available here, he will die within an hour.

'Thus you have rather less than sixty minutes to make over this company. Otherwise, you should send your servants to remove your son-in-law's corpse to your tower of silence, to be devoured by the carrion birds, as is the custom under your religion.'

'If I had not seen you before,' said the Parsee slowly, measuring out each word painfully, 'I would be convinced you were mad. What you propose is intolerable. It is blackmail and attempted murder. And I thought I was dealing with an English *gentleman.*'

'And I foolishly believed I was dealing with a man of honour. As you told me, a promise is a debt. I am offering you the opportunity of paying that debt. You have about fifty-seven minutes in which to do so.'

'I could make over this little company to you, doctor, and then you might be murdered and flung into the sea. Or you could be blacklisted by every merchant and trading company in the East.'

'I could be,' agreed Gunn. 'But not by you, because blackmail is a sword with two sides. And at the first sign of any reluctance of *any* individual to trade with me, I will publish your secret. I am not concerned with continuing the practice of medicine, so I am indifferent to what you say about me. You now have barely fifty-five minutes in which to make out those papers.'

The Parsee picked up his telescope and focused on the *Hesperides*.

Gunn crossed to the window by his side and opened the casement. The myriad sounds of a tropic day rushed in. Casually, he took Bonnarjee's red silk handkerchief from his pocket and wrapped it around his left hand. The Parsee pulled a bell tassel, and spoke rapidly to his servant. The man glanced at Gunn, went out and returned with the four men who had carried the sedan. They were squat with broad shoulders, shaven heads and cruel, slanting eyes. One wore gold earrings. All carried bamboos and they stood with their bare feet spread well apart like wrestlers.

'These men,' said the Parsee, smiling, 'will deal with you as you should be dealt with. *Then* we will seize the *Hesperides* and bring in my son-in-law. I own other ships with guns.'

'No doubt,' said Gunn. 'But if you apply your telescope again to the *Hesperides* you will see that the ten pounder in her bows is trained on this house.'

He leaned against the window, unwrapped the handkerchief and held it outside. A puff of warm wind made it tremble slightly.

'Touch me with your ruffians and I will drop this handkerchief. At once, MacPherson will open fire. Admittedly, I may be killed but so may you. And, of course, inevitably, your son-in-law. You are a man of decision, so decide now what you want to do. We have talked enough. But remember, I can drop this handkerchief before any of these rogues reach me. And I will.

'I suggest therefore that you do not resort to force or even the threat of violence, as with peasants who disagree over the ownership of a cockerel. Instead, accept that violence is only fit for those who cannot win a duel with words. Now, what is your answer?'

The Parsee swallowed with difficulty. Anger constricted his throat. He would avenge himself on this Gunn somehow;

but if not now, then later, in his own time, in his own way. He nodded to his servant. He and the four men bowed and walked backwards. The double doors closed behind them.

'Fifty minutes,' said Gunn, taking in his hand.

'Let me warn you, doctor, that between us there will now be war, and war is made up of many battles,' said the Parsee. 'You may win this first skirmish. You will never win the last.

'It is written: "Let a man avoid evil deeds as a merchant, if he has few companions and carries much wealth, avoids a dangerous road; as a man who loves life avoids poison."

'You love your life, doctor, and I recall from our earlier conversations that you love the prospect of wealth. You may gain your wealth briefly, but you will lose your life.'

'I will also quote from what is written,' replied Gunn. ' "He who has no wound on his hand may touch poison with his hand. Poison does not affect one who has no wound. Nor does evil befall one who does not commit evil." You are poisoned in your mind, Parsee, and you have wounds in your soul.

'You also have about forty-eight minutes in which to give me an answer.'

The Parsee crossed to his desk, took a sheet of paper from a drawer, sat down with his quill and began to write. He handed the paper to Gunn in silence. Gunn read: *I, the undersigned, do hereby make over all my shares in Crutchley & Company to Dr Robert Gunn.'*

Gunn handed it back to him.

'Add the words, *"in consideration of his services rendered and the return of my cheque for three thousand pounds",'* he said. 'Then call in your man to witness it.'

The Parsee sat down again and wrote at Gunn's dictation. He scattered fine sand from a silver casket to dry the ink. Then he pulled the tassel; the servant came in and signed his name. Gunn folded the paper neatly, put it in his inner pocket, and handed the Parsee his cheque.

'Do not have me attacked on my way back to the *Hesperides,* or our discussion will have been in vain, he told him. For again, as Buddha says, "Riches destroy the foolish, and the foolish, by their thirst for riches, destroy themselves".'

'And you have today destroyed yourself, Dr Gunn,' replied the Parsee in a voice so soft it sounded like the hiss of a snake. 'I would remind you that in your Bible in the Apocrypha it is written, "Gold hath been the ruin of many".'

'And I would remind you,' retorted Gunn, 'that lack of gold has ruined far more people.'

'We shall see,' said the Parsee, as though the matter was of no further interest. 'Tell me one thing, doctor. What are you going to call your company now?'

'Mandarin-Gold. I will be seeing a lawyer about the necessary paper work when I leave you.'

'So the two things you wish for most, power and money, are united in one name. How revealing! As I say, Dr Gunn, we shall see. Sometimes we can best leave revenge to the gods. The sword of heaven is in no haste to smite. But it never leaves a debt unpaid.'

He turned away, back to the window, as though dismissing an inferior. Gunn waited for a moment and then left the room, walked past the servant, and the four men, along the corridor and out into the waning afternoon sun. His mouth was dry with reaction and he felt suddenly weary.

It was rubbish, of course, that he had the only antidote for the Parsee's son-in-law. He had no such thing. Bonnarjee would recover very quickly on his own. But the Parsee did not know that. Audacity had triumphed — as it had triumphed when he had seized the *Hesperides* and marooned Crutchley; as he was convinced now that it always would. Faint heart never won anything but the chance to be feeble again.

As Gunn walked, however, the Parsee's words echoed and re-echoed in his mind like a gong booming in a well: *'You have today destroyed yourself, Dr Gunn.'*

What could the man mean? This was only a business deal,

and he was learning that such deals were hard, that inevitably someone must be hurt. The Parsee was angry, of course, and understandably; but Gunn could not shrug off the remark as one simply made through pique.

He had come a long way from that morning when the *Trelawney* had docked at Whampoa, and he had learned that Marion had gone away with another man. True, the road he was following now was not the one he had intended to take when he had first qualified as a doctor. But was that altogether a bad thing? Surely a man could follow many paths to fulfilment and success?

Yet, by so speedily abandoning his principles, and the pledges of the Hippocratic Oath, perhaps he had not only lost his way. Perhaps he had also lost himself?

IN WHICH SPECIAL COMMISSIONER LIN ACHIEVES ONE AIM, AND DR GUNN ANOTHER

Captain Elliot bowed to Mackereth, who sat down nervously in a high-backed wicker chair. Through the window of Elliot's office in Macao the sea blazed like blue glass, the sails of the junks were fluttering fans.

'I have asked you here,' said Elliot — who did not like the man and so spoke more roughly than he would normally have done — 'because, apart from Gutzlaff, who is at sea, I understand you speak Cantonese and can read the characters. Am I correct in this assumption?'

'You are, sir,' agreed Mackereth.

When he had first been summoned to Elliot's office, he had wondered uneasily whether tales of boys who visited him in his rooms had reached Elliot's ears; and if they had, whether their accounts would be believed or his. He had prayed long and earnestly beside the narrow bed on which he had lain with so many of these boys in the past, but somehow he had risen from his knees without any comfort from the Almighty.

If the British used their influence to put him out of

Macao, if they *wanted* him out — perhaps hoping to injure this newcomer Gunn, who had within months taken over an established company and become so successful with his forays along the coast, for they realized Gunn would never find another interpreter — then where could he go? There was nowhere left in all the world. If he moved in any direction, he would only be going back, and to what? To a bank that had failed, to a memory of wealth no longer his, to old age alone in a cold country.

Now Mackereth sat, legs crossed, hands tightly clenched so that the blood was squeezed from his thin knuckles, eyes fixed intently on Elliot's face.

'We have had a hasty translation done of this Edict from the new Commissioner Lin,' Elliot went on, tapping the paper. 'I'd like you to just read it through to me in the original, and see if you agree with our translation.'

He handed the document .over the desk to Mackereth, who mouthed a few words and then began to read aloud.

' "I call upon you to hand over for destruction all the opium you have in your ships and to sign an undertaking that you will never, bring opium here again, and that you are aware that, if you are found to have done so, your goods will be confiscated and you yourselves dealt with according to the law."'

He paused.

'That tallies,' said Elliot. 'Go on!'

'It's a long Edict, sir, in the usual flowery Chinese. Can I just paraphrase it for you?'

'It you wish.'

Mackereth began to read.

' "Today I stationed armed patrol ships at all the approaches to the quays — that's in Canton, of course."'

'Yes. Goon.'

' ". . . To prevent foreigners from embarking or disembarking. You foreigners have had a week to make up your minds about my earlier Edict, in which I gave you three days to surrender the opium. I have had no answer, so today I have-given orders that all loading and unloading of any foreign vessel will stop.

All craftsmen, employed by foreigners are to leave their service forthwith, and anyone who enters into any agreement or negotiation for service with them in future will be dealt with according to the clause of the Celestial. Code that forbids secret relations with foreign countries."

'That means death,' said Mackereth hoarsely. 'Death. He goes on ..."If there is any attempt to evade these restrictions, I, the Governor General and the Governor, will obtain permission from Peking to close the harbour to them and put a stop to their trade for ever ..."

'He says that the British Sovereign will surely take strong measures against you if the trade is stopped, and he gives reasons why he thinks the opium should be surrendered at once. Foreigners must surely dread the wrath of heaven which will punish them if they continue to ruin so many Chinese homes and kill so many opium smokers and opium dealers, for the death penalty is in force for both of these offences.

'Again, British, American and Portuguese ships carrying opium are, like all seafarers, in particular danger from gales, thunderstorms, crocodiles, dragons and the giant salamander. Do they not fear that Heaven, if further offended by these continuing offences, will use these creatures and unnatural forces as instruments of their anger?'.

'Apart from the giant salamander,' interrupted Elliot, 'is all the rest just bluff?'

'With anyone else here, I would say it was,' said Mackereth. 'With Lin, I just do not know. My friends among the merchants say he is entirely incorruptible. He does not want money, or women, or even — and here Mackereth's voice dropped to a whisper — boys. He simply wants to do his duty, and his duty here — as he sees it — is to destroy the opium trade. He thinks he will. I think he can.'

'You confirm my fears,' said Elliot, standing up. 'I had better return to Canton.'

'What course will you adopt there, captain?' Mackereth asked him.

'One that will not be popular with my countrymen. I agree with Commissioner Lin that the opium trade is_ foul and degrading. Why should we force a poisonous drug on these wretched peasants so that a handful of dealers can live like kings and retire to buy honours and squiredoms in England?'

'There is a lot of money involved,' Mackereth pointed out anxiously. True, Gunn had drastically reduced his fee from one thousand pounds a voyage to three hundred, but three hundred was still a very large sum.

'Money is not all important,' replied Elliot. 'You, as a man of the cloth, will be the first to admit that. In my last appointment, I made myself unpopular with the owners of slaves because I insisted they treat them as human beings, not as beasts of burden who happened to walk on two legs.

'They hated me for this. They had a punishment, Mr Mackereth, of awarding slaves fifty-five stripes for almost any offence. Or they locked them in the stocks for three days, or shut them up alone in a dark room for the most trivial misdeed.

'I made every owner keep a true record of all punishments meted out to the slaves. And if these records were falsified or the punishments were too hard, they had to explain the reasons in court. I can tell you, I became most unpopular, Mr Mackereth. But as a man of God you know that the popular way, the easy way, does not always lead on to the true glory. And my policy paid handsomely.

'When I landed in Guinea no taxes were being collected, and it was only a matter of time before those poor black wretches flung themselves on their oppressors and murdered them all. But the owners could not see the advantages of a more liberal policy without persuasion. So I persuaded them. Now the colony is on the way to prosperity.

'I, therefore, fully understand the interest of our compatriots in sustaining the opium trade here. But theirs is a shortsighted view. When, we can open the whole of China to legitimate trade and British and American enterprise — what a glorious prospect that would be not only for our countries, but for the Chinese themselves! Is not *that* aim deserving of some temporary unpopularity among the merchant classes?'

'I entirely agree,' replied Mackereth, moved by Elliot's obvious sincerity.

'I am glad that you do,' said Elliot, and rang a bell for his orderly.

'Have a fast gig prepared to take me to the factory immediately. And lay out my best uniform. As the Sovereign's only representative here I must not disgrace that honour.'

When Elliot's gig approached Canton, past the merchant ships anchored in the river, he scanned the shore for any sign of activity. As he lowered his glass, he heard the boom of a gun behind him. Flocks of starlings flew out from pagoda roofs. He turned in the direction of the noise and the gun boomed a second time. He saw that the orange flame flashed from a British-merchant ship.

'Turn about,' he ordered the captain. 'Pull alongside that ship.'

'Aye, aye, sir.'

The gig approached the merchantman, which was anchored fore and aft against the outgoing tide. A rope ladder hung down on the starboard side. Elliot jumped on the bottom rung and climbed up on deck. As he did so, another gun fired, and the whole ship trembled and creaked with the recoil. He heard laughter beyond the main cabins, and ran across an unscrubbed deck littered with uncoiled ropes that smelled of seaweed.

On the port side, facing Canton, half a dozen British officers lolled in cane chairs smoking cheroots, glasses of whisky let into the arms of their chairs. Two Lascars, stripped to the waist, long hair bound with tarred string, were sponging out the barrel of a cannon.

'What the devil's going on" here?' asked Elliot.

None of the officers had seen him, and three now stood up in surprise, while the others leaned forward in their chairs, regarding him with a mixture of anger and contempt.

'Where's the captain?'

'Here. I am the captain,' replied the nearest officer, a burly man in his late forties, uniform jacket undone, armpits dark with sweat. He held a beaker- of whisky in his right hand. 'What are you doing aboard my vessel?'

'By right of my rank. As Superintendent of Trade, I am in charge of all British ships in the Bogue. What target are you firing at?'

'That junk over there.'

'You mean you are firing at a Chinese vessel?'

'That's what I said, didn't I?'

'Why?'

'Because I wanted to. And because it's the Sovereign's birthday, and I had a bet here with the First Officer we could reach the vessel with half charge.'

'We bloody didn't though,' chortled one of the others from the chairs. 'We've fired nine cannon balls and all have fallen short. So that's twenty pounds you owe me.'

'You idiot!' shouted Elliot. 'Do you realize what your lunacy can lead us into?'

'I don't like the tone of your voice, sir,' said the captain coldly, putting' his beaker down on a chair. 'Get off my ship or I'll throw you off.'

He took a step nearer to Elliot, his pig-eyes narrow as half-healed cuts.

'If I have any more insolence from you,' replied Elliot coldly, 'I will have you clapped in irons on board your own ship, and the lot of you flogged and dismissed the service.'

'You haven't the power,' said the captain, but his fist went down; the heat was out of his voice.

'One more word from you, sir, and you will witness the power I have. In your drunken state you probably cannot appreciate the delicacy of the situation in Canton. A new Chinese Commissioner has just threatened to withdraw the privilege of trade from our compatriots *for ever.*

'Do you think that your idiotic behaviour of discharging nine cannon balls at a defenceless Chinese vessel, right under his eyes, is going to influence him in our favour? If he stops our trade, not only will the Company be brought to ruin, but I personally will see that none of you ever serve in any position of command in any British vessel.'

'My God,' said the captain, suddenly sobering, and seeing the gold braid on Elliot's uniform. The sun had been in his eyes, and whisky had fuddled his brain.

'Well may you call upon your Maker. What is your name?'

'Captain Bartram, sir. Commanding the *Sunflower* out of Calcutta.'

'I'll give you your orders, Captain Bartram. Set sail now. If you are not under way by the time I reach Canton, I will send *Andromache* after you to arrest your vessel, and all of you aboard her.'

White with fury, Elliot turned and walked across the deck, and climbed down the rope ladder to the gig. How incredible that anyone of his race who could reach the rank of captain in a Company ship, would be so lacking in common sense as to behave in this boorish manner! He would explain that the shots were not intended to harm or alarm, but would Lin believe this explanation? Would anyone, in these circumstances?

As soon as the gig touched the quay Elliot jumped ashore and went into the British factory as quickly as he could without running. The money-changers, or schroffs, squatted by their scales and weights and piles of coins. Some wore small sets of scales at their belts; they were always eager for business — and in their own money-changing shops, for Canton had no banks, they even sold the privilege of lifting the floors once a year. This gave the buyer the right to rummage for any loose coins or silver scrapings that had dropped between the tiles in the previous twelve months.

The manager sat writing with a quill pen at a desk in front of the granite treasury where the factory's money was stored. He stood up when he saw Elliot.

'Be so good as to send for the senior Hong merchant immediately,' Elliot told him.

The manager nodded, went out and returned in half an hour with the spokesman for the Hong merchants. No-one knew his real name, but the nearest anyone got to pronouncing it was to call him Mow. Because of his rank, a gutteral sound, Qua, was added, like Esquire; so he was always called Mowqua. Now he stood, trembling with fear. His usually bland soft face had sunk in on itself as though the skin had been originally intended for another man with a bigger skull altogether. His lips kept blowing and he stood in front of Elliot, washing his long-nailed hands without water.

'Can you interpret?' Elliot asked the manager.

'Yes, sir. If he does not speak too quickly.'

'Well, then, tell him that the nine shots he has heard are nothing serious. They were not intended in any way to aggravate Commissioner Lin. A foolish drunken man aboard one of the ships was firing them as a form of salute. He has been reprimanded.'

The manager translated. The Mowqua said something in reply.

'Commissioner Lin has already sought his advice about the firing,' the manager explained. 'He made up some similar story to him, but the Commissioner Lin would not believe it. Accordingly, thinking that the firing has some hostile purpose, Lin has ordered all opium to be surrendered by *tonight*.

'In the meantime, at dusk, every coolie and other labourer will be withdrawn forthwith from the docks. No provisions will be allowed for us in the factory, and. no shopkeeper can trade with us under penalty of death.'

This was worse than Elliot had anticipated.

'Can *I* see Commissioner Lin?' he asked.

More conversation in Cantonese, heads laid on one side, hands turned, palms upwards, to heaven.

'That is impossible,' the manager translated. 'He wants all the opium surrendered before *anyone* has an audience with him. And even then we will still have to use the Hong merchants as intermediaries. There will be no direct contact.'

'Don't translate this,' said Elliot, 'but tell me in English. Have we any opium we can surrender as a sop to him?'

'Not here, sir. But there should be thousands of cases at Whampoa.'

'Then get them up here.'

'What about compensation to their owners, sir?'

'There can be no compensation at present, if at all. The owners know full well that this is an illegal trade. And we cannot have our legal dealings jeopardized by their selfish and illegal actions. We must have as many chests as you can find quickly to give to him, if we have to. This token of goodwill, an earnest of future co-operation, may soften his attitude. Are any officers from Whampoa here?'

'I have seen some on the Point'

'Then tell them to report back immediately.'

The Mowqua began to speak again. The manager translated.

'Commissioner Lin has also ordered New China Street to be barricaded with wooden bars, and they are stationing police across it. Other police will stop anyone entering Old China Street, and all other streets behind the factory are being bricked up now, as we speak. In addition, sir, Chinese troops have commandeered the tea boats and the chop-boats and are anchoring in the river to watch us. By evening, Lin says he will have five hundred men with sticks and spears surrounding the factories to stop anyone leaving or supplying us with food.'

'All the more reason for you to make haste,' said Elliot. 'How many chests do you think you can give the Commissioner?'

'Difficult to say, sir, without checking. But I would think a very large number — perhaps, twenty or thirty thousand.'

At five hundred dollars a case this-would be worth at least two or three million pounds sterling; this was a fortune to put at risk. Elliot had not imagined the stock would be so large at that time of year.

'Jardine and Matheson have their new clippers ferrying mud regularly now from Calcutta,' the manager explained, 'so there is more at Whampoa than anyone knows what to do with. Which is why the companies are trying so hard to make contact with new buyers up the coast.'

'This development should save them that necessity.'

The manager translated for Mowqua's benefit. Now the Mowqua became alarmed.

'What for you pay so big?' he demanded in pidgin. 'No wantee so muchee. Six, seven thousand so would be enough. Muchee more than enough.'

'No,' replied Elliot. 'We have to make this a real gesture of goodwill. To show Lin we are genuinely willing to stamp out this trade.'

'*Are* we, sir?' asked the manager in surprise.

'*I* am,' replied Elliot simply.

Commissioner Lin sat in an upstairs room at the Yueh-Hua Academy in Canton, where he had set up his headquarters. The ceiling was high and the room felt cool. He was keeping his diary, and his brush flickered swiftly over the scroll of parchment.

'Today I stationed armed patrol ships at all the approaches to the quays to prevent foreigners from embarking or disembarking.'

He paused; what else had he done? He had posted spies to report on the reactions of foreigners to his Edicts. He had written several letters to friends in Peking. And that was all. Not a very inspiring or busy day. He put aside his brush, and looked out through the window over the rooftops towards the distant sea, and the gaily painted junks. An orderly knocked respectfully on the door, came in, prostrated himself on the floor, beat his head on the ground in ceremonial *kow-tow* and then stood up.

'I have, Excellency, a note by way of the Guild merchants from the Barbarian Elliot. They have prepared twenty thousand two hundred and eighty-three chest of opium which they wish to surrender. They await your instructions as to the day and hour you will receive it.'

'Good,' said Lin. Maybe the day was not going to be so dull as it had seemed. How right he had been to pursue a policy of firmness as soon as he had arrived in Canton! Doubtless, this number of chests was only a small part of the vast amount the Barbarians must have secreted in their floating warehouses at Whampoa. However, it was a start; that was the main thing. He now had something positive to report to his Emperor. Within days of his arrival, he had achieved most encouraging results; far more than Lu had achieved in months, and their predecessors in years.

'Send in the secretary,' he commanded the orderly, who bowed, and went out through the hanging bead curtain. Another man came into the room carrying several scrolls and brushes and small pots of coloured ink.

'Write,' commanded Commissioner Lin. 'First, I wish that a present of beef and mutton and other Chinese foods is sent immediately to the Barbarian Elliot and his staff as a token of our felicity at the news that he is surrendering stocks of opium.

'Next, I will write to the Emperor and inform him of our success so far. See you arrange the speediest rider to take this message. It is essential that the Son of Heaven receives it with the minimum of delay.'

Lin paused and stood, hands in the sleeves of his long robe, looking out at the sea, imagining the journey the rider would have. First, out on the plains, his horse still fresh, past the fields fertilized with human hair from the city's barber shops, then past the corpses of those who had recently died, lying in their open coffins by the roadside, awaiting an auspicious day for burial, for on some days it was fitting to be buried and on others it was not, and only local holy men could give accurate decisions.

Lin also thought of Viceroy Lu, who had left Canton in disgrace after his arrival. He would not be hurrying like the swift messenger on his northward journey, but would dawdle along the way, delaying his arrival at Peking as long as possible. How different to be a bearer of good news! For good news warmed the heart of a man even more than the sun's heat; it helped him to see in the dark even without the moon.

Commissioner Lin could imagine the Emperor's pleasure at receiving such swift confirmation that his policy was being so successfully carried out. It was not impossible that the Emperor would reply by sending to Lin the response most sought after in all the Kingdom: a strip of dried roebuck flesh, which was the Imperial way of saying without words that a subordinate's speedy promotion was assured.

Lin gave a sigh of anticipatory pleasure and clapped his hands for a special dish of black tea to be brought.

He had carried with him from Peking a stone canister of Bohea Padre Souchong, which had been given to him as a special present by His Celestial Majesty. This tea took its name from the Woo-E Hills of Fuh-Keen, where it was grown by priests of the Temple of The Silver Moon.

For generations the same family of priests had tended three small tea' trees near their temples, and every year each tree produced roughly one pound of tea. This was held to be so valuable that it was all presented to the Emperor, who, as a great favour, would give two or three ounces to mandarins and officials to whom he wished to show favour. They drank it sparingly, and only on days of great rejoicing or celebration.

As Lin sat and waited for this tea, and servants pressed

damp warm towels on his face, he felt that this was surely such a day.

'The *Hesperides* is due at Whampoa today, sir,' the head clerk told Jardine. 'She is expected to sail north tomorrow.'

'As you know, I am leaving for England very shortly. I wish .to see Dr Robert Gunn before I sail. Ask him to call upon me as soon as he can.'

'We have already done so, sir. He wonders whether six o'clock this evening would be convenient?'

'I will await him here at that hour.'

Some weeks had passed since Gunn had left the Parsee's house; He had not known what to expect in the way of retaliation from the Parsee, but nothing had happened, nothing whatever, and this surprised him. He had sailed down-river to load a new cargo of opium at Lintin, half expecting to meet obstructions or delays or unpleasantness of some kind, but all had gone smoothly.

Gunn had even received a courteous invitation to call on William Jardine, and now he sat in the back of the longboat — *his* longboat, while Lascars, *his* Lascars — rowed him towards Creek Factory at Canton.

'Wait here until I return,' he told the boatswain as they tied up. 'I will probably be back within the hour.'

He walked up a long flight of stairs to the pillared verandah. A Chinese servant bowed, and opened the ' green painted front door with its polished brass handles. Inside, the room was cool, and shades had been drawn to filter the afternoon sun. Wicker chairs were scattered about, with lacquered tables and oil lamps on stands. The whole room had a relaxed, lived-in air about it.

Jardine sat reading the latest issue of the *Chinese Repository,* a quarterly edited and published by an American Protestant missionary. His company owned its rival, the *Canton Press;* he sometimes found it instructive to compare two accounts of the same happenings. As Gunn entered the room, Jardine threw the paper to one side and stood up, hand outstretched.

'I have not had the pleasure of meeting you before, doctor,' he said. 'I know that, like me, you were once a ship's surgeon. And I hear that like me also, you have abandoned the calling of Galen and Aesculapius for trade. Indeed, you are now a major shareholder in Crutchley & Company, which I learn, you have renamed Mandarin-Gold. I thought that it might be agreeable, and perhaps advantageous to both of us, if we could meet. Will you take claret or whisky?'

'Claret, if you please,' said Gunn. His eyes took in the other man's urbanity, the expensive cloth of his suit, his polished shoes and manicured hands, his spotless linen. Jardine had the casual air of one who is above all consideration of counting any cost. Yet there was nothing ostentatious about him: he was successful and he looked it; and he was successful because he had audacity and courage and common sense. Well, thought Gunn to himself, these qualities are not peculiar to him. Our careers have already had much in common: they will have much more.

'I understand,' Jardine continued as he raised his glass, 'that you have had some negotiations with an occasional business colleague of mine, the Parsee?'

'Yes,' admitted Gunn.

'He tells me some surprising news. That Crutchley has apparently decided to abdicate from his position as our nominee and to go ashore up the coast? Moreover, before he set sail on this strange voyage of individual exploration, Crutchley made over to you his share in the company, and now the Parsee has also seen fit to make over *his* controlling share in the company?'

'That is quite correct,' agreed Gunn.

'You must be a gentleman of remarkably persuasive powers,' said Jardine. 'I speak, of course, as a shareholder in Crutchley & Company, and therefore, I assume, in your new company, Mandarin-Gold. Would you care to divulge to me the details of this transaction?'

'As the majority shareholder,' replied Gunn suavely, 'I do not see any cause to add to what you already know. And indeed there is very little I could add. Your information is quite accurate. But should you feel dissatisfied with the way I conduct the new company, Dr Jardine, then I would be prepared to purchase your few shares at their value.'

'That is most considerate of you, I am sure, Dr Gunn. But, of course, you will appreciate that these shares — and indeed yours — have no value unless *my* company *allows* them a value.'

'I do not quite understand you, sir?'

'Then I will explain. I have had a report from Captain Ferguson of the *Bosphorus* that you undercut him deliberately, despite his warning to you. Indeed, your unfriendly conduct forced him to sail for several more weeks before he could be rid of his cargo.'

'He could have cut his prices,' Gunn pointed out. 'I offered him that option.'

'Perhaps not a very generous option, since Ferguson is a wholly employed man, not a shareholder, who was under orders from his directors to sell at a fixed price.

'You will readily appreciate that since my company has virtually the monopoly of Indian opium here, and our only serious competitors are the Americans with their inferior Turkish mud, it is not in our interest to cut prices. We also have considerable overheads, of which you may not be aware. For instance, I pay one local mandarin twenty thousand Spanish dollars a year not to trade with any other freebooters of your type.'

'Perhaps then, sir,' said Gunn, smiling, 'I should offer him twenty-five thousand to trade only with me?'

'Where would you raise twenty-five thousand dollars?'

'From the same source as you, sir. The Chinese. Through selling them mud.'

Jardine sipped his drink. Despite his own. involvement, he

could not help being amused by Gunn's bravado; the fellow must realize he had no possible chance of succeeding as a free-lance opium dealer, yet he showed no sign of repentance or regret.

'I feel I am not making the situation clear enough to you, Dr Gunn,' he-said at last. 'You can only trade because we permit you to trade. We have an infinite number of boats. You have one. If you put your one vessel into any harbour where we have dealings, we will put one of ours alongside, with orders to undersell you anywhere along the coast, until you desist from your challenge to us. You will appreciate, I am sure, that it does not take many voyages to break a man with only one boat and no capital.

'Then how would you pay your crew? How would you vict-ual your craft? How would you buy your mud? We have been reluctantly forced to pursue this course on several previous and unhappy occasions and each time the freebooters have withdrawn from the scene. What makes your situation any different, doctor?'

'One thing,' replied Gunn, draining his glass, and holding it out for more wine. 'I am involved here, and I was not con-cerned in these other unfortunate cases you mention. I admit that you are infinitely more powerful than me, and in every way more astute than I am — or will possibly ever become. But surely, speaking as one medical man to another, you would not bring the vast weight of your great success and in-fluence to crush my very modest-and individual enterprise?'

'Your enterprise might not always be modest. It could grow, and eventually even threaten ours. It is easier, therefore, to cut it down now before such a situation could arise. If you owned six boats, say, or even three, we might not wish to come to what is virtually open commercial warfare between two gentlemen of the same profession. But because you have only one, I think that you should trade in another area, and with other goods.'

'Thank you, sir, for your advice. I am sorry that you view me as a possible predator on your profits. It is not my wish to engage you as an enemy, but to seek you as a colleague, a companion of the same calling in a distant land.

'I submit, sir, that we all have a right to live and ply what trade we can. After all, you and Mr Matheson had to begin in a relatively small way yourselves. So, sir, having thanked you for your warning, I will therefore withdraw.'

'You mean, withdraw from the trade?' asked Jardine hopefully.

'No, sir. From your company. The *Hesperides* will sail north as planned on the morning tide.'

IN WHICH DR GUNN TREATS A PATIENT AND MAKES A DEAL

Mackereth came up on deck unsteadily, shambled over to the starboard side of the *Hesperides* and leaned thankfully on the rail, balancing a bunch of leaflets on the smooth wood.

Sampans were moving out towards them like painted boats on a shining, waveless sea. One, with the local mandarin seated in the stern, under his. red silk canopy, crossed beneath the bows to the port gangway. Three others came alongside under him. An official in a rattan hat called up: 'You wantee sell number one chop? Wantee buy any good thing, what you have?'

'I give special you all number one speakee topside long fellow up yonder,' Mackereth shouted down to him, pointing with his left forefinger towards the burnished sky. He scattered a few leaflets into the sampan. The Chinese oarsmen scrambled for them, and began to read slowly, mouthing the characters, brows crinkled in perplexity.

'It is the word of the Lord,' Mackereth shouted hoarsely. 'Believe on this, and ye shall be saved. Yea, though your sins be as scarlet, they shall be white as snow. Isaiah one, verse eighteen.'

He had been drinking again, and was unable to translate into pidgin all the swarming poignant thoughts that crowded in his mind, for anything sounded absurd in that ridiculous tongue. Instead, he spoke in the local dialect.

'And the Lord said, Go ye out into all the world and preach the Gospel. Blessed is he who is bathed in the blood of the Lamb, for he shall be washed clean. That is the way of love and salvation. Be still then and know that I am God. Psalm forty-six, verse ten.'

The Chinese looked up at him, even more puzzled. Who was this strange Barbarian with the red unhappy sweaty face and dirty shirt and these pieces of paper? What god was he speaking about? Did he not know that many gods dwelt in the air, and others in the forests, and even beneath the surface of the earth and seas?

How could he speak so familiarly of one without offending the others? But then he had the glazed frantic look of a Barbarian who slaked his thirst on firewater. And, of course, so many of the Iron Rats were mad in one way or another. They should be humoured. The oarsmen smiled hopefully and called again: 'You wantee sell, you wantee buyee, say what you wantee, yes?'

Gunn walked up to Mackereth, and leaned over the rail beside him.

'They're taking off fifty chests on the other side,' he announced in a satisfied voice. 'What are you doing? What's in those papers?'

'They are religious tracts,' Mackereth explained with dignity. 'So that the Word may spread and cover the face of the earth, as the waters cover the sea. I've spent all I earned on my last trip to have them printed. And what you pay me after this voyage I will spend in the same way.'

'So we are offering opium on one side of the vessel, and you are selling eternal life on the other?' said Gunn in amazement.

'What else have I to sell?' asked Mackereth. 'My whole life has been a struggle to help the unbelievers. Blessed is he who bringeth one soul to heaven.'

MacPherson came up silently, barefoot, behind them.'

'Mackereth has the right idea,' he said. .'I believe that if people weren't meant to smoke opium, then there would be no opium in the world.

'Have you ever thought how strange it is that men, hundreds of years ago, living in the jungle, or in remote mountains, surrounded by flowers, trees and bushes of every kind, subject *one* flower to all kinds of experiments? They cut it, they bleed it, they bake it, they roll it up in balls, simply so that it can produce the essence of dreams and oblivion.

'Why do they pick on this one particular flower? What guides them to it, apart from all the others? There's a thought for you, doctor, something you'll never find in your medical books.

'Alcohol and opium. Wouldn't you agree they are both valuable? Beyond price sometimes?'

'The Greeks and Romans thought so,' agreed Gunn. 'Alcohol was the gift of Dionysus, and opium the gift of Morpheus. One reconciles you to living, and the other to dying.'

'Just what I would have said if I could have thought of the words,' said MacPherson triumphantly.

'And whether a man smokes opium or not is his own decision,' Mackereth pointed out. 'Just as we must decide whether to drink alcoholic liquor — in moderation, of course — or whether to abstain. You give these heathen wretches the chance to buy Lethe — a little brief oblivion. Out of your profits from that transaction — good or bad, I do not wish to argue — I offer them something of infinitely greater value, the priceless chance of eternal salvation.'

'I'd rather have the chance of a certain profit,' replied Gunn, narrowing his eyes against the horizon. 'And from what I see this may be denied us. There's another ship coming up. Hand me your glass, MacPherson.'

He raised the lens to his eye: the *Bosphorus* was heading towards them.

'Captain Ferguson,' he said slowly. 'He will cut us down in price, I wager.'

'What are you selling at?' asked MacPherson.

'The usual. Ten dollars a pound.'

'Then I suggest you offer the mandarin another fifty at eight, so long as he loads quickly. Just in case there's any trouble.'

Gunn walked across the deck to the mandarin. It was never wise to run when Orientals could see you; they invariably associated unseemly haste with hirelings or alarm. Mackereth followed to translate.

'He says he esteems the friendliness of your most honourable offer.' said Mackereth. 'But he recognizes the ship. Also, he knows the captain. He thinks he will make contact there first, lest the honourable captain be offended. As he says, dealers come in numbers, like a gathering of the clouds.'

'Tell him we can only make this offer because then our holds will be empty, and we wish to return to Macao.'

'He knows that is a lie,' said Mackereth disapprovingly. 'He has looked into the hatches. He sees you have at least another two hundred to go. He means to play us against the *Bosphorus*.'

'Damn him,' said Gunn bitterly. Ferguson would undercut him until they were both giving the mud away. The *Bosphorus* was about two hundred yards away now, and turning in a wide sweep. Gunn could hear the shouted commands; the sails cracked like dry bones breaking as the wind left them. She sailed within twenty yards of the *Hesperides* and then her anchors went down, fore and aft. He made out Ferguson in the wheelhouse, voice trumpet at his mouth.

'Good morning, Dr Gunn,' he called cheerfully. 'What are you selling at today?'

'Find out,' Gunn replied shortly.

'Gladly.'

Sampans were now bobbing against the shining tarred hull of the *Bosphorus*. Chinese officials began to climb up the rope ladder to the deck. There was a hurried consultation. Ferguson shouted back: 'Eight dollars, eh? Well, *five's* my going rate. Beat that if you can.'

'What will you do?' Mackereth asked Gunn.

'Nothing,' interrupted MacPherson bitterly. 'If we stay here, he'll only force us down, whatever price we quote. If we head north, he'll follow us or overtake us. That clipper can beat anything afloat. She is also probably carrying twice as much mud as us, anyway. We are wasting our time taking them on.'

'I'll decide that,' said Gunn sharply, but he knew MacPherson spoke the truth. He turned to Fernandes.

'Batten down the hatches as soon as the mandarin has gone. Then all speed north, up the coast towards Amoy.'

Fernandes began to shout orders. Ferguson called again, mockingly.

'What, leaving us, doctor? Why so soon? We will just have to follow you, wherever you go. And, by God, we'll beat you whenever you stop!'

As he spoke, Gunn remembered the Parsee's words to him in that quiet room, overlooking the Praya Grande.

Gold hath been the ruin of many. How ironic that other men's gold and power and prosperity should crush him before he could accumulate enough to squeeze others!

'Your master Jardine has declared war on us,' he admitted to Ferguson. 'You may have won the first battle, but one battle is not a war.'

'We'll take you on any time, doctor!' roared Ferguson triumphantly. 'You're not the first to try this, remember. You will learn like the others.'

The *Hesperides'* anchor chains were coming up, screaming through the hawse-holes. Then wind took her sails and she moved forward slowly, turning to the north. Behind them, Gunn could hear Ferguson shouting orders to his crew. They were going to be tailed up the coast. Ferguson would defeat him by his speed and the capital behind him.

Gunn went down into his cabin and sat on his bunk, thinking. It would be dark within three hours. Then he could head out to sea, and wait for dusk, and with all lights doused, he could head north under every sail. To confuse Ferguson, he could lower a boat with a fixed sail and a lantern at the top of the mast. Ferguson might follow the light, or he might not. It was not a very good deception, but it was the only way he could think of delaying them. He called Fernandes to his cabin and asked his opinion.

'It will not work, doctor,' Fernandes said at once. 'Ferguson is one of their best clipper captains. He will simply lower a longboat and row after the light. When he finds you've tricked him, he will guess we have gone north because there is nothing to go south for. And then he will beat up the coast himself. There is a half moon tonight. He would catch, us by midnight.'

'What do *you* suggest, then?'

'I have nothing to suggest, doctor. You are fighting a company so big they are like an iceberg. Only the tip is showing. The real power and weight and muscle is hidden.'

'You're a defeatist,' said Gunn. 'If Jardine and Matheson had listened to you they would have achieved nothing. There *must* be a way of putting him off the scent. And, by the devil, I have thought of it. Have we any gunpowder?'

'Of course. But you're not suggesting we fire on them?'

'I'm suggesting nothing,' said Gunn. 'I'm asking questions. And the first question is — what if we put a charge against his rudder and blow it off?'

'Well, he couldn't follow us then, obviously. Not until they had repaired it. But how do you propose to do this?'   I

'Those devices the Chinese used when the *Andromache* and *Imogene* wanted to sail up to Canton. Those barrels of gunpowder that floated off in the river, set to explode when anything touched them.'

'You will want a detonator,' said Fernandes. 'The Chinese use a glass tube of acid.'

'I have a dozen test-tubes in my medical supplies. And sulphuric acid. Make me up a charge of gunpowder, in some waterproof container, and I'll provide the detonator.'

'How will you carry it over to the *Bosphorus?*'

'Swim. You wrap the whole thing in some tarpaulin to keep it dry, then tie it on a wood raft and I'll push it through the water. It's calm as a pond. Then we'll put on lots of lights, and swing round. He'll turn, too, his rudder will crush the tube, and — bang — he's rudderless. Then we sail north on our own to sell our mud.'

'Jardine won't forgive this sort of behaviour,' said Fernandes cautiously.

'He won't hear of it for months. He's going back to England.'

'It's a risk.'

'Agreed. But what have we left to lose if we fail? We lose everything if they follow us up the coast. You admit that?'

'I do,' agreed Fernandes wretchedly.

'Right. So go and make up that charge. We'll cruise in a circle until dusk, but not far enough away to make them come after us. They'll think we are seeking to anchor here.'

Fernandes hovered uneasily in the doorway like a fat in-decisive moth.

'The sea here is full of shovel-nosed sharks,' he said.'

'So is the land!' retorted Gunn. 'Why do difficulties always argue themselves most eloquently? I am not asking *you* to swim with the charge, man. *I* will swim.'

'Yes, sir,' said Fernandes, and went out along the deck and down the companionway to the hold where the gunpowder was kept.-

Gunn unlocked his medicine chest, took out a bottle of sulphuric acid and a test-tube, filled the tube, stopped it, and propped it on the top of his locker. A shadow darkened the doorway. MacPherson came into his cabin.

'Fernandes says you are planning to blow the rudder off the *Bosphorus?*'

'I intend to try.'

'It is madness to swim here. The sea is full of sharks.'

'So Fernandes has already informed me.'

'Damn Fernandes,' said MacPherson. 'Ling Fai says they're man-eaters. The locals won't dive here for pearls or anything else because of them. These sharks can skin a man within seconds of diving in the water.'

'You can help me.'

'I'm not swimming with you,' replied MacPherson quickly.   .

'I'm not asking you to. I'm only going to ask you to throw a chunk of meat overboard when I set off, for the sharks to attack. That should give me five minutes to do my job. Now, what about Ferguson? What's he doing?'

'Watching us through a glass, as we are watching him.'

'Good. Keep turning until dark, then drop anchors. At the same time, lower the longboat. The noise of the anchor chains should cover it going into the water.

'Get in with some of the crew. Take Mackereth — and start shouting at each other. That will draw their attention. Then drop the meat.'

MacPherson went out and along the deck. Slowly, heat deserted the day, and the sun sank down into the milky evening sea. In the few moments of tropical dusk, the whole coast glowed in a green ethereal light. Then it was dark.

Ling Fai came silently into Gunn's cabin.

'You go makee long swim?' she asked.

'Yes.'

'I miss you most much.'

'I'll come back,' Gunn assured her.

'I come see you long, long time tonight. Yes?'

Gunn put out his hands and held her slim body. She had been crying; her face felt damp and soft with tears. She seemed so forlorn, so appealing, that he wanted her then; not just physically, but to know she was close, that he could reach out and feel her, warm and reassuring. But it was wrong to have the woman who belonged to his friend. Yet *did* Ling Fai belong to MacPherson? Could anyone belong to anyone else? Once he had thought that Marion belonged to him. Were we not all cast in the image of God, free to make or break alliances and associations?

'I want you, too, Ling Fai.' But 'you are MacPherson's woman.'

'Ling Fai not anyone's woman. She is her own woman. And if one man can love many women, why not one woman love two men? Ling Fai can. So let her wish you good happiness. As we say, may favourable winds and friendly tides help you. Understanding?

'Yes. Understanding."

She went out, and Gunn stood watching the open doorway and the purple dusk deepening beyond it, hoping she would return, but she did not. He took off his shirt, trousers, and shoes, and wearing only his drawers, rummaged in his locker for a length of thin manilla rope, and wound this in treble thickness around his waist.

From the shore he could hear music thinned by distance and the night; the wail of flutes, the boom of beaten gongs. Lanterns flickered along the beach, and up in the hills. Both ships rode easily at anchor, and mist came rolling out over the sea. Soon it blurred the outline of the *Bosphorus,* her masts and rigging. Within minutes, her lights were only dim haloes in a pale fog. MacPherson came into his cabin.

'Ready when you are,' he announced. 'The longboat has been lowered over the port side, and the cooks have a pig carcase ready to throw overboard.'

'I'm waiting for the charge,' said Gunn.

'Here it is,' said Fernandes from the outer darkness. The three men crowded into the cabin. Fernandes put down a small rum barrel on the table. The top was covered by a square of canvas tied by a rope, with two loops, one on each side of the barrel.

'I'll fill a second tube,' said Gunn. 'Just to be sure.' He did so and carefully pushed in the rubber stopper.

'I'll leave this on top of the powder. The acid will eat through the rubber in half an hour and set it off, in case the other one fails.'

He cut a hole in the tarpaulin and positioned the tube carefully.'

'Ship's carpenter has made a raft for you to push, sir,' said Fernandes.

'Good.'

As Gunn turned down the wick of the, cabin oil lamp, he saw his face in the mirror, hair dark and long, skin pale from the strain of what he was about to undertake. He could hardly recognize the face that had looked back at him from the mirror of his cabin in the *Trelawney*. He had been a boy then. And what was he now? A privateer? A physician? A merchant? Or was he just at last a man?

He walked out along the still-warm deck. The raft lay in the longboat, about four feet square, planks nailed together, with a rope tacked around the edge. He climbed down the ladder, and lifted the raft silently into the sea. Fernandes lowered the powder barrel at the end of a rope. Gunn put it on the raft, then went over the side himself into the warm water. As he did so, Mackereth's face loomed out of the darkness above him, like a white, frightened melon.

'May the Lord go with you,' he whispered hoarsely.

'Certainly no-one else is coming,' replied Gunn, and pushing the raft with outstretched arms, he began to swim.

From sea level, the hull of the *Hesperides* soared up like a black cliff. He saw, the dim lights of the *Bosphorus* and struck out for them. Behind him, he heard a splash as the pig carcase went into the sea, and he hoped the sharks had wind of it before they had wind of him. Then he heard a creak of oars and MacPherson shouting.

'I tell you, doctor, you're mad to think you can beat them at their own game! There's only one end to this. You *must* know that.'

'I disagree,' replied Mackereth, his voice slurred with drink. 'The doctor is in command. The Lord is working in him!'

Gunn swam on. Someone shouted from the stern of the *Bosphorus*.

'Ahoy, there! Who are you?'

'We are from the *'Hesperides,'* MacPherson shouted back. 'Taking an easy row! All's well.'

Water chuckled against the raft. Gunn held his breath and listened. Would he hear a shark — or would it move silently, like a deadly shadow in the sea? The first thing he would know, if one attacked him, would be the grip of a hundred sharpened teeth, and then the unspeakable agony of a limb being severed, or the even worse anguish of being dragged beneath the sea, powerless to resist.

He kicked more vigorously to drive these horrible thoughts from his mind. He was almost up to the *Bosphorus* now, and a little too far along the tarred hull. One of the crew was playing a mandolin on the after-deck; the notes sounded like liquid drops of music. The current was carrying him towards the vessel, and he struck out strongly, heart pounding. It could be dangerous, perhaps fatal, to hit the hull. And it was unlikely anyone would hear him swimming past, however strong his strokes. Even if they did, they would think the noise was caused by waves.

He reached the rudder and wedged himself against the lower hinge, holding on with one hand. With his other arm through a loop on the raft, he untied the manilla rope, and wound this around the hinge, encrusted with rust and barnacles, and then around the barrel.

He tightened the rope, secured it with a reef knot and then tied the test-tube to the barrel with the loose end, close to the hinge. As he pushed against the barrel to check that it was firm, a gurgle of water sounded above him, and a sewage pipe discharged on his head.

Gunn ducked under the water to clean the stinking mess

from his hair, and as he ducked he felt a rasp like sandpaper against his flesh. He kicked out as a shark turned on its back, its white belly a pale ghost in the green water.

Gunn took a huge breath, kicked with both feet, hands outstretched above his head, and then swam with all his might to the *Hesperides*. Every second he expected to feel the grip of teeth on his feet, and his heart thundered in his chest like a mighty drum. If the shark followed him, he was dead. Somehow he had to reach the rope ladder and haul himself out of the sea before the shark finished its meal of turds. He saw the dim dark outline of the *Hesperides* tower ahead of him and gasped hoarsely and desperately: 'Here! I'm here!'

Instantly, MacPherson lowered a ladder. Gunn clung on to the bottom rung, sobbing for breath, and then began to haul himself out of the water, dripping like a seal. MacPherson was waiting on deck, a beaker of Queen Anne in his hand. Gunn drank it thirstily.

'Truly,' said Mackereth, 'the Lord has poured his blessing on you.'

'I'll delay judgement on that until tomorrow,' replied Gunn. 'I've had something less salubrious poured on me just now.'

He turned to Fernandes.

'Give your orders as loudly as possible, so they'll hear you. Sail south. Then turn a hundred and eighty degrees north and we'll know if what Mackereth says about the Lord is right. Maybe Captain Ferguson is also praying.'

'Nothing avails like the prayers of a righteous man,' said Mackereth.

'Agreed,' replied Gunn. 'But who among us here would dare to give ourselves that description?'

He walked along the deck into His cabin, picked up a towel, and began to rub himself dry. The deck slanted as wind filled the sails. The mist had cleared, and the moon was rising. From the *Bosphorus* lights danced like long; lit windows on the sea. A look-out was calling urgently from their crow's nest: 'Ahoy, below! *Hesperides* is sailing!'

A rattle of chains, a shouting of orders, and the *Bosphorus* began to turn slowly behind them. Gunn stood at the porthole, watching her rudder move in a swirl of water. There was no explosion, no spurt of fire or flame; nothing. That tube must have fallen into the sea. Then he remembered the second test-tube of acid on top of the gunpowder. Fernandes appeared at the door.

'They are following us, dead astern,' he reported. 'Five hundred yards behind.'

'Clap on all the sail you've got,' ordered Gunn, keeping disappointment out of his voice. Surely that gunpowder *must* explode? It was a chemical reaction that nothing could prevent — unless water had seeped in beneath the cover and the charge was damp. He turned away for a moment and in that moment the powder caught. His cabin flared red like a furnace mouth.

He dashed to the porthole. Clouds of white smoke billowed over the *Bosphorus'* stern. Men were shouting in terror and surprise. The stern post had gone and the rudder with it; the sea was boiling like a kettle.

The crew of the *Hesperides* began to cheer wildly, an animal reaction of relief and triumph. They sailed on, the wind freshening, while behind them the *Bosphorus* wallowed uselessly. Her crew began to scramble over her sides to rig a makeshift rudder before wind and current ran her aground on the sands. Gunn wiped his face with his towel. It was damp, not with seawater now, but sweat. *He had done it!* This wasn't the last battle he had won, true; but it wasn't the first, either. There had been the Parsee; then Crutchley; and now the might of Jardine and Matheson. And in each case, ruthlessness and resolution had overcome the opposition.

He stood naked, looking at himself in. the mirror, grinning with triumph. Then he heard a voice behind him. Ling Fai stood framed in the doorway against the moon.

'Come here,' he said roughly, and drew her towards him. He

felt his body harden as she slipped out of her silk shift, and he took her there as they stood, her firm buttocks pressed up against the wall of the cabin, her legs entwined against his waist, mouth to mouth, stabbing her as though he would die if he stopped.

All through .that long hot passionate night, the *Hesperides* sailed north; and then through the next day and night, and the following day, with the wind still behind them. It was dusk on the third day when Fernandes sought, permission to draw closer to the shore and drop anchor.

'The charts are very vague here,' he admitted, 'but I hear that a friend of the mandarin we dealt with at Whang-pi is the new governor. He's also related to the Hoppo in some way. He has just been posted here, so he is probably willing to start up trade.'

'We'll find out in the morning,' said Gunn, scanning the' coast through his glass. Two war junks with high sterns and painted eyes to watch for the enemy were moored near the usual flotsam of sampans. Beyond the beach lay a handful of brick buildings with straw roofs. Their arrival must have been noted.

That night, as on the previous two nights, Ling Fai came to him in his cabin, and they loved the hours away.

'You have been in Chinese house, yes?' she had asked him.

'Never,' Gunn had told her. 'No-one has invited me.'

'We have custom above outer door to write, "May the five happinesses enter this abode" You understand, yes?'

'No.'

'We believe the five happinesses — the most happy ones — are long life, muchee riches, good things said about you, love of virtue, and at end of all, natural death. These are the five maintime happinesses.'

'There should be a sixth.'

'And what would that be?'

'To love and be loved,' he said, and meant it.

When dawn streaked the sky, she flitted away to her own quarters like a shadow. Gunn was growing obsessed by her, and his obsession overcame the guilt he felt about their association. She was there for the taking, and his need seemed mirrored by hers. And if MacPherson claimed her as his woman, then he should be able to guard her and keep her for his own. But MacPherson did not even appear to notice whether she was with him or not. He had his rum and he moved blindly; it was not for Gunn to open his eyes.

It was equally useless to wonder what might happen if MacPherson discovered he was cuckolding him. That event could argue itself. You enjoyed the moment. You lived for those climactic seconds when, back arched like a drawn bow, you pumped your seed into her willing, sobbing body, and then, damp with sweat, all passion spent, life drawn out of your being in the long pearly thread of love, you waited until she aroused you again. What did tomorrow matter when this was tonight?

Fernandes stood in the doorway as Gunn shaved. 'There's a ship approaching,' he announced. 'The *Golden Swan*. A Jardine and Matheson clipper.'

'Do you know the captain?'

'Only by name. Captain Peabody. One of their toughest.'

'So he'll cut us down?'

'I would think so.'

Gunn finished shaving, wrapped a towel around his naked loins, and looked through the porthole. The clipper was coming in under full sail. She would be alongside within an hour.

'What about this mandarin fellow?'

'He's on his way. Several boats are already rowing out from shore towards us.'

'Then we'll try and offload all we can to him as soon as

possible. Have some wine set out on the deck and a table and chairs, while I dress.'

The sun was already half-way up the sky, and the scrubbed deck planks stretched fresh and clean under Gunn's feet. The shore seemed greener than any green in England; the sea shone blue as porcelain. All colours were so much more intense in the tropics than in the cold northern climate, and life and its passions were correspondingly intensified. Surely this was a large part of the ceaseless burning attraction of the East?

The mandarin came ponderously up the gangway, bowed, hands in his sleeves, and sat down in the cane chair. The cabin boy poured him a glass of claret. Mackereth hovered in the shade of the cabin wall. The mandarin spoke first; Mackereth translated.

'He says, doctor, that as wheels revolve, so may sales and supplies continue. But he is surprised to see two ships where none have ever been before.'

'Tell him we share his surprise. Tell him also that we are friendly rivals. We will be honoured by his custom, but because of these rivals, we lack time to treat this matter of trade with him with the dignity that the mandarin's superior position deserves. Make sure he understands we seek no insult to his illustrious person by asking him, before our rivals approach, whether he will take some chests or not. And remember, we are carrying three hundred cases of best Patna mud.'

Mackereth translated. A bowing of heads, a further sipping of claret. The mandarin spoke again.

Mackereth said: 'He'll take a hundred chests at eight dollars.'

'The going rate is ten.'

'He knows,' said Mackereth. 'He also knows the *Golden Swan* is almost here.'

'Make it nine.'

'He will not. I have tried. Eight it is.'

'Damn him!' said Gunn bitterly. 'Make it a hundred and fifty at eight dollars then.'

'A hundred at eight, last price.'

'The *Golden Swan* is anchoring,' warned MacPherson. 'The captain's holding a voice trumpet. He is going to hail you.'

'A hundred it is,' said Gunn shortly.

He nodded to Fernandes. The crew heaved open the hatches, and the heavy smell of damp opium drenched them all with its honey-sweet scent. The *Golden Swan's* captain called: 'Dr Gunn, I presume?'

'What do you want with me?' asked Gunn.

'You are trading in our area,' replied the captain. 'I have instructions to order you to desist.'

'No one *orders* me to do anything,' retorted Gunn. 'I don't *take* orders, captain. I give them.'

He watched the little sampans bob their blunt bows against the *Golden Swan's* hull. Already men were scrambling up rope ladders; a chance to set one shipload of Barbarians traders against another did not come every day.

The captain shouted again.

'So you've sold a hundred at eight. We are offering His Excellency a hundred at *five!*'

A stocky figure in a wide-brimmed hat appeared beside the rival captain.

'That's Gutzlaff, the missionary Jardine uses as an interpreter. The fact he's aboard means the *Swan's* calling in at a lot of new places where they won't speak pidgin.'

Gutzlaff began to shout in dialect; the mandarin inclined his head briefly.

'He's agreeing their terms,' said MacPherson bitterly. 'Sitting here, drinking *our* wine, and buying *their* mud!'

'We can't stop him,' Gunn replied. 'Therefore, count out his money while he's here.'

The mandarin's servant produced a leather bag from the folds of his robe, and began to count out little silver coins on the white deck. The mandarin checked the sums on an abacus. Mackereth accepted the coins and recounted them. Over their heads, all the while, men with hooks and ropes scooped the boxes from hatches and over into the sampans. They were doing the same thing, of course, aboard the *Golden Swan.* Both crews finished at the same time.

The captain called ironically: 'Where to now, Dr Gunn? I had expected to meet Captain Ferguson in. the *Bosphorus* here. But as he has not arrived, we will have to stay with you on our own. We have four hundred chests still to go.'

Gunn had two hundred. The *Golden Swan* could break him and sail away to sell the remainder at any price they chose. He had been too confident too soon. He could not blow the rudder off every ship in their fleet. What was his one vessel, as Jardine had said, against so many of theirs?

Gunn sat down wearily, poured out two more glasses of claret, and toasted the mandarin ironically.

'Tell him,' he told Mackereth, 'this is the last time he will see us.'

'You're not giving up?' Mackereth asked anxiously. 'But you were going to beat them.'

'I was,' agreed Gunn, 'but what more can we do with only one ship? Jardine was right. They are too powerful for any opposition. If we'd started a few years ago, when they were smaller, we would have had a chance.'

'Maybe we could negotiate a sub-contract from them?' suggested Mackereth hopefully, seeing his fees vanish like mist on a morning horizon.

'I am not going back begging for favours, with my tail between my legs. I'll try elsewhere.'

'There *is* nowhere else,' said MacPherson. 'The market's on this coast only.'

The mandarin began to speak. Mackereth translated.

'He asks if you know the Hoppo in Canton?'

'No,' said Gunn shortly. Then he remembered, when he had first landed from the *Trelawney,* the fat man in the sedan looking at him intently as though he wanted to remember his face.

'I saw him once. A long time ago. That is all. Why does he want to know?'

'He is a relation,' Mackereth explained. 'Says the Hoppo told him you are an English doctor of medicine.'

'Yes,' said Gunn. 'But not practising much at present. What's his trouble?'

'He says it is private.'

'Which means pox, I suppose?'

This affliction, whether in a mild form, as in MacPherson's case, or in one of its more serious variations, was as common among the Chinese as cold or croup in England, and just as little regarded. Fathers, mothers, children were infected, then infected others, only to be reinfected themselves.

'Tell him I will treat him, then,' said Gunn resignedly. After all, the man had bought a hundred chests. More conversation; heads nodding, shoulders jogging up and down.

Mackereth said: 'It is not him personally. It concerns his son of twenty.'

'Where is he?'

'In the mandarin's sampan.'

'Get him aboard, then.'

More shouting; the mandarin clapped his hands. A young man with jet black beard climbed up the gangway, and bowed low to Gunn.

'I'll examine him in my cabin,' said Gunn, and turned to Mackereth. 'You come, too, to interpret.'

After the open deck, the cabin felt hot and stuffy. The sun, reflected off the tossing water like heat from a burnished metal mirror, was burning into the wood walls.

'Tell him to undress,' said Gunn.

The young man slipped off his clothes and stood, naked. Gunn saw the wet scabs across his chest, the cicatrices on his neck. The skin under his beard was pocked with ulcers, encrusted by a concretion of yellowish discharge that oozed from scabs the size of sixpences.

239

He examined the groin; the mandarin's son winced as Gunn touched his flesh; it felt dry and hot and scaly, and his pulse was a hundred and three. His back was covered with a minute eruption, as though he had been sprayed with grains of red sand; all the signs of a textbook case of syphilis.

'Warn him that the treatment is unpleasant,' said Gunn. 'And it will be long and painful.'

Mackereth translated.

'He says he is willing to endure anything if he can be cured.'

'A lasting cure is difficult, and often impossible,' Gunn warned. 'But I'll do what I can.'

He opened his medical chest, selected a phial of mercury ointment, and transferred some with a spatula into a wooden pill box.

"Tell him to rub this into these spots and ulcers three times every day and night. I will also give him some Peruvian bark to chew and sarsaparilla essence for him to drink every hour. Explain that this mercury will give him even worse pimples, and more pain. His skin may turn green and his mouth grow so painful he can barely swallow. But that is the strength of the cure fighting the disease. He may also need to be bled to relieve the pressure of blood in his body.'

Mackereth translated; the young man spoke; Mackereth translated again.

'He asks how you will treat him if you do not come here again — if you stop trading?'

The cabin door opened before Gunn could reply. The mandarin came in and closed it quietly behind him. He said something to Mackereth.

'His Excellency says he also wishes you to treat his son on your return.'

'Perhaps he could come to Macao?'

Gunn supposed he would be there, at least until he decided what to do, whether to take passage again as a ship's doctor, or to try some other branch of trade.

The mandarin spoke again.

'He could not travel to Macao for some months, as he has only recently, taken up this appointment. But if you help his son, he could help you.'

'How?'

'He says he owns the controlling shares with the Hoppo, and under a nominee's name, in Rona Lloyd.'

'Who are they?'

'Traders. They own five ships. Mostly old country wallahs, but useful for all that. Lloyd died a few months ago, and Rona is going back to Scotland. He has made his money. He does not wish to fight Jardine and Matheson and all the others. He wishes to retire.'

'Why have they let him trade up to now?'

'Because he was mostly in tea and silk, and only dabbled in mud. Also, he used the Portuguese flag. He married a Portuguese.'

'I'd then have six ships,' said Gunn slowly.

'Yes,' said Mackereth, smiling at the significance of the number.

The mandarin was also smiling. Maybe he realized the precariousness of Gunn's position? Maybe he wanted Jardine and Matheson to have more competition, because then there would be no monopoly in mud, and he would be able to play the companies against each other?

'What terms does he offer?'

'Seventy-thirty,' said Mackereth.

'His way or mine?'

'His.'

'Tell him fifty-fifty all clean number one equal split down the middle. Yes?'

Mackereth translated the mandarin's reply.

'Fifty-fifty no good. He says last-price sixty-forty.'

'No. I do not wish to pursue this conversation. Fifty-fifty or nothing. And tell him that the nothing means no treatment for his son. Tell him absolute last price. No more speakee. Ever.'

'He says, yes.'

'Why did he give in so quickly?' asked Gunn; he had expected a tussle to continue for an hour or more.

'He says that he wants his son cured. He is his only son. Also, seventy better than sixty, sixty better than fifty, but fifty better than none.'

'True,' said Gunn. It was. true for him, too. The mandarin had no idea how near he had been to ruin. Or maybe he had guessed? Gunn felt his back clammy with sweat at the thought of the prospect that would have faced him without money to pay off his crew.

'Yes,' said the mandarin in pidgin. 'All clean equal split down middle. Me velly happy. May wealth flow in abundantly.'

They shook hands.

'Hear, hear,' said Gunn, beginning to rub the mercury ointment into the young man's skin. 'And tell him it is a condition, of our deal that he takes the rest of my stock at middle price. Seven dollars a chest.'

'Mandarin says his middle price six and-a half dollars.'

'My middle is seven,' said Gunn.

The mandarin smiled.

'You velly hard man,' he said in English. 'But I take.'

'Because his son has been too often a very hard man, he is in the position you see him now,' said Gunn. 'Tell him he'd better abstain.'

And then he thought of Ling Fai, and her body against his; who was he to advocate morality now?

'Tell him nothing,' he said, grinning. 'Except we have a deal.'

IN WHICH THERE IS A FAMOUS VICTORY

As the bows of the *Hesperides* carved a sharp white arrowhead of foam through the dark and glittering sea, the moon painted a silver path from the upper deck to the distant, shaded shore.

Ling Fai leaned, on the rail and smelled salt spray, and felt the deck creak and move like a living thing under her bare feet. She had never been so far out to sea before. The immensity of the empty ocean, and the comforting size of the masts and their spread of sails against the blue vaulted dome of the sky were curiously peaceful. She might be the last person left alive in all the world.

She thought of MacPherson; his whisky breath, his unshaven cheeks, the matted hair on his chest, his kindness to her. Then she thought of Gunn: tall, narrow-hipped, hard in brain and body as the brass rivets in the rail on which she leaned. She liked them both, in different ways: she needed them both in different ways.

She had never met men like them before. They were so unlike the Chinese men in her family; her old father and her two brothers, with their quiet unquestioning acceptance of whatever the gods might have in mind for them. They asked so little of life; a bowl of rice, some plantains, strips of boiled fish and dried lychees once a day; and at night a shelter against the dews of darkness. She would never be content to return to that ordered, humble existence now, and yet what else could the future hold for her?

She had heard that England was an island on the other side of the world where nights were never as warm as this, where even the sea was cold and the sun was pale. The air was often milky with mist and smoke, and people crowded together in brick and stone building, in towns far larger than anything she could imagine. She had no place there.

MacPherson and Gunn had slid into her life, her sheltered existence, as they had slid into her body. They had changed her attitude towards inevitability: you did not need to accept without question whatever the gods decided you should have. You could mould your own life as the potter moulded clay. You held the key to many decisive things in your own mind; your actions could guide your destiny.

These things she had learned by watching them, listening to them, lying with them. And one day they would leave, and then she would be alone, because no Chinese man would take as his wife a woman who had been fondled and stroked by a Barbarian.

She had had no idea that these men would enter her life, and equally she had no inkling when they would leave. But it was certain as a sail must fill with wind that one day they would go. Other, younger women — perhaps Chinese, perhaps from their own country — would claim them and she would belong to the past. Then her memory and her influence would dwindle as the coast dwindled behind a ship; she would become only a face, then nothing but a name, half-remembered, half-forgotten.

But she would always remember them, both of them, as they were now: the quirks of their speech, the scent of their skin, the feel of their bodies in hers. And in the years to come, when she was awake, as now, when all the rest of the world seemed asleep, and only the stars kept watch with her, then she would wonder where they were; and whether they loved anyone, and, much more important, whether other women loved them.

It was true what Gunn had said about the Sixth Happiness. That was the greatest, the most important of them all. Which, no doubt, explained why so few people ever knew it existed, let alone dwelt in the wonder of its warmth.

Commissioner Lin was feeling unusually happy; in one day, he had received two communications from his Emperor, the Son of Heaven.

The first was what he had so fervently hoped to receive, a strip of dried roebuck flesh, which meant Promotion Assured. The generosity of this communication so overwhelmed Lin that he respectfully lit a stick of incense and *kowtowed* nine times in the direction of the Royal palace at Peking. Then he rose ceremoniously from the floor and opened the second scroll.

Although this had been sent some weeks after the first, it had been delayed by floods and lame horses. It contained permission for his request that he should reward everyone who had surrendered opium with five catties of tea — about six and a half pounds, as the Barbarians measured weight — and a reply to his question about disposing of the surrendered opium.

He had proposed sending it to Peking so that none could doubt that it had been destroyed and not stored secretly for him to resell at some later date. Colleagues at Canton had pointed out that if he sent opium worth a fortune in silver to Peking on a journey that would take months, very little would actually reach the capital. Then those who envied Lin's promotion would say he had not despatched the right amount.

The Emperor, while not admitting to such failings in the characters of his officials, now told him to destroy it near Canton.

So Lin called in his secretary and issued instructions for the Barbarian Elliot to transport the opium to Chuenpee, a town on the coast near Whampoa. He then gave instructions for a wooden pavilion to be built immediately at Chuenpee so that all interested people could join him in witnessing the final destruction of this foreign, poisonous mud that had so dangerously weakened the physical calibre of his countrymen and also the currency of the whole country.

The messenger pulled a third-scroll from the leg of his right boot. This was written by a Censor, one of the Emperor's personal advisors. Why, asked this writer, when Lin had been sent to Canton specifically to stamp out the importation of opium *for ever,* had he not produced a permanent plan for doing this?

True, Lin claimed he had confiscated some opium, and presumably he had extracted a guarantee from the Barbarian traders that they would not transport opium in future.

But there was no necessity for them to do so, since they could maintain their lucrative and illegal trade simply by using Chinese agents. Lin must therefore speedily devise some proper plan to stop this obnoxious trade completely, not just temporarily.

Lin folded the scroll thoughtfully. It was so easy to issue orders from Peking, but how could he carry out such lofty instructions, when Barbarian ships were infinitely faster than the swiftest vessel he controlled? He had to rely on the goodwill of the Barbarians, and the extent of this was hard to estimate, for he had no personal contact with them, and, of course, in his position he would not expect any. Thus he always had to gauge their mood by second-hand opinions. Ah, well, he would have to do the best he could. He clapped his hands, and a servant entered instantly.

'Have my boat made ready immediately. We will sail south to see the mud destroyed.'

'It awaits your departure, Your Excellency,' replied the servant.

Lin followed him out to the sedan that carried him down through the narrow teeming streets, into the baking heat of the quay. A boat with fifty oarsmen waited for him. In the stern hung a welcome shade of crimson silk to shield him from the sun; on its sides, against a black ground, details of his rank were painted in gold letters.

They set off, rowing in midstream, past the houseboats, the chop-boats, then past the graceful tea clippers anchored at Whampoa, waiting for Certificates of Release, which he would issue when all the opium had been surrendered.

Their British crews, anxious to be home, shouted obscenities and waved their fist's at him as he passed. Some even exposed themselves on the upper deck, urinating at him to show their intense displeasure, as his fifty gilded oars dipped and swung through the yellow water.

This was Barbarian behaviour, of course, and to be expected from such crude sailors from beyond the Outer Seas. Lin felt that he had just taught the Barbarians a lesson that they would do well to remember; maybe, one day, someone would also teach them civilized manners.

His boat docked and he allowed himself to be assisted out, up the specially built wooden steps and into another sedan. Bearers carried him to his pavilion and he sat down and looked with interest at the network of trenches that surrounded his seat.

At first, he had thought of burning the opium, but he had rejected this idea, because the residue would still be noxious, and no doubt some opium would escape the flames and be sold.

Instead, he had ordered that deep trenches should be dug and filled with river water. On either side of these trenches stood pyramids of salt and lime, with new wooden spades to shovel it in. Coolies waited, ready to jump down into the trenches, and as the opium balls were flung in, to pound them to powder, which the salt and lime would then neutralize.

A subordinate bowed before him.

'All is ready, Your Excellency,' he announced.

'Before we begin,' said Lin, 'we must make a sacrifice to the Spirit of the Southern Sea and warn her to take her subjects the fish and other of her creatures away from this area, where the poison will pour out into the river.'

'We have already prepared hard bristle and soft down, with clear wine and sweetmeats for such a purpose,' the subordinate assured him.

'Good,' said Lin.

The hard bristle referred to pig; soft down was the official way of describing a sheep. Both were sacrifices that, as was well known, the Spirit of the Southern Sea was always pleased to receive.

'Burn them,' Lin commanded. 'As they roast, I will make my prayer.'

The subordinate bowed, and gave the necessary orders. Lit papers were placed against dry wood chips underneath the two carcases skewered on bamboo poles. As the flames caught and the flesh began to crackle and blister in the heat, Lin held out his hand and began to speak.

'Spirit, whose virtue makes you a chief of divinities, whose deeds match the opening and closing of the doors of nature, you who wash away all stains and cleanse all impurities, warn your watery subjects in time to keep away, for we will burn poisons that may corrupt the rich oceans that beat around our coast.

'We could have burned this filthy thing, which has been poisoning the whole body of our land. But if it had been cast into the flames, charred remains might still have been collected. Far better to hurl it into the depths, to mingle with the giant floods.'

As Lin ended his peroration he nodded to a servant who beat on a huge brass gong to one side of the pavilion. As he beat, the coolies, wearing only loincloths and rattan hats against the heat, passed cases of opium from hand to hand, and tipped them on one side of the trench so that melon-sized lumps of the stuff splashed into the muddy water.

Other coolies, passively standing up to their knees in the burning corrosive mixture, whacked the compressed opium balls with their spades. They burst apart with a sharp, sweet, syrupy smell. Some of the opium had been adulterated with clay or mud and molasses and even cow dung and the gummy resinous juice of Bengal quince. This was sometimes done by natives anxious to increase their earnings, because clearly the more they could appear to roll in a day, the more they were paid. Now their secret malpractices were exposed, for these adulterated opium balls were covered with greyish-yellow mould; when they split apart, they stank like a rotting corpse.

Lin watched, his face inscrutable, despite the foul smell. He did not know the reason for the stench, but believed the rumours that human faeces and even the bodies of dead babies were pounded up in the manufacture of opium, and that this accounted for the disgusting odour.

Hundreds of locals had gathered to see the astonishing sight of a fortune being deliberately destroyed. Because the risk of theft was so great, Lin had ordered that a fence of sharpened stakes, should be set up round the trenches so that everyone could watch, but none could enter. All through that day he sat, counting the number of cases, and at dusk he pronounced himself satisfied. As he rose from his chair, he suddenly remembered something, and called a secretary to him.

'An Edict,' he announced. 'All these coolies are to be stripped naked and their body orifices thoroughly examined before they leave for their shelters tonight, in case they are smuggling any mud out of this place.'

The secretary bowed his acquiescence. Lin then proceeded to his boat, and the oarsmen took him smartly up the darkening river. It was evening when they reached the dancing paper lanterns of Canton.

Captain-Elliot sat at his desk overlooking the Praya in Macao, drafting a letter to Lord Palmerston, the Foreign Secretary in London.

It was a difficult letter to write, because it was inconclusive, and yet he had to write it or miss the ship, and then wait for weeks or maybe months, in the present climate of events, before another sailed.

Also, Elliot knew that whatever report he posted on the evening tide could be out of date by morning, and certainly would be totally irrelevant to the situation in Canton by the time it reached London. However, he was under orders to submit regular reports, and so his pen spluttered and scratched loyally on the thick, official notepaper. First, he had to announce that twenty thousand odd chests of opium had been delivered up for destruction, and more were promised. Next, sixteen British merchants who had been concerned with smuggling, had been warned by name that they would never be allowed to enter Canton again; one was James Matheson.

As a safety measure, because Lin was obdurate that no provision's would be allowed into any of the foreign factories until every chest of opium had been destroyed, Elliot, had ordered the British staffs to leave Canton. Some had sailed to Macao and others were aboard ship, anchored between Hong Kong Island and the mainland at Kow-Loon. The factories were therefore deserted.

American merchants still remained in Canton, however, simply because they had not been named as undesirables. After all, their smuggling activities were on a smaller scale, and some American companies nobly refused to deal in mud at all. As a consequence, they hoped, of course, to pick up the lawful trade that the British were being forced to abandon. Meanwhile, they had agreed to act as commission agents for tea and silk and other legitimate goods on behalf of British merchants. The American flag, known to the Chinese as 'the flowery flag' because of its stars and stripes, fluttered alone on its mast in front of the factories.

Elliot wrote grimly: 'This rash man Lin is hastening on in a career of violence which will react upon this empire of China in a terrible manner.'

He guessed that Palmerston and the Parliament would not allow the forceable seizure of British property, whether it belonged to smugglers or not, without some active mark of displeasure. Indeed, he declared that the proposals constituted 'the most shameless violence which one nation has ever yet dared to perpetrate against another.'

Clearly, the British Government must take charge of affairs on the China Seas, otherwise what anarchy would not result? And while he agreed that opium was a most shameful trade, it was not impossible that some completely legitimate aspect of commerce would be used as a lever against all Western traders.

Not a very inspiring report to write or to read, he thought wretchedly, but it was true, and he could not alter facts.

Elliot blotted the pages with sand, then drew another sheet of paper towards him, and on the impulse wrote a personal appeal to Lord Auckland, the Governor-General of India. He felt peculiarly vulnerable to any Chinese attack, whether planned or spontaneous, and the presence of a British man-of-war would undoubtedly have a steadying influence on the whole sad situation. Not least, the British would feel that they were not entirely at the mercy of the Chinese; and Lin would realize he would have to act with caution and not in a mood of unrestrained aggression.

By the same mail-boat, although Elliot did not know it, British merchants in Macao were also sending a round robin letter to Lord Palmerston, urging him to indemnify them speedily for their losses, and to take most vigorous action against the Chinese concerned. And their losses indeed were high. The usual price of five hundred dollars a chest had now doubled, which meant that a loss of twenty thousand chests was now worth the enormous sum of twenty million dollars, roughly five million pounds, approaching the total annual revenue of the East India Company.

Elliot could only foresee one way in which such an inflated sum could ever be repaid — by forcing the Chinese to pay it. And the only way to force them was by a punitive expedition.

Another name for this, of course, was war.

Lin sat in his room, a warm damp towel around his head, listening to his trusted messenger who poured out an extraordinary story.

Some sailors from British and American ships anchored in Hong Kong Roads, had gone ashore, drunk too much native liquor, and become involved in a fight with villagers. As a result, a Chinese labourer had been killed.

'Was this a deliberate act?' asked Lin.

'It is impossible to say, Your Excellency,' the man said evasively. 'There are many confusing accounts.'

Lin therefore guessed that it had not been deliberate. No. doubt it was only chance that an American or British sailor had not been killed as well. However, the incident was very fortuitous from his point of view. Perhaps the gods, in their wisdom, had decreed that it should happen, because it provided Lin with an immensely strong lever to use against the Barbarian Elliot.

'What other news do you bring?' he asked the messenger.

'Only what no doubt Your Excellency already knows. That more foreign mud has arrived at Lintin from Calcutta.'

'I was not aware of that,' said Lin sharply. The affrontery of these red-bristled Barbarians!

'Four clippers came in yesterday. Two are Jardine and Matheson ships, and two belong to this new English Barbarian, the physician Gunn, under the Mandarin-Gold flag. He has been trading for twelve months now; Your Excellency, and some say that if he continues at this rate he will eventually be the richest *taipan* on the coast.'

'But are not our sailors vigilant? Are not our customs officials seeking out these felons under penalty of ignominy and death?'

'They work like tireless ones, Your Excellency. But the coast is long, the nights are dark, the seas run high. It is not always possible to intercept all contraband.'

'I know,' agreed Lin with resignation. 'However, we must try. When a man sees water leaking through a dam, if he says that the hole is too difficult to repair, then the wall may crumble and the entire valley be flooded. If we do not stem this evil leak of poison into our kingdom, it will also increase until it swamps our civilization. Remember this! Vigilance!'

'That will be our watchword, Your Excellency.'

'Well, what *are* we going to do about it?' asked Gunn. 'If anything?'

'I do not know. I can only tell you what I have done. I have sent a man to the village with three hundred pounds sterling in specie for this dead Chink's relations. We have paid another hundred and twenty five pounds to the local mandarin, just to show him who his friends are. And we have distributed twenty-five pounds to the children in the village, as a general *pourboire.*'

'That is generous,' said Gunn approvingly. 'But *I* hear that Lin is still on the warpath?'

'Unfortunately, yes,' said Elliot. 'He is demanding that either the Americans or we give up the culprit to him. But, damn it, we don't know who the culprit is! Thirty or forty sailors get fighting drunk. They're fighting each other as much as the villagers — you see it all the time, when sailors come ashore — and a man is killed. No-one knows who killed him. It was clearly an accident.

'I have asked the captains of all our vessels to interrogate their crews, but although they admit there *was* a brawl, they do not know who killed the Chink. That is the truth of the matter.'

'But Lin will not accept this?'

'No. He wants to use this as an excuse for stopping all trade again. He probably knows that more mud is getting through.'

'That is true, captain,' agreed Gunn, lighting a cheroot. 'With a hundred odd miles of coast, and most of it empty, the Chinese cannot patrol it all. And, of course, most of the patrols take bribes from us. We pay them more for keeping out of sight on one night than the Celestial Emperor pays them for six months' vigilance!'

'It is an evil trade,' said Elliot sadly. 'You are making a lot of money at it now, Gunn, but it is like a debt. The interest payable on this will last for a hundred years.'

'Well, we will not be here to see that, will we?' asked Gunn easily. 'Now, what will happen about this villager?'

'It is impossible to guess. I put six of the rioteers up on a charge of murder before a special court in a merchantman, but they have all been acquitted. I couldn't really expect any other verdict, but at least I have done my best to find the man responsible before Lin carries out some retaliation. What I intend to do now is to get every Englishman and all their families away from here.'

'You mean we will leave Macao?'

'Yes. This is a totally indefensible position if there is any trouble. We are living here in luxury, with our tropical gardens, our fish "ponds and ornamental trees and dozens of servants each — and we are all naked to any attack by the Chinese.

'My feeling is that Lin will now sail here with a show of force. Then another unfortunate incident will occur — either by accident or intent — and God knows how that will end. As a precaution, I am going to order everyone to sail down to Hong Kong. They will be safer there.'

'That will cause panic here.'

'Possibly. But a little local panic is still preferable to falling into the hands of the Chinese.'

'Do you really think it is a serious risk?'

'I do. At the least, Lin will wish to take hostage some British subject, and then maybe he will kill him when we cannot produce a culprit for him, on the basis of a life for a life. And we could do nothing to stop him. Nothing at all.'

'My God!' exclaimed Gunn indignantly. 'What a disgraceful

position for Englishmen to be in!'

'I agree, doctor, but you and your fellow traders have helped to bring us to this pass. So now you must help us to escape. I want all your ships, and every Portuguese ship you can lay your hands on, to be here this afternoon. Every schooner, lorcha, clipper, gig - anything capable of carrying passengers or their belongings.'

'We are running away,' said Gunn sadly.

'Only to come back,' replied Elliot optimistically.

The Parsee nodded a greeting to his son-in-law, and indicated that he stand next to him at the window overlooking the bay, now filled with a flotilla of fleeing vessels.

'Do you think they have gone for good?' asked Bonnarjee uneasily. He did not relish the prospect of being abandoned in this tiny enclave off the China coast. The British understood the need for trade and profits; these were also matters dear to his heart, but the Chinese were not concerned with them. He feared them with their hairless bodies, their bland, smiling faces, their endless courtesy, even when insulted.

'The English are a strange people,' the Parsee replied. 'Not unlike us in some respects. They may lose many battles, but in the end they win the war.'

'There has not been a war,' said Bonnarjee quickly. 'Not yet.'

'You are wrong, my son,' said the Parsee. 'The East has been fighting the advances of the West for two hundred years, as a maiden fights a passionate lecher who disgusts her. There has been war here in all but. fighting, the War of the Iron Rats, I call it. The Barbarians against the Sons of the Celestial Kingdom. And soon, I regret to say, there will also be fighting.

'The Chinese will lose because they are inflexible. They are like those animals of ancient days that could not adapt themselves to change. Now if His Excellency Lin would have met that very gentlemanly Captain Elliot, they could both have easily agreed to solve their differences. And think what they could have achieved! But, now if only. If only!'

'When is Lin due here?'

'Within minutes. He arrived on the other side of the island some time ago.'

Down on the Praya, the head of a long procession was already appearing. It consisted of Portuguese troops — Goanese, half-breeds, negroes — in odd snatches of uniform and cast-off clothes — all marching as smartly as they knew how. Their officers rode on horseback and behind them came Chinese beating brass gongs, and others holding banners, and then two lines of Chinese troops carrying bows and quivers of arrows, and fuse matlocks, wearing quaint outfits based on the uniforms favoured by European armies two hundred years earlier.

Behind them again the Viceroy's magnificently lacquered sedan was borne high on the shoulders of eight bearers, with the Portuguese Governor of Macao riding at his side. They paused at the brow of a hill to meet a deputation of local Chinese magistrates who wished to demonstrate their loyalty to the Celestial Throne by setting out a row of presents; silver tankards, bullocks with scarlet ribbons in their horns, pigs newly scrubbed and ready for slaughter.

'What are they going to do?' asked Bonnarjee.

'I will tell you exactly,' the Parsee replied. 'They will drink many bowls of tea together. Then they will visit some landmarks of the city. Guns will fire in their honour. Fireworks will explode to drive off evil demons. Local Chinese residents will bring out all manner of festoons and scrolls proclaiming their loyalty. They will then take these presents — and they will all go home.

'And nothing whatever will have been achieved. Nothing at all. For this is purely a visit to threaten the British — and they are not here to see it...'

The Emperor sat on his hill-top in Jehol, beneath the shade of a willow tree, his usual table with the crystal bowl containing three goldfish placed before him. The weather was changing, and growing cooler; every day, like every year in an old man's life, was a little shorter than the last. Soon he would have to return to the stench of Peking, and this fresh place would be only a dream of past pleasure; a hope for future summers. Then far away, along the secondary road, he saw the familiar tell-tale smudge of dust which meant a messenger was approaching. Inevitably, this implied bad news to cloud a day already tinged with autumn.

Within minutes, the young man of noble birth, who now regularly brought him tidings from Canton, knelt before him and presented his Scroll.

The Emperor began to read. So Lin had forbidden the Barbarians to trade because they had not punished a guilty Barbarian sailor. That was good. But what was this? The Barbarians had withdrawn from Canton and Macao. What if they did not return? After all, they had been forbidden to trade, and so they had no reason to come back, for trade was their life.

What if they obeyed this order after generations of insolently disobeying such Edicts? How would his kingdom then be rid of its tea and silk and rhubarb? More disquieting, from a personal point of view, if there was no trade how would, he replace the Imperial levies and dues and taxes which the Hoppo zealously collected from these traders and forwarded to him? Obviously, if they conducted no trade, there could be no taxes. He would lose a vast proportion of his income, and this at a time when the value of money was falling every day.

'We would know *your* views of the situation,' he said gently. 'You are young. You are not corrupted by bribes or softened by riches made by other men's sweat. Speak! It is Our command!'

The young man swallowed; fear and awe scattered his thoughts like swallows on a summer breeze.

'Your Most High Exalted Majesty, the Barbarian ships *have* gone. Relations in Macao also tell me the Barbarian womenfolk and their children were very sad to leave, for they have no plans for returning.'

'Where exactly are they, then?' asked the Emperor.

'At sea, moored off Hong Kong Island.'

'How will they live?'

'I do not know, Your Majesty, for His Excellency, Special Commissioner Lin, has ordered that no-one, whether official or civil at Kow-loon, must sell supplies to the Barbarians so that they may be put in fear, and become willing to pay tribute.

'He realizes that the Barbarians, out of hunger, may attempt to land and purchase provisions by force. He has therefore made a personal proclamation to all the gentry and elders and shopkeepers and inhabitants of the outer villages along the coast, allowing them to buy arms and weapons. He has given permission for *anyone* to fire on the Barbarians should they land, even to collect water. They can kill them or take them prisoner.'

'None of this is in his report,' said the Emperor suspiciously. These proclamations sounded uneasily on his ears. The Barbarians were a proud and wayward people; empty threats to them would achieve nothing.

'It may be, Your Majesty, that these events of which I speak have taken place since the report was written.'

The Emperor nodded. This was possible. It was even more likely that events had worsened since the messenger left Canton.

'Return now,' he said. 'We will make Our commands through other channels. Obey! An Imperial Edict!'

The flotilla of little ships bobbed like floating stepping stones between Hong Kong Island and the mainland. Barrels of lime juice and drinking water were lashed to the decks. On some vessels the crews had wisely taken pigs and chickens as well as crates of dried biscuit, sacks of flour and rusks. The unfamiliar farmyard sounds of these pigs and poultry and the cries of little children, fractious in the heat, drifted over the water to the villagers.

Gunn, aboard the *Hesperides,* surrounded by his clerks and their families, brooded on a letter home. What could he tell his parents about the present situation that would not alarm or distress them?

In the years he had been away from home he had grown so far away from them and their small safe life on the Kent coast that almost the only things they still had in common were shared memories of the past; and with the passing of each year even these faded.

When he had left home, he had been a newly qualified doctor starting his first job aboard ship; now he was a rich merchant. With the mandarin whose son he had successfully treated for pox, he had taken over Rona-Lloyd and absorbed the company into Mandarin-Gold. What could his parents know of such complicated business arrangements? They were quite beyond their comprehension and so he deliberately told them little of his achievements, lest he should confuse them or they might think he was boasting.

And yet, without boasting at all, he had succeeded beyond his wildest imaginings. In a few years he had risen from the post of ship's surgeon aboard a second-class merchantman to become one of the most influential traders east of India.

As he sat now in his cabin, portholes pegged wide open, a glass of claret in his hand, he thought how strange life was that it allowed such a change and so quickly — and all through peddling a drug about which he had known nothing, apart from its medicinal qualities, before he arrived in the East. And if Marion had not gone away with her shopkeeper, he might still have been as naive as he was then.

He wondered what she was doing, where she was, how his parents looked. He wrote to them by each mail boat, as he was trying to do now, and he read their letters, but between them was this unexpected and unwished for gulf of experience and wealth as wide as the gulf that had separated Dives from Lazarus in the Bible story he had heard at Sunday school aeons of time ago.

He must go home, and see them before it was too late, for after they died there would be no reason to return. He still thought of Herne Bay as home, yet here was his home if it were anywhere. He was highly regarded by other merchants and accepted as one of the most successful men in commerce. And once accepted, Gunn had held his share of the coast trade — and then had branched out into other areas of speculation.

He was turning his attention to more legitimate trade, shipping tea and spices, lending money, at high interest rates, generally broadening the base of his operations, just in case China did suddenly open up its frontiers.

For local politics to impinge seriously on profits was a hazard he had never anticipated.

He felt in some measure responsible for these pathetic Goanese clerks and their families aboard his ships. But why had none of them ever sought to branch out on their own as he had done? Why would they rather remain subservient to him? They sought security under his authority, of course, but really he could guarantee them nothing they could not have secured for themselves, and on far better terms.

Captain Elliot's gig bumped against the *Hesperides,* and scattered Gunn's thoughts. He put away his paper and ink as Elliot came aboard.

'What's the news?' Gunn asked him.

'The Reverend Dr Gutzlaff is visiting the war junks near the shore, carrying two letters to the Chinese admiral. The first is a request for water, and the second, for food.'

'Why bother? We have enough of both to last us a week at least.'

'Not all are as fortunate.'

'I was not fortunate. I simply used foresight. But I will put Mackereth over the side to help.'

He called to him.

'Your brother in holy orders, the Reverend Dr Gutzlaff, is attempting to persuade the Chinese to give us food and water. You speak the dialect as well as he does. Pray put off in the longboat. Gutzlaff is visiting the junks on the starboard side. You approach those on the port side.'

'What about an escort?' asked Mackereth fearfully.

'There are two navy ships due from India,' Elliot explained; he was sorry for the wretched man. 'The Governor-General is sending the *Hyacinth,* an eighteen-gun frigate and another frigate, *Volage,* with twenty-eight guns.'

'You'll be safe enough,' Gunn said, grinning, enjoying the American's discomfiture. But why should he find such satisfaction in humiliating him? Could it be because Mackereth represented something, maybe some belief in God, that he had long ago lost, for now he believed only in himself?

Lin listened patiently to his emissary's report. 'And then, Your Excellency, the Barbarian Elliot and the Barbarian Gunn sent two other Barbarians, Gutzlaff and Mackereth, to plead with the captains to supply food and water.'

'With what result?'

'With this result, Your Excellency. They were ordered away speedily from each junk and advised to approach the next. When they reached the last of the line, that captain's answer was to send to the shore ordering the batteries to load their guns.'

'An excellent response,' said Lin approvingly. 'So what happened?'

'The two Barbarians spent six hours rowing in the Roads trying to persuade these captains from the course of their duty, without any success whatever. They returned to the Barbarian Elliot.'

'And?'

'And almost at that moment, Your Excellency, two British ships, with many guns pointing at the shore batteries, arrived off Hong Kong.'

'I see,' said Lin slowly. This put a different complexion on affairs. Despite the constant, reports of the feebleness of the Barbarians as soldiers and sailors, he knew that their guns could wreak terrible havoc on the junks. As with a spring tide under a strong moon, control of events was suddenly receding, from him, and he felt cold fingers of dismay around his heart.

Four men sat in Elliot's cabin, their faces grave.

The third man was a naval officer, Captain Henry Smith, who had been rowed over from his command, the *Volage.*

'There has been no response whatever from any of these captains,' Gunn reported.

Elliot nodded.

'I expected as much. But then it is probably death for them if they help us. They owe their duty to their Emperor, just as we owe ours to the Sovereign.'

'We have not come all this way, gentlemen, at high speed, to be made fools of by a lot of slit-eyed, pig-tailed, yellow-faced people in funny wooden boats,' Smith said gruffly. 'I suggest we take some speedy action against them.'

'I agree,' replied Elliot, surprising himself by his vehemence. 'I think they should feel the weight of our shot. We have tried everything else we can. I've been here for months, *years* in fact, Smith, urging moderation, and a temperate approach — and what do I get? *This.* We are now on the verge of being driven out of the China seas altogether.'

'I am not a man of war,' said Mackereth carefully. 'But rowing among the junks, I counted their guns, and they sport at least twenty times as many as we mount, not including the shore batteries.'

'To the devil with that,' said Smith. He was a big, hard, bluff man, eager for promotion. The best way to secure this speedily was to win a battle, and the greater the apparent odds, the more notable the victory. Caution and timidity were poor companions on any officer's journey to high command.

'We'll engage them before they can take aim. So I have your permission, Captain Elliot?'

'Yes,' said Elliot. 'I will deal with the junks to starboard. You take the rest and the shore batteries. And may God be with us all.'

'He is always on the winning side,' said Smith confidently.

'Amen,' said Mackereth.

Smith returned to the *Volage,* and for half an hour the ships rocked gently at anchor on the swell, and the sun moved relentlessly across the sky, and the children cried and the pigs grunted. And then the British guns began to fire.

Flocks of birds flew in terror from village temples, and in the singing silence after the broadside, the air was filled with the whacker of their frightened wings. The junks replied at once, but their cannonade sounded thin and feeble, like fireworks exploding, against the thundering broadside of nine guns from the *Hyacinth,* and then fourteen more from the *Volage,* with the crackle of lighter weapons from Gunn's *Hesperides* and other armed vessels.

For half an hour they fired, blowing away the sails of the junks and shelling the forts. Then the junks put out oars like long spindly fingers and the crews began to row frantically for the relative shelter of the shore. Smith, his guns recharged, followed them and picked them off one by one.

The sun began to glide down the sky; soon it would be dark. A white fog of powder smoke rolled across the milky sea of evening. Elliot sent MacPherson over to Captain Smith to urge him to break off the engagement. After all, they had punished the junks, they had upheld the honour of the British flag; there was nothing more to do.

He sat down in his cabin and wrote a report to Palmerston; the *Volage* could take, it back as far as Calcutta. Elliot's anger at the stupidity of the Chinese had evaporated as the first gun fired. Now he felt subdued, for this had not been a battle; it had been a massacre. Yet when the Chinese would not listen to the voice of reason, the only argument left was one for the mouths of the guns to utter.

And how could Lord Palmerston, sitting in his office in faraway London, with a coal fire to warm him and fog shrouding the streets, comprehend the mounting frustration of being confined for days in the stifling, sweating heat of an anchored ship, with water and provisions in short supply, and the knowledge that, on your decision alone, a whole Empire's eastern trade could depend?

So Elliot wrote carefully: "The violent and vexatious measures heaped upon Her Majesty's officers and subjects will, I trust, serve to excuse those feelings of irritation which have betrayed me into a measure that I am certain, under less trying circumstances, would be difficult indeed of vindication."

In other words, Elliot told himself bitterly, I lost my temper. Have I also lost everything for which I have been working out here?

Lin was worried.

'Are you *certain* that our war junks have been defeated?' he asked his emissary incredulously.

'Absolutely, Your Excellency. I was there. I saw them break and run.'

'This knowledge must be kept secret.'

'That is impossible, Your Excellency. Villagers saw it, hundreds of them. This news will spread like fire in summer grass.'

'Then we shall issue a proclamation saying that a great victory is ours. No, more than one. *Six* victories. That is a goodly number. Send in the secretary.'

'With speed, Your Excellency.'

The man turned and went out, and Lin sat, looking at the sun on the Pearl River, wondering how best to mould his account of events so that the Emperor would not blame him.

Still out of sight on that river, the English flotilla was slowly moving north to Macao. The Hong merchants were waiting for them, smiling. They knew who had won the engagement, whatever Chinese officials would no doubt later claim. They also knew the advantages of being on the winning side. There would no longer be any need for British crews to worry about decapitation should their ships be found to be carrying opium. After all, how could such sentences be enforced?

'So you see,' said Gunn, when Elliot told him this, 'Jardine *was* right all along. A little force can teach a very big lesson.'

'That has never been in doubt,' replied Elliot dryly. 'But who has learnt the lesson?'

IN WHICH ONE ACTION LEADS TO ANOTHER, AND THEN TO A FRIEND

Mackereth sat in his cabin in the *Hesperides,* whisky at his elbow, candles burning low in the globes. The night was oppressively hot, and sweat had pasted his shirt to his soft flesh.

On the table in front of him lay a sheaf of papers, some covered in Chinese characters he had painted carefully and neatly with a brush, others with English scriptural texts. He was finding it more difficult than usual to translate what had happened nearly two thousand years ago in Palestine and Judea and along the shores of Lake Galilee, into terms that illiterate peasants on the shore of the China seas could understand and accept.

He felt like a man making maps for a journey through a country from which no traveller had ever returned. He believed there were certain guide-posts and milestones, because others had told him they existed; but by the time he would discover whether this was so or not, it would be too late to warn those who came behind him.

Mackereth sipped his drink. It seemed an age since Jardine had first come to see him because Gutzlaff was ill, but it was only a few years. Now Matheson had returned to England, buying a great house and estate in Sussex, for something over half a million pounds sterling, it was said; and Jardine also was on his way home: Mackereth had heard he hoped to become a member of parliament. And all he was doing here was growing old.

Mackereth felt uneasy about his future. Gunn had become harder and more ruthless with each step he took towards greater wealth. Now he rented a Portuguese mansion over-looking the Praya in Macao; Mackereth's boys had told him of the grand parties that Gunn had given there, importing delicacies from Calcutta and even live turkeys from Manila. As many as sixty guests would sit down at polished tables to eat from silver plates with French wines served from crystal goblets, and. then there would be entertainments, music, dancing, flirting.

Always, Gunn seemed surrounded by beautiful women. The Chinese authorities would not permit the wives and daughters of European merchants to travel to Canton. And the heat, Mackereth knew, warmed the natures of these ladies to such an extent that any man of the slightest pretension to virility could pleasure one every night; and some, like Gunn, would pleasure several.

He contrasted Gunn's growing opulence and influence with his own declining standards. Even his boys brought him little pleasure now. There had been humiliating incidents when all he had been able to do was to press his soft flaccid, pale, pustuled body against their firm young limbs and sob out his love and longing for them. And, once or twice, they had laughed at him. Imagine, Chinese coolies' half-caste sons laughing at an American! It was degrading, mortifying. He had flung them from him and stormed into the other room, and then stood naked, panting, looking at himself in the wall mirror, and seeing a frightened old man look back.

There were other worries, too, apart from these private and personal torments of unperformance and envy. It was openly said now that war could break out any day between the English and the Chinese. Gunn, he knew, would be for any action that could open up the country to what he called legitimate trade; These were words that Mackereth had also heard from the American merchants; from the Portuguese, the French, from Russians and Austrians. Their wish for legitimate trade seemed to amount to very little more than talk about its undoubted advantages. But the trade they really, sought was illegitimate; the Coast Trade, the forbidden trade — opium. That was where the greatest and the easiest profits could be made.

Mackereth had seen what the drug did to those who smoked it; how soporific they became, how indolent, half asleep like giant, turgid sloths. He had also seen what effect opium had on those who trafficked in it. How it made them hard and greedy, eager for profit to pile on profit, although if they lived a thousand years, they could barely spend all the wealth they had already made.

It was as though the sweet poppy juice turned to iron in the veins of the men who sold it. It tainted their blood just as dangerously as it poisoned the lives - of those who smoked it or chewed it. This was the forbidden fruit, which ruined all who came into contact with it; now it was changing Gunn's character, with disastrous consequences for Mackereth. Gunn had already whittled down his price from a thousand to three hundred pounds, and was now threatening to drop him to two-fifty, because he disapproved of him peddling his tracts.

'I'm not paying you as a missionary,' Gunn had told him angrily one day, when Mackereth had gone to see him at his splendid house. 'I pay you as an *interpreter*. If you want to spend so much of your time hawking tracts about eternal life over one side of the vessel, you cannot expect me to pay you the same fee as if you were using all your energies and devoting all your time to interpreting for me on the other side.'

'Have I ever let you down, doctor?' asked Mackereth quietly. 'Whenever you have asked for me, I have been there. I have always given you a faithful translation of the most difficult dialects. Never once have you found me wanting. But no man can serve two masters. As it is written, no man can serve God and Mammon.'

'You appear to have done pretty well so far,' said Gunn sharply, 'so I feel you should accept a cut in salary. If you wish to distribute your own tracts, then make your own arrangements to do so. If I allow you time and opportunity to distribute them, then acknowledge that your time is my money.'

'There are other things in life but money, doctor. You must be rich now. More rich than you ever imagined.'

'How do *you* know what I imagined?' asked Gunn bitterly.

'You still seek so much, and yet I do not even own a roof over my head.'

'Then it is time you did, and time you thought about physical necessities, as well as spiritual possibilities,' Gunn told him.

And, of course, Mackereth had thought about them; indeed, such problems were rarely out of his mind. The Good Book had adjured him to take, no thought for tomorrow, for what he would put on or what he would -eat or how he would fare, for the Lord would provide. But nevertheless Mackereth sometimes felt that the Lord could do with a helping hand.

What would happen to him if there was a war, and all foreigners were driven out? He had no home to go to, no savings, no trade or qualification that guaranteed a living. He, more than most men, was utterly dependent on other people. This was why he had swallowed his qualms about helping the opium dealers. He had not struggled against their offers, as he should have done, for he had needed their money; and now he needed it more desperately than ever.

As MacPherson had said once, it was indeed strange how out of all the flowers and trees in the forest, their ancestors had discovered that the poppy could be persuaded to deliver up its deadly milk. Mackereth had seen poppies growing in India; fields red as blood in the Himalayan foothills, and others white as snow around Patna and Ghazipore, where they cultivated the white-flowered variety. There seemed something symbolic in the colours: though your sins be as scarlet, they shall be white as snow, Isaiah, chapter one, verse eighteen.

That meant forgiveness, of course, but there was nothing about the poppy juice that held any mercy, whether the petals were scarlet or white. The opium seemed soft and sweet and harmless at first, and you welcomed the gentle oblivion that it brought. But once you had tasted it or smoked it, you rarely could escape from its terrible spell. The poppy's petals, soft as a butterfly's gossamer, wings, turned to iron; the attraction was that of the chain and the manacle. You could not break free from the bondage of the iron poppy on your own; and how" could anyone else help you when so many were so eager to see others enslaved?

And he, Selmer Mackereth, had played his part in spreading this evil drug, the fruit of the iron poppy, the flower that held the sweetness of the grave.

How I have fallen short of the glory of God, he thought wretchedly. But what if war came, and he could earn no money, even in so vile a fashion as interpreting the commands of opium-traffickers? What would he do then: What *could* he do?

Mackereth knelt down at the side of the table, his face pressed against the cool wood, and prayed to God that if this happened, there might somehow be a place- found for him. Or if he had nothing left to do on earth, would it be possible for the Almighty to accept his servant at last into Heaven?

Gunn hurried into Elliot's office in Macao.

'Have you heard about this merchantman, *Thomas Coutts?*' he asked him.

'What about her?'

'Her master has taken some lawyer's opinion in Calcutta as to whether your order forbidding British ships to go to Canton is sustainable. He says it is not. Since the ship is not carrying mud, the lawyer says he has nothing to fear. He has accordingly applied personally to Commissioner Lin, and had been given a safe conduct pass.'

'The damned fool!' shouted Elliot, jumping up from his seat. By doing this the captain had placed a British ship and crew in Lin's power. Lin would now insist that *every* ship could only sail on the same conditions. Those who refused could be threatened with destruction.

How incredible that a British captain seemed incapable of understanding that every order Elliot issued had a meaning, and was part of his strategy for restoring equilibrium to the area, not simply a personal whim or wish!

'How many ships are waiting down river?' asked Gunn.

'Sixty, at least. And Smith's two frigates. I'll inform him of this immediately. Have you a fast gig to send him a message by MacPherson?'

'Of course,' said Gunn. 'It can leave within the hour.'

Elliot sat down to write his instructions. First, in this grave conjuncture menacing the liberty, lives and properties of British subjects, Smith was to collect the entire merchant fleet and anchor it opposite the village of Tungku, near Chuenpee, the position of which he already knew.

Then he was to take his two frigates to the Bogue and address a moderate but firm communication to the Chinese admiral there to the effect that they could not be held to ransom in this fashion.

MacPherson delivered the letter personally to Captain Smith aboard the *Volage*.

'This looks like trouble,' said Smith, not without some pleasure. He had felt a fool waiting for six hours in the hot sun, while Gutzlaff and Mackereth rowed around the junks asking for provisions. He had thoroughly enjoyed the brief action that had followed, but. such a one-sided engagement could not be dignified by the name of a battle, even in his most optimistic despatch. But what Elliot now proposed might well be eventually described in such terms — if he handled his side of things properly.

It was not, in Smith's nature to wait. He believed that the man who got his blow in first invariably won the fight; and nothing in his career so far had disturbed his faith in this belief.

'I used to be mate in the *Black Boy*,' said MacPherson, gauging his man: 'You'll have a strong wind against you if you're sailing up-river.'

'We sail better against the wind,' retorted Smith sharply; he did not need some ex-merchant sailor to instruct him in the art of seamanship.

'We also passed a big fleet of Chinese junks waiting for any approaching vessels.'

'The bigger the fleet, the better the target,' replied Smith shortly, and went to his cabin to draft out two letters, one to the local Chinese admiral, with a copy to Viceroy Lin.

That evening, the two frigates sailed north, tacking laboriously against wind and current. They took four days to reach Chuenpee, where they thankfully dropped anchors a mile beneath the shore battery.

Ahead of them lay fifteen war junks with painted eyes and painted guns, and fourteen fireboats stacked high with kindling wood and saltpetre. If the Chinese released these vessels at night, with sails lashed and rudders locked, they would sweep down river and either collide among themselves or hit the British frigates. In either case they would start an inferno that, with the wind, could reduce all ships in the area to floating stacks of kindling-wood.

A number of armed British merchantmen, and all Gunn's clippers, with armament mounted and charges ready, now joined the two British men-of-war. Elliot arrived in a gig as MacPherson, with Mackereth to interpret, was setting off in the *Volage's* longboat, against the running tide, to row to the Chinese flagship.

They shouted up the sheer wooden wall, ornamented with grotesque red and blue and yellow dragons with staring eyes, and garish representations of blazing cannon mouths. An officer received both letters, engaged in some high-pitched chatter with Mackereth, and then they rowed away.

'What's the admiral's name? asked MacPherson.

'Kuan T'ien-P'ei. He's a great friend of Lin. They paint fans together and write couplets. He is a scholar as much as a sailor, and a very fine one, I hear.'

MacPherson grunted; he had nothing in common with such a man. They climbed up the ladder into the *Volage*.

'Well?' asked Smith.

'An officer accepted both letters,' Mackereth reported.

'What about a reply?'

'They will deliver their answer to us tomorrow.'

'Until then,' Elliot told Smith, 'I want every ship to mount a double watch in case swimmers with explosive mines, or fire boats, are put out against us, or even come against us accidentally if their moorings break. Lin has either to engage us or back down. I am not sure which choice he will take.'

Next morning, at nine o'clock, the Hour of the Snake, as the sun turned the river to liquid gold, they had their answer. A fast crab, a small boat bristling with oars, bumped alongside the *Volage* and an officer handed up a package, bowed, smiled, and withdrew.

'Open it,' ordered Elliot tensely.

Mackereth, expecting a scroll with painted Chinese characters, cut the string with a knife and carefully unwrapped the paper. Inside, lay Captain Smith's letter to the Chinese admiral, unopened.

'There's your answer,' he said flatly. 'They are going to fight.'

As he spoke, the look-out from the crow's nest called down: 'Chinese squadron approaching.'

'Prepare to engage,' said Elliot briefly. 'But hold your fire. Let them come well within range.'

The flags making the signal fluttered up to the mast-head. On every ship crews, stripped to the waist, bodies brown with the sun and oiled with sweat, their long hair in tarred pigtails, leapt to the guns. One man with a glass aboard each vessel watched the *Volage* for the signal flags that would give them their orders.

Not knowing all this, ignorant of the significance of the flags, one above the other, and secure in their own delusion of supremacy, the Chinese junks and fire-boats came on downstream, moving fast with wind and current.

'When shall I engage, sir?' asked Smith. After all, Captain Elliot was in command of all British vessels, and so, would claim the credit if the day went well. Since he advocated allowing the Chinese to approach what Smith thought was unnecessarily close, it was only right that he should issue the crucial order.

As the junks and fireboats came within two hundred yards, Elliot was about to say, '*Now,*' when the. Chinese captains dropped anchor and the strange fleet, long banners streaming in the wind, stopped.in a line that stretched from bank to bank.

'Send another message to the admiral,' said Elliot. 'This looks like a show of force. I think they are bluffing. Order them to turn back.'

'And threaten them if they do not?'

'Not yet. Just give them that order.'

Again, the longboat set off to the admiral's, flagship. This time, the admiral gave orders for it to wait while he composed a reply.

Back aboard the *Volage,* Mackereth translated in a trembling voice: 'All that I, the admiral, want is the murderous Barbarian who killed Lin Wei-Hi. As soon as a time is named when he will be given up, my ships will return to the Bogue. Otherwise, by no means whatsoever will I accede. This is my answer.'

'Who is Lin Wei-Hi?' asked Smith curiously.

'A Chinaman some drunken sailors killed in a brawl in a

village months ago,' said Elliot. 'We could never find out who killed him. I have explained all that to them time and again.'

'They do not seem to have accepted your explanations, sir,' said Smith.

'You are right, Smith, they do not.'

'I don't trust them, sir,' said Smith. 'We are gravely outnumbered, and all the batteries on shore will be trained on us.'

'They cannot traverse their guns,' MacPherson reminded him.

'We have been anchored here so long they could practically build new batteries, with all guns laid on us',' retorted Smith bitterly. 'It seems to me, sir, that I have only two choices. One is to retire downriver to our merchantmen, and the other is to engage these yellow swine.'

'It would never do for the Navy to retire,' said Elliot slowly. But, on the other hand, how could he sanction what was virtually war between two empires, one young and restless and expanding, the other old and soporific, locked in its fading dreams of a past when there had been no gunboats, no steam engines, nothing at all of danger or value beyond its own Great Wall?

Elliot bit his lower lip in perplexity. The waves lapped and chuckled beneath the bows of the frigate, and beams creaked as the running tide persuaded her hull against the anchors. He had no idea what the government in London proposed to do about the pressing matters on which he had sent them reports, or if they intended doing anything. It would be months before he had their replies, if indeed he ever received them.

And here he had to decide within minutes, otherwise it was possible he might not have the opportunity of making any decision at all. If the Chinese released their fireboats, they could be beaten before they had begun to fight. Yet to retire now would be a loss of face from which they might never recover.

'I would engage them,' said Gunn, guessing Elliot's thoughts. 'We did not make an Empire by running away, or waiting for instructions from people at home who have never been farther east than Herne Bay.'

How odd that homely name sounded in this context of a battle no-one wanted!

'I do not *want* to engage them,' replied Elliot. 'I have always believed that discussion is more adult than force.'

'They aren't adults,' said MacPherson shortly. 'They're Chinese. Heathen.'

'Until the Lord moves among them,' said Mackereth hastily.

'Even if we do retire, sir,' said Smith, 'and they follow us and put their fire-boats in among our merchantmen, I submit I can do nothing to save our ships. Nothing at all. We couldn't even rescue the poor devils aboard them. As I see it, we have *no alternative* but to fire. With your permission, sir?'

'You have my permission,' said Elliot sadly, and turned away.

Up went the signal: *Engage.*

One by one the British armed merchantmen fell into line behind the *Volage.* A sudden wind filled their white sails which swelled like the breasts of giant pouter pigeons, and they began, to run broadside across the Chinese line. Up went the next signal: *Fire.*

The first broadside, from the *Volage* hit a fireboat, which blew up with an explosion that numbed Gunn's ear-drums. The second lifted a war junk right out of the water. Men, arms and legs waving frantically, spars, fragments of the latticed, sail, ropes, gun barrels, fluttered up and then down into the sea, already foaming from the fury of the attack.

The Chinese were also firing, but their guns were locked in one position and could not move. And as their ships were anchored, they could not raise the anchors in time to steer into the men-of-war. Also, the, British ships were now so close that the Chinese cannonballs were trundling harmlessly twenty feet above, their decks to splash into the sea two hundred yards behind them.

The Chinese crews wrenched at their anchor chains to turn

and scatter, for they were like pinioned targets. Some were blown to pieces; others sank instantly on their anchors. Several crews deserted their ships in fast crabs and rowed away furiously. The Chinese admiral Kuan T'ien P'ei, astonished and mortified by the overwhelming fire power of the supposedly effete Barbarians, stood bravely on the high stern of his junk as it sank slowly, shouting desperate orders that none of his crew heard, and could not have carried out if they had heard.

The *Hyacinth* ranged alongside, her guns trained on this most important target. One whiff of grape, and his sinking junk would be like the rest, a mass of jagged beams, stained red with the blood of her crew.

Every gunner on both sides seemed to be reloading. There was a sudden silence, punctured only by the screams of the wounded, the crash of splitting wood and breaking masts. Elliot seized a voice trumpet and shouted to the captain of the *Hyacinth*.

'Don't sink him! Let the admiral go free! He has fought well!'

The *Hyacinth* turned away reluctantly in search of other targets, and the waterlogged junk, like a wounded, broken-backed sea beast, moved slowly on towards the shore, and the humiliation of defeat.

Volley now followed volley, until the river was littered with floating beams from shore to shore, and desperate swimmers and drowning men waved their hands hopelessly for help. One by one they sank, and the cries of the wounded grew fainter as the current carried them away, and then the water was dotted with, hump-back bodies, floating like bundles of bloodied rags.

The banks of the river were crowded with villagers come out as though to see some great sporting spectacle. They were cheering, and their voices sounded shrill and thin across the troubled river. Chinese gunners had left their forts and climbed on the turrets for a better view. Smoke .blew thick and white, hanging like a strange acrid mist above the shining river, mercifully blurring the outlines of blazing fireboats and sinking junks.

'Disengage,' ordered Smith laconically, and the signal ran up to the masthead.

'Well,' said Elliot, 'that was a sharp action.'

It had also been astonishingly short; only forty-five minutes by his German silver hunter. How quick it was to decide an argument by force, that would have taken months to resolve by discussion, waiting for advice from London! It was true, of course, that you had to make your own decisions in such peculiar and unparalleled circumstances. It was also true that in these circumstances you often made decisions you felt were wrong, or at least not wholly right, because you had no time to reach better ones, and the other side were too stubborn and obdurate to allow you that time.

Now the Chinese had lost all advantage and credibility as an opponent to Western will and influence. They were as vulnerable as their paper houses. There must be a lesson here somewhere, he thought; maybe it was that painted guns fired no bullets.

Elliot should have felt elated. Instead, he felt immeasurably sad, sickened by the needless slaughter, depressed at the damage to a nation's pride, which he guessed would take generations to remedy.

'What are our casualties?' asked Smith. He had a report to make, 'and it would make good reading. He felt almost cheerful.

'One sailor wounded aboard our ship, sir,' replied the first officer. 'Nothing serious fortunately. And one killed by a splinter aboard the *Hesperides*.'

'Who?' asked Gunn in a hoarse whisper. This was his ship, his first, his special charge. Fear gripped his throat like a strangler's hands.

'No-one special, Sir. Only a Chink woman. Sort of camp follower; Name of Ling Fai.'

The street lamps wore dim soft haloes in the London fog that muffled the clop of the horses' hooves and the faint cries of the street-sellers. Jardine climbed out of his carriage, and hurriedly walked up the steps of the Foreign Office to meet Lord Palmerston. After the prodigal heat of the East, he hated the chill and the cold that made his joints creak like rusty hinges.

He had been in London for some months, but news travelled very slowly, and the Government had many other matters of concern, so that what had appeared of great importance in Canton or Macao on the far side of the globe seemed infinitely less pressing here. Its significance diminished like a scene viewed through the wrong end of a telescope, and it took its turn behind more urgent domestic problems.

But now, at last, after appointments made and broken, Jardine had received a letter from Lord Palmerston asking him to attend on him, to explain what he considered should be done over the irritating matter of China trade.

Jardine was in a far stronger position to urge the use of force to solve a problem that had dragged on in various degrees of intensity for more than a hundred years, than when he had first arrived, in London.

Since then, the directors of thirty-nine Manchester cotton firms had addressed an urgent petition to the Government, explaining that they had exported cotton goods worth half a million pounds sterling to Canton. Because of the intransigent attitude of the Chinese, all these goods were at risk — and so was their money.

As a result, some of their firms faced imminent financial ruin, and thousands of workers, largely women and children already on starvation wages of a few shillings a week, would now be thrown on the resources of their parishes as paupers.

In addition, the directors of ninety-six London manufacturing firms, had sent a similar petition regarding their goods, and other merchants in Blackburn and Bristol, in Liverpool and Leeds, had also urged the Government to take swift and positive action to protect British subjects, and British goods in China for which they had not yet been paid.

The Whig Government realized the damage that inaction could do to them politically, but they cherished a reputation for enlightened thought and action—such as providing free education and improving the Poor Law and abolishing slavery. They did not wish now to be accused of going to war to succour opium smugglers. Accordingly, they had prevaricated and done nothing, hoping that these problems would somehow solve themselves. But instead, they had grown worse. Jardine was now determined that this indecision should end.

'The Foreign Secretary is awaiting you, sir,' the butler told him, as he gave his name, and opened the inner doors.

Palmerston stood behind the huge table that dominated his room. He was wearing his favourite suit of dark green tweed. His hair was still dark and thick, and hot yet flecked with grey, which, in years to come, he would tint carefully to appear younger than he was.

He had been Foreign Secretary for nearly ten years, except for a short time under Peel's Tory Government, and he watched Jardine with interest as they shook hands. They both spoke the same language of action. As Palmerston had written: 'Half-civilized governments, such as those in China, Portugal and Spanish America; all require a dressing every eight or ten years to keep, them in order.'

Various officials filed in and were introduced, and then took their places around the table.

Jardine sat at Palmerston's right hand, and explained in his quiet unemotional voice the background to the situation in Canton. He produced maps and charts to show the depths of water off the coast, the terrain of the country should troops be needed, the location of roads and towns and wells.

'Now, sir,' said Palmerston, as he finished, 'we are much in your debt for this cogent summary of a long and grievous problem. Assuming for the moment that you, sir, were in my position as Her Majesty's Foreign Secretary, what action would *you* feel justified in taking? Remembering, of course, that the opium trade is not a cause over which our supporters would wish the Government to go to war.'

'I have given this matter much thought, both in China and since I have been here in London. Were I in your position, Minister, I would proceed in the following manner.

'First, having attempted over many years to understand the Chinese, conundrum, I would advocate a stronger approach to their intransigence. Our minimum requirements for such an approach would be at least seven thousand men in transports, with a naval force of two ships of the line, plus, say, two frigates and two other, vessels of shallow draught able to sail up any river. I would prefer these last two to be steam paddle-boats, independent of any wind.

'I would assemble this force at the mouth of the Pei-ho River that leads to the capital, Peking. From there I would send a message to the Emperor demanding an apology for repeated and gratuitous insults to the British flag, to the British sovereign, and to British subjects, individually and collectively.

'I would also demand payment for the twenty thousand odd chests of opium your representative, Captain Elliot, has seen fit to surrender for reasons that are by no means clear to me. Thirdly, I would demand a treaty that allowed free trade with all western nations through four ports which could each become as busy as Liverpool. These would be Amoy, Foochow, Ningpo and Shanghai.'

'Those are very serious demands to make of any ruler,' said Palmerston, much impressed. 'What if the Emperor refused them, as I feel he would be bound to do? After all, China has a huge population and, I am informed, a considerable navy and army.'

'In numbers, yes,' agreed Jardine. 'But in achievement and armament and calibre of fighting men, both can virtually be discounted. Assuming, Minister, that the Emperor refused my demands — and they are *demands,* not requests — I would immediately seize a number of islands along the coast, or one large island, such as Chusan, until the demands were met. The Chinese could not afford to lose face indefinitely, so they would have to submit — simply because they could not be rid of us in any other way.

'This would end — I hope for ever — this nonsense of Hong merchants, vast bribes and an artificially short trading season each year at Canton. It would also throw open the whole country and its enormous potential markets to the commercial initiative of Britain and other manufacturing countries.

'Various Governments have tried to do this by diplomatic means over the last century or so, but they have not succeeded, because the Chinese, like other Eastern races, only understand one persuader — *force!*

'There would be a second benefit, too, in that the Coast Trade could be put on a far sounder and more secure basis than it enjoys at present. But there would be no need at this stage to mention this very great advantage.

'The first would be a glittering prize enough for any administration when it came to re-election. The righting of a great wrong. A huge foreign country made to swallow its insults by virtually a handful of British soldiers and Jack Tars!'

'Parliament would debate it, of course,' pointed out Palmerston.

'Of course,' agreed Jardine. 'But you could then put up some orator like young Lord Macauley,' the Secretary of State for War. He would surely carry all with a speech on the lines that our Empire has been built by men of spirit who have treated orders from England as so much wastepaper.

'Should the Opposition claim that you gave Captain Elliot no specific orders about stopping the drug traffic, he would reply that *of course* you did not, for the trade was impossible to stop. Here in England, we maintain a preventative service of Customs officers, all brave and skilled, no less than six thousand strong. I am informed they command an annual budget of half a million pounds. We also maintain fifty cruisers around our coasts and *still* about six hundred thousand gallons of brandy and a corresponding amount of tobacco is said to slip through their watchful fingers *every year.* How many more men, how much greater expense, would your government incur if they had attempted to stop *all* smuggling in China, *ten thousand miles away?* Minister, with that argument you would carry the day.'

'I incline to the view that you may very well be right, Dr Jardine,' said Palmerston slowly. 'Tell me, have you ever thought of a political career for yourself?'

'Frequently.'

Jardine did not add that some of his rivals thought this an impossible ambition for him, but he knew they were wrong. He kept his promises, and promises were the pivots by which orators swung voters to their view as rudders turned his fleet of clippers.

'I will ascertain what seats may become available in time for the next election,' said Palmerston. 'A man of your ability, Jardine, with your commercial acumen, your professional sense of integrity and your considerable rhetoric would be a great advantage in any Parliament.

'Now, unless there are any questions, gentlemen, I will ask Dr Jardine to let us have a note of his recommendations and then I suggest we adjourn.'

There were no questions.

'Earth to earth, dust to dust; the Lord giveth and the Lord taketh away; blessed be the name of the Lord.'

Mackereth's voice droned on above the grave. Behind him, the bell in the church of St James the Apostle, Macao, boomed out its lonely, solitary knell.

'I never knew she was a Christian,' said Gunn afterwards, as they walked back to his great house. In fact, he had known very little about Ling Fai. She had been there when he wanted her, like a servant or a hireling. She had been the second woman he had known sexually which would never be the same as the first, but still it meant more, a little more, than the dozens he had slept with since. But she had still only been a Chinese, even if she were a Christian.

'She became a Christian,' MacPherson explained, 'just after we took over the *Hesperides*.'

'She never mentioned it,' said Gunn, remembering her scented body hard against his, her clutching fingers, her warm tongue like a darting snake.

'Oh, yes, the Reverend Mackereth accepted her into the Church.'

So much happening, and he had known nothing about it; all he had been concerned with was cutting down the opposition and then in building up his trade and his fortune. Well, it was too late to alter things now; years too late.

'She was attached to you,' MacPherson went on.

'And I liked her,' replied Gunn carefully. 'Very much.'

'I don't mean *liked*. I would not say that a Chink woman can love, doctor. But Ling Fai came very close to it.'

'You mean, loving you?'

'No. *You!*'

'I never realized that,' said Gunn. And of course he hadn't. It had just been a physical thing to him; and yet he had *liked* her. And he missed her now she was no longer there, so far as he missed anyone; now she would never be there again, would never come silently to his cabin at dusk, or early morning; never again lie with him.

There had been many other women in Macao and in the *Hesperides;* in the new house he was building at Singapore, and the other mansion he rented in Manila, because Spanish merchants there were eager to invest in the opium trade. But of them all, matrons with husbands away at Canton, or daughters fresh and passionate and soft as wild hibiscus, he only remembered a few.

The Parsee's daughter and Ling Fai were both like gentle voices on the evening wind, brought back by a sudden scent or a snatch of melody that transported him instantly over chasms of time, down the long cold aisles of the past, where unforgotten things remained.

It was better that they should remain there, too, he thought, for if they came too close, if they impinged on the present, they proved you were not as self-sufficient as you seemed. They would show others that deep down inside you lay a patch of longing and loneliness that might grow and colour all your achievements, if you allowed it to do so, as you never would, because you could never dare to.

But MacPherson was still talking, splintering his dreams; MacPherson, who had saved his life, who trusted him; who he had rewarded by seducing his woman; and now she had gone from both of them.

'Glad to see the home government is acting at last Sixteen men-o'-war, twenty-seven troop transports packed with Irish, Scots and Indian troops, four armed steamers from the Company's fleet — all to teach Lin a lesson.'

'We taught him a lesson back at Chuenpee,' said Smith, anxious to establish his importance with these two richer men.

'I hear that he didn't pass on to the Court what *actually* happened there. He made it put to be a victory. Said he'd had *six* victories, in fact. He called them the Six Smashing Blows. I wonder if the Emperor believed him?'

'Even the Son of Heaven has to believe someone,' said Gunn. But then, he thought, we all do; even when it is only ourselves.

'They'll be forced to believe we mean business now,' said MacPherson. 'It will change life here, though, as we have known it for years.'

'For the better,' promised Gunn.

'I wonder,' said MacPherson. 'I really do wonder. Truth is, doctor, I like living here as it is. I like the food, the atmosphere, the sun. I even quite like the Chinese. But it will all change now. Even the Chinese. The good days are ending, doctor.'

'Everything's ending,' said Gunn. 'But it will see our time out. Come up and have a claret with me and the Reverend Mackereth. I was very touched by his service.'

'He'll be saying one for us one day, no doubt,' said MacPherson lugubriously, as they began to climb the stairs into the coolness of the huge stone house.

Lin laid down his fan, listening intently as the emissary's astonishing story unfolded.

'Are you *certain* about this number of Barbarian troops?' he asked him.

'Absolutely, Your Excellency. Our agent has relations in Singapore. They personally counted the number of men aboard each vessel.'

'We still outnumber them ten thousand to one.'

'Agreed. But they have qualities our troops do not possess, Your Excellency. *Discipline. A plan.* Also, they are not half asleep through opium, or in the mud-smugglers' pay, like so many of our soldiers and their officers.'

'You are right,' agreed Lin bitterly. 'Our leaders are no doubt admirable calligraphists. But they know nothing of war as the western Barbarians wage it. Now — withdraw!'

The man scuttled away, and Lin was left alone with his thoughts. They made sombre, unhappy company. What would the Emperor say to this news? The approach of the Barbarians in such numbers could not be ascribed to rumour and lying report. And that they were determined to march on Peking as well as Canton? This was desperate news.

Lin knew how easily the painted fortresses with their painted cannons would fall before any determined assault. He knew how thousands of locals would turn out enthusiastically to look at the Barbarians, just as they filled the streets to see travelling circuses with sideshows; anything to enliven dull lives. They would not realize the danger these Red-Bristled Ones represented, but then they offered no danger to the peasants, for the peasants had nothing to lose. The Barbarians were only dangerous to mandarins, to governors, to the Emperor, who could lose everything.

How deplorable that events should have come to this! He had heard surprisingly good reports of the Barbarian Elliot; that he was a gentle, kind man who worshipped his own strange God, who adhered to the odd code of honour the Barbarians called their own. If only it had been possible for them to meet over black tea or rice wine and discuss their problems and search for a happy and just solution. But now their discussion would take place through the mouths of cannons, and the tongues that talked would be tongues of flame and death.

Lin gave a sigh of sadness at the folly of it all.

Then he straightened his shoulders. He would have to inform the Emperor what he had just heard. Or at least as little of it as he thought prudent to pass on. Reluctantly, he rang his bell and called for his secretary

The Emperor looked up slowly from his three goldfish in their crystal bowl into the unhappy eyes of the familiar young man of good family who had brought him the news.

'You mean that these unspeakable Barbarians are even now approaching Our capital, the centre of the Celestial Kingdom — as well as Canton?'

'Not only does His Excellency the Commissioner Lin say they are approaching Canton, Your Majesty, but I have seen their vessels and heard their soldiers sing as_ they sail towards Pei-ho River. I have seen their guns and the iron ships propelled by fire and steam. They will be here within days.'

'Days!' repeated the Emperor in astonishment. Days are nothing in the face of eternity. We are the timeless ones. We will absorb them and destroy them, and those who do not die We will send back naked and ruined. Are We not right? Answer, with honesty! The Imperial Wish!'

'Since you seek an honest opinion, Your Majesty, however

unworthy I am. for that honour, it is with deepest humility and the greatest respect and reluctance that I have to disagree.

'The Barbarians have guns of such, power they can fire from so far away that they cannot even see their target. They have ships that will outsail our whole fleet. And they have determination, because they are far from their own barren little islands. This last quality, Your Majesty, is one that some of our commanders, with generations of easy living behind them, would appear to lack. They have nothing to lose, but Your Majesty has everything.'

The Emperor looked at the young man and realized he spoke the truth. He felt also much to blame for this incredible situation. He had allowed himself to be cocooned in a world of make-believe and illusion, where a painted gun was as deadly as one that fired, a reported victory as important as a proper conquest. Fantasy had replaced reality, and he had been lulled into a soporific dream by the honeyed words of men who told him not what was happening, but what he wished was happening.

Of course, as the Son of Heaven, the one man in all-the world who stood closest to God, Tao could never admit fallibility. So he would have to throw the blame on the weakness and gullibility of others. That would not be difficult; he was surrounded by dissemblers as a great tree in the forest is hemmed in by hollow, rotten elms.

The Emperor dismissed the messenger and sent for his secretary.

'To Special Commissioner Lin,' he said briefly. You have dissembled to Us, disguising in your despatches the true colour of affairs.

'So far from having been of any help, you have caused the waves of confusion to arise. A thousand interminable disorders are sprouting. You have behaved as if your arms were tied. You are no better than a wooden image. And as We contemplate your grievous failings, We fall a prey to anger and melancholy.

'Your official seals shall be immediately taken from you, and with the speed of flames you shall hasten to Peking, where We will see how you may answer Our questions. Respect this! The words of the Emperor.'

Lin read the Emperor's Scroll and then rolled it up, no inkling of his feelings showing on his face, as deliberately expressionless as a water-melon. He nodded a dismissal to the messenger, and only when he was alone did he stand wearily, shoulders hunched, allowing himself the rare luxury of showing his feelings in his face.

He looked into the ornamented mirror in the, wall and a defeated old man stared back at him. He had achieved more than any other Commissioner for a hundred years in subduing the Coast Trade. He had even set up a clinic outside Canton, where the worst opium addicts were admitted: men with distorted necks, fingers clutched like claws, teeth blackened, gums separated, their skins yellow as lemons, too enfeebled to walk or even to think for themselves. Here these living caricatures, had responded to a special treatment of. hunum-aloes, crushed orchid petals, and saxifrage, a rock plant whose yellow and red flowers symbolized his bright hopes, now all withered and dead.

He had also proved to the Barbarians that a Chinese Edict could be backed by Chinese determination, and that all officials were not corruptible. But what were these achievements by a man who had made his own way, against a nest of aristocratic sycophants at Court? And now he knew he was beaten, not only by them, but also by distance and communication; the time a message took to reach Peking, and an answer to return, the basic weakness that the Emperor knew nothing about events and conditions in Canton, and could not be bothered to learn.

For how could Lin alone deal effectively with Barbarians when even the Chinese marines stationed in Canton boasted that their official pay was but one hundredth part of what they received — and the other ninety-nine came from .opium dealers? Was it likely that such troops would act with vigour against the unspeakable Barbarians who had made them rich?

He realized what fate awaited him in, Peking: the long and humiliating trial with its predetermined end, and then exile in some remote mountainous spot where winds howled end-lessly like hungry wolves, where mists blotted, out the jagged peaks, and the damp humours of high altitude would, eat into his joints like rust into iron. And because he had tried so hard, and had so nearly achieved his Emperor's aims, his fall would be all the greater, all the harsher, and the more grievous to bear.

But at least he was not to be led away over the mountain roads on chains like so many other officials who fell short of some impossible Imperial edict. Even so, how different would be his departure from his triumphant arrival a year before! Why — and Lin smiled at the thought — he might even meet his predecessor, Viceroy Lu, in exile. No doubt they would find much to discuss.

But it was useless dwelling on what might have been, and what so nearly could have been. He would accept defeat, hu-miliation, even the ultimate disgrace of strangulation, if the Emperor so wished, as he had accepted his successes of the past months. How wrong that piece of roebuck flesh had proved! It was not promotion of which Lin had been assured, but degradation and defeat

'I hear Lin's gone,' said Gunn, pouring more claret.

'Yes,' agreed Elliot. 'The Emperor's sent down a new viceroy, a Manchu. One of his own family. A very rich man, apparently. Name of Kishen.'

'How far are our troops now from Peking?' asked MacPher-son.

'They could take it at any time they like,' said Gunn. 'They've already blockaded the mouths of the Yangtze River and the Pei-ho.'

'It's impossible, dealing with these people,' said Elliot testily. 'I received a personal letter from Lord Palmerston, marked for the Chinese Government, by the last mail ship. It described these chests of opium we gave up as being the ransom for the lives of all of us in Canton, and demanded that this opium must be restored or its equivalent in money paid. But how the devil am I to deliver this?

'I gave it into the hand of one of the men-of-war captains, and he took it to Amoy and attempted to land in a small boat under the flag on truce. But the Chinese had never heard of such a flag and refused to let them land. So we can't deliver the letter that contains the terms under which we'll stop fighting! Did you ever hear of such an absurd situation?'

'They are asking to be destroyed,' agreed Gunn. Even as he spoke, he felt uneasy that all this was happening. The attack in such force had been unnecessary, and neither side would be the victor. Both would nurture their own legends of duplicity or glory, to be inflated and handed down in the folklore that schoolmasters dignified by the name of history.

If only it had been possible for both sides to talk, to explain what they wanted, what they could not allow, what concessions they were prepared to give, how different the outcome would have been! If only. Were they not the two saddest words in any language?

He poured himself more claret; He felt suddenly overwhelmingly weary, jaded and jaundiced. Maybe he had been out East for too long; perhaps the heat and humidity were to blame.

'Did you hear what's happened to Gutzlaff?' he asked Mackereth; anything to break the spell of gloom that would otherwise cast its chains around him.

'No.'

'They've appointed him a magistrate at Ningpo, one of the four new ports where the Chinese are to grant us trading rights.'

'Gutzlaff has done very well,' agreed Mackereth, and bitterly contrasted his own wretched situation and indefinite future. He should have managed things better when he had money and authority, for now he had neither. He was an object of contempt, not only to the Chinese and the British, but worst of all, to himself.

He turned and went out of the room, and walked back to his own house. He walked slowly because his eyes were blinded with tears of mortification and defeat.

IN WHICH SOME WINNERS APPEAR AS LOSERS

Kishen the Manchu sat in Lin's chair and sipped his milkless, sugarless tea, his narrow eyes flickering like lizards' tongues around his predecessor's room.

Of course, Lin was only a peasant who had secured his promotion by the immense effort of passing countless examinations. He had not been born to wealth and ease, and the room reflected his spartan, simple character. Kishen would have to alter this; it would need complete redecoration. He would set the work in hand just as soon as he had dealt with this tedious matter regarding the Barbarians.

The Emperor was as remote from all realities as the sun is estranged from the moon, so he would send him soothing messages, assuring him that the trouble at Canton was not worthy of the briefest of his Holy Glances. It was entirely a matter between the Red-Bristled Barbarians and corrupt and inefficient Chinese officials of the lowest and most insignificant class. It would all be dealt with speedily, as such unimportant altercations were always resolved when men of the high traditions and ancient lineage of Manchu turned their attentions to them.

This Barbarian Elliot, for example, was thousands of miles away from his own Government; and possibly his rulers were as ignorant of the true facts as the Emperor. Kishen would cajole and praise and flatter him, and somehow undertakings that would last at least long enough to see Kishen put of Canton and back on his vast ancestral estates, would be agreed.

He accepted the supremacy of British firepower and their troops, and those black soldiers from India in their outlandish uniforms, who would doggedly advance on a heavily defended fort and put to the bayonet or musket all its defenders, without regard to their own casualties.

Life was full of problems, and like a chess game, with real people as pawns, each possessed its own exhilaration. Problems, after all, only existed to be solved, as rivers existed to be bridged.

But in those comfortable and, soothing thoughts, Kishen, plump, rich, infinitely soft, a connoisseur of women with small pointed breasts, of mature rice wines and scented, spiced meals, completely miscalculated the dogged, earnest character of Captain Elliot.

Sitting in his room overlooking the Praya in Macao, Elliot, received deputation after deputation from Kishen promising discussions, talks, anything but action. Finally, unable to accept any further procrastinations, and mindful of the approach of the rainy season; when all military activity would slow down, Elliot gave permission for British troops to seize two forts at the mouth of the Bogue which commanded the approach to Canton.

This was intended as an indication of what would follow if Kishen did not come to terms, and the main merit of the engagement was that it was short. The dying January afternoon ended with Chinese soldiers throwing away their bows and arrows and scattering across the paddy fields to escape the terror of British cannon.

Within an hour, both forts were taken and the Union Jack fluttered from the highest pinnacle. The advancing troops counted five hundred-Chinese dead and three hundred lying wounded. On the British side, there were no casualties whatever.

The way was now open to seize Canton, and at the same time; and at the other extremity of the Kingdom, to storm the ramparts of Peking. Kishen was astonished at the rapidity and success of the attack on the forts. Immediately, he sent out emissaries to secure an end to the fighting. The terms Elliot offered him were harsh, but he had no alternative but to accept. They included an indemnity of six million dollars, to be paid at the rate of a million a year over six years, to recompense the merchants for the opium they had surrendered; Hong Kong would go to the British Crown; trade would reopen again at Canton, and also at four other ports, Amoy, Foochow, Ningpo and Shanghai.

All this was exactly as Jardine had proposed to Lord Palmerston in London, with the exception of Hong Kong. He had favoured the larger island of Chusan, but he was more familiar with that than with Hong Kong.

Elliot sat back in his cane chair in his office, justifiably pleased with what he had extracted from a shambles of indecision and no decision from London. Hong Kong, he knew from his own experience, possessed one of the best harbours in the world. He preferred it to Chusan for this reason, and because the natives on the island were friendly towards those Westerners already living there.

The British companies could build new warehouses, on Hong Kong Island and carry on their trade secure from all Chinese interference. The bribery of the Hong merchants would thus be a thing of the past. Opium could be stored on the island by the ton, and distributed with far greater ease than from the rotting, floating hulks off Lintin. The indemnity of six million dollars would pay for the cost of the military expedition.

Kishen also allowed himself some congratulations. With no cards to play, either military or political, he had ended an invasion before it had properly begun, and saved his country from collapse. Hong Kong, so far as he was concerned, was only an island of scrub and swamp and serpents, with wretched peasants digging for clams or fishing. Such an unimportant island was a little price to pay for freedom from complete subjection by Barbarians.

By agreeing to Elliot's terms, Kishen also secured the release of a considerable town, Ting-hai, on the road to the capital. From this, Nanking, China's second city, could have been threatened, and the vast Yangtze River blockaded. The Barbarians had apparently not appreciated the strategic value of Ting-hai,. and had willingly withdrawn.

The indemnity of six million dollars Kishen would easily extract from the Hong merchants, each of whom were individually worth two or three times as much. So what could have been a war of swift annihilation had ended with honour to both sides.

The Emperor would have to allow foreign ambassadors across his frontiers and trading from four ports instead of one, but this was bound to happen eventually in any case. Otherwise, life in China would continue as it had continued for centuries. In all the unhappy circumstances, Kishen felt convinced that no other negotiator could have secured such fortunate terms for his Emperor.

So, some time after this agreement had been reached, Kishen allowed himself a small celebration with a few friends, and rice wine and music and tumblers and jugglers; just as Elliot gave a dinner party to which he invited those colleagues most closely involved as his personal guests. Both men were glad to relax, for both had extracted from other people's errors very considerable gains for their two countries.

But both received — ironically, almost at the same time — news from their masters, which shattered their satisfaction and their dreams.

Elliot was called to the door of his house to accept a sealed envelope from the hand of a messenger who had sailed in one of Gunn's fast clippers, just landed from Calcutta. He read it, cigar in hand, under the flickering flames of the candles in his hall, and could barely believe the words on the page.

The letter was a personal communication from Lord Palmerston, who began bluntly: 'You have disobeyed and neglected your Instructions.

'You have deliberately abstained from employing the Force placed at your disposal; and you have without sufficient necessity accepted Terms which fall far short of those you were instructed to obtain.

'You were instructed to demand full compensation for the opium which you took upon you two years ago to deliver up. To ask Parliament to pay the money was out of the question. You have accepted a sum much smaller than the amount due to the opium holders. You were told to demand payment of the expenses of the expedition, and payment of Hong debts. You do not appear to have done one or the other.

'You were told to retain Chusan until the whole, of the pecuniary Compensation should be paid, but you have agreed to evacuate the island immediately. You have obtained the cession of Hong Kong, a barren Island with hardly a House upon it. Now it seems obvious that Hong Kong will not be a Mart of Trade, any more than Macao is so. However, it is possible I may be mistaken in this matter.

'But you still will have failed in obtaining that which was a Capital point in our view: an additional opening for our Trade to the Northward. You will, no doubt, by the time you have read thus far, have antici · pated that I could not conclude this letter without saying that under these circumstances it is impossible that you should continue to hold your appointment in China.'

So Elliot was dismissed. With glazed eyes he read his instructions about handing over his title and authority to a successor; and then details of his new posting. This was as far away from England and the East as his Government could locate: a position as British Consul in North America.

He read this news of virtual exile to a former colony with a mounting sense of irony and sadness. He had worked since his arrival for an understanding between Britain and China. Against all those who advocated war, he had hoped for peace until the very end. Now, he would have his wish; peace undisturbed in a diplomatic backwater.

Almost at the same hour, another messenger, red with dust from his long journey across the mountains, delivered a Scroll from the Emperor into Kishen's hand. He dismissed the man and read the Scroll with equal disbelief and horror.

'The Celestial Empire treats the Outer Barbarians with favour and compassion,' the Emperor began with a calm statement of fact.

'When they are obedient, We never omit to show them friendliness and goodwill, for We strive for universal peace. The English Barbarians, however, knew not to repent, but daily increased their insolent violence. It would not have been difficult for Us to call forth Our troops and annihilate them utterly. But we gave consideration to the fact that the said Barbarians presented addresses in which they asked for redress of certain grievances.

'To insure fairness for all, We delegated bur Grand Secretary, Kishen, to proceed to Canton and there examine the matter. On arrival he explained everything to the Barbarians, but they still dared to make excessive demands. We had declared them long ago to be fickle of temperament. Wherefore We have instructed the best provincial troops to hasten to Canton and there to extirpate them.'

He read on, the background of chatter and laughter from the inner room where his guests were gathered, now as totally unreal as the impossible orders he was being given.

The Barbarian Elliot was to be subdued immediately and brought in chains to Peking. The Emperor clearly knew nothing of the hard realities of the situation, for he wrote of moving armies that did not exist, of manoeuvring a navy that was already beaten like wheat beneath a thresher, of a situation that had been so misrepresented to him that it bore as little resemblance to reality as a devil mask bears to a human face.

But, of course, in his reply, Kishen could not mention these gross delusions. He would have to use guile, and humility and hope he might thus succeed in avoiding the Holy Anger.

Immediately, he called his secretary and began to dictate a reply to be carried back to Peking.

'After I, your slave, have perused the Sainted Words commanding me to wage war rather than follow diplomacy, I have this to submit.

'Whatsoever concessions I promised the Barbarians were made with the understanding that I should on their behalf petition for their grant. But Oh! I am ignorant and what I have done will not meet with the approval of Your Majesty. I tremble more than words can describe. As I, your slave, thought over the situation, I concluded that what happens to me can only be insignificant, but what affects the whole nation is of tremendous importance.

'I, your slave, have actually abandoned all food and sleep, so deeply concerned am I by the situation. But the Barbarians have pledged themselves to return all they have captured. I beseech the Heavenly Face to take the lives of the masses into consideration, and grant, to us poor mortals extraordinary favour. The work of extirpation can be carried out later. I, your slave, have throughout acted for the general welfare. There is not a shred or sign of timidity in me.'

As the secretary finished the last ideograph on the ' scroll and carried it away to dry, one of the Hong merchants came out to find what was keeping Kishen from his guests. Usually, Kishen would have given some easy answer, but tonight his fear showed on his face. He explained the horror of the Emperor's message.

'What will happen to me?' he asked in an extremity of apprehension. The merchant was both rich and wise: he had survived the disgrace of Lu and Lin, and their predecessor who had failed to subdue, the Golden Dragon King. He would still be here after Kishen's departure.

'You will be taken to Peking in chains,' the Hong merchant replied immediately, his voice showing neither sympathy nor concern. 'Your property will then be confiscated, and you will be sent to some remote part of the Kingdom, which is forever drenched with rain or white with mist. There you will rot out your days, dreaming of what might have been.'

'You lie!' shouted Kishen, furious at the man's presumption. It was idiotic of him to have sought the opinion of one who had no long lineage, who was only a merchant, a usurer.

But even as Kishen spoke, he knew he was deluding himself. The Hong merchant was right; this was what would happen. Kishen leaned against the wall, eyes shut, trying to focus his scattered, terrible thoughts, to reassemble the detritus of his dreams, while all the time, out of sight, flutes wailed and gongs beat and his guests demanded more wine. Truly, his efforts to carry out his Emperor's orders had ended with strange results.

He had found peace and lost his career. He had achieved victory and won defeat.

MacPherson poured himself a pint of claret and took his usual chair in the corner of the room.

'I hear Elliot's going,' he said to Gunn. 'In disgrace, poor fellow. It's a dam' shame, a total misunderstanding, for he, of all people, tried to secure an honourable agreement without bloodshed. And look what's happened to him! He's going to be sent as British Consul to Texas in North America. That's equivalent to exile in the far frontiers of the Celestial Kingdom — which is what is going to happen to his Chinese counterpart, this man Kishen.

'First, Viceroy Lu. Then Viceroy Lin. And now plenipotentiary Kishen. It makes me thankful I am not a politician. As a merchant, I may go bankrupt — but at least I will never be banished.'

MacPherson was already slightly drunk. Sweat damped his white starched shirt and glistened on his forehead; alcohol slurred his speech. He admired Elliot; his calmness recalled other professional naval officers under whom he had served years ago — men of courage and. principle, who had been entirely detached from trade and bribes, and such commercial considerations which now weighed so heavily on him.

'Can't we help Elliot at all? A letter to the Government, or something?'

'No,' replied Gunn. 'We are all bidding for high stakes out here in different ways. Elliot played for peace with honour. He won, yet the Government think he lost. Kishen extracted the best terms he could, but his Emperor thought they were not good enough. So he lost, too.

'You cannot make an omelette without breaking eggs. And you cannot have peace without war if rulers on both sides live in make-believe worlds!'

'I suppose *your* world is all real?' said MacPherson caustically, pouring out more wine.

'Entirely,' said Gunn; and that of course was the tragedy. It was all too real in terms of wealth and securities and bonds and gold ingots and ships on the seas. There was nothing of the spiritual nature of man about it; no time for dreams or gentleness, let alone love.

You used people all the time; their value was in direct proportion to their importance in your plans. You had no time to like them for themselves. Soon, you grew unable to like them only to use them. Had not the Parsee warned him, long ago, that he sought to acquire a fortune, and one day, too late, he could find that it had acquired him?

Gunn was rich now in everything that money could buy, except for the priceless qualities, like happiness and humility, that no currency could command.

'What you need,' Gunn said now cruelly, to MacPherson, to exorcize these uneasy thoughts, 'is another drink.'

'I have drunk enough,' MacPherson replied, speaking slowly so as not to slur the words. 'And have *you* forgotten you have invited fifty guests to dine with you tonight?'

'No,' said Gunn; but, incredibly, he had. They were only guests, that was the reason. They were not friends. They accepted his invitations because he was who he was, because he was rich and influential. And he invited them because he might need to use them and because it flattered his vanity to be surrounded by rich, important men and pretty women, on equal terms. Not as the local physician being shown into the servants' entrance of the big house, but as the host who commanded their presence at his table.

Equally, they did not accept his invitations because they, wanted to, but because they felt they ought to. They were his guests, but not his friends; Gunn had no friends.

IN WHICH DR GUNN MAKES AN IMPORTANT DISCOVERY

MacPherson came unsteadily into the dining-room and stood for a moment, looking over the shoulders of the chattering guests at the long, polished table.

Candles glittered amber and red on glasses of hock and claret, and winked back from silver knives and forks. Through the wide open window, indigo with evening, paper lanterns along the quay glowed orange and green.

Gunn looked up at MacPherson enquiringly. He hoped the man had not drunk too much. As host, he sat at the head of the table, glass in hand, gold cufflinks agleam, long dark hair smoothed back. His face was still handsome, but under the flush of wine, it seemed slightly coarsened, like a portrait seen out of focus through a glass.

'You're late,' he said half-accusingly, treating MacPherson as an inferior, a hired man, as he had done increasingly and openly since Ling Fai's death. Gunn knew he had been growing more autocratic in other ways. He hated guests being late for his invitations; he felt no need to endure what he considered the smallest slight, whether imagined or unintended. He was a man of means now; he had a high position to maintain. After Jardine and Matheson, Mandarin-Gold was the most successful company on the Coast; and everyone knew who was the most successful man.

Gunn's six clippers had become ten. He had opened a depot in Manila and had successfully negotiated for a warehouse site on Hong Kong Island. He had overtaken the Parsee's agencies in Singapore and Rangoon and Calcutta. He was no longer the raw young doctor who had pleasured a native girl; he was a man of money who could write his name to a bond with a million pounds sterling; and he was still not thirty-five. Yet, although his success was universally acknowledged; he had to keep reminding himself of it, as though if he did not, it might disappear or at least diminish.

Also, for some time past — he was not positive for how long — weeks certainly, probably for months,, he had been growing progressively less interested in his career. Maybe he had overworked, and this was the reaction; or maybe the heat and humidity and the frustration of dealing with Chinese who said one thing and did another, had affected his constitution. Whatever the reason, he knew he was becoming more irascible, and he found a salve for his inner discontent in abruptness to his colleagues and rudeness to those he considered his inferiors.

MacPherson crossed the polished floor towards him.

'I went for a short walk,' he explained, 'and saw the *Hesperides* arrive from Calcutta. A very quick run. Eighteen days.'

'Anything for me?' asked Gunn mechanically, not caring greatly. Others opened his commercial mail. He had Chinese clerks on high stools scratching away with their pens and gritty ink, invoicing bills, sending receipts, acknowledging bonds and debentures. Sometimes, less frequently than before, his mother wrote. He always read her letters, not because she had much to say that interested him now, but because a letter was something she had gone to the trouble to write. Not many people did things for him now without hope of reward; in fact, he could not name a single person.

'One letter,' MacPherson replied. He put it down among the

glittering silver on the dark, glowing wood that reflected his hand and also the poor quality of the envelope. Gunn picked it up and glanced at the post mark: Herne Bay, Kent, England.

So it must be from home, and yet he did not recognize the handwriting. He probably received six or seven letters a year from his mother and sent back as many in reply, but her news of a neighbour's death, or of the new railway from London through Chatham to the coast, seemed as remote to him here as his news to them of a thousand chests of mud at fifteen dollars each, or the cost of maintaining his house in Macao.

He sent money to his parents, of course, from time to time, but not so much as he had originally intended, and not as often, either. Gunn told himself that this was not because he was mean, but because he did not wish to boast about his wealth; and to his parents fifty pounds was a sum they could appreciate and equate against their needs, whereas five hundred or five thousand would have been a gift beyond all relevance to their circumstances.

But now, as Gunn sat at the head of his table of guests, all drawn to him by the irresistible triple magnetism of youth, power and wealth, he felt a sudden spasm of guilt, and a longing for a different life; for a time long since past, when he had also been a different person; when money and ruthlessness had only been words and not integral parts of his character.

He picked up a silver bread knife and slit the envelope, ignoring the chatter that went on like the shrill cawing of birds; oblivious of servants in splendid white and gold livery who moved silently with crystal decanters of wine, and of others who waited behind each guest to remove their plate. Gunn shook out the letter. It was from his father.

'Dear Robert,' he read, 'I do not know how long this letter will take to reach you, but I feel I must tell you that your dear mother has been unwell for some weeks.

'As she explained in her last letter, old Doctor Golightly has retired, and the new physician does not yet know us as well as he did. He has caused your mother to be bled and has regularly applied leeches, but her general condition is not responding to this treatment.'

What *is* her general condition? thought Gunn irritably. Who was this unknown doctor indiscriminately abstracting the life-blood of his mother? Damn it, he was a doctor, too, and her son. He had a right to know. He read on.

'I know that you are very busy with your own affairs which we here find so difficult to comprehend, because our lives go on quietly as they have always done, but I would esteem it more highly than I can express if you could return to see us this summer.

'Your mother does not know I am writing in this way, for she has resolutely insisted that I do not inform you of her illness, which she assures me is only temporary and unimportant. I would not presume to go against medical opinion, but when you have been married to someone for nearly forty years you know them as well as you know yourself, and I feel — I hope without cause — that your mother is seriously ill.

'It would lighten her life like a month of sunshine if you could write to say that you were on the high seas, coming back to see her and your father, who shares her pride in our only son's great achievements.'

Gunn folded up the letter, put it in the envelope and then into his jacket pocket.

'Bad news?' asked MacPherson. His voice seemed to come from a great distance, and the conversation of the others was as meaningless as the roar of surf breaking on the sand.

'Yes,' said Gunn shortly.

'Anything I can do?' asked MacPherson.

Gunn shook his head. There was nothing anyone could do now. He could have visited his parents a dozen times, and combined each trip with business in London, but the chances had passed, and like the river rushing south beyond the paper lanterns of Canton, the tide of time only ran one way. Maybe, even now, it had gone out for his mother:

'You look pale,' MacPherson went on.

'It is nothing. Just the heat.'

Gunn picked up his glass and drained it, and immediately it was refilled, and he drank that, too. He would go home by the next boat. If need be, he would take one of his own. Extraordinary, that now he could command an entire clipper to convey him home, while others had to wait for weeks — or even months in the season — for a cramped passage aboard an East-Indiaman, and then often be asked to buy furniture in the cabin as well.

Now the furniture was his, the cabins were his, the ships were his. He had paid for them all with his integrity and years of effort, and in some other unquoted currency, the value of which he was not yet quite certain.

This was what years of trading in mud and breaking other rivals, crushing all opposition, had done to him. You could not touch pitch and stay undefiled; you could not do what he had done without some damage to your soul.

He glanced around the vast room, at the flushed, sweating faces of the men, staring lasciviously at the pushed-out, almost bare breasts of the women. Their husbands were, of course, in Canton, and the women were free and available; and after the meal they would pair off to a dozen different bedrooms. When the dawn came up, their mouths would be dry from far too much drink, their heads beating with the dual drums of disillusion and worry lest their husbands should discover yet another infidelity.

None of these, people cared a damn whether he lived or died; Gunn knew that. If he dropped dead at the head of the table in front of them, they would mourn perfunctorily for a few days. A drunken parson — probably Mackereth, he thought bitterly — would address an audience who did not hear, or, if they heard, did not wish to understand. Then someone else would own the clippers, someone else would equate what they had once been with what they would become. In the blood and bone of some other young, ambitious man, the juice of the poppy would turn his will to iron.

Gunn stood up. He could bear the heat and. the wine and the foolishness of the chatter no longer.

'Excuse me,' he said to the woman who sat on his right. 'I have business to attend to.'

He had intended to lie with her that night, but now the prospect seemed disgusting. He had indulged too many appetites — lust, greed, avarice, cruelty — far too long. He must escape. But where — and how?

Gunn went out of the room into his bedroom and stood on the dark verandah overlooking the Praya. He would not be able to sail tomorrow because a new clipper was being delivered and he had to check this himself, otherwise he might be swindled, for a subordinate could take a bribe.

The following day, he had a dinner engagement with the Portuguese Governor in Macao, and after that he had arranged a tour in the new clipper up the coast, to meet mandarins and personally to renew contacts and contracts.

He would put them all off. If he did not, he would always find new and urgent reasons for delaying his departure. But first he must speak to someone who would understand how he felt, who could assuage his sudden guilt. But who was there? Ling Fai was dead. And even if she had lived, she was only a body, a soft warmness in the dark, a heart against his own; only a girl who had never been out of China. How could she have understood how he felt about England and a Kentish mist; about his longing for the smell of drying hops, or a fresh wind from a colder sea?

There was MacPherson, but Gunn would never lower his mask in front of him, not after what had happened with Ling Fai. And MacPherson was in any case his inferior; he would lose face if he confessed his feelings to him.

He knew no-one else he could trust, for everyone absorbed the confidences of a rich man as greedily as blotting paper soaked up ink. Then they rushed out to pass them on to other people, suitably amplified and distorted, for another man's weakness minimized their own.

What he needed was some impersonal confidant bound by an oath of secrecy, who would listen and not condemn, who could pour some balm on his raw misery; another physician, maybe, or a priest.

He suddenly thought of Mackereth, the only priest he knew, if one could call a Son of Zebedee a priest. On the impulse, he walked down the stairs, out of the side door, past the watchman who saluted, and along the narrow streets to Mackereth's house. The white-washed walls had stored up a whole day's heat of the sun, and the air was still warm, sharp with the smell of sewers and the salt of breaking waves.

It was not usual for Gunn to walk; Europeans rarely walked when litters and sedans were so easily available, but he enjoyed walking, and there was something more personal in going alone instead of arriving at the home of a poor man surrounded by your servants. It was almost like doing penance, or making a pilgrimage.

He reached Mackereth's house, and beat on the front door. A half-caste boy showed him in. Gunn had not expected this; he had imagined that Mackereth would be alone, perhaps reading the Bible or at prayer, or however priests spent their spare time. He had not imagined he would have the company of a boy. He felt a sudden disgust at the thought of the old: missionary pleasuring himself with this youth, whose eyes were wide and frightened. The boy recognized Gunn, and guessed that the visit of such a *taipan,* such an important merchant, must have some unusual significance.

'I want to see joss-man Mackereth,' Gunn announced. Joss was pidgin for God, a corruption of the Portuguese word *deos;* and Mackereth, thought Gunn, was himself a corruption of a man of God.

The boy led him through a long, tiled corridor, smelling slightly of cats, past the few water colours Mackereth had collected about him, and into the main room. Mackereth sat at a table, the remains of a meal pushed away from him. Two whisky bottles were at his right hand, one empty, the other half full. Candle flames trembled in the wind at Gunn's approach, and mosquitoes whined. The room did not smell fresh, and he made a sudden mental comparison with the luxury of his own house, and the seedy, rundown squalor of this.

If Mackereth could not achieve more in this world, he thought, how could he possibly claim to hold the keys of the Kingdom of Heaven? Was he really the only guide available to lead him through the swirling mists of eternity? What comfort could such a failure give to one who was so successful?

But then, Gunn answered himself almost immediately, surely all holy men, even Christ himself, would have been, judged failures by the crude commercial terms of reference he had considered so important for so long?

Mackereth looked up at him now, his face creased with concentration as he tried to focus his bleary bloodshot eyes.

'It's you, doctor!' he cried hoarsely, in surprise. 'What's wrong?'

'*Must* there be something wrong?' asked Gunn.

'You never come to see me unless there is some crisis,' Mackereth replied, his voice thick and slurred as a muddy river. 'Usually you write *no — command* me — to attend you at your more — ah — salubrious residence.'

He tried to stand up, but the room spun as he moved, so he sank down thankfully in his chair again and the walls steadied reassuringly.

'Send the boy away,' said Gunn. 'I want to speak to you privately.'

The boy was standing in the doorway, watching them. He shut the door silently. Gunn sat down farther up the table, facing Mackereth. How could he strip his mind and misery naked in front of this drunken charlatan? And yet who else was there to help him?

'I am going home,' Gunn began.

'What do you mean — home?'

'To England. To see my parents.'

'Very pleased for you,' said Mackereth, and belched. The cheap whisky tasted bitter as bile in his throat. This rich swine sitting opposite him, boasting of going home! How could he realize what it felt like to have no home, the misery of having no-one in all the world who cared whether you lived or died? And to admit that you didn't even care greatly, yourself? Honour thy father and thy mother: that thy days may be long upon the land which the Lord thy God giveth thee. The fifth commandment.

'I just wanted to tell you,' said Gunn. He must pierce the drunken fog that clouded this man's brain and reach his comprehension, because he knew no-one else who could even begin to understand his loneliness.

'When I am away you will be paid five hundred pounds — no, one thousand pounds — a voyage. I want to help your work.'

He was trying to be friendly, dealing in the only coinage he understood; money.

'You haven't done much so far towards my work,' said Mackereth grudgingly.

'I have at least paid you three hundred a trip.' Or was it only two-fifty? The sum was so unimportant, he had forgotten the amount.

'And made thirty thousand a trip yourself. You would hardly have made a penny, doctor, if I had not been there, ready to interpret, risking my life in those fevered swamps up the coast.'

'I could have hired Gutzlaff, like Jardine.'

Why did every conversation seem to degenerate into arguments about payments and profits? Was there no escape from bargaining? Could he never have any relationship without cost being involved and bickered over?

'Why didn't you, then? I will tell you. Because you could

buy me cheaper, doctor. That's why.'

'I did not come here to argue about money, Mackereth,' said Gunn, swallowing his irritation. 'I came to say that I realize, perhaps very late, that I have not been as generous as I could have been, and to try and make amends.

'But you only see one side of the picture — the part that affects you. I had to cut down on fees to save money to build up the business. You do not realize the overheads, the bribes, or the enormous corruption that exists among captains and crews.'

'I know all that. This is a corrupt, rotten world, and you and your kind have made it that way. You have also made your fortune, Gunn, and I am glad you have. It is what you wanted.'

'I wanted it then,' agreed Gunn. 'But now I seek your opinion as a priest, not as an employee. I am rich as bankers count wealth, in money, but that is not the only measurement of happiness. I have neglected other values, Mackereth. I believe my mother is dying. She may even now be dead. I could have done so much to help her, but I did very little. I meant to do more, to go home. But I never did.'

'Honour thy father and thy mother: that thy days may be long upon the land which the Lord *thy Gunn* giveth thee,' said Mackereth thickly, raising his glass in a toast, and spilling whisky down his sleeve as he drank. He wiped his mouth with the back of his other hand. Gunn saw with distaste that his nails were black with dirt.

'You're drunk,' said Gunn suddenly, with contempt and sadness for himself as much as for Mackereth. He could never pierce the misty armour of alcohol deep enough to reach Mackereth's fuddled, sodden brain. He was wasting his time. He stood up regretfully and wearily.

'I came here to ask advice,' he explained, 'but you have nothing to give. Get back to your boys, Mackereth. Drink away your days, for soon it will be dark, for all of us. Live in your own world of illusion, as I live in mine. Peddle your tracts portside while we shift mud, starboard.

'You're worth nothing more. You're lucky you have as much. And it is only through my generosity — which you are always so quick to abuse — that you have anything.'

Now Mackereth staggered up and almost fell. He kept his balance by holding on, to the back of the chair. The legs scraped a protest on the tiled floor.

'That is my life, agreed;' he said. 'We all have sinned and fallen short of the glory of God. I was rich once, too, but I lost my money. I had to take what jobs I could find. I had to equate the sin of poisoning thousands of people with filthy drugs, against the virtue of staying alive to preach the Gospel.

'The only way I could do this was to convince myself — as Gutzlaff convinced himself — that the trade was a necessary evil, because how else could we raise money to spread the word of the Lord?

'I have never actually peddled your mud, doctor, although I admit I have profited by it. But I have ploughed back my profits to help these Chinks. Maybe out there, somewhere along that dark heathen coast, a handful of people *have* read my tracts and now believe-that God *is* love. Maybe they know the comfort of admitting the one true God.

'It's not much of an achievement, I admit, by your standards. I own no clippers, no godowns, no mansions, nothing. Why else do you think I drink like this? I drank at first to remember, to fight the fever. Now I drink to forget. A broken and a contrite heart, O, God, shalt Thou not despise. Psalm fifty-one, verse sixteen.

'But what have *you* achieved, Gunn? You and your bloody Hippocratic Oath! You and your high-minded principles! What have *you* done with your life? You have made money, agreed. Now you can go home and buy yourself a seat in your English parliament or become a squire and ride over your acres.

'But you, like me — like all of us — are only living on time borrowed from God. Maybe the loan will be called in sooner than we know.

'Don't you ever fear, sometimes, as you dine in your great house, or when you lie with your Chinese whores, that all the souls of those tormented people you have condemned to a living death of dreams and drugs, will one day rise up against you? And if not in your lifetime, in the lives of those who will come after? And one night, as for the man in the parable, as for all of us, thy soul shall-be required of thee.

'You have sown a great fortune, doctor. But those who follow will reap the bitter fruits of abomination, for you and your like have sold posterity for a quick profit.

'I tell you this,' and Mackereth thrust his sweating, contorted face close to Gunn, 'I would rather be in my wretched squalid room here, having failed — agreed — at everything I have attempted, but at least having attempted *something* of nobility, rather than be like you.

'You're drugged by the poppy as much as those poor ruined peasants who smoke your mud. It's an iron poppy, doctor. A flower with an iron hook in it for them, that will never let them go though they live to be a hundred. A flower that hardens your heart so there's no room for any kindness, any compassion, any love — nothing but lust for more money, more power. There's more iron in a single poppy bloom than in your whole great clipper fleet, doctor. And it's all in your heart and soul.'

Gunn stood up now. His face was hard as stone in the candle glow.

'You will never work for me again,' he said quietly.

'I do not wish to work for you again. Or for that drunk MacPherson. Or for Jardine or Matheson, if ever they return, which I doubt. Or for the Parsee. Or for any of you people who have a price for everyone and everything. I would rather take my own life and end it cleanly, and go to meet my Maker, and say, Father, I have sinned, than be like you and bribe bishops to pray and say masses and toll bells.'

Mackereth staggered across the room and lurched against the table. The bottle tipped and fell on its side. Whisky slopped over the stained wood. Neither of them noticed it.

'Good-bye,' said Gunn. 'I will give MacPherson my instructions about you.'

'That's all you give anyone. Instructions! Orders! Demands! That is why you come creeping to see me at night because you cannot face me in the day to *ask* something. You must *demand* it! So you come here in, the dark, when no-one will see you, because you are lonely. Because under all that rich suiting, all that flesh you have put on, and in those great houses, with the whores with whom you have surrounded yourself, you have no friends. You are frightened and lonely.'

Mackereth lunged at Gunn with the empty bottle. He slipped on the tiles, damp with whisky, and fell groaning and gasping. As he began to claw himself upright again, Gunn crossed the room. Mackereth was demented, of course. He should have recognized the symptoms long before, but he had been too busy. How tragic and absurd to expect help and comfort from a lunatic!

The frightened boy was listening outside the door.

Gunn swept past him, unlocked the front door and hurried away from the house, until he came to the Praya, and then he stood, facing the luminous phosphorescent waves, breathing the warm, scented comforting breeze blowing in from the ocean.

Mackereth listened until Gunn's footsteps faded and the front door slammed. The boy came into the room diffidently; he did not know whether Mackereth would want him how and he did not like to ask. The *taipan* had an unpredictable temper when he had been drinking.

Mackereth saw him hovering uncertainly in the candle glow, his shadow huge on the wall behind him, and waved him away. He wanted no-one to see him now, alone and defeated. His tongue had taken possession of him. The tongue no man can tame; it is an unruly evil. The General Epistle of James. Chapter three, verse five. Now this untamed tongue had cost him his job. He had nothing left to live for: no-one else would employ him. He should have been wise, like Gutzlaff, and made a new career for himself.

The whisky bottle was empty, and he could not bring himself to pray. He imagined Gunn laughing at him, telling MacPherson. Even the boys laughed at him now he could no longer pleasure himself with them at will. His mouth was dry and his heart began to pound in his thin chest.

He crossed the hot foetid room, opened the cupboard and took out a pistol, and examined it cautiously. The weapon appeared to be primed. He pulled back the hammer and looked down the small, dark, barrel-mouth, peering into a tunnel that led to eternity.

He had only to squeeze this trigger, and all his troubles would be at an instant end. Yea, though I walk through the valley of the shadow of death ... Thou art with me.

As he remembered these words, from which he had so often drawn comfort, he found the ability to pray, and in a hoarse dry voice, with his hot breath, rasping in his throat, he whispered: 'Oh, Lord, unto You I commend my spirit. Have mercy on Your servant, who has failed You and himself in every way, and who is no more worthy to live in Your image. Receive him now and find some task for him to do.'

Mackereth's eyes had misted with tears of self-pity. The walls of the room were clouded by a haze. He peered at his silver hunter: eleven o'clock, the Hour of the Rat, as the Chinese counted time. He felt that this had some significance, but could not quite understand what it might be, and he had no-one to enlighten him. He wished he knew someone to whom he could say good-bye, someone who could wish him Godspeed on his last and longest journey, but there was no-one. He had sent the boy away and he was on his own.

He had fallen short of the glory of God and the fellowship of man. But at least he had the courage to acknowledge this, and to end this sham existence.

He took a long breath, and slowly, almost lovingly, he squeezed the trigger and watched the hammer fall:

When Gunn reached his house, MacPherson was still waiting up for him. All the other, guests had gone, and Gunn felt a sudden rush of unexpected warmth towards the Scot. MacPherson was fatter now, of course, and more grizzled than when he had saved him on the coast years ago, but he was loyal, and loyalty was beyond all price. Gunn had treated him as a subordinate all this time, but MacPherson had never minded. He had gladly accepted his secondary role in their relationship. He had never complained.

He was sitting now in one of the cane chairs with holes cut in their arms for glasses. The room was hot, for the curtain was drawn against night moths and mosquitoes. In the candle-glow, MacPherson's face shone with sweat like a redstone carving.

'I have been to see Mackereth,' Gunn explained and sat down opposite him and poured himself, a whisky. 'I do not wish to employ him any longer as an interpreter.'

'You're going home, aren't you?' said MacPherson. 'That's why you're telling me this.'

'How did you guess?'

'Because for months you have been talking in your sleep. Your women sometimes tell me what you say.'

'And what *do* I say?' Gunn asked, suddenly wary.

'Nothing important, usually. Things about your boyhood. Whitstable oysters. Coal barges with red sails. Spring mist over the marshes. A hot day in a cornfield. When you go home, it will be like the prodigal son returning.'

'It is nothing like that at all,' retorted Gunn angrily. The man had been drinking too much. These people had such gross flaws in their characters. Why had he surrounded himself with the drunk and the depraved?

'The prodigal son went back, poor and wretched, having wasted all his inheritance. I am going back rich. Why, if I wanted, I could be a Freeman of the City of London — even Lord Mayor.'

'*If* you wanted,' echoed MacPherson. 'And who the devil would want that? You are rich in money, Gunn, but you are poor as a church mouse in everything else.'

This conversation was intolerable, and somehow familiar. MacPherson had never addressed him by his surname before, always as doctor. The man was far more inebriated than he had seen him for a long time; he must cut down on the amount of claret and whisky he consumed or he would have a seizure. But the night was hot, and MacPherson was growing old. He should make allowances for that. Instinctively, because he needed MacPherson now, Gunn dredged to find excuses for his behaviour.

'You don't answer me, do you?' said MacPherson tauntingly. 'That is because you can't. I tell you, there are coolies out in the streets, running barefoot with rickshaws or carrying loads on their heads, far richer than you.'

'I think you had better go,' said Gunn, keeping his temper. 'I will call a sedan for you.'

'You'll call for nothing for me. I'll go when I'm ready. I'm taking no more orders from you.'

'I have never given you any orders. They have always been requests.'

'That's another word with the same meaning so far as you are concerned. You *request* me to do this, that and the other thing. Find you a new woman, buy another clipper cheap, beat down some middle-man.

'You *request* Mackereth to translate, to sail among the junks at Hong Kong for food and water. You *request* that poor miserable wretch to take three hundred pounds a trip instead of a thousand. He couldn't ignore your *requests* because he needed the money.

'You use people and don't give a damn what happens to them after that. You're like a ship being launched, that rolls down the beach to the sea on logs. We are all the logs, supposed to be grateful if we can help your passage to greater glory.'

'You're drunk,' said Gunn coldly.

'Of course I'm drunk,' agreed MacPherson. 'How else could I stand this filthy job?'

'I would think it is better than being a mate in a wooden grain ship, and to be seized by pirates and marooned on a hostile coast!'

'It's better paid, but by God, I earn the money. When I was at sea, at least I slept nights. I didn't wonder what was going to happen when we'd poisoned all the Chinese with our mud, to make *you* a greater profit.'

'Your conscience does you credit, but I feel that its pangs trouble you rather late. You must be worth a million pounds now, at least, MacPherson. I would have paid more heed to your heart cries had I heard them before you were so rich.'

'I'm not saying I'm any better than you,' said MacPherson. 'I like money for what it buys. But for me most of what it buys is oblivion. The kind our customers seek in mud, I find in the bottle. I drink two bottles a day now, since Ling Fai died. And *you* killed her, Gunn.'

'Don't be ridiculous. That was a total and tragic accident. I liked her, as much as you did.'

The irony was that he had not even known she was in the *Hesperides* at the time. He was with Captain Smith, and had assumed she had stayed in Macao, with Chinese relations, for there had been no need for her to leave; she had not been a Barbarian:

It was ludicrous, and quite wrong for MacPherson to make such a terrible accusation. And he *had* liked her; as much as he liked anybody. But that was all; a face in the night, a body when he needed one.

'*Liked!* You had her time and again, didn't you? And you thought I didn't care or didn't know. Well, I didn't *want* to know, because I wanted her to have what she wanted to make her happy. And who, if necessary. Even you, Gunn. *I* loved her.

'You have nothing to say, have you?' MacPherson went on thickly. 'That is because you don't know the meaning of love. It is only a four-letter word to you.'

'You're wrong,' said Gunn. He had also loved once, but as you grew older you found other distractions, other involvements that became more important. And the real tragedy was that your capacity for love diminished as the sun's heat decreases with autumn. You could tell yourself that a day in October was really as hot as one in June, but you were wrong; it was not, and never could be.

'You loved no-one,' said Gunn in a level voice. 'You're just a drunken old sailor looking for a quarrel. I will ring for a sedan. Maybe you will feel differently about things in the morning.'

Gunn pulled a bell tassel. MacPherson stood up, swaying.

'I'll never feel differently about anything concerning you.

'*Request a* sedan! Request the bearers and the coolies and every other poor devil you own. You can order them all, and they'll do your bidding, because they must.

'But how many of them would do anything for you out of *liking?* Go home, Gunn. Sail back to be Lord Mayor, like Dick Whittington. Have your great house in London, your warehouses along the Thames. Become an MP and write letters to *The Times*. And when you've done it all, and you come crawling back here, don't look for me, because I am leaving.'

'I don't understand what has happened to you,' said Gunn puzzled. 'When I left the dinner party you seemed perfectly normal. You'd had a little too much to drink, perhaps, but that is not new. Now you're a different person.'

'When people in the villages around Vesuvius left their homes one morning, Gunn, everything was no doubt also perfectly normal. But when they came home at night, the volcano had erupted. The earth had had enough and was on fire. That goes for me, too. It just happened that what I have been considering for months — years — reached breaking point tonight.'

Two servants appeared at the door in answer to Gunn's summons. They each took one of MacPherson's arms and led him down the stairs out into the street to the waiting sedan. He walked unsteadily, and he did not look back.

Gunn opened the curtains and walked out on to the balcony. The moon had turned the sea to silver, and the Praya was deserted except for the sedan, with its four bearers, jog-trotting into the distance. He stood and watched until they turned a corner, and then there was nothing in the empty street but beggars curled up asleep in doorways and a cat prowling for scraps.

He would never see MacPherson again, any more than he would see Mackereth. Their lives had touched briefly and run together, and now they had parted. Something had turned their minds, of course; heat or whisky or loneliness; or maybe all three had fused together to destroy their faculties. Or maybe it was simply because they had become involved with him. He was sorry for both men, of course, to a limited extent, but he was also sorry for himself.

Where would he ever find two others like them, if he had need of them?

The clipper hove-to outside Bombay. The sea streamed yellow with churned mud, and kite-hawks screeched and dived for scraps, and then turned and wheeled away, huge black parentheses in the sky.

'Longboat's ready, sir,' reported Fernandes.

Gunn nodded. He was wearing one of his new suits; dark jacket, a silk cravat with a pearl pin, and carrying his top hat. He handed this to a servant who swarmed down a rope ladder with it while Gunn walked down the gangway and took his seat in the stern. He was glad to sit; a kind of vertigo had attacked him during the last few days at sea. He was grateful to be going ashore, however briefly.

Oar blades dipped and flashed. Within minutes, he stood on the quay at Bombay, a quarter of his journey home from

Macao behind him. His agent was waiting for him, and doffed his hat respectfully.

'I want you to take me to Mr Bonnarjee's residence. Up on Malabar Hill.'

'Is he expecting you, sir?'

'Does that matter?' asked Gunn coldly.

'Not at all, sir,' the man replied hastily. 'Why I asked is that I believe he left for Macao last week.'

'Then no doubt there will be someone else at home who can receive me,' said Gunn, and climbed into the sedan.

Bonnarjee's house was built of white stone with ionic pillars commanding a splendid view over the huddled rooftops of the city. Half a dozen ships lay at anchor in the bay. Two of them flew the flag of Mandarin-Gold.

He could still keep the name, even if MacPherson retired. Change was bad for business; companies liked the reassurance of continuity. He had been wise to keep both their names out of it. It was bad enough being tainted by Mackereth's suicide; you did not expect a man of the cloth to take his own life.

Somehow, the sight of the flag cheered Gunn, and he sat back in the sedan, as far away from his agent as possible in the confined space, willing the man to silence. He did not wish to waste breath on small talk of no consequence. The fact was that since he had left Mackereth, and probably even before he had visited him, he had not felt quite so fit as he usually did; the vertigo was one symptom. A certain lassitude was another, brought on, no doubt, by the heat, by the humidity and the constant worry over the movement of capital and clippers, the fear that subordinates might be swindling him in the endless fight for commercial supremacy in changing markets, a changing world.

Gunn needed a break from all this work and worry, and this trip home would set him up, restore his vigour and his keen appreciation of business. He had _not taken a holiday since he had left England. He had always convinced himself he had neither need nor time for one. Now, he admitted he had both.

The bearers lowered his sedan gently under the porch. One pealed the door bell and Gunn climbed out.

'Wait here,' he told the agent. 'I will not be long.'

A bearded Indian servant in white uniform with a red and gold sash appeared at the door and bowed.

'Mr Bonnarjee,' said Gunn, handing him his card.

'Bonnarjee sahib *nay hai,*' replied the servant.

'*Memsahib hai?*' asked Gunn.

The servant nodded and opened the door. Gunn walked into the hall. It was grander than he had imagined, with a high tessellated ceiling, and little gilt-edged tables set around white walls. He stood on pink-veined marble tiles, inlaid with the points of the compass. The servant padded away hurriedly on bare feet, and reappeared almost immediately and bowed.

Gunn followed him into a large room overlooking the sea. Two tapestried punkahs moved gently from the ceiling, and a mynah bird chattered in a bamboo cage. There were settees and oil. paintings of men in turbans, and small soap-stone figures and porcelain ornaments. A gilt French clock ticked loudly on a wall. The Parsee's daughter was standing in the middle of the room holding his card.

'Why have you come here?' she asked.

Suddenly Gunn felt awkward, and bowed to conceal this unusual sensation.

'I am on my way back to England,' he explained. 'I do not know when I will return. I wanted to see you before I sailed.'

'You waited a long time,' the woman said tonelessly. 'Years.'

Her voice was not as he remembered it, laughing and bright like dancing water, but flat and already old. Perhaps something had gone out of her life, too?

'I have not been in Bombay before. Business has kept me on the Coast.'

'I know. My father told me.'

'What exactly did he tell you?'

'That you started your company by using our association to blackmail him into selling his shares in Crutchley & Company.'

'That is not true,' replied Gunn heatedly. 'He tried to have me marooned first. I could have died.'

'I don't believe that,' said the Parsee's daughter firmly. 'I have known my father for far longer than you have, Dr Gunn. He is a good, kind man. What brings you here, anyhow? You have not broken your journey just to tell me lies about my father, surely? We said good-bye years ago. Or rather, we did not. Remember?'

'Yes,' said Gunn. He remembered other things, too: his body in hers, and the smell of her hair, and her face damp with the sweat of love in that shaded upper room overlooking the Praya. He had been young in mind then and young in experience, which was not the same as being young in years.

'Have you come to try and blackmail *me?*' she asked quietly.

'My God, no,' said Gunn, shocked. Why did people assume the worst so quickly? 'I just wanted to see you.'

'If you wanted to see our son, he is not here. He is out with his *ayah.*'

'You are the one I came to see.'

But it was somehow gratifying to know he had sired a son, even if he would never see the boy. He must be seven or eight now; already a tenth of his life was past, and Gunn had known nothing about him. And if he ever told the boy he was his father, he would never believe him. The ironies of life!

'You have met my husband, I believe?'

'I saw him briefly, once.'

'He is not here, either. He is on his way to Macao, so if you wanted to tell him about us, that will have to wait.'

'Why on earth should I do that? That belongs to the past, and to us. But tell me, have you any other children?'

She shook her head, not speaking. He was glad, in a pointless way. Maybe this woman *had* liked him, and more than like him, almost loved him. The thought warmed the cold corners of his heart. He wanted to tell her he was pleased, but he could not; his tongue would not form the words.

Instead, he stood looking at her in silence. She had thickened since he had last seen her — yet this was to be expected. Each year in a hot climate ripened women; from being young they suddenly matured like overblown roses. She did not attract him physically now any more than he attracted her; they were two strangers, who, long ago, had been close in a far country to which neither belonged. But even then, not all that close; he still did not know her name.

'There is nothing more to say,' said Gunn. 'Except what I came to say. Good-bye.'

'We will be taking tea shortly,' the woman said unexpectedly, as though she regretted her earlier remarks. 'Will you stay?'

'No, thank you,' said Gunn. 'My ship will sail on the afternoon tide.'

There was nothing to stay, for now, for what had linked them once, proximity and the passion of, youth in a burning land, had long since disappeared. It was odd to think that in all the many women he had possessed since he had taken this woman in the Parsee's house, he had sought *her* face, had felt for *her* body, and searched for *her* spirit. And now that they were face to face, she was someone else altogether. But then, so was he.

'Good-bye,' he said again, and held out his hand. Her skin felt warm to the touch. Just for a second, a wild, fleeting, splintered flash of thought, Gunn contemplated seizing her, forcing his mouth on hers, tearing up her sari, and having her there as she would have loved to be taken years ago. But instead he bowed formally and turned away, and walked to the door and, like MacPherson, he did not look back.

The bearers picked up his sedan, and as they began to trot down the hill he turned and looked up at the window of the big room. She was standing half behind the white silk curtain, looking down at him, and then the sun caught the window in a reflected blaze of gold and she was gone.

'Is there anything I can do to help you, sir, in Bombay?' asked his agent nervously. He had never met the firm's founder before, and such an opportunity, if fully used, could only advance his own fortunes.

'There is nothing,' said Gunn. 'Nothing anyone can do. But thank you.'

As soon as he, was aboard the clipper, Fernandes came into his state-room to ask permission to sail.

'Of course,' said Gunn. 'Whenever you are ready.'

Fernandes saluted and went back to the wheel-house. Gunn poured himself a whisky, and listened to the familiar screech of anchor-chains, the shouts of sailors up on the yards. The coastline turned through the porthole, and he toasted the view, drinking the whisky greedily, as though its fire could warm the cold weariness he felt in hipbones.

He had half expected to feel either elated or sad or warmed by the sight of the Parsee's daughter, but instead he felt nothing save this weariness that used to be quite alien to him.

He sat down in a cabin chair and poured himself out another whisky; it might have been water for all the effect it had on him. Perhaps he was sickening for something? Maybe it was some latent fever encountered in the swamps of China when he had been building up trade, and energy and overwork had kept it subdued, but now that he was at leisure, it was finally showing its strength?

What Mackereth and MacPherson had said about him was quite true, he thought. He had used people, because they were there to be used. He had never realized this until he had sailed East, because until then all his life had been a struggle; to pass examinations, to keep up appearances, to strive on his own, for what he really did not know.

But perhaps he was not entirely to blame, for people were like soft clay; they yearned to be used.

The Parsee had allowed himself to be used by paying him more than he need have paid. Then Mackereth was willing to be used, for by what other means could he earn any money? And MacPherson had sailed through life like a rudderless vessel until he found Gunn and allowed him to steer him in the direction Gunn thought fit.

The girl Ling Fai he had used as a creature for his pleasure, and now she was dead he felt strangely guilty. She alone had left an empty place in his mind that would at best be filled with uneasy and shameful thoughts. True, it was only a small place; but it was there, and the only one there.

So he had used them all, and they had stayed where they were, while he had gone forward, and now nothing could stop him. He could easily become a Member of Parliament. A knighthood was within his command; so was a peerage. For everyone had their price, and money was the key to all the currencies of corruption. And now he had money, more than any man could spend in a lifetime.

Gunn stood up again and looked at his face in the mirror above the pewter washbasin. It was surprisingly sallow, like the face of a man who rarely saw the sun. He looked again more closely, and suddenly felt fear's cold fingers clutch his heart. He *must* be ill to look like this. Then he glanced out of the porthole; the sea off Bombay was always yellow, and this had simply been reflected in the mirror.

Of course! How foolish to have forgotten this — and yet why did he feel so overwhelmingly relieved? Had he subconsciously been expecting some sign of ill health? Maybe this wretched lassitude, the enervating humidity of the sea voyage, had induced this attitude of mind? He was tired, that was the trouble; tired and lonely; the trip home would help him.

He poured a third whisky, and wind took the high sails and the ship leaned eagerly towards the west like some great white-winged bird. Gradually, the coastline faded and sank away. The yellow pigment left the sea, and the water grew green, then lapis lazuli, and finally blue as a Ming vase. Flying fish scudded and flickered like arrows above the smooth and sunbright waves.

Gunn stood up and looked at himself again in the mirror. Instantly, all his comfortable reassuring thoughts vanished like the coast of India.

The sea was blue, but his face was still sallow. Now he could see clusters of small brown freckles, like grains of sand, around his eyes. He sat down shakily on the edge of his bunk, then lay back, still wearing his jacket and his boots. He lay like a dead man, hearing the creak of the timbers and the roar and chuckle of the water on the other side of the hull. Someone came and knocked on the door with afternoon tea, but he did not reply and presently Gunn heard the footsteps die away.

He lay, listening to the beat of his own heart and the boom of the sea. He knew what this yellow colour meant, what the freckles and the weariness and lassitude signified. These were the signs of anaemia, but not the harmless kind from which pale young women suffered, and for which he had so often prescribed a diet of lean meat and porter and oysters. This was the type for which no human held the prescription. He had seen other men, even children, with' this sallow skin, these freckles, suddenly wither away, their flesh falling in on their bones until they resembled nothing so much as walking corpses. Redness left their blood as life left their bodies.

The cabin darkened and Gunn dozed uneasily and dreamed, and started up from his sleep, thinking he had endured a nightmare. He lit the lamp and examined his face again in the mirror, but this was no dream; his flesh was still as yellow as parchment, and the freckles were the mark of death.

Involuntarily, he glanced at his watch. Eleven o'clock. The Hour of the Rat, as the Chinese accounted time. He smiled ironically, remembering the Chinese description of Jardine as the Iron Headed Old Rat. The War of the Iron Rats. How long ago it seemed, and how very brief it had been! But every war had unknown casualties, and he was one of them. The Parsee had been wise not to take revenge himself. As he had said, the sword of heaven is in no haste to smite, but it never leaves a debt unpaid.

Gunn sat on his bunk in the hot stuffy cabin, looking out at the stars, another whisky in his hand.

He had achieved everything he wanted and he had achieved nothing. He was one of the richest men in the East, and one of the poorest. For what use was wealth unless you had health to enjoy it? As much use as light to a blind man, or shoes to a man who had no feet. And why should this happen to him, when he had worked so hard and had achieved so very much more than anyone he knew? Why, oh, God, *why*?

Gradually, the moon came up and the sea stretched like a shimmering silver floor on to the outer edge of darkness. And still Gunn found no answers to these questions. For there were no answers, no answers at all.

THE END

Dr Robert Gunn returns in *The Chinese Widow* and *Jade Gate*. Both are available as e-books and in paperback.

ABOUT THE AUTHOR

James Leasor

James Leasor was one of the bestselling British authors of the second half of the 20th Century. He wrote over 50 books including a rich variety of thrillers, historical novels and biographies.

His works included the critically acclaimed The Red Fort, the story of the Indian Mutiny of 1957, The Marine from Mandalay, Boarding Party (made into the film The Sea Wolves starring Gregory Peck, David Niven and Roger Moore), The Plague and the Fire, and The One that Got Away (made into a film starring Hardy Kruger). He also wrote Passport to Oblivion (which sold over 4 million copies around the World and was filmed as Where the Spies Are, starring David Niven), the first of nine novels featuring Dr Jason Love, a Cord car owning Somerset GP called to aid Her Majesty's Secret Service in foreign countries, and another bestselling series about the Far Eastern merchant Robert Gunn in the 19th century. There were also sagas set in Africa and Asia, written under the pseudonym Andrew MacAllan, and tales narrated by an unnamed vintage car dealer in Belgravia, who drives a Jaguar SS100.

www.jamesleasor.com Follow on Twitter: @jamesleasor

BOOKS IN THIS SERIES

Dr Robert Gunn Trilogy

It was the year of 1833 when Robert Gunn arrived on the China coast. Only the feeblest of defenses now protected the vast and proud Chinese Empire from the ravenous greed of Western traders, and their opening wedge for conquest was the sale of forbidden opium to the native masses.

This was the path that Robert Gunn chose to follow... a path that led him through a maze of violence and intrigue, lust and treachery, to a height of power beyond most men's dreams — and to the ultimate depths of personal corruption.

The Chinese Widow

James Leasor's two preceding books in his chronicle of the Far East a century and half ago - FOLLOW THE DRUM and MANDARIN-GOLD were acclaimed by critics on both sides of the Atlantic. THE CHINESE WIDOW is their equal. It combines the ferocious force of the Dutch mercenaries who seek to destroy Gunn's plan; the pathos of a young woman left alone to rule a fierce and rebellious people; the gawky humour of Gunn's partner, the rough, raw Scot MacPherson; the mysterious yet efficacious practice of Chinese medicine, handed on through thousands of years...

When doctors in England pronounced his death sentence, Robert Gunn-founder of Mandarin-Gold, one of the most prosperous Far Eastern trading companies of the nineteenth century-vowed to spend his final year in creating a lasting memorial to leave behind him... to pay back, somehow, his debt to the lands of the East that had been the making of his vast fortune. He had a plan - a great plan - but to see it through he had to confront a fierce and rebellious people, a force of Dutch mercenaries and the Chinese Widow. Who was the Widow? What was her past-and her power...?

Action, suspense and the mysterious splendour of the Orient are combined in this exciting and moving novel.

Jade Gate

Robert Gunn, founder of the Mandarin-Gold trading company, had always been quick to seize new opportunities. That had been the making of his vast Far Eastern trading empire. And when the change from sail to steam in the world's shipping made coal "as valuable as gold. Gunn saw his way to another fortune. Vessels on the Eastern seas needed local supplies of fuel — and the man who discovered coal in the East would command the whole area. Enormous power for his country ... and himself. Gunn believed that Jade Gate Island, off Borneo, hid coal deposits, and there were others who shared his belief. In a land where life was cheap and the prize incalculable, the race for coal was likely to be a fight to the death ...

'Jade Gate' is the final book in the Robert Gunn trilogy, following on from the acclaimed best-sellers, 'Mandarin-Gold' and 'The Chinese Widow'

BOOKS BY THIS AUTHOR

Follow The Drum

'Once in a while, a book comes along that grabs you by the throat, shakes you, and won't let go until you have read through to the last page.' - Hal Burton, Newsday

'Follow the Drum is superb reading entertainment' - Best Sellers

India, in the mid-nineteenth century, was virtually run by a British commercial concern, the Honourable East India Company, whose directors would pay tribute to one Indian ruler and then depose another in their efforts to maintain their balance sheet of power and profit. But great changes were already casting shadows across the land, and when a stupid order was given to Indian troops to use cartridges greased with cow fat and pig lard (one animal sacred to the Hindus and the other abhorrent to Moslems) there was mutiny. The lives of millions were changed for ever including Arabella MacDonald, daughter of an English regular officer, and Richard Lang, an idealistic nineteen-year-old who began 1857 as a boy and ended it a man.

Ntr: Nothing To Report

"Superbly authentic atmosphere, taut narration. Mr Leasor would have delighted Kipling." - The Observer

"The most clinically accurate description of India and Burma about the time of the Kohima breakthrough I have yet seen." - Daily Telegraph

"Mr. Leasor brings to 'Nothing to Report' a journalist's straight-forwardness, and an on-the-spot sureness about how frightened men behave, that are both refreshing and effective." - Spectator

In the early spring of 1944, when the British fortunes of war in the East were low, the Japanese invaded India.

Viewed against some other catastrophes of the war, this was only a minor invasion; an intrusion of some 20 miles or so on the North-East frontier. But, at the time, it was considered very important indeed. Political discontent was rife in India and there was constant fear that the British would withdraw as they had already done in Malaya and Burma. If this invasion were not checked and the Japs flung back there might be revolution in India.

The story concerns a draft that was sent to help repel the invasion. An odd lot, that draft, and not quite sure what it was all about. The author tells of men in adversity, some shrewd, some cynical, some loved and others lonely. In the end they sent back the message N T R—Nothing to Report. The reason behind this, illustrating all the futility of war and its consequences, is related in this moving and realistic novel.

Open Secret

Max Cornell had survived the Katyn massacre and the Russian camps. Now he wanted a new life - and the money to enjoy it - in England. And the price of a passport was three years' work for British Intelligence, running the Russian codenamed Butcher.

Asimir Vasarov, once camp commandant at Katyn, became Stalin's closest aide - a man whose political loyalty was assured and whose power was unlimited.

But the successful British businessman and the man from the shadows of the Kremlin share more than memories of the past. In the post-war world of high politics and backstreet crime, they are linked by an explosive truth which could rock governments if it ever became an OPEN SECRET.

'Fast-moving... a nice seedy atmosphere' - SUNDAY EXPRESS

Ship Of Gold

Only months before, Anthony Carter's hopes of a promising military career had been shattered overnight. Now he is an out-of-work swimming instructor with nothing before him but the prospect of a chilly Portuguese winter. So Mr Serrafino's offer of employment comes as a lifeline. Carter is to supervise the team of tough German divers who will be raising gold bullion from a sunken treasure ship. But Mr Serrafino may not be quite the respectable businessman he appears to be... And the ship of gold may prove to be a cargo of lethally dangerous fool's gold...

Tank Of Serpents

Benares, India, 1945. Captain Richard Blake stands trial at a court martial, accused of stealing a million rupees from one of the wealthiest, most powerful and dangerous men in India. Eight years later, he begins his quest for retribution...

'Unlike Jeffrey Archer, James Leasor seems to have a natural ease with words; and this fluency means that his book moves along at an altogether faster clip." The Times

'Well up to the standard we have come to expect from one of Britain's best thriller writers.. .a superb study of revenge! Evening News

Most books by James Leasor are now available as ebook and in paperbacks. Please visit www.jamesleasor.com for details on all these books or contact info@jamesleasor.com for more information on availability.

Follow on Twitter: @jamesleasor for details on new releases.

Jason Love novels
Passport to Oblivion (filmed, and republished in paperback, as Where the Spies Are)
Passport to Peril (Published in the U.S. as Spylight)
Passport in Suspense (Published in the U.S. as The Yang Meridian)
Passport for a Pilgrim
A Week of Love
Love-all
Love and the Land Beyond
Frozen Assets
Love Down Under

Jason Love and Aristo Autos novel
Host of Extras

Aristo Autos novels
They Don't Make Them Like That Any More
Never Had A Spanner On Her

Robert Gunn Trilogy
Mandarin-Gold
The Chinese Widow
Jade Gate

Other novels
Not Such a Bad Day

The Strong Delusion
NTR: Nothing to Report
Follow the Drum
Ship of Gold
Tank of Serpents

Non-fiction
The Monday Story
Author by Profession
Wheels to Fortune
The Serjeant-Major; a biography of R.S.M. Ronald Brittain, M.B.E., Coldstream Guards
The Red Fort
The One That Got Away
The Millionth Chance: The Story of The R.101
War at the Top (published in the U.S. as The Clock With Four Hands)
Conspiracy of Silence
The Plague and the Fire
Rudolf Hess: The Uninvited Envoy
Singapore: the Battle that Changed the World
Green Beach
Boarding Party (filmed, and republished in paperback, as The Sea Wolves)
The Unknown Warrior (republished in paperback as X-Troop)
The Marine from Mandalay
Rhodes & Barnato: the Premier and the Prancer

As Andrew MacAllan (novels)
Succession
Generation
Diamond Hard
Fanfare
Speculator
Traders

As Max Halstock

Rats – The Story of a Dog Soldier

Printed in Great Britain
by Amazon